M

Volume One

(Books 1-5)

By

David McWhinnie

Madeline 1

Madeline 1

Prologue

With striking good looks, evident from an early age, Madeline was never short of admirers. By the time she was sixteen she had developed into a woman of grace and beauty and thus became the aspiration of all menfolk to have her as their wife. Unfortunately for Madeline, these admirers included married men.
And therein lay trouble…..

*

Chateau d'Estelle, France 1796

They were freezing to death.
Cowering on their hard pallet with its soiled straw, she pulled the thin, fraying blanket tighter around them as she tried her hardest to warm her child through body contact.
She stared hopelessly at the wooden bowl but still it remained empty, the guard being late with the food once again. She knew he did it on purpose, trying to evoke some reaction from her. But she was harder than that. She had suffered far worse in the past and the tardiness of the food was, to her, but a slight inconvenience.
It was her five year old son she was concerned for.

Her catgut-stitched chest bore no breasts with which to suckle her child, so her son had been raised on sour goat's milk, which he had regularly vomited back. Since then, he had to endure what sustenance there was provided by a jailor who knew little of how to cook, it being each day a thin, tasteless soup with the occasional piece of fatted meat and stale bread. And she knew for a fact that he had, on occasions, urinated in it for his own sick pleasure.

She wished, at least once, the soup had been hot, then perhaps it would have given them some warmth against the harsh weather, its ferocity penetrating their cell through the half-enclosed barred window. And having nothing to block up the gap, they had endured the wrath of the biting wind for five consecutive winters now.

They had survived on these paltry offerings two years since after a brief respite, when, for a time, there had been a guard with which a special pleasure could be exchanged in return for extra food. So, on regular occasions her hand was to be found down the front of his britches while the child lay asleep with a full stomach. This trade-off, unfortunately, had been short-lived and, upon his replacement, they were back to basic rations within months, the current guard unwilling to continue with the same agreement. This, she knew, was not his aversion to women in general but to her alone, her deformity and scarring off-putting to him. The fact that she still wore the same clothes as she had on her arrival six years hence, and the lack of cleaning facilities, added to his displeasure. Her body reeked as badly as their cell, with him refusing to empty their toilet bucket until it slopped over onto the floor.

And very rarely did they have the luxury of silence in which to find sleep. With the frenzied screams and mutterings from the other inmates keeping them awake, they caught only brief naps between this and the constant banging on the cell doors.

If this was the hell her Christian Mother had spoken to her of as a child, then she was well and truly in it. If only she had heeded her warnings.

Hearing the guard's key in the door, she automatically pulled her child closer towards her. Holding a muck-encrusted pail in his hand, he entered the cell and, without a glance, aimlessly tipped some of its contents into their bowl. His back to them, he pulled two pieces of moulded bread from a tattered sack and threw them down next to it. And with languid pace, he dragged his feet towards their toilet bucket and casually kicked its side. But totally unaffected by some of its contents sloshing onto both the floor and the handle, he picked it up by the latter and, grinning to himself, exited without word. She knew full well that it would not be returned for some while. It was his intention for them to relieve themselves in the furthest corner of the room and then scrape it by hand into the bucket on its return, this being yet another of his many ways of seeking amusement at their expense. She remained still until she heard the key turn in its lock and, when it did, she roused her son from his hungered torpor.

Looking down at the colourless soup, she saw the thick green glob of saliva floating on its surface. But somewhat relieved that this could be more readily removed than the frequently compounded urine, she scooped it off with her splintered, wooden spoon. What meat there was within the insipid consommé was eaten first. And she made sure her son chewed it well to ensure whatever goodness there happened to be in it was maximized. It pained at her to make him do so, for she knew very well that his gums and teeth were tender and painful through malnutrition. This part of the procedure over, she unclasp her hand and let the contents slip into the bowl. Grinding the dissected bugs, that she had accumulated earlier, into the mixture, she looked into her son's eyes, who desperately awaited further sustenance. She, herself, dipped her own bread into the thin liquid but only to soften its staleness and, as normal, ate just sufficiently to sustain life, preferring her son's indulgence to her own.

And within a minute the bowl was empty yet again, both staring straight at it and unknowing when it would be refilled. Her heart sank once more, as it always did, when he raised his face to meet hers and she saw, deep within his eyes, the misery, despair and a pleading to a mother who could not give him relief from his suffering.

So, despondently carrying him towards the corner, they resumed their previous positions, sheltering from the icy wind which blasted its way in from the window and cut into their very souls.

Her eyes opened with a start.

With the sound of the key turning in the lock, once again, she was taken by surprise. So soon, she thought. Surely not, this was highly unusual…this was worrying. The door was pushed open and the guard casually walked in swinging his keys. But to her astonishment he was not alone. Pulling her child tighter towards her, she cowered in the corner and watched, in disbelief, as two dark cloaked men were led in by an elderly Nun. These individuals, apart from her various guards in the past, were the first people she had set eyes upon in over five years.

"Leave us," voiced a curt command from the taller of the two men. With this, the guard made a solitary grunt and moved towards the door.

The Mother Superior, who held a cloth to her face to suppress the smell, spoke with muffled tone, "Take the child with you."

On hearing this, she pulled her son even closer and protectively twisted her body into the wall. But her failing strength put up little resistance to that of the powerful guard who, without care, pulled the startled boy from her and callously dragged him kicking and screaming along the hard, stone floor towards the doorway. She leapt up at him only to feel the backward force of his free hand on her face. Knocked to the floor and momentarily stunned by the impact, by the time she had regained her wits, they were lost to view, and as she scrambled her way towards the closed door, she heard the faint cry of

her son as it faded into the distance. As she did, so her own tempered, but silent scream took its place.
The three, meanwhile, looked upon the scene unmoved.

Lifting herself from the hard ground, she looked up towards the Nun and with hatred in her eyes, spat out in her direction. And knowing full well that reprisals were forthcoming, she shuffled herself back into the corner.
As before, the taller of the two took the initiative. Approaching her, his outstretched hands tugged at her tattered top, and once again she found herself too weak to counter her assailant. But although he sought to pull the garment from her, she did not recognize brutality in his doing so, and certainly not the savagery she had encountered on numerous occasions before at the hands of so-called men. There appeared respectability in his touch, and a much more sympathetic feeling towards her, that, for many years now had been all too absent in her life. But she could not afford them her trust as yet. Too many times had she in the past put her faith in someone only to have it slapped back in her face. No, she would continue to play the game her way, and keep up her side of the bargain.
Lying bare, with her tattered chest and body exposed to them, she felt violated once again, with the three looking down upon her deformity like that of some depraved demon.
Flicking her matted hair to the side, he moved her jaw to the left and saw the scar upon her throat. The deep cut that had taken her voice from her six years ago.
"Then it is true," the other spoke.
He nodded his agreement. "It appears so!" Taking both sides of her garment in his hands, he closed the gap, covering her wounds. And with calmed voice, offered instruction. "Sit my child."
She had to consider his words very carefully. Not a single word of compassion had she heard utter forth from another's lips in all these years, so pulling the tattered cloth tighter in towards herself, she looked questioningly up into his eyes seeking confirmation.
Knowing fully well what was required of him, he took hold of her hand and gave pledge of his words. "Your suffering has been much my child," he informed her, "but it ends here, now."
Feeling the reassuring grip of his hand and seeing the geniality of his smile, she closed her eyes tight wishing it not to be a dream. But when she heard the cell door open and instantly feel her son once again in her arms, it felt to her, real. But no more real than when she was taken by the arm and escorted towards the door.
But standing still upon the threshold, she hesitated, pausing upon the brink of freedom to ponder over her surroundings. She peered back, over her shoulders and into the room she was leaving. For over five long years now she had suffered the tight confines of this cell, a cell where without trial or jury she had been condemned to rot. But the hardships and brutality of her

incarceration she had endured, and endured well with only one thing in mind…to seek out and rout from power and station, those who had been responsible for having her put there in the first place.

Clutching her son's hand with her left, her right hand, through stealth, pulled free from beneath her clothes that which she had concealed now for all these years. So, in tandem, as she stepped across the boundary to step free and cut loose from the confines of her cell, so did she from the confines of her restrictions.

Paris would soon know of her return and feel once again the extent of her power over it. Many would indeed suffer her wrath, but just as many would reap the benefits…

…Monarchy included.

*

Madeline 1

Chapter 1

Escape!

Born and raised a strict Catholic by her parents, it was her authoritarian matriarch who relentlessly instilled religious fervor into the whole family. And, in particular, Madeline, who, being the only daughter of six, found herself the target of her Mother's vehement doctrine.
With striking good looks that were evident from an early age, she was never short of admirers. Her long, black hair and eyes of similar hue, made her shine out among all the young townswomen. By the time she was sixteen she had developed into one of grace and beauty and thus became the aspiration of all the men folk to have her as their wife. Unfortunately for Madeline, these admirers included married men…
And therein lay trouble.
This preferential attention had not gone un-noticed by her Mother and, as harsh as her dogmatic zeal had been in the past, this was now sadly laid upon Madeline tenfold.
Stringent prayers six times a day were now commonplace, with her having to seek God's forgiveness for having such favourable looks and thus soliciting, in her Mother's mind anyway, libertine responses from the array of would-be paramours.

So, held within the confines of their house, she was neither permitted to see or be seen by anyone who, in her Mother's eyes, could tempt her into the ways of promiscuousness.

Beauty had apparently come at a price, Madeline thought, and had she been given a choice in this matter at birth, she would now have gladly accepted austerity of looks in lieu. She sought the ordinary life of her siblings, devoid of this harsh treatment which she was undeservingly enduring as a woman. Why was it that her brothers were encouraged to seek wives within the community while she had to endure an emotionless life akin to an old maid?

"I cannot answer your question Maddie," he replied with all honestly, "mother takes it upon herself to smother you at any given chance. We, all of us, that is, cannot understand why."

Childishly, she stamped her foot. "As well I know, and father does not escape her asperity also."

Landis, her eldest brother and also her favourite, sat patiently beside her on the garden bench. "Father is weak, his health ails him and he has not the strength to counter mother's will."

Madeline watched him wave a bluebottle from his face before answering. "I am well aware of that, but I see no help from his sons in this matter. You all seem to take it."

Still struggling with the persistence of the fly, Landis countered. "Mother can at times be as equal in strictfullness to us boys you know Maddie, we're not all immune."

She doubted that. She knew they got far more leniency in their socializing within the town, whereas she was severely monitored even at her schooling. "Your diplomacy does not wear well Landis, and you are as bad a fibber as you are with your grammar."

He sat upright. "What do you mean?"

"I mean that there are few, if any, restrictions given to you, whilst I am confined to the house." She opened her fan and waved it repeatedly. The summer day appeared to be getting hotter as it progressed...or was it her temper, she thought?

"I didn't mean that, I meant with my grammar."

"Oh, pooh the grammar," Once again, the hard soil underfoot took the wrath of her boot. "I just want a life."

Aware of her temper and having to pull back his head as she swiped out at the bluebottle with her fan, Landis tried his best to appease her the best way he could. "Madeline, you are only sixteen. You have your whole life ahead of you yet."

She seethed. "Almost seventeen, and spent most of my time at prayers. I cannot take it much longer Landis."

Even he could see he was making little headway with her. But still he tried. "We all have to pray, little sister. We have been raised fully knowing this."

She could see no conclusion to this conversation. She had thought that, out of all her brothers, at least Landis would have come to her aid. "But not all of

us six times daily," she snapped in return, "I have yet to see this town let alone visit the city of Paris. I will be old and gray before I am permitted even leeway in my aspirations."

Taken aback at this announcement, Landis requested clarity. "And to what do you aspire little sister, pray tell."

She turned, and ignoring his condescension, faced him full on. "I can see only two alternatives to my plight." She intentionally left the statement open-ended, hoping he would take the bait.

He took it, and leaned forward, intent on listening. "And?"

After which, she explained. "Well, as I see it, I can either wait until mother dies, which could take forever," She noticed his stark reaction to her proclamation so immediately progressed to the second. "Or I just run away…which I will."

As equally astounded with her resolution as he had been with her initial alternative, Landis burst out laughing, his hands repeatedly hitting his knees. "Oh Maddie, Maddie, the tears of laughter are never far from my eyes when I'm in your young, naïve company."

Madeline sat frozen to the spot, shocked at his dispassionate response. But her temper soon got the better of her. "I see no reason for jest."

As she stood to leave, he grabbed her arm and sat her back down. "Madeline, I did not mean to make fun of you. I see how you suffer at mother's hand but it will be short-lived, I promise."

How could he say that? What reason could there possibly be that would change her mother's attitude, or her way of thinking. She could see none and had made up her mind already. She was leaving. If her good looks and body shape were as desirable to men as many in the town had commented upon, and her mother had reacted to, then why shouldn't she take full advantage of it? It had never been her intention in life, nor had she been self-centered about her looks, but her mother had now driven her to this decision. Her goals were simple, set out in her head. She would seek out a life in Paris where, hopefully, a wealthy husband awaited her, even now.

Unfortunately, her ignorance of the world, in that a good sum of money would be willingly paid as procurement of these currently suppressed looks, eluded her, and that a path in life taken by many ill-fated individuals could very well await her.

She stood, once again, in self-defiance. "I have made my decision Landis," but as she made to leave, she paused before turning, "and with regards to your grammar, there is no such word as 'strictfullness'."

Two days later, her determination had faltered none.

Fresh fruit cake was being handed out to all and as Madeline looked around the room, she saw all of her brothers smiling, it being Garmon's eighteenth birthday. As she did so, her eyes fell upon her father, who seated in his usual armchair look up to the waiting salver. Watching on, as he gingerly accepted, with shaking hand, the selected piece from the plate, Madeline saw him lose grip and the cake fall to the floor. And, as was normal with her mother and embarrassment to himself, he was the recipient of her acrimony once again. Even with such a minor failing as this, she did not spare the verbal rod upon him.

Madeline tightened her fists in anger. It infuriated her the way she treated him. Like a child. Through no fault of his own he was sick, but, at any given opportunity, she sought to humiliate him and was blasé about who stood testimony to it. He, unfortunately, like Madeline, suffered greatly at the hands of their dominator and was powerless to do anything about it…or at least, for her, until now.

Her displeasure at this was obviously noticed by Landis, who was making his way from the fireplace towards her. And, on noticing her empty hands, commented, "No cake."

She shook her head. "I would choke on it."

"Oh come now, it's your brother's birthday cake," He looked across the room and finished, "not mother's."

The entire company carried on oblivious to her mother's present derision, which infuriated Madeline as this now appeared to be generally accepted as routine. "Am I the only one in this family who cares about father?"

Landis turned on her, shocked. "You do your brothers an injustice there, little sister. Of course we do."

"Then do something about it then." She unconsciously stamped her right foot in rage, but fortunately this was hidden by the hem of her dress and no-one noticed.

"And what do you suggest we do?"

She looked him straight in the eyes. "Be a man!"

Without waiting on his reply, she moved towards her father and, on reaching his chair, knelt down beside him. Ignoring her mother's cursory tone, Madeline held his hand in both hers and did not need to utter a word. He returned her smile immediately upon receiving it. As she looked into his eyes, she thought of what she was leaving him to. Unlike her, who had now made plans, he had the rest of his life to spend like this. She would miss him, miss him dearly. Miss him so much that it would break her heart to leave. And yet there appeared recognition in his gaze, one of understanding. One of discern. Did he know? Was he aware that her departure from the house was imminent? Her questions were rewarded with a deeper smile and a slightly prolonged nod, a nod that not only signified acknowledgement of her plight, but that of sanction. She rose slightly and leaned over to kiss him. And as she did, she felt his other hand take hers. Wrapped tight within the grip was folded paper and she knew straight away what it was. Her Father was not only giving countenance to her actions, but endorsing them through patronage. And with this, she felt the tears fill in her eyes and a hole develop in her heart…

…it would be the last time she would see her father alive.

Encumbered with both clothes bag and satchel, Madeline left her bed chamber and closed the door behind her as quietly as she could. Her face automatically tightened with the sound of wood scraping upon wood. She remained still – listening in the dark. Satisfied with herself that no-one had heard it, she turned to go. Proceeding barefooted and blindly within the murky shadows of the hallway, she tip-toed her way along the upper floor towards the stairs. Pausing briefly outside her mother's room, she waited a moment before continuing. She could feel her heart almost beating itself right out of her chest. Had she been caught, she thought, heaven knows what would happen to her? With legs a-quiver, she carried on. Familiar with the house, even with her eyes closed, she knew it geographically enough to hasten her pace until she reached the stairway. Squinting with her eyes tightly together in order to focus, she looked down into the descending abyss. Then attempting to prevent any the boards from creaking, she light-footedly made her way down the stairs, one cautious step after another, her bags brushing against both wall and banister. She was convinced that someone, somebody would hear her. But with a sigh of relief, she eventually reached the bottom without incident or discovery.

Laying her bags on the floor, she slipped on her soft leathered sandals which she had removed earlier in her room. Then, gathering her belongings together, she headed towards the kitchen, where a faint light cast from a waxing moon illuminated the room just sufficient enough for her to see where she was going. She had to get some food for the journey.

Selecting three of the best looking apples from the basket on the table, she added them to her already bulging satchel. Looking around in the semi-darkness to see what else she could take, she spied the left-over birthday cake. She dismissed the thought immediately. Squeezing her eyes tightly together once more, Madeline considered the consequences of her actions yet again. Who would take the brunt of her leaving, her father? Certainly not her brothers, for Madeline knew only too well that not one of them could ever do any wrong in their mother's eyes. What she, as her only daughter, had done to deserve such treatment was beyond her.

Even after the revelry of the party, she had been made to strip from her afternoon dress into her everyday house clothes and sit within the makeshift chapel once again. Not that any prayers had been forthcoming, on the contrary, she had replayed her impending departure over in her mind until it hurt. Now, here she was, actually putting her plans into action. She felt her body shake at her imminent escape - an escape from all the humiliation and despair in her life. Escape from all the hardship and daily rituals. And worst of all....escape from her family. This was the part that she hated most.

"So you mean to go through with it?"

Madeline gasped at the suddenness of his voice. And on doing so, unwittingly let the bag drop hard to the table, resulting in partial contents spilling from its now open hold, onto the floor.

Garmon approached from the doorway with a solitary candleholder in his hand and upon reaching Madeline, bent down to help her retrieve her belongings.
He helped collect the now, rapidly bruising apples. "You cannot survive on fruit alone Maddie."
Madeline lightheartedly nudged her elbow into his side and whispered in tone, "You gave me such a fright there".
Giggling together, they paused in mid-gather and looked up in unison, gazing into each others eyes. It was Madeline who broke the awkward silence between them. "I have to leave Garmon, I can't take it any longer."
Garmon recognised the pain in her eyes and with an inward sigh, nodded slowly. "I know little sister, I know."
"And you intended to flee before saying goodbye to us all?"
Mutually startled by this unexpected voice, both heads turned in accord and faced the doorway.
Noticing yet another candle, this time in Landis' hand, Madeline straightened up. She walked towards him. "And if there is any further light in this room, then the entire town will be aware of my flight to freedom."
Taking his cue, he extinguished the candle in one rapid expulsion, returning the room into the dimness of which she craved.
When she reached him, she leaned to the side and peered round his shoulder. "Oh, no." Standing in line behind him stood her three remaining brothers.
"They had to know Maddie." He shook his head. "You can't just leave. You at least owe them a farewell."
She knew him to be right of course, but her stubbornness had dictated that she sneak off into the night, thus preventing any emotional farewells that may in turn have stopped her leaving. Spinning on her feet like a ballerina diva, and her prowess evident, she marched towards the table to retrieve her baggage. "Well I'm not changing my mind".
Landis followed her. "No-one's asking you to Maddie." He placed his hands on her shoulder. "We just needed to see you before you left. Surely you must understand that?"
Oh pooh, she thought. Why did she love him so much? As much as she cared for and loved each and every one of her brothers, it had always been Landis who had been there for her with an understanding ear and a shoulder to cry on each time she needed to. She turned around and let him embrace her, and as she did, she felt her eyes fill. On releasing his hold upon her, each of her siblings stood in line to take his place. With each embrace in turn and their individual best wishes and fond farewells, her cheeks moistened even further.
She would miss them dearly.

Three other passengers filled the coach with her but not one did she have an inclination to converse with.

Deep within her own thoughts, she considered her decision-making on leaving her home. Had she made the right move, had she been too impatient, too foolhardy in her fortitude? Her mind was racing. A mixture of trepidation and excitement of both leaving home and heading for a new life in Paris. Then it suddenly occurred to her that, in her impulsiveness to leave, she hadn't really thought of what she would do when she arrived. Yes, her mind was set on finding a loving and possibly wealthy husband but how does one go about it unescorted? With no-one present for the introductions needed in society, how would she ever meet a person of standing? The reassurance that the money her father had given her would, at least, help ease the burden of this. But she was a young, naïve sixteen year old woman in a big city and the prospect of this suddenly dawned on her.

"Do not worry, my child," spoke a soft comforting voice. "The carriage is quite safe."

Madeline looked up from her unconsciously clasped hands to find the owner of this soothing tone. And, much to her expectations as to the maturity of the voice, sat an elderly lady veiled in sheer lace, the colour of which signaled a recent bereavement.

Aware that this woman had mistaken her clenched fists as fear of the rocking carriage, she smiled at her. "Merci Madame, but alas it is not the rough track and the shaking of the coach which distresses me."

"Oh, then forgive me, Mademoiselle, for my mistake."

Madeline shook her head and smiled further. "No, no, please do not misunderstand me, Madame, it is true what I say, but your concern for my well-being is very much appreciated."

"Well, well, a young lady with good manners." She turned condescendingly to face the young woman to her left. "Now that is a rarity these days."

Madeline looked upon the face and, with the young woman being of similar age to herself, took this to be her granddaughter. Being small, plumpish and sporting tight curls of red hair, the freckles in multitude upon her face, made her look spoilt. And as she pulled her crossed arms tighter into herself and sighed, this now confirmed it.

Madeline turned her attention back to the elderly woman. "You are travelling to Paris?"

"Yes, I am visiting my daughter, I stay there on occasions." As she spoke this, she raised a small, silver-handled cup to her mouth but before drinking, she raised it slightly. "For medicinal purposes, of course." She beamed mischievously.

Madeline knew that brandy lay within its hold, as she could smell it even from there and smiled at the audaciousness of such an elderly lady. She liked her immediately.

Delicately raising the black veil from her face, just enough to take its size, she sipped from its edge. But as she lowered it, she let release a small hiccup, this being much to Madeline's amusement and her granddaughter's mortification.

"Grand-mama."
"Oh be quiet child," she shooed her.
Madeline could tell that there was not a lot of love lost between the two of them. But even with only one hour into the journey, this elderly lady already appeared quite tipsy. And with so many miles still to travel, she wondered in what state she would arrive in Paris.
Flicking the residue from the cup, she replaced it in her bag and looked up again in Madeline's direction. "You are so young to be travelling unescorted and such a distance. You have relatives in Paris?"
What could Madeline say? How could she tell her that she had absconded from home, ran away from her parents. Would she inform the authorities? Would she be made to return home? All these questions raced around in her head but before she could summon up an appropriate answer, or lie, the lady continued.
"The uneasiness I commented upon earlier is now reinforced by your hesitance in replying." She leaned forward slightly. "I assume the answer is no and that you are alone?"
Madeline looked to the granddaughter who, all of a sudden, had taken an interest in the conversation; and then to her left, to the fourth traveller who, she noticed, was fast asleep. Now refacing as before, she looked directly at the lady and shook her head. "No."
"No. No to what... that you have no relatives; or no meaning yes you are not alone?"
Confused at the wordplay and on how to reply, Madeline answered both questions one at a time.
"I take it then that your parents know not of your whereabouts?" she enquired through concern, as opposed to a stranger's inquisitiveness.
Madeline dipped her head and answered with solicitude. "No."
It was clear that this woman was not going to give up without answers. "Then may I ask what your intentions are?"
Madeline's mind floundered. To seek a wealthy husband! What kind of answer would that be, she thought? She would sound foolish and, in particular, did not want to be thought of as such by the granddaughter, who now sat staring, wide-eyed, awaiting her response. She spoke to the lady direct. "I seek an education."
Her look of surprise expressed the bewilderment she felt. "An education," she continued, quizzically, "In what?"
In the rules of subterfuge Madeline now thought, immediately regretting this falsity. But as with the policy of deceit, one lie automatically leads to another. "The arts." She finished, not knowing where she was going with this fabrication.
"Oh!" She looked even more taken aback with her reply. "And in what form does this craft take, painting, sculpture or the written word perhaps?"
Madeline tried to keep pace with the old woman's questions, and her own lies. "The written verse."

"Oh my, a poet no less. I, myself, am taken with the written works of Christine de Pizan. You have heard of her perhaps?"

What had she gotten herself into here? Madeline shook her head. "No, I have not had that pleasure."

"Then I recommend you read her works upon your arrival in Paris. I should consider it good reading for an independent woman such as your good self. I imagine you will find it enlightening as you would have much in common with her views on life."

Madeline smiled whilst nodding her appreciation. "I will Madame, merci." She looked to the carriage door, evading her eyes as if inviting an end to the conversation. She wanted this lie to finish.

"Start with 'Book of the City of Ladies', you will find it intriguing."

Madeline nodded once more as she repeated the title out loud and thanked her once again.

She was fooling no-one and knew that this wise, old owl, who sat staring at her, saw right through her. If this was the extent of her ingenuity then, as a young woman, she stood little or any chance of surviving in Paris. She would have to be more alert, and on the defense at all times.

There and then she vowed to herself that no-one would get the upper-hand on her again.

- No matter what it took.

*

Madeline 1

Chapter 2

Freedom

Its fetid smell hit her immediately upon arrival.
The Seine, in all its contaminated glory, threw forth a stench she had never known could exist. And sweeping itself across the whole of Paris as a miasmatic cloud of hazed brown, it unwittingly violated the lungs of all its innocuous residents. She could only ponder the life expectancy of any one constantly breathing the air.
"You'll get used to it," the voice from behind informed her.
Being the fourth and last passenger in the coach, Madeline had spoken to this tall, shabbily dressed young man only briefly between his constant naps.
As a resident of Paris, he had informed her that not all good things come with size. She remembered smiling to herself at this unintentional double-entendre and when it had dawned on him what he had said, they simultaneously burst out laughing. But this was also to the chagrin of the old lady who looked on in disgust. The granddaughter, meanwhile, lost to its meaning.
During one of their short but concise conversations, he had introduced himself as Jacob and that he taught French at a school near the heart of the city. Estimating his age to be approximately middle to late twenties, Madeline was enamoured by his good looks and, in particular, his way of speaking. A curiously present but ever so slight stutter came forth when he spoke. And although such an affliction to any other would be a possible liability, with Jacob it appeared natural and at its ease with his perfunctory-self.

Their talks had been light-hearted and, as it turned out, easy on her ear. This was due to him asking very little about her, preferring instead himself, albeit not vainglorious, as the topic of discussion.

Madeline had been extremely conscious of the elderly lady eaves-dropping into the conversation in the hope that she'd let slip further snippets of personal information. So she volunteered very little. She was learning.

In the meantime, Jacob had rambled on about his teaching and various students. She had found his company very relaxing and had hoped that, by journey's end, he would ask to see her again during her stay in Paris. And thus, by accommodating her wishful thinking, he readily did.

"Café Neve on Rue Parfait, Saturday, ten sharp," he made her repeat.

Smiling at the thought, she stretched up and took her baggage from him atop the carriage.

"You won't forget now, will you?" he shouted, above the surrounding melee of horses and carriages as they maneuvered within the station.

She shook her head excitedly. "No, I will not forget." He appeared to be just as keen to meet her again as she felt about seeing him and it made her feel warm within. It was a good beginning. Granted, he was only a teacher and not the man of means she would eventually want to marry, but feeling happy within herself at her plans coming to fruition, she left the station content so far with her first day in Paris. She would now seek accommodation and, at once, set her feet to wandering the streets in awe of her surroundings.

Apart from the persistent smell and the filth littering the streets, the bustle of the city set her heart racing. The constant coming and goings of the pedestrians, accompanied with vendors' shouts of encouragement to enter their place of trade, had her smiling from ear to ear. This was what she had hankered after. This was what she had dreamt it would be like and a far cry from her home town.

As she turned the street corner, she heard the 'wolf whistles' from several similarly-aged boys as they loitered at the roads edge and if her smile wasn't big enough, it felt twice the size now. Encouraged by this attention, she wandered on. However, it soon became apparent that the further a field she walked, the more lacklustre her surroundings appeared. The shops were minimal, usurped now by sleazy-looking cafes and tavernes, the patrons of which looked dubious in character. She must be heading in the wrong direction she thought, if indeed she'd had a direction to head for in the first place.

Turning to retrace her steps, she was, in an instant approached by a young man she believed to be in his twenties.

His eyes fixed straight at her breasts. "How much?"

As naïve as she was, Madeline assumed he was asking after her satchel. "It is not for sale." She automatically clutched it up to her middle, defensively. "It contains my belongings."

"Wasn't after your clothes in there missy, was after what's under them's you've got on," Upon eyeing up her shape more intently, finished his question, "So, how much?"

"Please Monsieur." She attempted to sidle past him. "I wish no trouble from you."

With persistence he blocked her path. "No trouble missy, just tell me what them two beauties are worth?" He pressed his face in closer until she could smell the rancid breath from his black, rotting teeth. "Well missy, how much to get ma cock in 'etween 'em?"

Pulling the satchel up to cover her top half, she struggled free from his now threatening grip, and although shaken with the ordeal, finally escaped his grasp. As she hurried along through the crowds, her hectic pace did not falter until several streets later, whereupon finding suitably unthreatening surroundings, stopped for breath.

Within seconds she heard a voice approaching from her left. "Looking for lodgings are we?"

A kind-looking, middle-aged woman now stood before her and Madeline was instantly relieved at her benevolent but stern smile. Attired befitting church on Sunday, her pristine demeanor hinted at a convivial nature and one which Madeline immediately considered trustworthy. "Oui Madame."

Taking into account her baggage and travel dress, she added further. "I trust you have just arrived in our fair city?"

"Yes Madame, you are right, and I do seek lodgings." But she immediately thought of the cost before finishing, "as long as they are not too expensive and meet the extent of my purse of course."

"Then I am sure we will find something suitable to it." Her body turn suggested she should follow.

Madeline stood agape as she watched her leave, and, on hastily collecting her things together, eventually caught up with this woman's spirited pace. "My name is Madeline." she panted. But as she negotiated her cumbersome bags through the on-coming stream of traffic, the crowd, meanwhile, appeared to part on this woman's perpetual approach as if being her privilege.

Without faltering in her step, she declared her name. "Madame DeVille. You may call me Monique."

Her introduction was devoid of all cheer, Madeline noticed, but as she continued weaving in and out in her wake, she enquired as to their destination. "May I ask where we are going?"

"It is but a ten minute walk from here."

Unperturbed by her response, Madeline followed her without another word being spoken until they eventually reached their destination. As they entered into a street unlike all others she had seen so far, there stood a townhouse built upon two stories and which appeared to be her new home for the time being. Madeline's eyes lit up. She was led upstairs to the second floor and as she walked along plush carpet underfoot to the end of the hallway she passed by elaborate oil paintings hanging on each side. The door was opened for her and as she entered, she looked upon the room with joy. Like a child having been given the most expensive toy ever, her heart was aflutter with excitement. Sporting walnut and mahogany furnishings which consisted of a large heavy wardrobe and bed side tables, in addition to this and to her delight there was also a writing bureau and chair. With the room decked out in pastoral colours and sporting wide, curtained windows in which the sun shone invitingly across to her equally adorned bed, it was to her, perfect.

Beaming, she nodded her approval. "It is ideal Madame, I will take it, if the price is affordable."

It was. But she had to pay one month's advance rent. In open view of Monique, Madeline opened her satchel to retrieve her purse. And taking the required amount from her funds paid it out willingly.

"I am fatigued from travel, Madame, and would like to bathe once I have unpacked." She looked towards the door and along the hall. "I gather there are amenities?"

Monique followed her eyes. "Yes, along the hallway to the end. I may say that I am pleased to hear that you show good sense and wash regularly. Many here do not." She turned to go. "I will send water up presently, as much as I can spare. But do not expect too much in Paris, fresh water is scarce, so use it sparingly."

Surprised with the thought of many city folk not washing as it had been second nature to her living near a fresh water stream, she considered this to be a slight inconvenience, but one she could easily deal with. If she could even top and tail herself regularly then at least it would be something. She could live with that.

With Monique now gone, Madeline laid her bags upon the bed and made at once for the window to take account of her view.

- And was not disappointed.

A thoroughfare of shops and cafés lay before her and she heard the sweet sound of a solitary violin playing a familiar tune. So, as she turned lightly on her feet, she hummed along, and reaching for her bag, opened it up. How fortunate, she thought, that in so short a time, she had procured a room such as this. She smiled inwardly.

Her unpacking had taken only but the length of the tune and on pulling at the cord of her purse she emptied its contents upon the bed. Given the agreed cost of the room per week, she estimated this would accrue to approximately four more months rent, having already paid one in advance. She would have to be frugal with her expenditure as this board did not include meals. She would have to make it last. She also had to find a safe place in which to secure it. Although her landlady appeared honest, she could not assume that everyone in Paris would be of equal measure. She could not be so trustful. But before reaching a decision on its secretion, there came a knock on the door.

"A moment please."

She hurriedly gathered the money together and hid it temporarily beneath her empty bag. And as she opened the door, she was met by an ashen-faced girl about her own age, sporting a coif and holding a large, empty ewer in her hands. Announcing that her bath was ready, Madeline thanked her and accepted the proffered towel.

But after she had relocated the money back in her clothed purse, she looked around the room to consider the options. Apart from the obvious, she could see no real place to hide it. So giving up, she decided that she would, on this occasion, take it with her.

Following the instructions given, she made her way towards the indicated room and, once within, found the door to be without lock. Apart from the solitary metal bath in its middle, there was nothing else in the windowless room that could be pushed against the door for privacy. So removing her garments, she carefully folded them and laid them piled high at the bottom, thus, hopefully, preventing easy access. Stepping into the shallow, tepid water, she worked her way steadily down until she was as fully immersed as the eight inches allowed her. She looked down at the pale colouring and considered that if this was what was deemed clean fresh water then she could not see herself drinking much. But, as she relaxed in the soothing water, letting it cleanse the travel from her, she considered her first day. The thoughts of Jacob and their impending meeting; her own little room; and the sweet sound of the violinist, sent her head into an easy reverie. But she was suddenly aware of someone by her side.

Abruptly sitting up, she opened her eyes to see Monique standing over her. "Madame!"

Holding a small bottle in her hands, Monique let the contents run into the bath. "Eau de toilette my dear," she announced, watching Madeline raise both arms across her front in embarrassment. "A young lady such as you cannot be without fragrance now can she?"

Still Madeline cowered. "Please, Madame!"

On realizing Madeline's outrage at her privacy being breached, she continued, "Do not be alarmed Madeline, there is no malice in my actions. I wish only to bestow femininity upon you worthy of your natural appearance."

Madeline looked over towards her bundled clothes and noticed that they had been pushed to the side on her entering.

"Do not be concerned, your belongings are quite safe I assure you."

Madeline knew this for a fact. She was sitting on them. Tightly wrapped, impervious to water, her money lay safe between the cheeks of her rump.

Monique scanned Madeline's body within the water. "You have the full shape of a woman for one so young. May I ask your age?"

Still embarrassed with the situation, Madeline replied. "Sixteen."

"And your skin, so pale as it is, a sure sign that you are from a family in which you have not endured outdoor work."

In other words, she was not a pheasant from the fields, thought Madeline. "Please Madame. You are making me uncomfortable with your talk and your presence."

"Very well my dear." She changed the subject. "I trust you have not eaten since your arrival in Paris, and this being the case, then I wish you to join me in some repast, when you are ready."

With this, she left the room without awaiting her reply. Madeline could only sit in bewilderment at what had just happened. But the mention of food made her stomach rumble and she suddenly realised that, with all the excitement, she hadn't eaten since the previous night. And although she was tired, she would gladly accept the food beforehand.

Having secured her money within the lining of one of the heavy, draped curtains, she eagerly prepared herself for supper. Selecting one of her lighter fitting dresses from the wardrobe to accommodate the heat, she left her room and descended the stairs. Selecting the middle of the three doors as per her instruction, she was greeted upon entrance by a male stranger.

"Madeline, I gather." He walked towards her with hand held out.

Glancing briefly to her right she caught sight of Monique and quickly resumed her focus. "Oui Monsieur." She made a small curtsy as ntroduction.

Taking her hand in his, he gently raised it to his lips. "Enchante Mademoiselle." His head turned towards Monique. "She is, without doubt, the beauty you described."

As she approached, she spoke. "Ansel will not be joining us for supper." She led him by the arm towards the door. "He is here to call upon another of my guests."

"But Monique," his reluctance to leave apparent, "is there no chance?"

Cutting him off in mid-speech, Monique closed the door behind him and returned to Madeline. She led her by the arm to the centre of the room. "Men can be so persistent in their desire for women."

Madeline allowed herself to be seated at the dining table. "He is without doubt a very fine looking man."

Monique smiled. "I agree, but like most of their type, they have it in their heads that all women should fall at their feet."

Madeline watched as she poured from a decanter, two small glasses of dark red liquid, one of which was handed to her. "Then a fortunate guest you have to have him as a suitor." She took the glass from her not knowing what it was, but thanked her just the same.

Monique raised her glass in salute. "Now my dear, let us enjoy a fine meal together, along with, what I hope will be good conversation."

Madeline raised her own in response and as the door opened, two young girls entered with silver salvers laden with a variety of roasted meats and vegetables. Salivating at the sight, she prepared herself for a hearty meal.

Whatever the drink was, it was making her head spin slightly and she refused further after the third. The meal was to her liking though and she had eaten heartedly the wild game and fresh vegetables. But after an hour of food, drink and rather dull conversation, she felt tired. So, without sounding unappreciative, she excused herself for bed as diplomatically as she could. Reluctantly, Monique obliged and let her take her leave. But upon escorting her to the door, and without warning, leaned forward and kissed Madeline's cheek.

But as Madeline considered how she had always sought from her own mother, similar affection, Monique did it a second time. She looked deep into her eyes and heard her speak.

"You miss your home my dear. I can see it in your face."

Madeline nodded. "I do, Madame, I miss my family so very much already and it has been but two days." She hated admitting this to herself, let alone a complete stranger.

"Independence takes time to get used to." She smiled with reassurance. "I'm sure you will do just fine."

As hard as it was, Madeline returned her smile. "Merci Madame."

"Please, Madeline, its Monique."

She nodded. "Merci, Monique." After which, she left the room.

As she ascended the stairs Madeline thought of their conversation over dinner. Unlike the old woman in the carriage, Madeline had imparted far more personal information to Monique about herself than she thought she would have, given her earlier promise to herself to be more safeguarded. Whether this had been the drink that had loosened her tongue or just the relaxed and unimposing surroundings she now found herself to be in, she had no idea. Either way, Monique appeared to take a great interest in the fact that no-one knew where she was and although at the time it seemed unimportant, it now seemed to the contrary. But upon reflection, her parting words of comfort to her appeared sincere and, on consideration, thought herself paranoid. Surely someone in the world has to be trustworthy. Deciding on such, she continued to climb.

The upper hallway had darkened somewhat since her earlier departure from it and the dim light was now illuminated by candles mounted on holders either side of the wall. This lengthened its appearance somewhat and in a dreamlike fashion, extending it further than she thought possible. As she took several paces forward, she seemed uneasy and at once felt her legs flounder beneath her weight. Steadying herself against the wall, she shook her head to regain her bearings, and upon doing so, heard voices coming from the room just ahead to her left. Conscious of it being both male and female, she could vaguely make out what was being said, with her hearing now impaired slightly. As she inched her way along the wall, she felt herself lethargic in movement and a sudden sickness in her stomach. If only she could reach the door she thought, then perhaps she may ask for assistance from those within, but on taking further steps it made her worse. The entire hallway appeared to be spinning around her and the candles felt as if they were looming down ominously towards her from the walls. Struggling, she forced herself onwards, and eventually reaching the entrance, pushed the half shut door fully open.

Suspended in mid-sway, she focused her eyes on the scene before her and recognised the man as Ansel. But gone now was the debonair gentleman who had introduced himself to her earlier, replaced now by an unclad and sweat-ridden individual embroiled with an equally unclothed woman at his front. Standing naked, he held within his hand a goblet from which he drank, whilst the other had coiled within his grasp, the long, dark tresses of a female, who, upon her knees in front of him, had her head pressed closely to his loins. As Madeline stood wavering, trying to take in the sordid scene before her, she watched as he pushed forward allowing his stiffened manhood to slide deep into her mouth. In his drunken state, he raised his goblet and smiled at her. And with this, she felt her legs finally go beneath her and her body fall to the floor.

*

Madeline 1

Chapter 3

Contentment

In an attempt to bring her vision into focus, she encountered the morning's early light and instantly shielded her eyes from its intensity. Her head was spinning and as the previous night's events began to uncoil in her head, she became aware that she was lying in her bed, in her room, in Paris.
- Naked.
Feeling no restriction of clothing about her body, her lifting up of the cover slightly and peering under now confirmed it. How she had gotten to her bed she could not remember, recalling only the nausea she had felt in the hallway. So who had brought her to her room, and more importantly, who had undressed her? The cloudiness of her head sought answers but, after careful deliberation, came up with nothing. Then recalling the scene with Ansel, she pulled the cover up tightly to her chin in revulsion. Squirming at the thought of what she had seen, she found her hands shaking as they gripped the sheet. Such an act to her had been unthinkable and could only consider the woman, who had indulged in such a thing, a demon. In her naivety, she considered that for a woman to permit a man to empty his bladder in such a way as that was an abomination. Surely a receptacle of some sort could have been found. She wanted this vile thought from her mind as quickly as possible.

Looking around the room she saw nothing of her apparel and assumed whoever had prepared her for bed had attentively hung them up in the wardrobe. So, conscious of her situation, she coyly stepped naked from the bed, and bending over slightly to help conceal her vulnerability, crept towards it. With relief, her clothes hung within. Selecting the first one at hand - it being a dress of fine, beige wool - she was satisfied with the choice. She felt exposed, and a thick cloth, irrespective of the heat, would help cover this.

After washing her face from the shallow basin by her bedside, she donned the rest of her clothes and, on lacing her boots, headed for the door. Where she thought she was going, she had no idea. She just needed to be out in the fresh air for a while, or at least as fresh as the city provided. She needed to take stock of her situation, evaluate her predicament, and most of all clear her head.

Closing her door behind her, she locked it secure and headed along the hallway. She had decided that she would take breakfast in one of the outdoor cafes opposite, but once in the street, she kicked herself when she realised that, in her haste to leave, she had forgotten to retrieve money from her cache in the curtain. But reluctant to return so soon, she carried on walking, the smell of the freshly baked morning bread making her insides churn. Her perambulation casual, she headed in the opposite direction from the previous day and had it not been for her empty stomach, she would have enjoyed it immensely.

The summer's morning had all in high spirits, it seemed, and as she continued on from street to street her surroundings, once again, changed as before. In place of the rustic and relaxed atmosphere of her residential area, this part seemed more formal, more business-like. She saw very few women; and the men, who predominantly held sway over the street, she noticed, to be strait-laced and sporting business attire. This area, she assumed, was for the aristocracy alone as she saw no waifs or strays about the street. But it wasn't until she overheard part of their various conversations that she realised she was near parliament. These were politicians, the men who ran France, the men who managed the affairs of the state. Now this was where she wanted to meet her future husband. This was what she had dreamed of. To live the life of luxury and raise her family in a large chateau, drink the finest wines, eat the best food money could buy. And her clothes - she would have the wardrobe the envy of all France. But these were fanciful dreams, illusions in the mind of a child. Here she was without purse, bonnet or parasol, a commoner on the streets of Paris. How, indeed, would she meet someone of prominence inadequately attired as this? But she had one thing, she thought, her appearance. Just as Monique had mentioned the day before, she had the maturity in body of that of a woman. And hadn't her good looks been commented upon in the past? She had what most women desired - the face and the body to match. Or was she being too vain? Could she possibly be overstating herself? There was only one way to find out. She would try it here, now, in this very street, whilst surrounded by the very folk with whom she wanted to mix.

She selected a quiet café, out of full view, and decided on how she would conduct herself. Deciding on her plan of action, she approached the tables and in an instant was met by a smartly dressed, middle-aged waiter who guided her to a table.

"Thank you, no, I wish only some water, if you would oblige me?" She waved her hand at her face, the picture of innocence. "The morning sun has so parched my throat." She noticed the immediate response to her request, and from the seated customers. It was remarkable.

"Indeed, indeed, Mademoiselle, please sit." His moves were a flurry of excitement. "Alas we have no water fit for drinking, but perhaps some wine?" He was gone in a wink.

Somewhat taken aback at the fuss he had made over her, she had however noticed that it had drawn the attention of several gentlemen seated on both sides. Having looked up from their readings to the furor being bestowed upon her, their eyes had remained fixed and so much so she felt awkward seated as she was.

When the water arrived, he had placed in front of her a small glass of red wine. Yuck, she thought, the idea of drinking it after the previous night had her stomach churn. She thanked him, and courteously sipped at its edge. But still he remained, hovering over her. This would not do at all, she thought. How could she be seen to be available for conversation when he was here as he was? So, looking up at him, she thanked him once again. "And please, do not let me keep you from your work."

He followed her eyes and shrugged, meaning that he wasn't busy.

Oh go away, she thought, still smiling at him. But still he remained. That was until he was called over from a voice to his right.

Relieved that the leech had been removed, she sipped at her wine, her eyes surreptitiously looking around her. And within minutes the waiter was by her side again, only this time he held a tray in his hand. Madeline watched as he laid freshly made pastries on the table in front of her. Looking up, she panicked. "No Monsieur, I did not order these."

"It is from the gentleman to your right," He announced, his envious undertone apparent to her.

Madeline turned in the direction indicated and watched as a grey-suited gentleman approached. "Please forgive my clumsy introduction. A spur of the moment thing I'm afraid." He turned to the waiter and bid him leave by way of an upward flick of the head.

Madeline looked at the table and smelt the freshness. "Merci Monsieur." She looked up at him. "But I cannot accept."

"If you do not wish to eat alone, would you permit me to join you? I have not eaten as yet myself, so this way we can both enjoy them."

Her empty stomach and mind were in agreement. "That sounds like an invitation I cannot refuse." She nodded her acceptance to his invitation and with her open hand, invited him to take the seat opposite. But taking full advantage of her acceptance, he took the chair nearest, whereupon pulling it even closer to her, made the formal introductions after which they broke the sweet bread together. During their conversation, Madeline ate as gracefully as her empty stomach permitted. She hadn't realised how hungry she was until she had started, but as soon as she had, the plate was soon cleared.

Gaston, she learned, worked in government and as he explained, in layman's terms, the machinations of such, Madeline sat momentarily engrossed listening to his tales of bureaucracy within the system. This went far over her head but she tried to look interested and have an understanding of its meaning. But after a while its repetition bordered on monotony. The truth was she was bored with his mundane drivel. Granted it was the way of the world to govern a country but his endless talk of laws and bylaws sent her mind to sleep. If this was what she would have to endure to live the life she sought after, then it seemed too high a price to pay. Luxury could only come with comfort and her ears could not stand this wearisome talk, ad nauseam.

"Forgive me, Madeline, here am I going on about France's affairs when I have such a flower as you in front of me."

But before she could answer, she heard her name called from the street. She turned her head in the direction of the voice to see Jacob standing within a group of boys. His students, she presumed, and as she watched him approach, she stood to greet him.

Reaching the table, his excitement on seeing her was clear. "I thought it was you." But upon looking down at Gaston, he faced her again with saddened eyes. "Oh. Forgive me, you are with company."

"No, no, please." She spun on her feet. "Gaston and I are merely talking."

His dashed hopes now revitalized, he enthused upon her. "Then our appointment is still on for Saturday?"

She looked confused. "Of course, why would you think otherwise?" "Well, I thought, seeing that," He hesitated at Gaston's presence. "Perhaps you had…"

Knowing fully well what he meant, she cut him short. "Ten sharp you said, just as we planned."

He smiled at her recollection of his instruction, ten sharp. "In the morning I mean. I wish to spend the day with you."

She smiled. "I already assumed that." And without thinking, she leaned forward and kissed his cheek. But upon realising her impropriety, she sat down immediately, her face flushed red.

Jacob laughed out loud at her impulsiveness and bade her farewell.

As Madeline watched him leave, she thought of the difference in personality between him and Gaston. And knew in whose company she preferred.

Gaston, on the other hand, did not take this defeat lying down. "May I be permitted to call upon you sometime in the future Madeline?"

Taken aback with the spontaneity of his request, she sat for a second dumbfounded. Had she heard him right?

"I dare say a bit of rivalry in your life would make for a more pleasurable one," he continued. "And I would show you such sights in Paris."
Without thinking, she accepted his invitation, the reason of which was lost to her. Hadn't she just done thinking about morose he was, and comparing him to the jovial Jacob? "I reside in Rue de Lombarde, the house of Madame DeVille."
It was Gaston's turn to be struck silent and his reaction showed.
Madeline questioned his bewilderment. "Do you know the street?"
He nodded slowly. "Yes, and know the house." He looked Madeline up and down for several seconds before continuing, "I was not aware that you were one of Monique's girls."
She amiably nodded with innocent affirmation. "I have just recently arrived in Paris and have a room there.
Curiously, he nodded. "Do you indeed?"
"And I have to be getting home now, I fear." This wasn't actually true of course, but she used this as an excuse to leave. Feeling fatigued from the previous night, she needed to rest, so pushing her chair back she stood to leave.
He stood with her and allowed her to go on her way. "Of course."
"Thank you for the pastries, Gaston." She offered him her hand.
Without shaking it as she intended, he turned and kissed its back. "I look forward to seeing you again soon Madeline," His eyes stared straight at her. "Very soon."
"Au revoir Gaston, and thank you again."
They made no specific date upon which he should call, or a day convenient to them both, but knowing fully well that she had just secured the affections of one man of prominence, it had been a productive day all round. She had proved to herself her worth, but more important than that, she had met Jacob again.

Her walk, on return, was taken in half the time. This she put down to a fuller stomach plus a destination in mind. And as she reached her street she saw, further up, three women leave the house. Overly dressed, she thought, for the time of day but put it from her mind as quickly as it had come. But upon reaching the door, a fourth emerged similarly attired. She nodded in friendly salutation and received a curt one in return with no words spoken. Only a quick sweep of her form, from head to waist and back up, did she receive acknowledgement, and this had culminated in a begrudged sigh. Charming! She thought. Were all her encounters to be the same?
Monique did indeed have many other guests occupying her rooms, thought Madeline. It struck her funny though that they were all female. Perhaps Monique did not consider men trustworthy enough to reside in her lodgings, she wondered. It would be nice though to have friend, but until now, none had remotely hinted at amiability.

Quietly passing the doors on the lower level, she made her way up the stairs to her room. And once there, she relieved herself from the tightness of her boots and the restriction of her corset. Lying loose clothed and sprawled across her bed, she felt herself weary, still fatigued from her travel which the previous night's sleep had not yet taken from her and drained with the relentless heat. She lifted herself to open the window in an attempt to get some cool air flowing into the room, but as she reached the curtains thought of her money. She had forgotten about this, so to set her mind at rest, she bent down and sought after the loose stitching in which she had placed it. But its presence eluded her momentarily. Then, with increased agitation, her fumbling checked the entire lower half. Had she the correct curtain or was it the right one? Had she been so tired as to forget which one? She checked the other and, after a few minutes, returned to the left. She was positive it was this one. The loose stitching lay bare in full sight of her. But where was it? Where was her money? Scouring the floor to see if it had come loose, she reached the middle of the room before she accepted that it could not have possibly fallen that far out. And, once again, she returned to the curtain. Several more heated attempts to track its whereabouts followed and it soon became apparent that she was wasting her time.
It was gone.
All the money she had in the world was gone. Within twenty four hours of being in Paris she was penniless. And kicking herself at not even having the sense to buy provisions earlier, she now had no money for food. Rolling herself into a tight ball on the floor, she wept like a child, and in her mind were thoughts of her family...of their warnings and her father's departing gift. She had lost it all.
But had she lost it? How could she have lost it? Money does not just disappear. It had to have been stolen. Someone had been in her room and stolen her money.
In her haste, the fact that she was in a state of half-dress was forgotten about, and after pacing the hall at speed, she descended the stairs at an even greater pace. Without knocking as introduction, she barged her way through the middle door and as was hoped for, found Monique was seated alone at the table.
Midway through eating her lunch, Monique looked up from her plate as if she had been expected, and not looking at all surprised with her appearance, commented on her outburst. "Manners and etiquette in my house would be appreciated my dear."
Madeline ignored her request for formalities as this was quaint coming from someone who had entered the room unannounced during her bathing. "I have had money stolen from my room."
Losing no momentum with her meal, Monique appeared unconvinced. "Money stolen, in this house, I think you must be mistaken my dear."

"Madame, all the money I have, or had, was hidden inside the curtain in my room. It is now gone, I have this very minute checked. Someone has stolen it."

Monique placed both knife and fork on the plate before dabbing at her lips. "And when did you secrete this little fortune of yours, may I ask?"

"Last night." She took an uninvited seat at the table in mid-explanation. "Just before I had supper here with you."

Seeking further details of this alleged theft, Monique enquired further. "Was it there when you roused from sleep this morning?" Monique had uttered this question in such a matter-of-fact way that Madeline was growing impatient with her lack of concern. "I do not know. I left without checking."

"Then I suggest you must have moved it elsewhere. In the state I found you in last night it appears that anything was possible."

Madeline leaned forward. "It was you who put me to bed?"

"Yes, and no-one has entered your room since."

"But Madame, surely…?"

Her reply was brusque. "Enough, I will hear no more on the matter."

"But I have no money for food, or for my room come the month's end." Her eyes pleaded. "What can I do?"

Monique pulled herself free from the table and walked around in Madeline's direction. "Monsieur Travette was quite taken by your appearance last night." She explained. "You have caught his eyes."

Madeline looked up from her twitching hands and followed her as she rounded the table towards her. "Who?"

She reached her side and leaned on the table. "Ansel, of course."

Madeline closed her eyes at the thought of this man. He was certainly not the person he had appeared to be earlier in the evening. She sensed pressure beneath her chin and as her eyes opened, she felt Monique's curled finger raise her head up to face her. She heard her speak further.

"I do believe he would pay handsomely for the privilege of your company, Madeline," This she uttered whilst the same finger now caressed at her cheek, "As would many other gentlemen of my acquaintance."

Madeline shook her head in confusion. "I do not understand, Madame. Why would Monsieur pay me money for just my company?"

"Hmm, well…" She dipped her head to the side. "Perhaps a little more." She worked her way round to Madeline's back.

Madeline looked over her shoulder. "A little more?"

Taking her long, dark hair in her hands Monique slowly guided it into one tail. "The paleness of your skin and the shape you possess are an asset you should use to your advantage my dear. To sit in the company of one as beautiful as you would be sufficient for any man…" She paused, "But alas, not as fulfilling." She released the grip on her hair and took the loose hanging edges of Madeline's dress in her fingers. She opened it slightly before finishing "And certainly not as lucrative for you."

Madeline looked down to see that both her breasts were in view, with her having forgotten about her lack of corset. But for some reason she felt no urge to cover herself up. So deep in thought was she about what Monique was saying. She was beginning to understand Monique's way of thinking, she thought. "Would they give me enough to pay for my room, and food?"
Ah, such ignorance, thought Monique. "More than that my dear," she explained, "much, much more, and not only from Ansel. You would be paid for the privilege of being escorted to Paris' finest."
"It is that simple?"
Monique nodded.
My goodness, thought Madeline. If what she was saying was true, then why should she settle for some boring gentleman husband like Gaston when she could have the pick of any man she wanted? Be escorted by many around Paris as opposed to being kept by one, and be paid for the privilege of doing so. She smiled at the thought. Hadn't she already proved to herself that she had this capability at the café earlier? She looked behind her for further clarification but Monique had worked her way around and was now knelt down in front of her. "You will have coin Madeline, and enough to spend on clothes of the finest quality, I will have all Paris in line for you, my dear." As she extolled the virtues of such an alliance, she took hold of the sides of Madeline's top and let them slide down both arms. "You will be the toast of the city."
Madeline remained still as she watched Monique's face move closer towards her breasts and sat stunned when she placed her lips upon her left nipple. She gasped at the sensation and felt both Monique's gentle kisses upon her and her tongue move over it. Taken by surprise at her body's reaction to this stimulus, Madeline closed her eyes and felt an unfamiliar tingling in her lower half as she let Monique continue her soft caresses upon her. And on pulling her head even closer into her, felt the rush of blood to her head and a warm glow fill in her heart.

Madeline now understood the significance of the word 'more'. She had just experienced it for herself. She sat stunned by her body's reaction to Monique's touch. "I have never felt like that before Monique. It was a strange feeling."
Monique passed her over a glass of deep red wine. "It is but a sample of what you can expect as a woman my dear," She paused to reflect on previous encounters. "Well, under the right circumstances of course."
"Will I feel the same way again?" Her own finger touched her nipple to recall the feeling. "I mean, does that happen each time, even with a man?"
Monique shook her head. "No, my dear, regretfully not, and I do not wish it so either. You will have to remain distant from your feelings. Never let them rise to the surface. You have to be in control at all times. It is for their pleasure, not yours. Your time will come when once you're ready, until then…"

Madeline sipped at the edge of her glass and wondered why. "Do the men not like this to happen to the woman? Would it not be pleasing to them to see me feeling as such, or would this be a failure on my part?"

"No, my dear, do not think of it as a failure. You have to learn to gain the upper hand over these men. Keep them hungry for more. Let them be the hunter, you, the untamed prey."

To Madeline, Monique described this as a game. And, in some ways, it could be, she thought. But her mind was on what she would have to do to satisfy these men. "I cannot let them make toilet with me Monique."

Stunned by this announcement, Monique asked what she meant. And when Madeline had described to her what she had seen the previous night, she smiled at her. "There are many ways to pleasure a man my dear, that being one of them."

She sat with confusion on her face. "But how can this be pleasurable, especially for the woman who has to endure it?"

"He was not emptying his bladder into her mouth as you thought. He was being pleasured by the touch of her mouth, much in the same way as I did there with you. As I have explained, it is not the place of the woman to be pleasured." She leaned forward, "But to please."

She saw, still, the confusion in Madeline's eyes. "I think, my dear, you need a real hard lesson in men."

She refilled both their glasses.

Having explained to Madeline the meaning and technique of oral genital contact, Monique felt assured that she had described it satisfactory for the time being. "The simple fact being, my dear, is that most men like this type of contact, whether it be the intimacy of the act or possibly the feeling of dominance over the woman, who knows, it varies from man to man."

This, by comparison, led on to intercourse in the normal fashion. As Monique described in detail, over another glass of wine, the various positions possible during it, Madeline sat with mouth agape the entire time. And after yet another glass and a time lapse of over fifty minutes, Monique ended the lesson. "I guarantee you, my dear, where there is a hole in your body, there is a man out there who'll want to fill it." She smiled, "and willing to pay you accordingly."

Madeline considered what she had just said and then it struck her. "You don't mean?"

"I do indeed, my dear, and for that your price will rise dramatically."

"But Monique, I have never done such things before. How would I know what to do come the time?"

"There is time enough for tuition, my dear. It is sufficient that you know what will be expected of you in due course, but I think, for the moment, you have learned enough for your delicate head to handle for one day."

Madeline smiled back at her. "Yes Monique."

"And I would prefer it if you called me 'Madame' in front of the other girls."

The other girls! Of course, now she realised what Gaston had meant this morning, 'one of Monique's girls'. "Please Madame."
"We are alone Madeline. Monique."
"Sorry, Monique, How many girls are staying here?"
As if this question had to be pondered, she looked up slightly to her left. "Nine I think." She bit her lip in thought. "They come and go. Yes, I think nine at present."
"Do they all have rooms here?" This was asked in the hope that she might make at least one friend her own age.
"Hmm." She rocked her head slightly. "Some do, some don't."
Finding this vague reply unsatisfactory, she pushed further, "But how many stay here in the house as I do?" But as she spoke the words, she remembered her own dire situation. She was still without money, still unable to provide herself with food and everyday accessories. She was in a word…broke.
Monique, on noticing her mood swing, drew her from thought. "I will now inform you how I wish for us to proceed." And, upon standing, began pacing the room. "As you are without adequate funds at present to subsist, I will furnish you with all your requirements. Firstly, this will include meals here in the house but not in here with me I may add, that has to be understood. I can show you no preferential treatment in front of the others." She paused in thought. "Well, not presently anyway."
Continuing to walk round the table, she expanded further, "Secondly, as you are in the same position regarding new clothes, toiletries, etc, I, again, will provide these. The cost of which will be deducted from..."
Madeline finished her sentence for her, "...My first payment."
"Touché, my dear."
And with it, Madeline's face beamed.

*

Madeline 1

Chapter 4

Assignment

Monique had explained further. Her lodgings would be provided to her in the same way as her provisions. Madeline was pleased with the arrangement as her money worries were over. All seemed right at last, so as she sat on her bed's edge she stretched up her arms and fell back upon it, happy in what looked to her, a good future ahead.
Paris would be hers, she thought. She would have it all.
On hearing the solitary violin begin its familiar tune outside in the street, she felt contented with life; and with the full stomach provided by Monique, she closed her eyes and let sleep take her.

But this sleep was short lived it seemed. And although the dimness of the room signified evening, she still felt as if she had only just shut her eyes. She heard Monique speak her name.
"Madeline, Madeline, waken up."
As her eyes drew accustomed to the semi-darkness, she focused in on her.
"What is wrong Monique? I mean Madame."
Her instruction was brief "Get dressed, quickly." She lit the candle at the bed side.

"Why, what is the matter, has something happened?"
Monique's head nodded abruptly. "Happened? Yes, yes something has happened. A chance for three months rent to be made, that's what's happened," Her words appeared to be falling over themselves.
Madeline rose from the bed and with sleep still clinging to her, dawdled across to pull closed the curtains.
Noticing her languid pace, Monique pulled her back. "I'll do that. You get dressed, and make it your finest. The best you have." She left the curtains and made for the wardrobe. "On second thoughts, I'll pick it for you."
Madeline sat herself on the bed, still half asleep. "What is this that I have to do?"
"To do, to do?" On turning, she held up Madeline's favourite cream dress for inspection. "This will do nicely."
"Monique, you have not answered me. What must I do?" She rose to her feet and took the dress from her.
"Nothing," She shrugged her shoulders. "Nothing at all, that is the beauty of it." With her answer as cryptic as her actions, she headed for the curtains.
Confused, but doing as instructed, Madeline stripped off the clothes that she had fallen asleep in and stepped into the fresh cream dress. But as she turned around to face Monique, she caught her staring directly at her, silent, unmoving and mouth agape.
Madeline inched her way towards her. "Are you alright Monique, you look faint?"
She sighed, and shook her head. "Yes, yes, I'm fine, now let me see you." Reaching up to Madeline's face, she moved it from side to side. "My, my, even from sleep you are without blemish, how lucky you are to have such a skin texture. But put water to your face anyway," Her instruction exact.
Monique paced the room while she waited. Had it been anyone else then she would have made certain their face was made up, but Madeline's complexion was so untainted and pure, she not such enhancement.
After a while, Madeline presented herself for inspection. "Will I do?"
Monique sighed once again. Standing before her was a picture. She had pulled her hair to the side exposing more of her face and having had the freshness of water upon it, she looked divine. "Charming, my dear, just charming."
Madeline smiled in response, pleased with her efforts.
"Monsieur Leone awaits our arrival downstairs. And he is, without doubt, my dear, the easiest money you will ever earn." She stood up to describe his trait. "His desire is, now how do I put it, ah yes, one limited to that of show."
Madeline listened intently but understood nothing of what she was saying.
"You need do nothing, my dear, but sit, listen and talk as freely as you wish." She stopped dead. "But most importantly of all," She paused again, "look but do not comment. This is extremely important." She nodded. "Very well, let us see how you do."

Madeline followed her as they exited from the room and nothing more was said between them until they reached the bottom door.

"Now remember, my dear, do not comment or react in any way." She looked down at Madeline's body and noticed her shaking slightly. "Do not be afraid, I will be there with you."

Concerned now about what lay within the room, Madeline forced a smile and nodded. "Thank you Madame."

Monique noted the use of her title. Good, this girl learns fast.

The door was opened and as Monique made her way in, Madeline followed in at her back. But so close was she to her back that when stopping abruptly in mid-room, she almost banged into the back of her. She heard Monique being greeted by her male guest.

"Ah, Signora DeVille, a pleasure to see you again."

"Please Ramone, Monique. We are old friends, are we not?"

Remaining still and partly out of sight whilst the salutations were exchanged by way of several kisses to the cheek, she could just see passed Monique's shoulder. Recognizing the accent as Italian, he appeared to sport the uniform of a soldier, or perhaps navy, it was hard to tell. An officer, no doubt, by the looks of things and mature at that. Going by his rugged face and hair colour, Madeline placed him around sixty years old. And tall, even at three feet away, she found herself twisting her neck to look up at him.

As Monique continued talking, Madeline noticed his curiosity rise with her presence.

"Forgive me, Ramone." Monique turned gracefully on her feet. "Please permit me to introduce Madeline."

When he had stepped forward to within a foot of her, Madeline found that she had to bend her neck up somewhat just to see his face. He must have been at least six foot six, she thought, and very handsome with it. It was plain to see why Monique had said to look, but for the life of her could not understand why she was not permitted to comment upon it. Was he ashamed of or embarrassed about his height perhaps?

"Madeline has just recently arrived in Paris," Monique extended.

He grinned down to his left from a great height. "And you, Monique, have no doubt taken her under your wing."

With movements so swift as to be caught unaware, Madeline suddenly felt a kiss on either side of her face as he bent down to greet her. "Signorina Madeline, you are so beautiful I could almost take you for Italian." He laughed loud at his own comment.

Madeline returned his greeting with both nod and smile, but their encounter was short-lived as he was taken from her in an instant.

"Come Ramone, take some wine with me." She guided him by the arm to the drinks cabinet.

Redundant for the present, Madeline sauntered over to the fire and took seat next to it awaiting further charge. She looked around at the splendour of this new room and then over to the two as they talked whilst pouring the wine.

As Ramone stood with his back to her, facing Monique, Madeline once again took stock of his stature. Look, but don't comment, hah, if this was an easy way to earn money, then Monique had not been lying. But as Ramone turned during the course of their conversation, there appeared something odd about his uniform. Something was not quite right about his britches. She leaned forward slightly to make sure her eyes were not deceiving her. And they weren't. There, standing next to Monique, stood an officer with his manhood on show. Approximately three to four inches of naked flesh hung loose from his opened britches and with her having five brothers, she had in the past caught glimpses of such, so she knew for certain what she was looking at…but never as bold and on open show as this though. It was strange.

She noticed that Monique, who was obviously aware of the situation, carried on with their conversation and appeared completely indifferent to the situation, as if natural to them both. She inwardly smiled. So, this was what Monique had explained to her. Look but do not comment upon, to take this man exposing himself as natural and to say nothing of it. She felt herself grin. This to her was amusing. How could she possibly look this man in the face without reacting so? It seemed bizarre that he would want to do such a thing. But her thoughts were taken from her as Ramone approached her with two goblets in his hand.

"Some wine Signorina?"

Madeline looked up and took one from him. "Merci Monsieur."

"Please Madeline, call me Ramone." He twisted to his left towards Monique. "After all, it is my name." And, yet again, laughed out loud at his self witless comment. But on doing so, his stretched body lay bare and extended within a foot of her eye-line, his exposed-self.

Madeline felt the goblet within her hand tremble slightly, but with it came an unexpected mixture of emotions. A feeling of exhilaration, that in doing this simple task, she was making an old man happy, and with that of sorrow, in that fact that he had to do this to find pleasure. Looking up at this kind hearted looking gentleman, she felt sorry for him and quickly decided there and then that if this was his pleasure, then she would make this old man's pleasure that little bit more pleasurable for him.

"Well, well, my dear," Monique quirked, as she closed the door behind her, "Ramone was very taken with you tonight."

"Merci Madame, I mean Monique."

She approached Madeline, still seated by the fire, and took the chair opposite. "I must say I was most impressed with your conduct." Adjusting her dress to fit her confines, she continued. "Others in the past have not taken to this, rather unorthodox approach to fulfillment, easily, nor had indulged with such confidence. At least, not as well as you had tonight that is."

Madeline sat silent, knowing by her voice that she wasn't finished.

"Perhaps, too much?"

With her tone inciting doubt, Madeline remained still.

Monique rose from her chair and paced the room. "My dear, Monsieur Leone is an old man, and with old age comes affliction. His, unfortunately like most men of similar years, is one where physical pleasure no longer remains an option for him."
Madeline sat engrossed, awaiting further information about this seemingly bizarre ailment, whatever it was.
Monique continued. "Thus being the case and a physical outlet for pleasure notwithstanding." Her choice of words appropriate, she thought. "Then the only alternative is in his mind."
Madeline finished what remained of her wine and held the empty goblet in her lap. Staring at it she contemplated this explanation in her head, but after deep thought, countered Monique's defense.
"But surely he could find pleasure through touch, as I did with you?"
Monique sighed. "Alas, Madeline, you know not of the male form."
The male form, thought Madeline, wasn't that what she'd been looking at for nearly an hour now? "I do not understand Monique, do men not get pleasure from touch also?"
"Of course they do, my dear. That is the whole point. But when a man is aroused, he becomes hard, thus enabling him to enter a woman and to void his seed. With Ramone now, all this is in the past. His only outlet is in his head by way of exposing himself. But this, I may add, is only here in the confines of this house of which he pays handsomely for the privilege of doing."
Still Madeline sat confused. "Then what did I do wrong?"
"My dear, Ramone's idea of pleasure has to be natural, as if it was commonplace for him to be laid bare. You made too much fuss and your awareness of it was apparent."
Madeline bowed her head slightly. "Forgive me Monique, I sought only to please him."
"That you did, my dear." She cupped her hand beneath Madeline's chin and tilted it up to face her. "For all your shortcomings, be them minimal," She paused to smile at her, "He wishes to see you again."

Madeline blew out her candle and lay naked on top of her bed.
Of course he wished to see her again. She had made sure of it. It had been Monique's wish to treat this man as old, decrepit and somewhat senile in his wants and to pander to his wishes in return for payment. But in the course of the evening Madeline had seen far more qualities in his character than deficiencies and had found him to be charming. Had she not been required to be an accomplice in this farcical role play, she would have found his impeccable company appealing. But with her mixture of emotions regarding Ramone and her loyalty to Monique's cause, she played her part with mélange. Both had their way in the end. But she had not only done it their way, but her own way as well, and had taken this game to its limits.

Carrying out Monique's instructions to the letter, she displayed no sign of awareness to Ramone's exhibitionism. But on three separate occasions during the evening did she reinforce this with a deliberate show of unintentional cognizance.
- And for Ramone's eyes only.
The first time had occurred when Ramone refilled her goblet. Standing before her, akin to their first encounter, he stood but a foot from her. Feigning the drop of her handkerchief, she had leaned forward to retrieve it, and with her face now a mere inch from his naked flesh, she remained still for several seconds in the pretense of searching upon the floor. But in all this time she had showed no reaction to what lay in front of her. She was also aware of what Ramone must have been thinking. Looking down he would have seen her youthful face an inch away from his manhood and feel her warm, sweet breath upon it. This, of course, was done out of sight of Monique, after which she had sat up straight and raised her goblet for refill. It was obvious thereafter what Ramone must have been thinking, as upon turning and walking towards the drinks cabinet, he had looked back in her direction again, somewhat confused.
Later, as they all stood admiring one of Monique's paintings, she had intentionally brushed the back of her hand against his flesh when turning. But, with the need for apology at doing so uncalled for, she had made none, nor, indeed, did she acknowledge the fact that it had happened at all. This she noticed had puzzled Ramone even further.
The third and last was when Monique had left the room for a comfort break. Ramone had been by the fire, standing upright in officer's pose with goblet in hand.
"You have a fine uniform Monsieur. You are in the Italian army?"
"Please Madeline, call me Ramone. And no, Italy, unfortunately, has no army, or at least none to boast of anyway." He brushed down his front buttons. "But I thank you for the compliment."
"It is very dashing, may I look at it closer?" she asked, "Your insignias and decorations I mean."
Needlessly clearing his throat, he nodded. "You may, if you wish." Spoken with a straightened back, he stared directly ahead as if on parade.
Madeline, taking her cue, rose with goblet in hand and moved towards him. But as she approached, she feigned, once again, a slight twist on her ankle, and with it, her wine flowed freely from her goblet upon his pristinely pressed tunic.
"Oh Monsieur, Monsieur," she quickly apologised. Upon doing so, she hastily retrieved the handkerchief from her sleeve.
Ramone stood with arms held out as she rapidly administered a clean-down of his uniform. This began in the fashion of downward strokes upon his tunic, but as she lowered herself, her hand worked its way down to wipe the dripping residue from his britches. As if they were fastened up, her sweeping motion brushed around and upon his naked skin and she watched, again at

41

eye level, as his penis moved freely about with her doing so. As before, even with him being inches from her, she played along and ignored its presence once again. When all was done, she rose to her feet, and looking up at him, smiled. "There, all done."
Ramone looked down, directly at her. "You play the game well, my child."
Her head leaned slightly to the side. "Monsieur?"
"Oh, come now, Madeline." Turning and heading for an armchair, he added. "I am not an fool, so please do not treat me as one." In doing so, he fastened himself up.
"I am sorry if I have offended you Ramone." It was her intention that she used his first name.
Now seated, he crossed one leg upon the other. "You play along with an old man's game well, Madeline," he remained silent, pondering for a moment, "but apparently with your own set of rules it seems."
She sat opposite him in the twinned armchair. "I only wished to make it better for you. Have I done wrong?"
Ramone laughed, this time with genuine pleasure. "No Madeline, you did not do wrong. But you did have me questioning whose game it was. Mine," He leaned over towards her, "or yours."
Madeline returned his smile and, at that, Monique entered the room. Making her entrance as bold as she could, she excused her absence. "Forgive me Ramone, I had to attend to one of the girls."
"Not at all Monique, Madeline has been a more than adequate host." Upon rising, he made his way forward to meet her. "And with that I will bid you farewell for the present."
"Oh, so soon, Ramone?"
"Alas, yes." He turned to face Madeline. "But my time here in your company has been, rewarding." He nodded slightly and smiled, "very rewarding indeed."
As she lay within the darkness of her room, Madeline considered Monique's closing remark. Of course he would want to see her again. After all, she had made it happen, and made it happen...
...her way.

*

Downstairs, Monique placed Ramone's payment for services rendered into her money box and closed the lid. As she tapped at its top, she considered what she had witnessed earlier. Through her concealed hole in the wall she had watched as Madeline went through the facade of spilling her wine and her jejune performance thereafter. This young girl had taken her instructions to the extreme she thought, and it was not to her liking. She alone set the standard and rules within these walls, not some fresh little minx from the countryside. She would have to keep a close eye and a tight leash on this Madeline if she was to have her under her control.

- And she knew the perfect man for the job.

*

Madeline 1

Chapter 5

Career

The following morning, Monique sat patiently awaiting her guest. If indeed such a person as Rubin could be construed as such. He was a part time employee who had, in the past, helped her out in some of the more extreme situations she'd had to deal with. But today's task was more run-of-the-mill. The door opened, and in he walked, all lumbering giant of him. And sat down opposite.
She looked on in disgust as he casually spat a mouthful of brown coloured phlegm onto her recently scrubbed kitchen floor, but as normal, she remained silent in her reproof of him. It would be cleaned up later. Looking up at his battle-scarred face with its stitched eye, she felt revulsion once again at his sordid appearance. She could never get used it, but he had played his part well and had been of use to her on numerous occasions in the past.
"You are to follow her when she leaves the house." Resolute in her instructions, she opened the box and on pulling some coins from within, she looked up once again. "I wish to know where she goes and who she meets." She handed him his payment. "Is that understood?"
Plucking the coins from her dainty hand with his grime-infested fingers, he stood up straight looking down at her. "A new one is she?"

"Who she is, is of no concern of yours Rubin. You will carry out my instructions without question. Is that clear?"
"Whatever you say Ma'am, whatever you say."

*

Upstairs, Madeline awoke refreshed and revitalized.
Stepping naked from the sheets, she casually walked towards the curtains, and standing just far enough back for decency, pulled them apart. Standing with arms open wide and unabashed with her nakedness within the privacy of her own room, she felt the warmth from the afternoon sun hit her skin. Leaning forward, she pushed open the window just in time to catch a breeze and upon closing her eyes to appreciate its brilliance upon her, she felt good within herself. She was in Paris and soon Paris would be hers. She would have it all.
With her stomach bereft of food, she readied herself to leave by donning a light dress of patterned orange and soft leather sandals. Descending the stairs, she made for the kitchen; and with a luncheon of cold meat, bread and cheese, she ate until full. After which, she headed out to the street.
Once there, she was undecided on what to do. She had come outside automatically. Be it with the sun drawing her into its glow or just a feeling of freedom to wander the city, she let her feet freely walk and she followed them where they took her. Unconsciously, they led her in the direction of the parliament buildings once again.
As she passed by the café where she had spoken to Gaston, the waiter, upon recognizing her, shouted a greeting, and more than happy to oblige, she responded with a smile and a wave.
She suddenly remembered Jacob and wondered at which school he was employed. It must have been local she thought, as he had several students with him the previous day. So, for the next hour or so, she roamed street after street in search of him. What the school building would look like, she had no idea, and eventually this thankless task suddenly felt to her foolish. So, making her way home, she was back in her room within thirty minutes.

Elsewhere, close at hand, someone not as nimble of foot as she had panted his way through the streets of Paris in her shadow. And as Rubin stood leaning against the wall outside the house, he coughed up a dry vomit and hoped to god that tomorrow she would stay indoors, or at least for his sake, walk slower.

*

Having retired early after dinner, Madeline had fallen asleep whilst reading a small book she had borrowed from Monique. Now, today, she felt as if she had slept for a week. Today was Friday, she thought, and in twenty four hours she would be meeting Jacob. So springing happily from her bed, she prepared for a good breakfast.

As she ate her dried oats and milk alone in the kitchen, Monique popped her head in the door.

"Madeline, come and see me when you have finished." This was more of a command rather than an invite, so when her breakfast was over, she headed for the parlour.

"Come in my dear." She nodded to a chair as an instruction to sit.

Madeline seated herself, as required, and said nothing.

"Your time of the month my dear, when is it due?"

Madeline looked puzzled. "When is what time due Madam?"

She turned to face her. "Your cycle, my dear, your monthly cycle, when are you to expect it?"

Madeline shook her head at a loss as to what was being asked of her. "I do not know what you mean, this cycle of which you speak."

Rising from her chair, Monique walked across the room towards her. "You mean you have not begun menstruating yet?"

Again Madeline shook her head. "I do not know what the word means." Her sorrowful face looked up. "But I can learn."

"Oh my dear, dear Madeline." She took the chair next to her. "Your mother has spoken nothing to you of such things?"

Madeline was lost for words. Her mother had spoken to her very little about a lot of things, unless of course she included what words lay within the bible. Again she waved her head in response.

As with her previous tutoring Monique explained to her the natural bodily functions of the normal woman.

"Then, until that time, I cannot be with child?" Madeline eventually understood and asked.

"That is correct, my dear. But that, I may add, is to our favour." She paced the floor, as was her norm. "Not only are you chaste but you cannot yet conceive." With this combination in mind, it spun in circles with the possible marketing potential, if, indeed, it was true.

"Sit upon the desk, my dear."

Madeline looked to her left and noticed the ornately carved writing desk upon which lay an assortment of materials and implements. She also noticed a basin of water, and heard Monique instruct further.

"And remove what undergarments you may be wearing."

Madeline sat in silence.

"Come, come my dear, I wish to examine you."

What she wished to examine by removing her undergarments, she was unsure of, but Madeline complied with this strange request. As she sat upon the edge of the desk, she rested her feet on either side of Monique's chair as instructed. She watched on as she raised her dress up to her waist.

"Did you ride as a child?"

"No Madame. Well once…"

Monique looked up. "Monique, my dear, we are alone."
"Yes Monique, sorry, no Monique," she jabbered, "I mean, I rode a friend's horse once... ouch!"
Pulling her hands free, Monique at dipped in the basin. "I gather by your reaction that there was some discomfort there?"
Assuming the examination was now over Madeline stepped down from the desk and lowered her dress. "Yes Monique, a cutting pain."
"Well, my dear, you are, without doubt, in tact." She proceeded to wash her hands. "The beauty of all Paris and chaste with it," she extolled with convoluted bravado. "…a child with the body of a woman, and a woman with the body of a child. How you have developed into such a mature woman without menstruating surprises me. You are, without doubt, a unique young woman, my dear."
Madeline smiled. "Is that good?"
"Good? Indeed it is my dear, indeed it is."

*

The young girl ran into her father's arms and as he tried to lift her up, he whirled her around in a circle as best he could. "You're getting too big for this sweetheart."
His wife hollered to him from the garden table. "You'll make her ill Gaston, you know how queasy she gets."
Letting her down, he patted her head to go play and made for the voice. "She hasn't eaten yet."
"I didn't mean her breakfast, I meant make her giddy." She refilled her teacup and poured Gaston a fresh one.
Sitting opposite, he raised it to his mouth. "Shouldn't she be at school by now?" He blew on the steaming hot brew.
Somewhat taken aback at this question, she raised her eyebrows. "Since when have you given any thought to our children's schooling?"
"Heavens dearest, I only asked." Momentarily distracted, he burnt his lip on the scolding tea. "Fuck!"
He heard the 'tutt-tutt' utter from her lips.
As he dabbed at his mouth with the table napkin, he looked at his wife Janis, her head as usual stuck deep in a thin paper book. His heart sank. What an existence. Long gone were the looks he had fallen in love with. Her prosaic, brown hair, tied back in a bun was like that of an old maid with a pallid, featureless face to match. Her toneless dress, sporting no style whatsoever, pulled at her shallow breasts and enhanced her ever-increasing overweight mid-rift. She had changed from a fair looking woman to that of an old crow. And he hated her. Hated what she had become, and hated her for making him what he was now.
He made ready to leave, and spoke out as pleasantly as he could muster. "I have to be going now, work beckons." But as he rose to his feet, the

expectation of acknowledgement to his pending departure left him yet again resentful of her.
"Mm-hhh!" This said without raising her head, but was added to soon after, "Remember, we are taking mother out to dinner tonight, so no dilly-dallying, straight home."
Spoken to like a child, he left the table, but beforehand, as had been customary to them for so long now, he bent to kiss her. But proffering the slightest of cheek, she received it cold.
As he trundled up the garden towards the house, he smiled to himself. 'No dilly-dallying eh! I'll show you fucking dilly-dallying you festering old trout.' He had already made his evening plans and they did not include dinner with his mother-in-Law and her bloody Christine de Pizan books. Tonight he would be visiting the house of another Madame….A certain Madame DeVille.

*

He arrived unannounced at seven o'clock while Madeline was bathing. Monique, her usual self, now entered the room, as equally unexpected, a minute thereafter. "He is in the parlour now. Do you wish him in your room?"
Shocked by the suddenness of it all, Madeline panicked "No Monique." But aware of her slip, she looked round towards the half-opened door. "Sorry, Madame. No, I do not wish to entertain this man in my own room. I hardly know him."
Monique handed her a towel. "Then use one of the others. Some of the girls have not yet arrived and are presently vacant."
Madeline wrapped it tightly around her and stepped free from the requisite eight inches. "It is not the use of my own room where my reluctance to receive him lies, but rather the private nature of it. What is to be expected of me now that he knows who, or what I am?"
Understanding her dilemma with what she would now consider to be Madeline's first client, she offered an alternative. "Very well, you may have the use of the parlour, if that pleases you."
"Oh, yes please, I'd prefer it that way as I am still unsure as to the nature of his calling. Whether it be cordial, or perhaps," She hesitated. "Is he a regular guest of yours? I mean, does he come here for…?" She lowered her voice. "I do not wish him to presume too much as I had met him in a café before I, well, before you, we…"
"Be calm, be calm. No, he is not one of my regulars, but he has asked for you specifically. I did wonder how he had come to know of your presence here, I had not yet made anyone aware of this."
But as Monique thought upon Gaston as a possible customer, Madeline hoped that his calling on her was in a more innocent fashion. Hadn't he said that some healthy competition, through rivalry with Jacob, could be

enjoyable to her? Well, she would have to see what developed during their evening together.
But first, she had to make herself presentable.

As she entered the parlour she spotted him at once, standing by the fire and exactly where Ramone had stood previously. He enthused over her on his approach.
"Madeline, Madeline," He took hold of her right hand with his both and fervently kissed at its back. "My heavens I had forgotten how beautiful you are."
And she was.
Sporting an off-white dress of tightened bodice, its laced length flowed with ease around her legs as the girdle enhanced the cleavage of her already full bosom to even greater effect. Her long, dark hair hung freely around her shoulders and her eyes shone like that of black diamonds. And with natural complexion, her face bore no powder or lips cochineal, for none were required as her natural beauty held sway over all ersatz décor.
"You surprise me with your presence Gaston."
Teasingly side-stepping his further advance and heading for her favourite seat by the fire, she continued. "I was led to believe by our last conversation that your knowledge of this place was known only to you by hearsay," And upon seating herself at the fire, concluded her homily, "But not location." She was deliberately inciting a reaction. "You have visited before?"
He immediately countered. "Certainly not. I had heard of this place previously, through an acquaintance, before meeting you and when you said you resided here I sought directions from the same person." Fidgeting, he moved towards her. "But only to see you again."
Madeline sat silent for a moment to consider the situation. If Gaston was aware of what Monique's house was and the profession of the residents therein, then in what capacity did he now place her?
"I am happy to hear it Gaston, but in what form does this visit take?"
Gaston, who had come to an immediate halt upon hearing this question, now paced the room with hands clasped at his back. "Well Madeline, that all depends on you. I had hoped to see you as any man would do after being taken by the charms of a woman such as yourself." He stopped in mid-pace and turned to face her. "But now I may well have to stand in line with the others."
She knew instantly what he meant by 'others' and was furious at his insinuation. But then, as she thought further upon his remark, he was correct in his assumption. She was, in truth, pure and simply, and by his own implication, one of Monique's women…
…And she should charge accordingly.

*

He laid the money on the table and with his outstretched hand, led her to stand. And as he held her in his arms, Madeline stared deep into his eyes. His conversation this last hour had been more exhilarating than their first encounter and she found herself lost within his words. He spoke of his affection for her and his plans for the future. And these, apparently, included her.

"I have thought of little else other than you, Madeline, since our first meeting," he admitted with unreserved ardor. "My waking day is filled with your image and that same picture still remains with me even in sleep."

Madeline was touched by his sentiments but felt that to feign a mutual feeling to such an extent on her own part would be unfair. Yes, her feelings towards him had increased slightly but her recent aspirations regarding her own future had altered dramatically. She decided she would play along and see what would develop. "So then, what would you like us to do?"

He returned her smile. "You decide. I want this to be as pleasurable for you as it is for me."

"It will be. I assure you."

At that, both felt a presence by their side. Scooping up the coins and noticing the gratuity left, the waiter thanked them.

"Let's just walk for a while Jacob."

"Of course, I have you for the whole day remember."

With Madeline intentionally arriving at precisely ten o'clock, they had both laughed at the exactitude of it, and for the next hour they indulged in whatever conversation took Jacob's pleasure. Nothing had changed there then, she thought, but she was content to sit and listen about his ideas of one day owning his own school.

Taking her arm now in his, their casual stroll upon the street let the morning sun shine its warmth down upon them. And with gloves, purse and parasol, Madeline felt aptly dressed now to do so.

As Jacob continued with his description of his dream school and his fervour regarding it apparent, Madeline considered what a favourable husband and provider he would be to the right woman one day. Unfortunately that woman would not be her, she had now decided. The previous night with Gaston had put pay to that thought.

His reply to her question regarding his visit had revealed to her two things. Firstly, she was, in his eyes, a common whore, though in her own mind that was not strictly true. She had not yet succumbed to pleasuring a man and even her time with Ramone did not enforce this thinking upon her. Secondly, she noticed more than just lust in his intensity. Even being as ignorant to the emotion as she was at such an age, she recognized what she possibly perceived as love. Whatever it was, she wondered how the two could work as one. Could a man possibly love a woman when he knew she lay with other men? Hardly, she thought. But Gaston had appeared to have been suggesting otherwise.

With her arm still locked in Jacob's as they walked, her mind wandered off to the previous night in the parlour.

"I care not what you do or what you are Madeline." She remembered him saying. "I seek only to attend to your every need."
So far advanced an emotion in such short a time had her confused. "Then how do you wish to proceed with this Monsieur?"
"Monsieur! Oh, please Madeline." Dropping down on one knee to clasp her hands, he explained further, his wants. "To begin with, it is my wish that you call me by name, not as some paying customer."
Madeline looked into his eyes and saw pain. With dark, tight, curled hair and a thinly trimmed moustache, his chiseled features portrayed a handsome man. A man any woman could easily fall in love with. But to her, she saw only one confounded by his emotions. "If that is what you wish Gaston, then I shall oblige."
What she thought she was obliging to, she was unsure of, but suddenly found his face, complete with tear-filled eyes, nestled in her lap. And as he sobbed like that of a child, her hand instinctively patted his head like one. Good gracious, what was happening here? But this childlike behaviour was short-lived and was soon replaced by a demeanour bordering on boorish.
He looked up, and stared straight at her. "I want you so much, my darling."
Tilting his head inwards towards her jutting neckline, he raised both hands to her breasts and held each one within his grasp. But as he frantically kissed at and around her cleavage, his grip upon her increased. Like an animal with its prey, he mauled at her.
Overpowered by his brute strength, her futile attempt to push him free failed miserably and she could only sit powerless whilst pinned to the chair. She could have easily shouted out for help from the heavy set man who was employed by Monique to safeguard her house when in business, but for some reason she did not.
"No Gaston, please no. Not like this. Please!" Her pleading took but seconds to penetrate his nefarious state and she suddenly felt his pressing grip upon her subside. She looked deep in to his eyes as his face raised to meet hers. "Please Gaston. Not this way, I can make it better for you. What is it you want me to do?"

But, as she walked arm in arm with Jacob now, she knew that in making it better for Gaston, she had signed off as redundant whatever plans for the future Jacob had in mind for her by way of marriage or any other association. She knew he would or could not accept her dual life as Gaston had done. He was far too righteous a man for that and it broke her heart to do so. She vowed there and then, that upon their eventual parting that evening, she would let Jacob go. She was determined that he would never discover her true existence.

Madeline 1

Chapter 6

Love and desire

As if the entire townhouse was made of Swiss cheese, Monique had witnessed the preceding night's scene through yet another of her clandestine spy-holes in the wall.
This Madeline was undeniably the little minx she had previously supposed her to be. She had tolerantly eavesdropped upon this spectacle with derision and had watched, once again, as Madeline twisted Gaston round her little finger. With her unwitting promise of 'making it better for him' on his first visit, he had reacted like a man possessed. And with Madeline having secured an extra curricular sum of money from him for services rendered, she herself had gained nothing from it. A subsequent search of Madeline's room, including the curtains, had left her even more infuriated as no tell tale sign of its secreted whereabouts could be found. This would not do, she thought. The sheep may not outwit the fox.
Last night, having been his second consecutive visit, it was, without doubt, the clincher. Whether it had been through her naivety or strictly controlled maneuvering, Madeline had Gaston pledge to her the world, or at least what he had of it.

But Monique knew for a fact that he was, indeed, a man of means, a Parisian well-to-do. He had devotedly endowed to Madeline assets far reaching even Monique's own expectations. A chateau, the envy of Paris, lay just outside its boundary, and although resided over by an inflexible and domineering matriarch-in-law, she knew that Gaston would inherit the family fortune in the not too distant future. Her ailing health dictating that her allocated years here on earth were almost spent. Furthermore, Gaston was a married man. But did Madeline know of this, she wondered?

As she looked across the table at her, she had pondered the consequences of such a union prior to Madeline's arrival at breakfast. She herself, as the 'Madame' would gain nothing from this unholy alliance. But with her knowing fully well that Gaston was married, she considered the options open to her at this juncture. Should she tell Madeline, in the hope that this would prevent further meetings? She should do, as she did not intend to let a comfortable future slip from her grasp, but in addition to this, she did not want to lose her. Her feelings towards this young woman was becoming much more than just a working relationship she now knew.

Pouring her third breakfast cup of coffee, she spoke out. "You must be making quite an impact on Gaston my dear. Twice now he has paid me over the odds to sit in your company. He is, without doubt, a generous man."

Madeline looked up from her plate to face her. She had been conscious of her silent stare since she'd sat down. "I wouldn't know of such things, Monique. You, yourself, have taken to deal with all business transactions in my stead."

Business transactions, business transactions! Who did this young girl think she was addressing her in such a tone? Business transactions, indeed!

Aware of the reaction she had just evoked in Monique, Madeline attempted a semblance of concord. "I meant to say that I have no experience in the affairs of money between customers and I am only too pleased that you are looking after my well-being." She fibbed.

Monique eyed her up quizzically. In such a short time in Paris she had secured the friendship of Ramone, had attained a tenable future with Gaston and, to her utter bewilderment, she had unmistakably scratched at the heart of a woman in the autumn years of life. Namely herself!

With an inward sigh, she looked upon the face of the heaven-sent angel who sat before her. Since her first encounter with Madeline, and taking her breast to her lips, she had fallen in love. Such an absurd thought in the past, would never had entered her head. These things, to someone as late in life as she, did not happen, even in their imagination. But she had been captured by this young woman. Everything about her she adored, and as much as she tried not to, she was still smitten. She could fully understand why the gentlemen of late had fallen for her. She was femininity personified. And although her professionalism as 'Madame' to the Parisian elite dictated that she should be devoid of such feelings, as hard as she had tried, her emotions as a woman countered them all.

She was in love.

On Gaston's initial visit, she had this professional attitude firmly tucked tight within her breast, but as she spied Madeline's teasing of him and innocently using a technique as yet understood or employed by any of her other girls, she hypnotically gazed on in admiration. And one of envy!
After Madeline had asked of Gaston what should could do for him, he had hasty unbuckled his belt and lowered his britches. She could still remember the look on Madeline's face when she saw his fully penis staring up at her. And with him placing her hand about it, and guiding her through the process until he ejaculated, she had found to her astonishment that her own hand had slipped beneath her petticoat. So, then, as it was, this picture of radiance had held both within her tight grasp as she came herself to orgasm watching on.
"Excuse me Madame."
Momentarily startled, she pulled herself swiftly from her thoughts and looked up at the waiting housekeeper. "Yes?"
"Please Madame, there is a gentleman caller."
So early in the morning, she thought. Surely not a client! "Very well, show him to the guest room. Tell him I will join him presently." Her rapier mind alert now to which of the girls were available at this early hour. However, her instruction was broken in mid-sentence as Madeline leapt from her chair.
"It is Ramone Monique, he has called for me."
Monique returned her gaze to the housekeeper and noticed the slight nod which confirmed this. "He asked only for Mademoiselle Madeline." She curtsied immediately, fearful of retaliation for being the bearer of bad tidings - such was Monique's dominance over the staff.
"Then make haste and ready yourself," she offered as politely as she could to save face in front of them both.
Madeline smiled at her. "Thank you," Then suddenly remembered the housekeeper by her side, "Madame." She made her leave with a spring in her step.
Monique sat in silence as she watched Madeline make her exit. Ramone, indeed, and when was she going to be informed of this?
Her mind drifted back to the night when she had woken Madeline and the sight of her undressing in preparation of first meeting him. Slipping from her dress she had noticed Madeline's shape from behind. Bending forward, her long, slender back curved into a gracefully, narrow waist and culminated in beautifully curved thighs, the likes of which Monique had only dreamed of. And with her long, pale legs extending down to her narrow ankles, she was perfection. In her mind's eye she had inched forward placing her hand upon her rear and instantly feeling the warm, silky skin beneath her palm. And as she gently kneaded the flesh, she had felt the heated sensation within her grow. Kneeling down, she'd placed her hands upon either side of Madeline's rear and, looking upon this derriere perfection, she'd gently parted its halves. She'd felt the instant surge in her loins, as she did now, when she beheld the delights before her. With pink, moist skin masked in a deep, black coiffure,

she'd inched her way towards it and, in veneration, immersed her face deep within.
Her body shook slightly with the mixture of her lust and the anger she felt at herself for succumbing to such thoughts. As Monique watched Madeline close the door behind her, she rose from the table and after dabbing her lips with the napkin, threw it on the table. "The eggs were not cooked to my satisfaction this morning." She followed in Madeline's steps. "I want the cook fired. Find a replacement, now." Damn this incessant girl for making her feel this way, damn her, damn her, damn her…but pausing at the door, she deliberated for a moment in thought, then nodding slightly with her instant decision making, turned on her feet. "Find Rubin for me and tell him I want to see him."

*

Gaston refilled his glass with the rich cognac and raised it to his lips. But before he sipped at its edge, he tilted it slightly in a self-congratulatory salute, 'Bravo Gaston. You have done well, my good fellow.'
Drinking this early in the day was not the norm for him and with little, if any, breakfast in his stomach, the effects had been immediate. He now swayed a little to the side. With this being his fifth in so short a time, he fell back upon his armchair and, with outstretched legs, half-emptied the glass in one go.
The euphoria he felt with the drink in his system was mixed with the pleasurable memories of the evenings spent with Madeline. In this semi-inebriated state, his thoughts raced back to their first night when, through sheer determination and a convincing act, he had made headway with Paris' finest. The recollection of this encounter was still a vivid picture in his mind, he soon noticed, as the bulge in his britches now clearly testified.
His plan, thus far, regarding Madeline had seen encouraging results.
Shrewd as Monique thought she was, it was widely known in her circle of clients that her spy-holes in the walls existed within each room of the house. So, knowing full well that Monique was watching their every move, he made sure that paying Madeline was in full view of her. This, he had hoped, would instill animosity between them both thus aiding in his plot to tear Madeline free from the house and Monique's grip. A two-pronged attack.
The extra payment, in addition to Monique's fee, was for Madeline's purse alone. And the time in her magnificent company was well worth it. She had made him feel like a real man. Long gone were the days when his wife showed any emotion towards him. His hatred of her now was now on a par with her contempt for him. And in cupping Madeline's breasts in his hands, he had made his desire for her even more. Her body, like that of a goddess, had driven him to passions unbound, himself unable to control his own natural feelings. Thus, totally out of character, he had acted like some crazed fiend mauling at her body.

Her words, 'she would make it better for him', had been music to his ears. He felt himself harden further within his britches even now at the thought of it and closed his eyes to recap on the delights of Madeline's soft touch upon him. It had been what he had planned for and with her obliging his needs, her gentle strokes had taken him to heights unknown. As the pleasure he had felt on both occasions was replayed in his mind, his free hand grasped at his front. The goblet meantime fell from his left as he felt his britches fill with the same warmth that Madeline had so easily taken from him then. He jolted his orgasm further until complete.

But as immature a reaction as this was to a memory, he felt no embarrassment with himself. So, casually pulling himself free of the armchair, and through drunken stupor, he staggered his way over to the washbasin. If he was to never see his sweet angel again, he thought, then this memory of her would indelibly stamped in his head. But this was far from his intentions. His plans were more than just a fleeting fancy, they were real. And this included gaining his inheritance sooner rather than later.

His wife's mother may own the chateau where they resided, but hadn't he worked hard to get to where he was today? Hadn't he been the one that, for many years, had to endure the company of the Parisian poseurs in order to gain respect in his own right? Suffered countless evenings during over-indulgent repasts with aging Lotharios and their talk of libertarian art, and the monotonous utterances of ministerial old goats of which he had nothing remotely in common with. These rampant thoughts were physically transferred to the struggle with his belt. And as he attempted to lower his britches in order to rinse himself fresh, his anger made even more headway towards its zenith. He had seen very little of the family wealth thus far. With his mother-in-law refusing to part with a denier, she clutched her riches firmly to her ever-increasing bosom. Even with the fleet of carriages she owned, she had still chosen to travel by public coach to visit them in Paris. This, in her parsimonious mind, would have saved on the cost of a driver.

His temper at bursting point, he lapped furiously at the water, soaking himself, until, with a final sweep of his hand, the porcelain basin flipped over and fell crashing to the floor. Looking up, his blurred vision caught sight of himself in the mirror. Standing with britches at half-mast and himself fully exposed, he rocked to the side slightly. Momentarily stunned at the pathetic image before him, both body and mind refocused. He planned to have Madeline whatever it took. If he could not have her, then no-one in Paris would. This he vowed - and turned to face the housemaid who now stood in the doorway, mouth agape.

*

"So where is he spending his time?"
"I do not know Mother."

"Then, as a wife, you should." She ignored the waiter as he topped up her wine.

Waiting patiently for him to leave, she leaned across the table and in an almost whisper, "Please Mother, lower your voice." She scanned the room quickly and returned with wide-eyed gaze. "I do not wish all of Paris to know my business."

"Pah!"

Resuming her upright position befitting a lady, she regained her composure. "He is a political man, he has friends and, as such, he is obliged to spend time in their company." Although knowing fully well that this feeble excuse would not appease her mother one bit.

"Yes, but do all gentleman of Paris smell of 'eau de toilette'?"

Janis knew her Mother to be correct in her assumptions. Gaston had returned home the last two nights and had certainly not reeked of his usual brandy and pipe smoke from his club. To the contrary, he smelled of another woman. And not just the artificial smell of scent, this was of natural odour, one of femininity…one of grace.

Her head dipped slightly and she let her eyes take account of what lay before them. As dowdy a dress she had ever worn, her present wardrobe being of similarly colourless and dull replicas. Her shapeless hips and waist spoke only of a middle-aged woman with the best part of her life now behind her, the bulge in her mid-rift seemingly ever more prominent with each day passing. Was it any wonder that her husband's eyes had possibly been drawn to that of another woman? She lifted her glass from the table and unconsciously let the wine swirl in her hand. As she looked deep into the red vortex, she wondered at what part in her life she had changed.

As a youth, her unlimited family budget permitted her free reign in the choice of the latest French fashion. She had taken full advantage of their fortunate wealth within the Parisian class structure. So much so that she was, undoubtedly, a woman much sought after as a wife.

In return, Gaston had fitted her own expectations of that of a husband from their very first meeting. Their relationship quickly blossomed into something special and four months later they were duly wed. Having a child in their first year of marriage meant that her body would never be as it once was. She knew Gaston had noticed this; and their frequent lovemaking in the past was reduced to the occasional two minute session of which his performance was often notwithstanding her wants.

Her eyes reluctantly pulled themselves from the now static wine and glanced around the room. Looking over her mother's shoulders, they were instantly drawn to the entrance where, if she had felt unwomanly before, the scene now before her reinforced it. Being led into the room by a uniformed gentleman of aging years was a sight to behold. A young lady, unquestionably his granddaughter, drifted towards their allocated table with such poise as to turn the heads of all seated in close proximity, both gentlemen and ladies alike. Janis could only look on in envy as this gracious being brushed her tightly bodice farthingale along the floor with smooth familiarity. A lace of pure white, which upon her left breast was placed a cameo, and her elegance outshone, by far, her luxuriant surroundings.

Janis swallowed what was left of her claret and, devoid of all etiquette, laid it heavily upon the table.

Conscious of her daughter's sullen thoughts but unaware of the cause, she attempted a distraction through encouraging discourse. "Perhaps, a change would do you good." She enthused, but immediately regretted the suggestion.

A change in what, thought Janis? Everything! Such a suggestion was the last thing she wanted to hear as this was admitting that she was, indeed, the frump she thought herself to be. Leaning forward as before, her words were now of a more solemn nature, "As a mother yourself, I had expected at least you would have noticed a slight change in your daughter's appearance of late."

Momentarily taken aback at her daughter's tone, her immediate response was once again regretted, "You may have gained a pound here and there but nothing of any consequence."

Still a mere foot from her mother's face she countered, "And has it not occurred to you why?"

She shrugged. "Well I naturally assumed that you have done what most women do when neglected...oh, you're not?"

Slouching back into the chair, Janis's head nodded confirmation. "Yes I am mother. I am with child." She closed her eyes at the prospect. "I am expecting Gaston's child."

*

Being led into the dining room by Ramone, Madeline was instantly struck by its magnificence. Such a room the likes of which she had never seen before nor ever imagined could exist. This was one of Paris' finest, Ramone had informed her, reserved for the privileged few, the French elite. A beacon of which was a constant reminder to the gentry of the extensive class difference rife in contemporary France at present. 'Surroundings to which Madeline was perfectly suited', he'd added.

Gone was the antiquated, politically correct, Baroque style of most rooms she had seen in the past, usurped now with the new Rococo method of asymmetrical designs. With curves of gold and pastel colours, this blended well with the ornamental mirrors and paintings which adorned the walls. The ornate furnishings of the highest quality sat proudly amidst some of the finest sculptures she had ever seen, one of which stood adjacent to their allotted table.

Letting herself be seated by the head waiter, she sat in silence and in awe of her surroundings.

Allowing her the due time to adapt, Ramone eventually put her at ease, "Such an ambiance was made for you, my dear Madeline." With a playful wink of an eye, he edged forward. "You look stunning by the way. Did you see all eyes turn as we entered?"

This had been clearly stated within earshot of their attending waiter which made Madeline's face flush pink.

But upon seeing her rapidly reddening face, Ramone playfully added further fuel to her fire, "What do think Gerard?" He looked up at the waiter. "Am I justified in saying such a thing?"

It was a general principle amongst waiters that they should willingly agree with any customer, this not only being establishment rules, but in the hope a huge gratuity at meals end. But on this occasion there was no need for pretext, Gerard had never seen such radiance in a woman before and he had served the most beautiful women in Paris. But replying with the degree of decorum and etiquette allowed, befitting his position, he briefly replied, "Without doubt." He abruptly changed the subject. "The usual Armagnac, Monsieur?"

"Hmm! Let me see." Upon looking at Madeline, he deliberated. "Yes, why not, I think this young lady can stand the taste of such." He nodded upwards. "Two."

With the waiter now gone, Madeline felt a little more relaxed. "I feel very special today Ramone. What a wonderful time I am having, and this." Referring to the dress that Ramone had purchased for her not thirty minutes previous, she felt the fine material underhand as she drew it across her waist.

"As much as I admired your dainty, little country dresses Madeline, they, unfortunately, would not go down too well here," He joked.

Madeline took stock of the room once again and returned his gaze. "Such affluence."

"I will repeat my earlier statement. This is what you were made for Madeline. Look around you. These are the upper echelon of Paris within these walls and you fit perfectly in this circle and not the house of Monique. Or is that what you are, or more importantly, is that what you want to be?"

What did she want, Madeline thought? Escaping the confines of her mother, her dreams of Paris had always been to meet and marry a man of influence and wealth. But her attitude to life had changed dramatically since arriving in the city. So much had happened. She had learned so much but there were still so many things she didn't understand. During the course of the day, when he had taken her by carriage around Paris, they had talked of many things. She knew he was a friend and confidant and now, conscious of his silence, she spoke out. "May I speak openly with you Ramone?"

He leaned closer. "Of course you can. What irks you?"

She innocently blurted it out. "I have pleasured a man twice now and for payment in return,"

Not many things, spoken in earnest, shocked a man of Ramone's age in life, but he sat lost for words. This was not in respect of the act which she had

supposedly been performed on said individual, but the blatant, preamble-free way in which she had announced it. "I must say, Madeline, you know how to leave an old man speechless."
But Madeline had heard very little of this reply as her attention was drawn to a remote table by the wall. Considering their opulent surroundings and what Ramone has said of her country dress not suiting, as lacklustre a woman as Madeline had ever seen sat at a table attired in what appeared to her to be very inappropriate apparel for the room. She was clearly upset as well, sobbing almost.
"You seem distracted, Madeline." He turned to follow her gaze.
What her preoccupation was with, he was not to find out. With the waiter's arrival at their table, his presence had not only drawn Ramone's attention back but had also blocked Madeline's view. So as the waiter exchanged professional pleasantries with regard to the day's food recommendations, Madeline surreptitiously peered round his frame. But a surprise awaited her.
The sobbing woman forgotten about, Madeline smiled to herself. Even at such an awkward angle, she instantly recognized the fellow diner as the elderly brandy drinker who had been her co-passenger on her coach journey to Paris. What a coincidence! And still dressed entirely in black, she noticed. But the elation was short lived when remebered in whose dignified company, and the surroundings, she now sat. Since arriving in Paris, and in less than a week, she had gone from the shy little girl on the coach, to this. Surely the subterfuge and lies needn't have to start again. She watched on as they rose from their chairs and after adjusting themselves in preparation of leaving, made for the exit, which was directly in their path. She would have to make herself disappear.
Ramone noticed the adjustment in her seating position. "Is something wrong, Madeline?" He watched further as her body leaned in towards the table and slumping down by her side. "Are the seats not to your liking?"
"No, no," she lied, "I think I may have a small pebble in my boot." She now leaned at a ninety degree angle to the table.
Confused, Ramone let her proceed. "I've taken the liberty of ordering for us both. I hope you don't mind?" Finding himself talking to the back of her head, "Bouillabaisse," he announced with bravado.
Half-hearing Ramone's ramblings about this being a very special fish dish from Marseilles, she continued the deception with her boot. How long she could keep this façade up she was unsure, considering they were high laced, but her question was answered by a voice from above.
"Well, well. What have we here?"
Madeline recognized the voice immediately and on raising her head to face her, forced a surprised smile. "Ah, bonjour Madame." The insincerity of her tone was fooled no-one.
"I thought I knew you from across the room. But no, I thought, surely this couldn't possibly be the young lady to whom the arts world was beckoning to join."

Madeline noticed the woman standing to her left. Her face red and eyes awash she remained unmoved, oblivious to the conversation. Apparently she had more important issues on her mind rather than to listen to the sarcastic 'talking down to' of a young woman.

Aware of Madeline's predicament, Ramone gallantly came to her aid. "You have me at a disadvantage here Madame." He raised himself slightly from his seat. This was done just sufficient to show good protocol but equally to show his discontent with her manner.

Recognizing this, she glanced at him briefly. "My name is of little consequence." She noticed his choice of dress. "As is the uniform you blazingly sport."

It appeared to Madeline that this woman showed no mercy when it came to formalities, so, in response to Ramone coming to her assistance, she did likewise. "Madame, I have noticed that your everyday choice of dress colour is in complete harmony with your denunciatory play on words. In addition to this, I see that you are callous enough in nature to allow the lady to your left, who is clearly upset, to remain so whilst you find it acceptable to stand and bandy words with near strangers. It would be better, would it not, if you dealt with the important issues at hand and this way you may not feel as uncomfortable with the conversation as we both do. Now if you would excuse us, we were in the middle of dining."

Even Ramone was shocked with her denigration, but inwardly smiled at her nerve.

"Well, I never," She turned on her feet and made for the exit, with Janis submissively following in her wake.

Ramone, although momentarily speechless, eventually found the words, "You know, Madeline, in all my years I have found that each time you are fortunate enough to make five good friends, in return you make one bad enemy." He leaned forward. "I do believe I've just met your first."

Madeline shook her head. "It matters not to me, Ramone." And recalling the coach trip, explained. "I have very little time for anyone who, whilst with a smile upon their face, would at the same time easily pierce your heart with a blade."

"I gather then you have met this woman before?" He raised the much needed Armagnac to his lips.

"Yes, on the coach journey to Paris. Ramone, she was kind to me. She felt my loss at me missing my family but as I conversed with Jacob and we became friends, her feelings towards me changed."

Ramone looked surprised. "Jacob?"

Running her index finger up and down the stem of her glass, she pondered on whether to explain to Ramone the entire story. Of her excitement on waiting for their café appointment and during which she had announced to him that she was she would not be seeing him again, and the reason why!

"There is much I have still to learn about you, my dear Madeline. But I'm a patient man, you tell me what you want and when you want to." He finished his drink in one swoop, and looked around for Gerard. "Another I think."
"I cannot see Jacob after what I have done, Ramone."
Gerard, on his approach, took Ramone's flick of the hand as an order to stay away. As he moved closer towards Madeline, his voice spoke in tender tone, "Madeline, if you prefer that we talk about this in more convivial surroundings we can leave now. I am willing to take you anywhere you want. I am your friend remember."
Looking up from her untouched drink, she saw the look of concern on his face. "I am aware of that, Ramone, and I am grateful for it."
"Then tell me. I may be old and not the youth I once was but I can assure you, my dear, I was young once." Upon leaning back into his chair, he tried to make sense of his own remark.
Madeline looked into his aged eyes and saw the maturity and wisdom that lay deep within. She smiled at him as readily as her heart desired. "You remind me of my father."
Somewhat shaken with this announcement, he offered council. "Well I doubt very much that your father would be at all pleased with the circumstances in which we had met, so I would remove that thought." He finished with an embarrassing cough.
Madeline's smile turned to a grin. "I find it hard to grasp now that you of all people," and blushing with it, "would be the first manhood that I would see."
It was his turn now to show reddened face, and as he looked around him for Gerard in search of a much needed drink, he found that he was too afraid to look her straight on. Catching his attention, he now demanded, through gesture, that Gerard should further his drink. Eventually he spoke. "You have me at a loss for words once again."
"Ramone, you have become my friend and have shown me such kindness." She paused once again, to admire the décor. "May I not give you something you desire in return?"
Overhearing this last remark upon his untimely arrival at the table, Gerard laid the drinks upon the table.
Ramone looked up. "If you value your job young man you will repeat none of this," he commanded, "Is that understood?"
Madeline pulled her fingers to her lips to suppress her laugh and watched on as Ramone's face reddened further.
Gerard, meanwhile, showed the utmost professionalism and replied accordingly, "Monsieur, I could hear the conversation but I assure you I was not listening." Leaving the table, he knew fully well that his gratuity in service had now immediately doubled.
"Surely you cannot feel embarrassed at what I say, when it was you, yourself, who made me aware of such things?"
"I made you aware. Me?"
"I had never seen a man until you, Ramone."

"My sweet, sweet Madeline, you know only too well why the visits to Monique's house are important to me. It's all that I have." Now feeling like a childish fool, he raised the drink to his mouth.
"Yes, but Monique has explained to me why. Can I not do to you what I have done to another man, it only takes but seconds?"
Ramone's Armagnac barely touched his lips before it was sprayed across the table. And noticing the dark specs upon Madeline's dress, his request to leave immediately had Madeline confirm it.

Gerard, upon calling them a carriage, received his well-earned gratuity underhanded from Ramone.
But as they descended the steps to enter the coach, they were approached with stealth from behind. Madeline turned in shock to face their assailant, only to see the six-inch blade held to Ramone's throat.

Madeline 1

Chapter 7

Unequivocal love

"You filthy swine."
She lifted the thin sheet from them both and flicked it in the air to release the stench of his flatulence.
"You've done it again," she continued, "You fuckin' pig."
Rubin, meanwhile, lay slovenly naked on the bed beside her, this being yet another one of his disgusting habits he made Annie endure during his visits with her. He knew only too well that he was a pig but he cared very little about what people thought of him.
Remaining motionless and semi-conscious, he heard Annie's persistent diatribe through muted ears. Allowing his sight time to get accustomed to the inside of his eyelids, he remained frozen, awaiting the inevitable pounding in his head to begin. His hangovers were getting worse these days he'd noticed.
Annie, as if impatient with this slow build-up, continued unremitting with her ear-shattering, high-pitched wails a mere foot from his head. Long gone

were the times, as a soldier, when he could drink for days after battle and still remain alert enough to fight on a whim. Capable of enduring canon fire and musket shot within inches of him, he now found himself unable to endure the simple rants of a woman when his head was throbbing. As strong and robust as he was, he recognized, only too well, the tell tale signs that he was getting old....old and repulsive. The full-length facial scar that he adorned had been hideously stitched together by a battlefield physician who had all the dexterity of a field-hand ploughman. The protestant sword which had laid waste his cheek had also taken many of his right teeth with it. So, all in all, he was not, by his own admission, the most sought after beau in town.

Annie, aware now of her fruitless endeavours to rouse a reaction from him, snuggled into his back. "You want seconds?"

With a solitary grunt, he pulled himself free from her clutches and draped his powerful, bare legs over the edge of her flea-ridden bed. Robustly shaking his head in an attempt to get some focus into his eyes, his hand simultaneously groped blindly for his wine that he was certain to be at his feet somewhere. Finally locating it, he uncorked the bottle and on placing it to his lips, guzzled down the contents in one continuous sweep. Looking down at the empty bottle in the vain hope that it would miraculously refill itself, he wiped his sodden stubble with the back of his hand and burped loudly.

"Pig."

Ignoring her empty insult, he burped again even louder and nonchalantly tossed the empty bottle over his shoulder, narrowly missing her head by inches.

Unashamedly sitting up and letting her massive bosom swing free, she punched repeatedly at his hirsute back. "You dirty swine."

Unperturbed by her pounding, he casually rose from the soiled sheets and went in search of his clothes within the dimly lit room.

Sitting cross-legged upon the bed, she folded her arms, giving her huge but wilting breasts some much needed support.

"That'll be five," she demanded.

Clearing his throat and spitting into the corner for the fifth time since his arrival, he made no effort, once again, to even remotely hit the bucket.

"Did you hear me?" repeating her demands with all the assertion she knew he would tolerate.

Sighing, Ruben dug deep into his pocket and pulled out a clasped hand. Throwing two small coins onto the wooden table, he proceeded to buckle up his wide, leathered belt as he watched one of them spin and roll off onto the floor. Grinning to himself, he looked down at her and noticed the silent reaction to the pittance he had just rewarded her for services rendered.

"Is that it?" Her tone despondent. "Is that all I'm fuckin' gettin' for what I've just done for you?"

Looking down at the shaven-headed, young girl as she pulled on and laced up her tattered, off-white top, he grunted, "Huh."

"What do you mean... huh?"
He dipped his head down to but an inch from her face. "You swallow next time and you might get more."
Straightening up, he fastened his waistcoat together and retrieved his sheathed knife from beneath the bed. Sticking it covertly down the back of his britches, he pulled on his three-quarter length jacket, thus covering the eight inch lethal weapon from view. He had a job to do.
With one final spit, he made his way across the bare, wooden floorboards towards the door. "Same time, next week." His right hand waved in a mock salutary fashion.
He heard her hard, wooden sandal hit against the door as he closed it behind him, and her rant. "Then have a wash first then you filthy bastard."

Avoiding the broken steps as he descended the stairs, he held onto the wavering banister for support. He had only just reached the bottom when a croaked and stammering voice came from the left.
"Annie free now is she, is she? Is Annie free now?"
Rubin looked down at the three foot high obesity and smiled back with blackened teeth. "Yeah." He glanced up at the stairs, "An' just ripe for the pickin'."
"So, you got any money on yah my friend?"
Rubin straightened his powerful torso up in disbelief. "What, I moisten the bitch for you and you want me to pay for her as well?"
With his short, portly legs all a fidget, he pleaded further, "Come on now, Rubin, you owe me."
"Owe you for what?"
Nodding slightly, he winked. "You know?" With this he continued on, but only after a quick scan of the room, "The night of the fire,"
He impatiently awaited Rubin's recollection of the time in question. "You know, the dead girl."
It wasn't hard for Rubin to lift him single-handedly by the shirt front up to face level. And as he watched him squirm with the tightness of his chest, he stared right at him, his rancid breath making him gag. "I told you to forget about that, Sach."
"Okay, okay."
Rubin's release made him drop four feet to the ground and as Sach brushed himself straight, Rubin dug deep into his pocket for the second time that morning. He had to think about how much he had left. The money that Monique had given him was almost spent. Between the women and his taste for the taverne's cheap wine, he'd nearly squandered the lot. He opened his palm and sighed once again. What remained of his payment didn't amount to much. Considering what he had done, and still had to do for it, he thought himself vastly underpaid yet again. He would have to come to a more beneficial agreement with Monique in the future. But then what do half-

blinded, ex-soldiers do to earn a coin if not the insalubrious demands of the wealthy.
"I can give you two," was all he volunteered, "an' that's more than I can spare, so think yoursel' lucky I'm in a good mood." And he was - he always felt good after a time with Annie.
"Two's fine."
On snatching them from Rubin's hand in mid-march, he made his way dancing and singing up the stairs. "Annie, Annie baby, here I come, my love."
Rubin shook his head, spat again, then made for the street. He needed a drink.
His eyes squinted at the sudden glare of the sunlight after the dimly lit surrounds of his favourite brothel. As much as he knew every thoroughfare, back street and rat hole in Paris, with his heavy head lounging on his shoulders it took him a moment to get his bearings. Important as his task in hand was, he needed to get some wine in him first. He'd make for Sally's place. She was open for anyone, anytime. And smiling into himself at the double meaning, he took a left down the street.

*

Jacob threw the manuscript to the floor. He'd had enough. He could not concentrate on school reports at this time. Leaning back deep into his hard, wooden chair, he lifted both feet and placed them heavily on the table in front of him. Oblivious to the reaction of his students, he raised both arms and, threading his fingers threw his long, waving hair, held his palms firmly to his head.
Why? Why? Why? He thought. And with each one word question within his head, his body reacted similarly with the heel of his boot thumping on the wooden surface.
Closing his eyes even tighter than before, he replayed the day spent with Madeline in his head once again. This, in the off-chance he had overlooked something that was perhaps said or done to make her finish their brief but blissful relationship so prematurely. He could think of nothing. His mind was blank. He had treated her with all the dignity and decorum he'd had within him. And yet she had still chosen to part from him. Why?
He recalled the afternoon when he had seen her at the café. She was in another man's company. He dismissed the thought immediately. Madeline had mentioned nothing of this tryst and why should she? With contradiction of thought, he was consciously aware of someone by his side.
"Sir."
He opened his eyes to see one of his eldest students standing a few feet from him. His mind taking a few moments to refocus, he noticed the young man patiently awaiting the release from his reverie, then eventually attempting further communication, "Sir, I need some assistance with a problem."

Sighing, Jacob resumed his seated position and looked at the question at hand. Noticing that the wording to which the student was referring, he felt himself madden. "For heaven's sake, Renee. We have covered this on numerous occasions before and yet you still fail to grasp the concept of it. Are you stupid man?"
Aware that he had said this in full earshot of Renee's fellow students, Jacob felt sudden remorse at his own stubborn outburst. Tugging at the restrictions of his knotted tie around his neck, he took a deep, inward breath. He needed air. He needed to breathe. He felt stifled within the confines of the school room.
"I'm sorry Renee. I'll explain later."
Standing, he picked up his leather satchel and threw it over his shoulder. "I will return in a short while. Continue with the...," he announced, but had to pause in mid-sentence as he couldn't recall the theme he'd given his students. "Well... just continue." His jabbering making his already blushing face redden further.
Leaving the room in a flustered state, he made for the open street.

He would walk aimlessly, he thought, try and rid himself of the pain. Erase the memory of her from his mind. But he knew within himself that he could not, should not. Madeline had burrowed her sweet, innocent-self deep into his heart in such a short time that he had thought of little else. In addition to this, he felt remorse and guilt at the neglect of his students. Their schooling had suffered severely with his sporadic periods of quiet introspection in class. So much so that their tuition in the last two days had amounted to nothing more than 'Rome was definitely not the capital of Spain', he himself making this faux pas. His recollection of this foolish mistake made him kick out at one of the stray curs which had innocently crossed his path as he walked. As it yelped at him doing so, he disregarded the startled looks from fellow pedestrians as he ambled on towards destination unknown. This, whilst venting his frustration out further upon the pavement debris as he went.
With shoulders crouched and head hung low, he unconsciously wandered onto the street. Oblivious to his surroundings, he neither saw it nor heard it. But felt the impact on every bone in his body as the carriage careered in his direction and struck him full on.

*

"Leave the bottle."
"That's your second." She announced whilst avoiding his grope. "And you still haven't paid for the first one yet."
Being too quick for her, he grabbed her by the rear and pulled her closer. "Since when have I ever let you down, Sally?"

"Hah, on numerous occasions," And on pulling free, added further "and I'm not talking about the wine either."
A riotous laugh erupted from the nearby tables on overhearing this remark. But ignoring them, Ruben let her go on about her business and uncorked the bottle. There had been a slight improvement in his head with the first bottle and he now hoped by the time he had finished this one, he would be back to normal. He leaned to the side but was interrupted in mid-emission.
"And stop spitting on my floor you filthy beggar," rasped Sally from the counter.
Swallowing back what he'd prepared to expurgate, he slated himself on the tepid red wine, emptying a third. After a loud burp, he rested the bottle on the lap of his outstretched legs and looked about him. Normal, he thought. But what was his normal? What was he reduced to now, chasing a young girl about the streets of Paris, lurking in doorways and spying on a romantic meeting. Huh, he was worth more than that, he thought. After all, hadn't he fought for his country? In fact more than just France, he'd fought as mercenary on numerous sides. His loyalty had been to himself, not to some poseur king or infantile queen or even to someone in Rome calling himself Pope. He was from Germanic blood and proud of it. Even though being an illegitimate son without knowing either of his parents, he'd been raised the hard way, fending for himself, looking after number one. What had they called him in the army? Ah yes, the toughest and meanest bastard in the regiment, he recollected with self-admiration. And he had lived up to that title on numerous occasions. On one such instance, bringing back to camp as a token of war, the helmet of the protestant who had sliced at his face, complete with the head still in it. This, after eviscerating the poor bastard and letting him die slowly while choking to death on his own manhood.
And now this!
Reduced in rank to beneath that of an ordinary soldier, could he get any lower, he thought?
And what was it with this new girl that Monique was so intrigued by? She had never been as over-protective with any of her other girls as she was with this young girl. Madeline, he'd found out from Rosie, her name was and he didn't mind saying, she was a looker to boot. In fact, in retrospect, he'd actually grown quite fond of her shenanigans. The youthful and innocent way she carried herself. Granted, she had run his arse all over Paris but it was safe to say he liked her just the same.
Nodding, while agreeing with his own thoughts, he raised the bottle again and downed another third. And as befitting the second third, came the mandatory burp. Without thinking, he turned and spat on the floor. Merde, he thought, looking up slyly to the bar. Sally had her back to him. Good.
He returned to both pose and thought. Or he would have, had an odorous smell not filled his nostrils, making his already fragile stomach turn giddy. Sally had started to prepare her daily feast of rabbit stew. How her patrons could stomach the muck she regularly churned out under the vise of food, he

couldn't imagine. Hadn't it occurred to anyone yet, that Paris wasn't exactly rife with rabbits? But as a savoury substitute, the city did have rats in abundance. He could stomach it no more, and had to leave. Throwing what coins he had left onto the table, he re-corked the bottle and stuck it in his coat pocket. Re-adjusting the blade at his back, he bade Sally a fond farewell and left her to her culinary delights.
He still had work to do.

*

Madeline 1

Chapter 8

Enlightenment

Madeline stepped out from her blood-stained dress and with complete indifference to the newly acquired garment, threw it in the corner. Hastily removing her undergarments, she guided herself into the consolatory comfort of the warm bath. Immersed to her naval, she sat upright and frantically rubbed at her hands and arms to remove the dried-in blood. After a moment, she held them out in front of her, palms down. They were still trembling. Pulling herself down, she fully immersed her face and scrubbed likewise, knowing full well that the spray from the neck wound had covered her. She had been momentarily blinded by it. The razor had dragged across the throat so acutely that the deep arterial fluid had, in one rapid jet, sprayed her upper half. It had all happened so quickly, and with her being pulled to the ground by someone unknown for her own protection, she was unsure as to the assailant. She could remember one thing though, whoever it was, their body odour reeked. She could smell it in her nostrils even now.

Wiping the dripping residue from her face, she sat up with her long legs fully stretched. This being Monique's private bathroom, the luxury of the deep enamel bath was a grand step up from the tin one used on her first night. She alone, out of all the girls, was now permitted to use this at her leisure. The exclusivity of this had not been taken lightly by the others who, on the previous day, had snubbed her friendly salutations during breakfast. As well as her rapidly growing friends and acquaintances list, Madeline noticed that she was also attaining an equal amount of opponents to her charms.
- Enemies almost.
But the invigoration of the warm water about her consoled her slightly to the extent that she considered the events of the day. And on recounting this in her head, she found herself not only shocked by the assault upon Ramone and herself but equally excited by it as well. This mixture of emotions had her mind in a spin. How could she possibly be abhorred with such a violent act and yet, similarly, feel this emotionally charged, and to the extent that her body reacted to this mental stimulus in a corporeal fashion?
She focused in on the attack. And in reaction to this, she felt a tingle in her lower half. Tensing her muscles to let the feeling take its hold upon her, she found her right hand involuntarily rising to her breast. Placing her middle finger gently upon her left nipple, she felt her eyelids automatically close in response. With a circular motion, she felt herself harden beneath its tip. Her body appeared to stretch out, head leaning over the edge and her legs parting, allowing the periodic spasms she felt to continue unabated. Never in her life had she felt this way, her entire body reacting to the tender touch of her own finger. And responding to its call, her right hand slid down her body and lay flat against her abdomen. Feeling the soft hair underhand, she allowed her middle finger to slip down further. Her back arched up immediately and with a deep, inward sigh she felt like the heavens had opened up to her. With a minor adjustment to locale, she found the definitive spot and kept it firmly fixed at that point. The gentle strokes of her finger elevated her body to heights that, until now, had been un-thought of. Even with her one and only sexual encounter, that with Monique, in which she had felt such pleasure, this now felt many times greater and to the extent that her entire body was shaking. The rhythmic movement accelerated, as did her mind on recent events. That of her escape; her arrival in Paris, Monique, Ansel, with his manhood firmly placed within the mouth of the girl; and finally Ramone, her first introduction to a man and her face being only two inches from it.
Her breathing gathered pace as both body and thought merged in complete harmony with each other. She thought of Gaston and his hardness within her grasp. Her small, delicate hand wrapped around a girth that had not only felt foreign to her touch but equally exhilarating. The power that she knew she had over this man felt truly remarkable. She could remember even now his promise of fulfilling her every desire, a pledge, there and then, to give her all that he had, to make her his own, even until death.

Her breathing now in unison with her racing thoughts, she had the overwhelming desire to have something deep within her. So, accommodating this urge, she arched her finger in towards herself and gently pushed it in, allowing her thumb to take its place in lieu. Her entire self erupted in one tremendous jolt.

She was indeed learning about her own body, her thoughts allowed. Not only did she know how to pleasure another person but how to be pleasured in return.

And as the recollection of the frenzied attack earlier replayed in her mind, her movements upon herself quickened…until. Her body froze, and yet shook frantically, as pulsation after pulsation made her gasp out between staggered breathe, a combination of pleasure and pain, and the feeling of tears filling in her eyes. With mouth agape at the severity of this sensation sweeping across her entire body, she felt herself push down repeatedly as if relieving herself.

As the feeling gradually subsided, she lay exhausted within the water and looked down between her legs. A thin, pink stream was emerging from her, sufficient enough to discolour the surrounding water. She smiled to herself in recognition. Gone was the young, naïve and innocent Madeline, here now, in its stead, was a woman.

- A woman who knew where her future lay.

*

"So who was this brigand?"
Ramone stood upright at his usual place by the fire and accepted from her his third brandy in only ten minutes. "Who knows Monique." He shrugged his shoulders. "But he'll not be trying that again soon."
Adjusting her dress to suit the confines of the armchair, Monique sat down in front of him. "Is he dead?"
Ramone laughed out loud. "Hah, well if he isn't, he now has a new gap in which to place his food."
Tutting at such a nonchalant remark, Monique shook her head. "I gather he was after your money?"
As if he was not standing erect enough, Ramone straightened his back up even further. "It takes more than a weedy low-life with a dagger to relieve me of my purse, I can assure you of that."
Monique knew him to be a proud man but she also knew his secret and that the uniform, he so pompously paraded in public, was but a guise. But as was customary with old and valued clients, she remained hushed about this information. Information was power and she knew far more about various men in standing than she let on. This to her was her reassurance for the future.
She noticed him pause and glance up to the ceiling. "It was young Madeline that I was concerned for, not myself." He now stood silent, gazing into his

whirling brandy, deep in thought. "Poor child was frightened out of her wits," he eventually announced; and finished his third drink in one swoop.
Rising to refill his glass, Monique enquired further, "Yes, but this man, did you know him, was he familiar to you?"
Ramone shrugged once again. "Never seen the man in my life."
Somewhat relieved, but confused with this answer, she replenished his glass. She knew that Ramone had frequently seen Rubin lurking around the house and would, therefore, recognize him immediately. She'd given him strict and concise instructions with regard to Madeline. So who was this unfortunate stranger who had inadvertently attempted to do her own bidding?
Her eyes, once again, noticed the blood on his tunic. "Your uniform is in dire need of washing, Ramone. Remove it and I'll have one of the girls tend to it now."
"No need, my dear." Shaking his head, he finished. "I am returning home presently, one of my own staff will see to it."
To what home was he referring she wondered. The one here in Paris he used to reinforce the façade he played out or to the real one with family she knew him to have in Provence.
He finished his drink and covered the glass with his hand, refusing her offer of a fifth. "No more Monique, some people know when they have had enough."
Smiling at him, as was expected of a good hostess, she replaced the decanter on the table and escorted him to the door. "I appreciate you bringing Madeline home, Ramone."
Somewhat taken aback at this statement, he turned. "My heavens, it was the least I could do. It isn't everyday that you see a man murdered before your very eyes."
"Well, I appreciate your concern just the same."
Astounded and dumbstruck at her insinuation that he would do anything less, he eventually spoke out, "And you still think there is no need for a physician to check her over?"
"She is in shock, Ramone, nothing more. I will tend to her needs the moment she returns from bathing." Stretching up to allow the proffered kiss to her cheek, she added, "Do not blame yourself in this matter, Ramone. The city is rife with waifs who, without thought, would take a man's life for a few coins."
"Very well..." He looked up again again. "Give her my fondest regards and inform her I will pay her a visit tomorrow."
"I'm sure she will look forward to it."
Fastening his full-length coat, he exited and made for his waiting carriage.
Closing the door behind him, Monique sat down, as before, and considered what she had just heard. And somewhat relieved to hear that Rubin had no part to play in today's events, she sighed. The last thing she needed was for anything to incriminate her. She valued little, if nothing, about the people in her employ and was not going to allow herself to be publicly associated with

any of them in something illegal. She had a reputation to uphold and had, in the past, been far too shrewd a business-woman to let anyone stand in her way of achieving what she desired.
She had plans for Madeline and nothing was going to stop her.

*

Ramone banged the tip of his cane on the roof, signaling the carriage driver to move off.
Drinking four full glasses of brandy on an empty stomach was taking its toll on him. Having eaten very little since breakfast, and with their meal being prematurely cut short, he was in need now of some sustenance. His stomach had been churning constantly since the incident. His bravado performance in the presence of Monique had exhausted him. But the brandy had been much called for.
The truth being, he was in shock himself.
Replaying the vivid scene in his head yet again, he felt himself the coward once more. He had panicked at the suddenness of it all. Unaware of what was happening around them, he had lost control of the situation they had found themselves in. He remembered descending the steep steps to their carriage and the ragged edge held to his throat but further than that, with the ensuing melee, his memory was at a loss. But, in an attempt to shield Madeline from any stray swing of the blade, he'd turned in defense of her, and vaguely remembered seeing her fall to the ground, her dress sprayed blood red.
When the eventual bustle had ended, he'd found himself holding the lethal weapon in his hand. He couldn't even recall how it had gotten there. But he was hailed the hero by all; and as he looked down at the ground he saw the throat splayed fully open, and the assailant's body twitch its way to death's door.
And like his whole life nowadays, it was a sham. He took the praise easily and in his stride. If there was no-one to say otherwise, he would gladly take full credit for saving Madeline's life. He bowed his head in shame and let the driver take him home…home to nothing.

*

Edging towards the bed in the dark, Rubin pulled the blanket back and crawled in beside her. Knowing Annie, with it being the end of her shift, she would oblige him with a free one, so he pulled her naked body closer to him. With his loins pressed hard against her rear, he felt her rouse from her slumber and gently push back.
"From the smell of you, I take it you've washed."
He acknowledged this question with a playful squeeze to her ribs.
Giggling, she turned and wrapped her arms around him. "And I also take it you've no money again?"
He shook his head, but uttered nothing.

"Good, I prefer it when it's not business."
Rubin turned on his back and lay watching as her head descended to his lower half.
Of course he'd washed, he'd had to. The man's blood had sprayed all over him as he drew the blade across his throat. Feeling the tenderness of Annie's lips about him, he considered his actions. This was how he felt rewarded for a good day's work, perhaps not by monetary means, nor the favour being bestowed upon him now, but that of his conscious. He felt good within himself…- A fait accompli.

*

Madeline 1

Chapter 9

Thoughts of the future and past

"Can it be traced?"
"You mean will it be identified as the cause of death?" He shook his head. "No."
Gaston watched on as the scrawny hands poured more of the liquid into the vial. "How much will I need?"
The aging doctor paused what he was doing and looked over his cracked, half-rimmed spectacles. "Well, I suppose that depends, young man, on whom or what you wish dead."
Gaston was not impressed with the old man's tone. Given his squalid surroundings, of which he desired a hasty exit, it was hardly any wonder that this physician had lost his license through malpractice. "Your fee includes your silence and, above all, secrecy, you will do well to remember that."

Ignoring the threat as inconsequential, and that of a foolish and foolhardy young upper class lout, he continued to fill the vial. "That should do it." He corked the top.
Taking the dark tube from his shaking hand, Gaston leaned in towards the room's solitary candle for a closer inspection. "How do I administer it?"
"Administer it?" Leaning back against his chair, he eyed him up. "My, my, we are professional in our approach are we not?" he had said it as condescendingly as possible.
It was evident to Gaston that both were equally ill at ease with one another but he, unfortunately, could not leave without finding out what he needed to know. "Yes administer it, get it into the old trout's system." Aware now that this immature outburst had given the old man the upper hand, he immediately changed his tactics. "Please. How do I use it?"
"Well I gather that the intended recipient will not be a willing party in this, so getting them to rub it over their entire body for the skin to fully absorb is not an option here." He leaned forward. "So I would suggest dropping a portion of it into a beverage of some sort."
Patronizing bastard, he thought. "Yes but how much, the entire contents?"
"No, not the entire contents, it goes according to the size and weight of the...," he paused at the word 'person' and proceeded with more caution, "recipient."
"Then if I don't require it all, why have you given me so much?" Now wishing he could use the remainder on him. It would have given him great pleasure to stand up and slap that fucking smug-looking grin from his face.
Removing his spectacles and needlessly wiping them clean with a rag, which Gaston thought would make then even grimier than they already were, he listened intently to his explanation.
"Take, for example, a fish."
"A fish!"
"Yes, the ichthyological species you mentioned earlier."
Gaston gave up trying to repeat the word after three attempts and finally settled on 'fish'.
"Yes, the trout you mentioned earlier, that would take only a few drops of this lethal concoction. A cat being twice the size would take double; a dog, double again. I'm sure you get the meaning?"
Gaston looked at the vial in his hand and tried to work out the ratio in his head, finally deciding on three-quarters full. "And it won't be traced?"
"I assure you, there is many a corpse lying within the cemeteries of Paris with this in their system, and none of which had a physician question why they had been placed there."
Satisfied with this conclusion, Gaston removed the purse of silver coins and, on standing up, threw them discourteously onto the table. "I assume the authorities know nothing of this place. And in addition to this, that the two young girls waiting outside have both within them an unwanted child that they wish to be rid of?"

It was evident to Gaston that this decrepit old man knew a threat when he heard one.
Without looking up, he opened the purse and squinted within. "My word is my bond."
Coming from a man who Gaston knew would, without thought, callously throw the aborted fetuses into the back alley for the rats to feed on, this bond to him didn't amount to much. But he had no choice in the matter. "Then, with that, I would say that our business is complete".
Without waiting on further discussion, he turned towards the door and as before, bent down low under the arch to exit. Once within the waiting room, he noticed that the amount of pregnant young women had doubled since his arrival. The vermin of Paris would, indeed, be feasting heartily tonight, he thought.

With relief, he stepped into the alleyway and at once took a deep inward breath. This release to the system came twofold. The damp, musty smell of the room had made him nauseous. And mixed with the odour of the various medicinal compounds on display, it had made him gag even upon entering. He could smell it on his clothes even now. Secondly, his attainment of a substance, which, if properly managed would see his way into gaining a vast fortune in return. He breathed again. Smiling at his ingenuity, he patted the outside pocket of which held the lethal poison.
Uncomfortable with his sordid surroundings, he attempted to retrace his steps back to the familiarity of everyday life. He hated being in such foul places as this and looking about him as he walked, he convinced himself that the middle-aged woman, who lay on the ground just ahead to his left, was dead. Upon arrival, he paused and looked down at her. The vacant, wide-eyed stare and her disjointed jaw now confirmed this and he felt sick as he noticed the flies burrowing their way into her sockets. Momentarily stunned, he was roused from the trauma of this by an overhead cry of 'gardez l'eau'. Looking up, he jumped to the side and narrowly missed the stream of excrement and urine as it splashed onto the ground beside him. Shocked by the whole revolting scene, Gaston backed his way down the alley, his mind in confusion at to how anyone could survive in such conditions. His slow momentum was curbed by his collision with another person.
"Looking for some company are we?"
Gaston turned on his feet and was met by one of the most repulsive human beings he had ever laid eyes on. So much so, that he was convinced that this 'woman' was actually a man.
"No I do not."
With this, he made a hasty retreat and didn't falter in his footsteps until he had reached what he considered semi-civilization. If he hadn't smelled bad before, then the splashed marks of pale brown upon his garments, he noticed, had now made it worse. Retrieving his handkerchief from his pocket, he proceeded to wipe himself down. This would not do, he thought. There was

no way in God's green earth he could go to work like this. He'd have to return home to change first. But pleased with his recent acquisition, he smiled as he went.
His plans were working out well.

*

Madeline roused from her sleep and was met by a stream of light shining directly onto her bed. The night had been humid with a sticky heat and she had slept with both curtains open and window wide. But with little breeze, the room had remained fixed in its unrelenting assault upon her. This on its own would have been sufficient enough to interrupt her sleep, but the restrictions of her tight undergarment had her tossing around the bed most of the night. She flicked the thin sheet to the side and looked down upon herself. Never had she slept in bed so attired, but the need for some sort of hold on the cloth had been necessary.
Returning from her bath the previous evening, she had noticed that the flow of blood was continuing, so utilizing what she had available to remedy this, she had torn one of her older dresses into strips.
- Rags almost.
And in doing so, she was reminded of her familiarization of such from Monique when she had called this practice being 'on the rag'. Madeline had considered this term somewhat vulgar in tone at the time but as she had went through the same procedure the previous night, she had recognized the relevance in Monique's words. Which in turn, now led her on to another problem, should she inform Monique of this. Would it make any difference to the plans that she knew her to have? After all, if what Monique had told her about her not being able to have a child would be to her advantage, would she now change her thinking about this? She considered the consequences of this new development. And with this word in mind, but with a totally different meaning, Madeline's mind went off in a tangent, as she scanned her semi-naked body.
She had indeed developed into a woman, considering what she had looked like two years previous. Although her favourable good looks and congenial nature had been frequently commented upon at school, her body had not yet progressed to that of desirability to men. Still treated with the respect due to that of a child, with convivial pleasantries offered as to her youthful complexion, it wasn't until after her fifteenth birthday that these pleasantries turned to a more serious nature with a more adult connotation. In particular, her breasts and hips.
Monique had commented upon this during their lengthy discussion about her body and had been totally confounded on how a woman could develop to such a staggering shape without her monthly cycle having started. She was, in Monique's eyes, unique amongst women.

To her surprise, a rogue breeze blew in from the window and sitting up immediately, Madeline took full advantage of it. Raising her arms aloft, she let the cool wind surround her body, and as she closed her eyes to bask in its freshness, her mind wandered back to her summer days at home.

Her father had not always been ill. On the contrary, he was, without doubt, one of the most energetic men in town. No task, to assist others, was an inconvenience to him, and to such an extent that the entire neighborhood treated him with respect and thought of him as a friend. And although he worked hard as cobbler, putting in many hours of work to accommodate the needs of his family, he had always found time to spare for his children, his favourite of course being Madeline, his only daughter.
With her male siblings excluding her from most games, that of pretend soldiering and fighting, she had found herself alone most of the time. This was not to say that her brothers disliked her or were any way jealous of their father's partiality towards her. It was just that with her being a girl, she did not fit snuggly into their way of things.
Madeline did have one close girl friend though, Louise.
But, coming from a wealthy family, they took holidays each year in Marseilles, which unfortunately for Madeline left her, once again, with the entire summer to spend by herself.
Why she had made only one close friend at school surprised her. She had been courteous and amiable to all, but found that the more attention she received from the boys, the less cordial the girls were in their approach to her. This infuriated Madeline.
But her father saw through her sadness and, on several occasions, took her on fishing trips with him alone. They would sit by the campfire during the evening, cooking the day's catch and sometimes found themselves talking all the way through until daybreak. These were perfect days, she now thought. She felt she could tell her father anything then, and she had. He, indeed, was wise enough to know that a person had two ears and only one mouth, so should, therefore, listen twice as much as they should speak. Not only was he a good listener and confidante, he advised her on many things. Perhaps some things that she didn't really understand or appreciate at the tender age of fourteen, but would prepare her as she approached the major transition into womanhood. In retrospect, these teachings had come to mind many times since her departure from the house. These had included, most importantly, his advice on her being truly confident within herself. She could hear his words of wisdom even now.
"Never be afraid of being alone Madeline. There is a vast difference between being alone and being lonely."
She remembered, at the time, and with a child's mind, having to deliberate over this statement, to try and comprehend the adult way of interpreting life.
Being alone, and completely content and at ease with one's own company, didn't necessarily mean that you were lonely, she had eventually worked out.

Her father had, had the patience and know-how to let her deduce this for herself. But he did recognize that at such an age, the need for friendship was an important, if not necessary, part of growing up. To the extent that Madeline knew he'd sometimes wished he'd had more daughters and fewer sons to counter-balance the situation.

And here she was once again, like then, surrounded by women of her own age within the house and yet none willing to offer the hand of friendship to her.

But was she lonely? No, she felt alone, but not lonely.

She smiled to herself, and with the cool breeze now spent, let her body fall back onto the bed.

Her thoughts, once again, on days gone by. But as she did so, the smile wilted quickly from her face.

Learning many things from her father - this being limited to that which a man can tutor a child - it was the personal things in life that a mother should teach a daughter that Madeline had severely lacked.

With her father's health slowly deteriorating, Madeline had noticed a distinct change in her mother.

Although she had borne six children, her appearance had by no means given away the fact that she was thirty-six years of age. To such a degree that Madeline, through the years of growing up, had always thought of her as looking more like an older sister rather than that of a mother and apparently never seeming to age.

Like her father, Madeline had known that her hospitable nature had effortlessly been received by all and in return, was considered to be the perfect wife and mother. And even though she had dressed in accordance with her position in family life, she exuded a youthful quality that, as a child, Madeline had been in awe of.

Her father, on numerous occasions, had been proud enough to comment to Madeline that with each child born to him, her mother, without effort, had quickly regained her figure and was able to wear her everyday clothes within weeks. So, with this, Madeline had grown up through the years with a seemingly immortal mother in her midst and who unwittingly appeared to hold the elixir of life in her blood.

But not once through the years had her mother comforted her, either with a tender embrace or even a reassuring hug when she was unwell, her five brothers receiving all her attention. This was not evident in her early years, but as she grew up it had become clear to Madeline that it was from her father that she would receive the love that she craved. Had this perhaps caused the change in her mother's attitude towards her?

As a fourteen year old, Madeline had stood naked in front of the full-length mirror staring at the reflection of a child. A year further on, in the very same spot, she had beheld a woman looking back.

But alas, as luck would have it, her mother, on one of her all too rare excursions into Madeline's bedchamber, had found her in such an innocent pose. This, unfortunately for Madeline, had been the major turning point in her short life.

Now, lying on the bed, she squirmed at the recollection of this and with it her body involuntarily turned to the left. And as a reaction, her knees automatically raised themselves to her chin as her emotional defenses showed through. Wrapping her arms around her legs, she now lay curled up with her eyes tightly closed, remembering further the horrors that had followed.

Startled by her Mother's presence, she had immediately cowered over with the shock and embarrassment of her situation. And in a hasty attempt to cover her nakedness with her hands, had fearfully cried out in defense, "Mama, please!"

"As I suspected," her mother had boomed on her approach, "I have a young harlot for a daughter."

Madeline had never heard her mother speak in such a voice and in so brusque a tongue. On her arrival, she was equally astonished when she felt her mother's hand hit hard across her cheek sending her stumbling to the floor. Momentarily stunned, she tasted the salt within her mouth as it began to fill and knew that a tooth had penetrated the skin. Sitting dazed, she watched as the thin, red liquid dripped onto her thigh but before she had a chance to wipe her mouth clean, she felt the hard tug on her hair. The mortification of being hauled naked across the floor was surpassed only by the utter loathing she now felt for her mother. With her exposed rump being drawn across the rough flooring and her mother's rants, Madeline felt shamed. If this was not enough for her to endure, she felt total humiliation when she was dragged into the upper hall and along the passageway in full sight of her two youngest brothers, who looked upon this scene in astonishment.

For twelve solid hours she had squatted with bent knees within the tight confines of the closet in which her mother had imprisoned her. With neither light for comfort, nor clothing for warmth, she had shivered her way through the long night; and without water, her thirst had become unbearable. But eventually the door was opened and she was permitted to step free from this degrading incarceration.

How anyone could be so cruel, Madeline could not imagine but as this thought ran through her head, she was totally oblivious to the further torments her mother had in store for her. Her pretty, auburn dress that she had worn the previous day was now supplanted by a hand-stitched rag of dire grey. As if hastily stitched together throughout the night by her mother, it was, by anybody's standard, one step up from a sack. This, Madeline was made to wear during her frequent prayer sessions within the house's little, makeshift chapel. On a normal day, this would be at a minimum six times.

At night, alone in her room, she would often cry herself to sleep, wishing her torment would end; and sometimes considered scarring herself with a blade to make her appearance more unsightly to others, thus hopefully ending her mother's reign of terror over her. Thankfully these thoughts passed as quickly as they came and she never had to resort to such drastic measures.

Locked in her room whenever her brothers' friends had visited during the summer days was particularly hard to her. She could hear the distant laughter in the garden as they picnicked in the sun while she baked in her airless cocoon.

As airless as her Parisian room was now, she thought.

But those days were long in the past now. She had a future ahead of her, and one of her own choosing, and of her own making. She would return home one day, and when she did, she would arrive victorious in her efforts. But she had this city to conquer first.

Rising from the bed, she decided she would have a cool bath before meeting Monique for breakfast. After which, she had been told, was to be her first of many lessons. Her tuition was in the pleasing of men, and she intended to set the president.

Her climb to become the toast of Paris would begin now.

Madeline 2

Madeline 2

Prologue

Chateau d'Estelle, 18th Century France

Darkness engulfed them.
The damp and murky walls encroached upon them as they descended the broken stone steps, deeper and deeper into the bowels of the island bastion; and with the putrid smell of urine and waste filling their nostrils, neither uttered a word. Holding the shimmering torch aloft in one hand, the jailor callously dragged her unconscious body along the hard stone floor until he had reached the allocated cell. Brusquely dropping it to the floor, he held the flame to one side and struggled with the heavy iron key caught up in the lining of his coat pocket.
"So, who is she?" uttered the second.
His search momentarily interrupted, the jailor looked down. "Don't know but she's a pretty, young thing... had a peek through the swathes earlier."
Nudging at her waist with his foot, the second enquired further, "What's with all the wrapping about her?"

With the key now freed, he found a home for it in the lock and fought hard to turn it. "Someone doesn't want her recognised, that's for sure." He twisted further. "Merde, this one hasn't been used in a long time. Here, hold this."
Taking the torch from him, the second bent down for closer inspection. His hand immediately felt out for the breasts ."Not much titties on her... and hard too."
The jailor turned on him. "Here."
Surprised at this reaction, he looked up. "What?"
"Leave her be." He nodded down towards her. "Poor cow looks like she's been through enough without you poking at her."
In defiance, he countered with seditious tone, "Says you that's just dragged the fucking body from the coach to the door." He probed further up and on reaching her neck, his hand was caught up in cobweb and soiled linen. He retracted in shock.
"Exactly, now shine that torch up here. I can't see a bloody thing."
Temporarily speechless, he raised himself up and stood by the door. Eventually finding the words, he spoke out with lips a-tremble, "Her throat's been cut."
"I know. I dressed it best I could with spider web and cloth, all I could find."
Taken aback at his cold heartedness, he demanded explanation. "But who in God's name has done this to her, and why leave her here?"
The jailor shrugged. "Not for us to know." He pushed the heavy door open and was met by a cold, icy breeze blowing in from the cliff-side window. "We just do our job, right. Let's get her in."
The second stood aghast. "But isn't anyone going to tend to her? And she'll freeze to death in there."
The jailor turned on the spot and, once again, looked down upon the pitiful sight before him. And with negligible compassion, shook his head. "I've done all I can for her." Bending down to grip her feet, he dragged the body in. "She'll probably not last the night anyway...."
He laid her body in the middle of the damp and rat-infested cell.
"....Or the child that's in her."

*

Madeline 2

Chapter 1

Reflections

**Paris, 18th Century France.
Some years earlier**

For five solid weeks Paris had endured a summer of unrelenting heat. And with it came the stench of decay - not only emanating from the highly contaminated Seine but from the very epicentre of this vibrant, cosmopolitan city. Alas, as ill-divided as any 18th century European conurbation, the gentry stood aloft by means of ancestral wealth, while the waifs begged upon the streets for bread merely to subsist. This, amidst the all too often cruel and unforgiving streets, where ready coin could be gained by the crafted or wise at heart but equally lost in the blink of an eye by the foolhardy in mind... a place of daily survival through cunning and deceit, if honest, hard toil was not suiting. But in some extraordinary cases, with freewill partly present, such equally extraordinary vocations in life were chosen for them. So as the sun bade its fond farewell to the city and the dusk rapidly approached with all haste in its stead, one such recipient of this kismet stood alone in her room… her future perhaps not as laid out and planned as others would have liked it.

Perched two stories above the streets, Madeline poured the cold water from the porcelain ewer into the matching basin and prepared for what was to be a cool and very much needed footbath. She could have had, if she so wished, the option of bathing downstairs but the room had no window and in the off-chance that she could catch a breath of air, decided to sit by her opened window. This and the fact that fresh water in abundance was so rare in Paris, the bath would have only been several inches deep. So, adjusting the chair and basin accordingly, she sat naked with feet immersed and let the coolness of the water rise up through her body. She breathed in deep with the pleasure of it and immediately regretted it, her lungs still not gotten used to the ubiquitous smell of the city since arriving in Paris some weeks earlier. This being one of the few things she missed about her home town - the fresh and unpolluted air and the smell of the countryside with its sweet scent of flora. And having been raised in the vicinity of nearby streams where fresh running water had been readily available, personal hygiene had been commonplace amongst the residents. She had noticed, even on her early arrival in the city, the foul body odour of its populace as well as their reluctance to even cleanse themselves with the merest of water, preferring instead to either disguise the smell with cologne or wash dry with white linen. This, she now knew, was sadly their belief that germs or miasmas could penetrate the skin through open pores caused by hot water. So, in an attempt to avoid such a malady, they remained in a permanent state of ill-smelling repugnance. She had even heard it rumoured that King Louis, himself, had only bathed once in his lifetime and that being on his wedding day. But with her Father being the inquisitive type and had always sought knowledge of these things, he had educated his family accordingly. So, contrary to the majority, Madeline made sure she bathed as often as she could. These comforting things were what she missed the most and, regretfully, nothing much else, she thought with saddened heart, apart from her family, of course. She wondered what they would be doing now at this very moment.

Having left home without bye or leave, save the brief farewell to her brothers on the night of her departure, she wondered if they were concerned about her. With her being only sixteen years old and absconding to a city, which her Mother had always stated as an evil place of ill-repute, would she be missed? And who, now, would her Mother be laying her wrath in her absence?... her Father, no doubt. As ill as her Father was, she knew her Mother would not allow this to be an excuse to vent her ire. Madeline felt her body temperature raise itself even higher upon thinking this, so, leaning over to the left, she retrieved a nearby cloth from the table and immersed it in the shallow water. Squeezing out the residue, she sat up and nimbly dabbed it to

her neck and chest. Closing her eyes, she leant her head back and wished so dearly for a breeze to miraculously appear and cool her down.
It suddenly occurred to her that she hadn't heard the lone violinist for some days now. Before, she had enjoyed this solitary music each evening and so looked forward to it. But of late it had not been present during her stays in her room. Even with her enquiries as to the owner of the soothing chords, she had not been able to find out from where it had originated. Certainly not on the streets, like so many others, in the hope of a coin or two in gratitude, it had come from someone's house, someone's room. She felt sad at its absence, as if part of her life in Paris had been taken from her. It was the very first memory she had of her room, the first day of her arrival. So many things had happened since then. So many people she had encountered, good or bad, her favourite, of course, being Ramone. And come to think of it, she hadn't seen him for several days now as well. She smiled at her thinking, surely he and the violinist couldn't possibly be one? Her smile continued at the thought of their first meeting and this elderly gentleman blazingly sporting his uniform with the britches undone. By no stretch of her imagination could she ever see him playing the violin stood thus, although the picture conjured up in her mind made her laugh aloud. She had noticed, however, a slight change in him prior to his absence, particularly after the incident with the attacker. She had him to thank for saving her life and she knew she would always be in his debt. A true friend he was.
She suddenly heard the beginnings of the Friday night revelry outside, so, standing slightly, she leaned over and peeked down at the street below. Aware of her nakedness, she did not feel exposed as the dimness of the room hid her from view. And as for the house opposite, she was certain that no-one could see her as their curtains seemed to be permanently closed, apart from several inches of gap in the middle. Surely they could have afforded that extra inch or two, she naively thought. In her ignorance, it had never occurred to her before that someone could be spying upon her through this space. She thought back on how many times she had been unclothed within her room with her curtains wide open. The thrill of this suddenly came upon her...and she liked it. Could it possibly hurt to know that someone was watching her through that gap and with his hands down the front of his britches?
She reseated herself as before. Her mind had, indeed, developed over the last few weeks and, in particular, since her first orgasm while bathing. In addition to this, with her first bleed, she was now a woman in the true sense. Long gone was the girl who left her family, here now sat a woman with her future planned out ahead of her.
Thus far, Monique had limited her to entertaining the gentlemen callers only. It still felt strange to her that so many men would pay handsomely for the privilege of just sitting in her company but Monique had assured her that, with her beauty, they would still be queuing out the door. Nine different companies had she sat in, and in nine such companies had she endured a long

and tedious night. She, herself, was erudite enough to hold a conversation and had had a fine education as a child but their monotonous talk had put her mind to sleep. She had to struggle to keep the smile on her face throughout. Didn't these men have anything amusing to say? Only with Ramone did she feel relaxed in the company of, he had a charm about him that made conversation flow freely from the tongue. And if it were not for him, she would have found this 'game' rather dull.

As for the payments for her company, Monique alone determined Madeline's fee and this she knew varied from client to client, according to the gentleman's purse. The more he could afford, the more he had to pay. Monique had it all figured out but Madeline had seen very little of her share. Granted, her room and board were being paid for, together with the everyday items she required, but actual coin in the hand, that was a far different matter. So, as she playfully stamped at the water with her feet and listened to the carousing below, she decided on a further five minutes before dressing for yet another night in the parlour. No doubt as uninteresting as the others.

She was soon to be proved wrong.

*

Madeline 2

Chapter 2

Rosalind

Rubin was used to the smell of death.
He had fought in the army as far back as he could remember, so the stench of decomposition was nothing new to him. The aftermath of a battlefield needed a strong stomach and he had become accustomed to this since his early teens.
Some jobs were not for the faint-hearted and he, along with Sach, had performed these tasks on numerous occasions for the same morally depraved employer – a medical man, of a sort, who paid handsomely for the work done, no questions asked.
Looking about him, it appeared more like charnel house than a hospital morgue. Rubin couldn't even contemplate what this corrupt physician had done to the bodies, with severed limbs and entrails strewn about the floor. He just did what was asked of him and received his money in return.
Hauling at the stained under garments until it was fully unclothed, Rubin threw the rotting corpse of the young man onto the cart with the others.

Counting as high as he was able, he reached his maximum eight before restarting and getting to six. This was the only way of counting he knew, the total sum now being eight plus six with the number fourteen lost to his uneducated mind. Deliberating over his numbers, he knew himself to be one short of the required eight plus seven, but had a fair idea of where the last one was. Spitting thick, brown phlegm onto the bloodstained floor, he reached into his right coat pocket and pulled out his bottle. His squinting eyes revealed that it was a third full. He would have the lot. Sach would have to do without this time.

"You finished in there yet?" he hollered, before emptying half of it in one swoop.

A muffled response came from the next room. "Coming soon, my friend."

Rubin walked towards the door of the adjoining room and, on reaching it, leant against the side panel. "Well get a move on."

As if an everyday occurrence, Rubin watched on as Sach dismounted himself from the naked body of a recently deceased woman and, pulling up his britches, smiled on his approach. "Pink this time, she was still tight."

Rubin shook his head. "You're one sick fuck, Sach." And nodding at the corpse, continued, "If you're finished with it, get it next door with the others."

Sach heard nothing of this instruction, instead fixing his scurrilous eyes firmly on the bottle in Rubin's hand. "Got some there for me, my friend?"

Rubin sighed and handed him the bottle as he passed by en route. He would get it himself, just to save time - Sach was dragging his heels tonight, he knew. But on reaching the table, Rubin was unprepared for what he found. Looking down on the face of the dead girl, Rubin calculated her age at just eight plus six and with a quick scan of her body, his assumption was reinforced. He stood unmoving and silent for what seemed like minutes, staring into her stark, glaring eyes. With thumb and middle finger apart, he closed them shut, knowing full well that it had been Sach that had prized them open before going about his business with her. Further to this, and himself unsure as to why he was doing it, he removed his coat and wrapped the body within. Carrying it through to the cart, and without a word, he placed it gently on top of the others. He sighed once again.

…Eight plus seven.

Pulling the rope as tight as it would go, Rubin fastened it to the side of the cart, thus securing the sheet neatly in place over the bodies. "Get a move on, Sach, we don't have all night."

Sach appeared from the door carrying a wooden pail, full-to-spilling with the scooped up entrails from the floor inside. "I seem to get all the good jobs."

Rubin looked down at the mess slopping onto the street. "What you complaining about, you've probably fucked half of that bucket. Show a bit of gratitude."

"Ha ha, seriously, what am I going to do with all this?"

Rubin shrugged.

"Oh come on, my friend, I'm not sitting up there with all this shit spilling over me."

Rubin moved to close the wooden door. "It's going the same way as the rest - into the Seine."

"Yeah, but we got to get there first."

Securing the door and leaving the building as they had found it, Rubin made his way to the front of the cart. "I'm the driver and the disposer." He nodded to the pail in Sach's hand. "You, on the other hand, carry shit. Now move."

Sach had worked with Rubin on numerous occasions in the past, most of which had been as unprincipled as this one. But coins were coins, without them you couldn't hope to survive in such an unforgiving place as eighteenth century Paris and there was very little that Rubin wouldn't do to survive. But Sach's treatment of the young girl had hit home some hard truths as to the code and ethics by which they survived. Sach would be paid dearly for his assistance tonight and, with this, he would be able to relieve himself with any number of girls in the taverne. So why do this to the young girl? He could not give countenance to such an act and was going to make sure Sach knew it.

With both on board, Rubin gee'd the horses on and they trundled slowly forward in response. He looked to his left and noticed that Sach had covered the open-top pail with his coat. Gripping onto the edges for fear of spillage, he now sat perched at an awkward angle. 'Good, suffer you little bastard,' he thought.

With a quick check on the night sky signalling a half-moon and very little stars, these were ideal conditions for moving covertly across the city. This was a consignment that was definitely not for public view, thought Rubin, and, if caught, would almost certainly send them both to the executioner.

Thirty minutes later they had reached their destination. As uneventful a journey as had been hoped for, considering the time of night, it had been mostly silent, with each of them deep within their own world of thought. More importantly, they had not aroused suspicion by either casual observer or officialdom.

Dismounting, Rubin set about untying the sheet. Sach, meantime, headed straight to the river's edge to alleviate himself of his load.

"Where's the spade?"

Sach turned on his feet. "What?"

"The spade," Rubin repeated.

Sach kicked himself. He'd left it on the floor after he had scooped up the mess and blood. "Eh, I think I left it back there." He cringed, awaiting the onslaught.

It didn't come as the verbal assault he expected - rather a physical one. Out of the darkness, he felt Rubin's hand about him and, before he knew it, was thrown into the water amid the newly floating viscera. Rubin knew that Sach couldn't swim but he would make him suffer before he went to his aid. So he watched as Sach thrashed repeatedly at the water, his head disappearing and submerging each time amid his cries for help, and only then did he eventually grab hold of his arm and pull him free.

"Bastard, bastard, bastard."

Rubin left him sitting by the edge, cursing and wringing out his clothes while he, himself, made for the cart. Flicking the cover back, his eyes fell at once upon his coat. He would leave her till last. What he had to do now took guts and a strong stomach, so, removing the girl's body, he placed it on the ground away from the water's edge. In complete contrast as to how he had handled the girl, with a random grip on a free limb followed by a quick yank, Rubin pulled a body unceremoniously from the cart. Then, dragging it to a place a few feet from where Sach was seated, he let the body slump to the ground, face up. With no metal spade to do his bidding, he would now have to find a heavy, and perhaps if luck was on his side, sharp-edged rock. It took him just under a minute to locate such an implement in line with his specifications, so, kneeling down next to the body, he positioned himself with exactitude. Sach looked on, his face squirming. He knew what was coming. To dispose of a body in the Seine, and particularly one which may have died in suspicious circumstances, you had to disguise it. And what better way to prevent possible recognition, if unfortunate enough to be discovered before its natural decay or by the rats and fish eating at the flesh, than to obliterate the features. In the past, he had found it a necessity. In doing this, he was not leaving anything to chance.

And Rubin was a master of such tactics.

With one fell, overhead swoop, he brought the rock down so hard upon the corpse's face that the whole bone structure collapsed immediately.

"Shit!"

Sach was seated in the wrong position. If he had smelled badly before, having being covered in human offal and that of the everyday stench of the Seine, he now positively stunk to high heavens. As the skull had shattered, the spray of the crushed brain had jettisoned its way out in his direction. He now sat stunned as the moist matter ran down his face. Rubin burst out laughing. Never in the past had he seen anything as funny and yet so incredibly sickening. Sach, meanwhile, was lost to the joke. Still chortling, Rubin stood up and grabbed at the left hand, hauled the corpse to the river's edge and pushed it down into the water. Being downstream from the city, the current would hopefully take it away from everyday view. Bodies in the Seine were commonplace but fifteen of them floating by a village would draw the attention of even the most antisocial inhabitant who, in turn, would feel duty-bound to inform the authorities. But tonight was different. He had no spade to hack with and dismember the odd few as he would normally do. And as sharp as his own knife was, he did not savour the thought of cutting through a boned leg. He would have to take a chance and let all remain in tact.

With the repeated task undertaken and completed within the hour, he had set sail to eight plus one corpses and had weighed down a further five with heavy rocks. He had only the young girl left to do. He sat cross-legged on the ground and undid the coat. Looking down on the face, he felt, once again, the inexplicable urge to get emotionally involved with his work. Pulling the coat free of her, he examined her body and, finding no physical injuries, pondered for a moment, her death. To die so young, so innocent, he mused. Rubin shook his head to rouse from his reverie. Was he getting soft in his old age, he thought? A battle-scarred veteran like him deliberating the demise of a complete stranger. He had seen countless dead bodies, brave men fighting and dying with honour, poor souls murdered for the price of a bottle of wine but never had he taken the time to think about them in such a way as this. He knew then that he couldn't leave this young girl in the river for the rats to feast on. He would bury her and at least give her a proper place in which to rest.
But he had no spade to dig such a grave.
Sach was at his side. "You thinking of having her before she goes in?"
Rubin felt the blood boil in his veins. He had known Sach for many years and although they had shared many an undertaking together, he had never considered him as a friend, certainly not in the way good friends should feel about each other. Of late, his feelings towards him had dwindled to such a degree that he had considered terminating their dubious relationship altogether. What each knew about the other could lead them to the gallows and he had noticed that Sach was becoming loose with his mouth more often that not whilst under the influence of the taverne's wine. And Rubin could not take that risk.
"Go on, my friend, she's a nice young thing, she worked for me."
With Sach being of little stature, it wasn't hard for Rubin to stretch his arm up to neck height. In one swift movement, he had unsheathed his knife and with immense strength, had drawn the blade across Sach's throat. So deep was the cut that it had severed the flesh straight through to the spine and Rubin had to lean to the left to avoid the spray. He watched as Sach's startled body fell to its knees and the head swing back loose on the neck. Kicking the twitching body to the side, he would leave it to drain before severing the head completely and tossing both parts in the river.
Meanwhile, he had a grave still to dig.

With a pocket full of coins, he drank heartily or at least as heartily as his head would permit him with his thoughts still of the young girl. Sitting in the semi-darkness upon Annie's only chair, he watched her sleep as he drank his wine and let his mind drift back to earlier that night. It had taken over two hours to scrape up the hard dirt deep enough to hold the body. Using whatever flat stones he could find, he had chosen a place beneath a nearby tree. His only regret being that he had to leave it unmarked but at least she would rest in peace, of that he felt pleased. Now questioning his motives for doing so, he felt himself confused. Something had stirred deep within him tonight, something very new to him, very strange and disconcerting. Never in his life had he felt this way. What happened to Sach had been a long time in the coming and even now he felt no regret about what he had done. But this young girl was a complete stranger to him, so why was he feeling the way he did now?

Annie stirred on the bed and turned in his direction. Her eyes opened slowly and she sat up immediately, startled by his presence. "Rubin, merde, you scared the hell out of me there. How long have you been here?"

"Just a short while. Go back to sleep."

Giving up thinking about how he had gotten into her room without her knowing it, she pulled the cover back slightly as invitation. "You coming in?"

Rubin shook his head. "In a bit."

Recognising his solemnity, she stepped naked from the sheets and crouched down on the floor beside him, arms resting on his knees. "You look tired, Rubin."

He remained still, but smiled at her. "You think so?"

Annie placed her hand on his scarred cheek and let it rest there. She liked the quiet moments with Rubin and it made her feel good when he allowed her to comfort him. He would speak when ready.

Staring deep into her eyes, he eventually spoke, "Sach is dead," he continued, "I killed him."

What made him volunteer this piece of information to Anna, he couldn't fathom, but he knew whatever he told her would remain for her ears alone, of that he was certain. She may have been a whore but even they had codes by which they lived.

Unshaken by this news, as she was familiar with Rubin's lifestyle, Annie recognised his disposition and tone of voice. "Do you want to talk about it?"

Rubin remained silent for a moment, pondering on how he would begin to tell her about the young girl, who he had, for some strange reason, began to think of as 'Rosalind'. Why he had picked that name, he was unsure. Perhaps she had looked like a Rosalind, who knows, he just had and he liked it.

"There was a young girl tonight."

Annie made moves to remove her hand from his cheek but Rubin was too quick for her. Holding hers in his, he kept it in place. "Not like that, Annie."

"Not like what?"

"Like in the way you're thinking. She was a child. A dead child and Sach..."

Aware of his reluctance to continue, she pressed on, "And Sach what... what did he do? Did he kill her?"

Rubin shook his head. "No, she was already dead."

There was no need for Annie to know the full story of what their work had entailed, so he skipped that part. It was sufficient enough to say what Sach had done to Rosalind as an explanation to why he had slit his throat.

Annie raised her free hand to her mouth in disgust. As a common whore she had, in the past, pampered to almost every sexual whim - from normal sex to the extremes of urinating and defecating on her customers - but this, to her, was excessive even by her standards. "The filthy bastard."
"I reckoned Rosalind was only eight plus six."
His method of counting known to her, she continued, "So you knew her then?"
Rubin shook his head once again. "No, never seen her before today."
She looked puzzled. "So, how do you know her name?"
Rubin felt like an old fool. "It's what I called her when I buried her. Silly, eh?"
Annie looked into his eyes and saw nothing but compassion. This, to her, was a new experience as well... but she liked it. "Come here, you big lump."
She raised herself to her knees and wrapped her free arm around him, unconsciously pushing her left breast into his face.
Feigning suffocation, Rubin joked with muffled speech, "Any chance of letting me breathe in here?"
Fully awake now, she released her grip on him and when she had resumed her previous position, finger-tapped the bottle. "You going to share that?" But judging by the sound it made, she thought otherwise. "Oh, there isn't much left."
Rubin nodded towards the corner of the room where five full bottles sat unopened. "I think I can spare a drop."
Smiling, Annie stood up and walked towards them. "Then let's drink to Rosalind, whoever she was."
Rubin watched her naked body sway from side to side and raised his bottle. "I'll go along with that."

The early morning sun was breaking its way into the room when they finished the final bottle. So, taking Rubin by the hand, Annie led him to the bed and, although worse the wear from the wine herself, helped him undress. Folding his clothes as she went, Annie laid them down by the bedside but, on doing so, noticed something missing. "Where's your coat?"
Rubin, who had drunk most of the wine, lay naked and slumped across the bed, sleep now beckoning him.
"Rubin, where's your coat, have you left it somewhere?" she repeated. Annie very rarely saw Rubin without his coat, perhaps the only one he had, so, to her, it was odd to see him without it.
Rubin could think of an answer but could not speak it. It wasn't an issue as he had money to buy a new one, so he drifted off, safe in the knowledge that his favourite and only coat was now being put to better use.
It was keeping Rosalind snug.

*

Madeline 2

Chapter 3

Unexpected Pleasure

At the tender age of sixteen, Madeline was now learning the art of pleasuring a man, not just sitting in their company, as on previous occasions, but by actual physical contact with them.
She would not come cheap, Monique had informed her. Her other girls commanded the 'run of the mill' prices for each sexual act performed but according to Monique, Madeline was anything but a 'run of the mill', young woman.
She was beautiful.
And beauty demanded coinage of the highest denomination.
Monique had imparted to her several techniques through discussion but today she was to be instructed in the correct method of what she had misinterpreted on her first night in the house. Mistakenly thinking that Ansel had been emptying his bladder into the mouth of a woman, she was now

informed that this was a particularly enjoyable and frequently asked-for service among her male clients.

"Any woman can take a man in her mouth, Madeline, but it is what you do with it when it is in there that is the real secret of success," Monique had announced.

Sitting next to her on a separate armchair, Madeline listened intently. She had been informed by Monique, at an early stage in her education, that she would be permitted to ask questions after but not during the session and to remain quiet, listen and observe. This she had done during previous sessions, albeit reluctantly, with her young and impatient mind at breaking point.

So, seated comfortably in Monique's sitting room, they awaited the arrival of the two that had been summoned earlier and for her next lesson to begin. With knees together and her clasped hands resting upon them, Madeline's eyes wondered around the room. This was where Monique dictated she should do her entertaining as opposed to her own room. Clients were far more reluctant to take advantage in less intimate surroundings such as a bedroom, she had been informed. And last night had been no exception, only this time, to Madeline's utter surprise, it had been a woman in whose company she had indulged.

Caroline had been sitting where Madeline was seated now as she had entered the room and Monique had immediately made the formal introductions. But having left them alone within minutes, it had been Caroline who had stood and made ready two glasses of wine. Wasn't it her job to do the entertaining, Madeline had thought at the time? Strange!

As graceful as any woman could be, Caroline's genteel manner had captivated Madeline's attention in an instant and before long their conversation seemed like two long-lost friends reunited after years apart. Her heavy but sweet scent filled the air and with her white powdered face and lips of cochineal, she looked, to Madeline, a picture of beauty. A black, silky beauty spot lay dominant beneath her right eye and although she knew it to be Parisian fashion, Madeline suspected it was also to conceal a small-pox scar which was rife among many these days. Another of equal size lay upon the top of her left breast, barely an inch from her cleavage. But Madeline had never seen such white hair as this, and with it tied up high and held with sheer white lace, she couldn't help herself but comment upon it, "I do so admire your hair, Caroline, it is in a style and a fashion I am unfamiliar with."

"Thank you, Madeline, my private coiffeuse does like to stay ahead of Parisian fashion. No doubt it will become commonplace within weeks and then I will have to try something new. And I do so despise the wigs one has to wear in an attempt to remain in vogue."

Madeline had beamed at Caroline's self-confidence and the belief she had in herself. She had held her own hair at the side. "I myself wear mine in only two styles, down..." And on raising it up over her head. "...And up."

Both had laughed together.

"Then we shall have to do something about that then, shan't we?"

For fifteen minutes Caroline had toyed with various styles and as Madeline held a hand mirror in front of her, the 'yes' and 'no's' continued until her curiosity got the better of her. "May I ask why you have chosen me to spend your Friday night with. Do you not enjoy the company of men?"

As brazen as this question had sounded, it appeared that Caroline had not taken it in the fashion that it may have appeared. "Of course I do, Madeline, I am married."

Married! It hadn't occurred to Madeline to consider this. "Then may I enquire further as to why you are here, now, with me?"

"There is variety in life, Madeline. Not good for one's soul to linger on a uniformed existence. If a cup is filled to brimming then is it not wise to lessen its volume somewhat?"

Spoken in part-riddle, Madeline had tried to make some sense from it. "So my company, here, now, lessens that load?"

"Spoken like a woman. There."

Madeline angled the mirror at various viewpoints and was content with the result. "I have never worn my hair like this before. Thank you." Tied back at the sides and with layers of plats, it was very new to her. She turned to look up to Caroline and suddenly felt her hands on her shoulders.

"And yes, Madeline, your company does lessen it so."

Madeline sat unmoving as she watched Caroline bend closer towards her and gently place her lips upon her own. And where they remained but for a second before Caroline parted them and let her tongue slip inside.

Or had she just imagined that part?

Caroline had been seated opposite within seconds. "It's just temporary, pinned up, it will fall down with the least movement but I'm sure you get the general idea."

Madeline had sat speechless. Had she imagined Caroline kissing her? Or had it actually happened? The rest of the evening had been filled with similar talk as to the likes of that prior to the hair incident. But it wasn't until Caroline prepared herself to leave did she hint at the possible scenario. "I have enjoyed your company immensely, Madeline. I would have dearly wished to have extended on our little hair-play session earlier but, alas, this in neither the time nor the place. You will come visit my house in the near future."

This had appeared to be more of an instruction rather than an invitation, Madeline had thought. And even now, in retrospect, she still thought it strange. To have her kiss her and then act as if nothing had happened. There were kisses and there were kisses and that kiss did not feel like the kiss of a friend. Indeed, had it not been for the possible contact, Madeline would have liked to have considered her a friend. My goodness, she felt she needed one. Apart from Ramone, she had none or at least not one in which to confide. Not a girl friend.

With Caroline perhaps being several years older than she, herself, Madeline considered them to be compatible in many ways. And although divulging very little information about her own life, she had seemed keen about learning more about Madeline's - enquiring after her family; the town in which she had been raised; and of her early years growing up. It wasn't until Madeline had progressed to her teen years did she falter in her telling. Aware that Caroline had noticed her hesitance to proceed, she, as a true friend, had not pushed the subject any further and for that she had been grateful. She had wished these thoughts far removed from her mind and did not want to sully such a pleasurable evening with sad contemplation of her Mother's wrath upon her. She had found a friend and someone with similar views, opinions and a mind equal to the thinking of her own age. She would do very well to take up Caroline's invitation to call upon her in the future. But her mind was pulled back to the present as the door opened and the two entered.
Her lesson was about to begin…
…One that would change the course of her life.

*

Gaston looked down at his untouched meal.
Casually moving the contents of the plate from one place to another, he deliberated in his mind, yet again, his plans for the evening ahead. He must have played this same scenario out at least two dozen times in the past few days, he thought, and all the while, although determined to see it through, had considered the many things that could go wrong.
Although being a prominent and influential figure in Parisian society, the authorities would still not take kindly to a son murdering his mother-in law. This was no Borgia state he lived in and matricide was considered a punishable offence, if not by death then that of life imprisonment. He certainly did not relish the thought of spending a lifetime in the infamous Bagne of Toulon and would gladly accept the former if given a choice. But this eventuality could be easily remedied if he took care and followed his plans out in a vigilant and resolute fashion. There could be no room for error. The dire consequences of which were apparent. But satisfied within himself that the ends did, indeed, justify the means, he raised his head and looked at his wife seated opposite. He noticed Janis immediately take this eye contact as an opportunity to start a conversation and thus break the awkward silence between them. "Is the meal not to your liking tonight, dearest?"
'Dearest'! Indeed, where had all this false-sounding and unconvincing sentiment come from of late, he thought. Was it by sheer accident that, since the time of him meeting Madeline, his wife had made genuine efforts to gain his favour and eyes once again? What had happened to her in this short time he was unsure of but, as futile as her approach had been, he was steadfast in his plans for the future. So, playing along with this game of hers, he kept up the façade of being that of a dutiful husband. Being employed within

France's ever-changing political circles, he feigned anxiety as an excuse. "Just work, I'm afraid."
Skeptical of his reply, she continued, "I have never in the past, Gaston, seen you been put off your evening meal with thoughts of parliamentary affairs."
This was, of course, true, he knew. He had always pride himself on the fact that he could, with ease, split his allegiance equally between work and that of family life. Very seldom had he brought home with him the humdrum subject of politics to their dinner table. Tonight was no exception but he continued with the lie just the same, "We are at lengths to try and pass through a rather cumbersome and laborious bill at present. It has been occupying my mind for several days now."
Knowing full well that what he was saying was pure fabrication, Janis changed the subject - one that she hoped would bring them closer together. "Mother has the children at present. If you have no plans for this evening, a night talking together in front of the fire would be pleasant." She paused in thought, before finishing, "Like we used to do."
Gaston could, at one time, recall vividly these pleasant times to which she had hinted. He, himself, had enjoyed their frequent after-dinner conversations every bit as much as she apparently had and he knew at what particular juncture in the evening she was alluding to when she had mentioned it. What in the past would have started as routine conversation would more often than not have lead to their lovemaking in front of the open-hearth fireplace with their passion holding no bounds. But these memories of her were lost in his head, distant thoughts replaced now with feelings of lust, nay, love for another, as well as deceit on his part and even plans of murder in his aim of marrying Madeline. Anything of a carnal nature regarding his wife was, to him, way in the past but in his predetermined scheme of things, this fireside tryst was what he had intended beforehand. By sheer quirk of fate, with her suggesting this romantic liaison, his wife had now unwittingly become an accomplice in the demise of her own mother... the death of whom would leave them a vast fortune as inheritance. Gaston smiled to himself. Of course her mother had the children with her tonight, hadn't he planned it that way? He knew that after several hours with them, she would return home exhausted and want to supper alone in her room.
And if things went as well as he hoped, then it would be her last.

*

Madeline sat speechless and wide-eyed at the spectacle before her.
If she had been permitted by Monique to say something, then she doubted very much that she would have had the capability at that moment to have done so...so absorbing and mesmerising was the scene.
Madeline knew the girl's name to be 'Rosie' as she had seen her many times about the house. But, as with the other girls, Rosie had made little, if any,

effort in the way of associating with her. This, Madeline had put down to jealousy. It had been evident to them all that Monique had taken her under her protective wing. With the preferential treatment apparent, by way of special tuition, it appeared to Madeline that there had been a unanimous decision, taken by all, to snub her presence. But she was learning to accept this now. She had her own plans for the future and they did not include the likes of Rosie or any of the others as friends. She would make her own and had, indeed, done so. She had a friend - Caroline.

Rosie's participant in this curious tutorial was a man she was unfamiliar with. It struck her as odd that this handsome individual, who appeared to Madeline to be from a class structure higher than that of the everyday minion, should be involved in such a public show as this. Guessing his age to be twenty or thereabouts, he appeared at ease with Rosie and it had soon become clear that they were fully accustomed to each others way of doing things.

This was no debut show, thought Madeline.

Upon their entrance into the room, Monique had, without preamble or introduction, set them to task immediately. So, removing his britches and undergarments, the man, who she now knew to be called 'Frederick', had sat on the chair opposite them, his legs wide apart and his sex fully exposed. Madeline's eyes had been transfixed and the comparisons had been instant. She had seen at close proximity, Ramone; and had held within her hand, on two occasions, Gaston. But this man was something for which she was unprepared. With his length and girth being twice that of Gaston, she had given up with her assessment of this in regard to Ramone's regretful inadequacy. She could only wonder at the enormity of its fully aroused state and, more importantly, how on earth Rosie would fit this monster into her diminutive mouth.

Remaining fully clothed, as it had been deemed unnecessary for her on this occasion to undress, Rosie had knelt down in front of him and at once clasped him within her right hand. With tender and rhythmic movements familiar to her, Rosie expertly manipulated Frederick from everyday normality to a size which had made Madeline gasp inwardly. With continued smiles at each other, both Rosie and Frederick appeared to have been enjoying the experience and Madeline had known straight away that, outside the employ of Monique, they were lovers. This had just happened to be part of their job but clearly there was emotional contact there and not just routine. Madeline had thought this strange, that a man could love a woman even though she sold her body daily to complete strangers. Hadn't she, herself, puzzled over a similar conundrum with regard to her and Jacob?

Stretching her mouth open to its limit, Rosie had leaned forward and let her lips slip gently over him, proficiently guiding in as much of his full ten inches as she could.

"Take it all in," instructed Monique.

Madeline could see that Rosie was struggling to reach his base and Monique had reinforced this assumption with further instruction.
"Relax your throat muscles, my dear, and keep your neck straight."
Madeline continued to watch as Rosie tried her best to complete this, now fruitless, task and was totally taken aback when Monique rose from her chair to kneel down beside her.
It was apparent from Frederick's expression that he was not overly enamoured with Monique, an antiquated, old maid placing him into her skin-cracked mouth by way of instruction. But this she now did.
"Allow me, my dear."
An indication that Rosie's participation in the show was now over, she reluctantly moved to the side, thus redundant. Competently taking over where Rosie had failed, Monique took his entirety in one swift movement. And to prove further that this had been no accident, she drew her mouth back and forward several times as expertly as any man could have wished. So erudite was her technique, it was obvious to Madeline that this had been gained through vast experience in days gone by, as she had Frederick gasping and squirming uncontrollably within seconds. So much so that all three women knew that his climax was imminent, especially Monique.
With true professionalism, she withdrew her mouth but still held Frederick within her hand. "Some men cannot control themselves." She paused. "So, it is our job to do the controlling for them."
Madeline was unsure of what Monique had just done but she appeared to have applied pressure with her thumb at some part of Fredrick. The resulting effect was immediate. Even Frederick was astonished to see himself deflate before his eyes. But within seconds of this happening, Monique had, once again, taken him in her mouth and, with skill, resumed his previous state. Repeating this procedure a further three times for Madeline's benefit, each time showing her different strokes with her tongue and fingers, Monique eventually rose as gracefully as she could from the floor and sat down beside her.
"Now, my dear, show me what you have learned?"

*

The fire crackled into life and spat a red glowing ember onto the floor.
With tongs in hand, Gaston leaned over from his chair and placed it back into the flames. Aware of Janis by his side, he turned to be greeted with the drinks decanter a few inches from his face.
"Another?"
Grudgingly accepting her offer, Gaston raised his glass and allowed her to refill it for the third time since their arrival in the library. Pouring in more than was her norm, it appeared to him that she was trying to get him drunk... her motives clear.
"Would you care for me to read for you or are you content with just talking?"

The thought of her reading to him at first seemed a far more exciting alternative to their otherwise tedious conversation thus far. Drinking as much as this had not been part of his plan but, to keep up the façade, he had accepted each drink knowing that it would have appeared suspicious and out of character if he had refused what his wife knew to be his indulgence. He had to try and keep his wits about him and with the amount of brandy he already had inside him, it would be wiser to stay alert through continuous dialogue.

"Talking's fine." He glanced at the clock and noticed the time. They were late. Where were they?

Unperturbed by his curt reply, Janis sat facing him on the opposite side of the fire. Her eyes swept across the room and absorbed its ambience, created by soft, glowing candles she, herself, had carefully positioned earlier for effect. And once again, as before, she attempted to lull him into sentiment. "I do so miss these times together."

Pulling himself from his thoughts, Gaston looked up. "Sorry?"

"I said, I do miss our times together like this. The way it once was."

And will never be again, he thought, if he had his way. But remaining true to the charade, he comforted her with false hope. "We have changed over the years. Children affect the relationship of even the most devoted of couples."

Recognising her smile as a response to his unintended reassurance that their failing relationship could be rekindled, Gaston quickly changed the subject. He did not want to go down that path. "Talking of which... where are the children? They're late."

"And so they should be." Her reply resolute.

He noticed that her smile had developed to that of a mischievous beam.

"What do you mean 'so they should be'?"

"Well, I thought..."

Gaston watched her rise from her seat and inch forward in his direction.

"...It would be nice to have time without them." And on stopping in front of him, elucidated further, "A special time without them."

Gaston hadn't noticed, until now, or if he had, he had unconsciously paid no attention to it but Janis appeared to be wearing a dress he had not seen before - one of fashion and not the standard everyday attire to which he had become accustomed. With her waistline pulled in to the extreme and her corset pushing her breasts out high above the cutting, she was almost passable for a woman again.

"Mother shall not return with the children until late," she explained. "I have arranged it."

Bending down to take the seam of her dress in both hands, he watched as she began to raise it slowly over her ankles.

Confused, and through temper, Gaston sat forward in his chair and looked into her face. "Arranged it, arranged what?" This was ruining everything, he thought.

"This." Her explanation concise, she had within seconds straightened up and with her hands now at shoulder height, let the edges of her dress dangle from her fingertips. With no undergarments apparent, she stood with her exposed-self a mere two inches from her husband's face.

*

Madeline folded the bottom of her pale blue dress to the left for fear of it creasing.
Kneeling down in front of Frederick, she looked up into his eyes. This visual contact was short-lived, she noticed, as his eyes moved instantly to the left in Rosie's direction. Madeline knew that this was him seeking approval from her of a situation he had no control over. Not that Rosie would have any choice but to agree, nor, indeed, have any say in the matter - if Monique wished it, then it would be so. Frederick was fully aware of the bitterness Rosie felt but as he looked back into Madeline's deep, black eyes, he was dumbstruck. This young woman was absolutely beautiful, he thought. And for her to do to him what she was about to would have been any man's dream. He could only wait patiently for her to begin.
Madeline was equally aware of the awkward situation she now found herself in, so sat for a moment wondering how she would proceed.
"Come, come, my dear," Monique coaxed.
Madeline looked down at his flaccid manhood and, on doing so, slowly stretched out her right hand to touch it. Running her delicate fingertips along the full length from base to tip, she could sense the atmosphere in the room. All three, in different modes of thought, waiting to see what she would do. She knew that Rosie would be loathing the sight of her man being treated as such by a woman far, far prettier than herself. And that Rosie would know that her Fredrick would be enjoying the experience every bit as much as she hated it being done to him. Monique, she was aware, remained silent, waiting, watching. Placing her hand fully on top to feel its mass, Madeline felt the warmth beneath her palm and a slight throbbing as Frederick suddenly came to life. Feeling the rapid growth beneath, she wondered why it had only taken the softness of her hand upon him to do this when it appeared that Rosie had had to work at it through movement. But it soon became clear that it was Madeline's own personal touch that was exciting Frederick, not just the sensation of being touched. Looking up, once again, into his eyes now confirmed this as she saw the pleading in his face, as if begging her to continue. And knew at that moment she had complete power over this man, the thought of which was exhilarating. The full extent of his aroused-state became apparent within seconds and Madeline found that, even with her hand clasp fully around him, her fingertips barely touched. How she would manage to fit this into her mouth did not bear thinking about but she would have to try. She could not let Rosie gain the upper hand and, in particular, let the other girls know she was incapable of doing it. If she were

to reach the heights in Paris that she aspired to, then this feat would not only have to be accomplished but surpass even Monique's high standard. Her instigation and approach to this she now considered would be, in part, that of Monique's procedure, a part of which Madeline had considered very passionate and exciting. She would lean down to the left and place her mouth at the base. Then running her tongue slowly up the full length until she had reached the tip - this all the time staring deep into Fredrick's eyes - she would then slide it between her lips. After which she would take in as much of him as she could and hopefully do herself justice in the way of natural aptitude. This was her plan anyway and she only hoped she could accomplish something from it. Imitating the earlier rhythmic movements of Rosie, Madeline slowly worked her hand back and forth and felt the skin move freely over its much harder interior. She looked up at Frederick to gauge his reaction and saw the pleasure on his face. With his mouth agape and his breathing intent, Madeline knew she was doing it in the correct fashion and to his liking. Looking down, her mind flashed back to the times when she had done this for Gaston. On the first occasion it had lasted barely a moment - with her touch upon him brief, he had surrendered to the sensation within seconds. The following time had lasted slightly longer and had confused her at the time. Considering the fact that if this was so pleasurable, then why would you not want it to last longer and enjoy it further? Monique's explanation suddenly entered her head, 'controlling the man'. She had thought previously that this had meant dominance over them but Monique's earlier explanation with regard to Fredrick now put a new perspective on things. Men had no control over their pleasure. It must reach a point when it was so pleasurable that they could not proceed any further. This intrigued Madeline but for the life of her she could not recall what Monique had done to prevent this. She was also aware of her duty at hand. Leaning forward towards her goal, she looked up at Frederick once again and fixed her gaze firmly upon him, where, if all went as she had planned, they would remain for the duration. She fixed her lips firmly to his base and prepared herself for her first proper contact with a man. On doing this, she felt him harden even further within her grasp and this was reinforced with a simultaneous jerk in his abdomen that she felt on her cheek and a short-lived tremble in his legs. So, with a gentle pace she started her slow ascent and instantly tasted the sweat of passion on her tongue.

*

Gaston pushed himself hard against her rear once again.
On her knees and with her arms resting on his chair, Janis felt sensational to his touch and with yet another deep thrust he knew it would not be long before he exploded deep within her. This being better now than he could ever remember it being with her in the past. He could hear her voice, as if far off in the distance, spurring him on. 'My dearest, my dearest.' And although his

earlier reproach of her use of this expression towards him had been justified at the time, he now found that these words were drawing him closer to the fulfillment he craved at this very moment. Feeling his heart pound within his chest and his breathing heavy, he knew that the beads of sweat rolling down his forehead were from the heat of the flames and the consumed brandy.
He heard her voice once again. "My dearest." And with it came one final thrust. Driving himself deep inside her, he remained pressed hard against her skin while his body shuddered to a climax, himself pulsating within her and his stomach twitching as if in death's throw. With weak and shaken knees, he slumped across Janis's back where he remained for a moment before pulling himself free and rolling exhausted onto the floor. Disorientated and spent, he lay still as the room about him shifted in and out of focus, its contents gliding around him with irregularity. He tried his best to comprehend the situation and, for a brief moment, a window within his confused state, there appeared vision and possible enlightenment. How he had gotten himself into this predicament with his wife he was uncertain. It had just happened. Be it the brandy or otherwise, this past twenty minutes had been out of his control. As if led on by an imaginary spirit or succubus, he had, and without forethought, done what he had promised himself never to do again. And, furthermore, didn't think capable of doing since meeting Madeline.
Make love to his wife.
Janis had cast a spell over him, his delirious and fevered mind now sought to blame.
Four brandies, albeit full glasses, had, in the past, never dulled his senses as much as they had tonight. He could easily remain in control after consuming far more than that. Drunk maybe, slightly inebriated but still capable of freewill, unlike tonight where he felt like he had been influenced by something far stronger than the potency of the drink
Suddenly aware of a weight upon him, he opened his eyes to see Janis sitting astride and looking down. He heard once again, as if far off in the distance, her voice speak to him in soft tone, "I'm not finished yet, my dearest."
Focusing his bleary eyes on her face as she drew down nearer towards him, he felt the touch of her lips on his. As she playfully bit at him amid gentle kisses, he lay frozen and powerless to her now seemingly addictive charms.
The voice spoke yet again within his head... 'My dearest, my dearest'. His mind had regained its confused state and with it, clarity of vision. Her face had vanished but he still felt her presence and the touch of her lips upon him. But lower down upon his chest, then lower still, deeper and deeper and he sensed within him her focus and the object of her desire.

*

Monique sat alone within her dimly-lit sitting room.
As was normal at this late an hour with most of her clients now left for the evening, it was her ideal time for quiet and a moment's reflection on the

day's events. But, more importantly, the daily finances. Having eleven girls now at her disposal to engage as she wished, she alone determined the prices of all transactions and the commission that each of them received in lieu of services rendered. Minus their room rentals and amenities, she knew that none would ever make their fortune in her employment. But their alternative was even worse. They could, if they so desired, ply their trade on the vicious and uncompromising streets of Paris but few wanted to venture into this urban wilderness of thieves, rapists and murderers, preferring, of course, the safety of her house. Thus, Monique could command her oversized share of every coin they earned. Each client known to her, she ran a strict and no-nonsense house. If any of the girls attempted to extort further payment as initially agreed by her, then it was the duty of the customer to inform her. This was one of her most stringent rules and many a client had been told in the past not to return, along with the girl in question. This rarely happened nowadays, Monique having made herself clear to all.
But an exception to this rule had been Madeline.
Having commandeered this young woman's money, through cunning, on her first day, Madeline was now under her control... to a point. She knew that Gaston had, on several occasions, paid Madeline extra over what had been initially decided. These payments had been for Madeline's company only, nothing else, but what had developed sought recompense through coinage of which he had happily parted. This, Monique had overlooked and for good reason. This was no young woman of which she wanted to be rid. Madeline was a woman who would make her a fortune. She had kept her isolated from the other girls for good reason. Not that it had taken much effort with them taking it upon themselves to do so. Although each and every one of her girls had their own unique individuality, style and special talents to accommodate any client requirement, Madeline still outshone them all with her natural composure and beauty. An air of jealousy and envy filled the house with regard to Madeline and, through no fault of her own, she was making few friends. But Monique was grooming her for higher things and her special tuition was part of it. Even before the start of today's lesson, Monique could determine its outcome. To her, it was clear. Madeline was unique.
It would have been absurd to consider a novice, such as Madeline, proficient enough to accomplish the task that even an experienced whore as Rosie could not achieve. Frederick had been chosen for two reasons. The first one apparent - his size; and secondly, the private relationship that Monique knew him to have with Rosie. Monique, herself, had years of practice and experience on countless men to be able to carry this out with ease but Madeline, she knew, would struggle from the start. And that is why Monique had chosen Rosie. She was renowned for her chat and a confidante she was not. If word needed to be spread, then she was the one guaranteed to do it. The outcome of today's lesson would now, she knew, be circulating not only within her group of girls but beyond the house walls; and certainly not in the

true sense, with Rosie's personal interpretation of the proceedings being far removed from what had actually occurred.

Monique had sat in silence and, unlike the others who were curious to see how Madeline would perform under these circumstances, let her begin, knowing full well that her protégé would not let her down. Taking into account the size and length of Frederick, Monique could look deep into Madeline's mind, who, after a brief period of deliberating, finally leaned forward to meet the nemesis she held within her grasp. Doing what Monique had suspected and hoped she would do, it was the complete opposite of what Rosie had done. Madeline had laid her mouth at Frederick's base. His body and mind had reacted to this even prior to the stimulus of her tongue rising and before she had reached the top, he was spent. Madeline, aware of the impossible task ahead of her, had changed the rules to suit her circumstances. So confident within herself to be able to bring Frederick to a conclusion without having to attempt the impractical, she had managed, through a combination of direct eye contact, to lure him and his thoughts of what was to come, and conclude the session in an acceptable way. Against harsh odds, Madeline had overcome them and if Frederick had been a client, then he would not have felt cheated.

Monique intended to exploit Madeline's natural ability and adaptability to its limit.

*

Madeline 2

Chapter 4

Sunday, Sunday

Part 1

Seated beneath the shade of the parasol, the elderly woman looked down at the breakfast table. "You seem pleased with yourself this morning."
Janis placed a teacup down in front of her. "Indeed I am mother, indeed I am. Milk?"
Bewildered, she looked up to her daughter standing by her side. "You know I don't take milk in my tea." And in defiance, faced forward. "Never have."

She reached for the sugar while seeking justification. "Did your planned evening go so well as to have sullied your mind as much?"
Her mother was right. To even suggest the unthinkable, that of putting milk in her tea, indicated to her that her mind was elsewhere this morning but she ignored her lame indignation and pressed on, "Better than planned I suspect." Stirring in two spoonfuls, she eyed her daughter, now seated opposite her, with suspicion. "Better?"
"Not to go into too much detail, mother." She beamed and leaned forward. "Well, not over breakfast anyway." Then resuming her upright position, continued, "Yes, better than I expected. I imagine Gaston may, at this very moment, be thinking similar thoughts."
Looking at the vacant place setting, she shook her head. "I doubt that very much."
Janis followed her gaze and smiled. "Oh, I don't know. I think I may have instilled a little warmth into our relationship last night, one worth remembering."
Her mother coughed with embarrassment. "Yes, well, as you said, there is no need to go into detail."
"Oh mother, how can you sit there and say that when it was you, yourself, who had suggested it?"
Sipping at her tea, she considered the part she had played in her daughter's seduction of her husband. Wasn't it her who had obtained the very substance that Janis had used - a powder known to few for its natural aphrodisiac effects? And with her being a lady of substance and knowing the right people who could procure this on her behalf, she had provided her daughter with the possible means of luring her husband back to her. "I do not intend to let Paris have its way with this family through gossip and scandal."
"I know, mother; and I appreciate all that you are doing to help."
"Then we will have to see what has transpired." Then looking at the empty place-setting once again, added "The moment he decides to grace us with his presence."

*

Through sheer determination, Gaston prized open his eyes and immediately regretted it.
He shut them tight.
His head was pounding and as he lay curled up beneath the bed sheet, he clasped his hands to his forehead as if to drain the tension and pressure he felt within. Never had he endured such a pain as this through the effects of brandy. Slowly opening his eyes once again, he tried to adjust them to the faint light shining through the thin, summer sheet. He wondered in which room he was lying as he had no recollection of going to bed. But with a summary scan of himself, he did notice that he was naked. And with this, some vague memories of the previous night came flooding back to him. He

thought harder. And on pulling off the sheet and sitting up, his suspicions were confirmed. He was in their matrimonial bed.
No!
Certain that he had, and for reasons unknown, made love to his wife, he now inwardly chastised himself for doing so. Furthermore, his carefully laid plans, with regard to his mother-in-law, were now in ruins. Nothing had gone as he had planned. What had caused this? He also felt his bladder full, so, reluctantly pulling himself from the comfort of the bed, dragged his frail body onto his feet. Locating the bedpan where he knew it to be, he prepared to relieve himself. But upon his touch, his body doubled over with the stinging pain. Looking down, he noticed he was red and swollen. Good god, he thought, what had he done to himself or rather what had Janis done to him? Raw and tender to the touch, he had to try and pull himself back just enough as to set an easy flow in motion but the more he persevered with this, the more painful it got. He would have to squat over it like a child and let nature take its course. But on doing this, he felt every heated drop as it passed through him, so, to try and alleviate the pain, he attempted to let it out in stages. Wincing in agony, he thought further on what had happened. But inwardly he knew. It was the result of fervent love-making with his wife, a wife that he had vowed never to go near again.
Damn it!
Sitting on the edge of the bed, he once again held his throbbing head in his hands. He needed a powder of some sort to dull the pain but would have to dress first before wandering downstairs in search of one. Looking about him, he sought the whereabouts of his clothes, their absence of which, both strewn about the floor or hanging over the chair, indicated to him that Janis had, with assiduousness, folded and hung them up in the closet.
His britches! The vial was in the pocket.
He ran across the room and hauled open the door. Rummaging as fast as he could through his various items of clothing, he finally located the pair he had been wearing the previous night. Pulling them free, he delved into each pocket repeatedly but to no avail.
It was gone.

*

Their plush garden extended down at a slight gradient towards the slow, trickling stream at the bottom. As a family they would often come down to catch the small, but insufficient, edible fish that swam there; or perhaps with a friend or two to paddle freely in the cool water when the summer's sun was too hot for them. But on this occasion, he felt himself wanting to be alone. He could hear the voices yonder at the picnic further up the garden. The others playing their various games as the elders shaded themselves beneath the spreading trees. Their conversations dull to him. Choosing a rock beside his favourite part of the torrent, he sat with porcelain soldiers in hand and watched its flow. He had risen early today, he thought, considering it was a Sunday, a day of leisure to do as one wants without the restriction of schooling. This, and the fact that he had arrived home late with his grandmother the previous night, he had spent very few hours in bed. He was young and didn't feel he required the amount of sleep that the older ones apparently needed - his father still being in bed at this late hour a prime example. Up from bed early, even before the house staff had begun their chores, he had breakfasted with two apples from the larder. Wandering the house when no-one else was awake had always been an adventure to him. He would enter the rooms which were not normally permissible to him by his parents. He could never understand why, so, on this occasion, he had entered the library, yet again, making at once for the cabinet which had always held his attention - the array of bottles within its hold seemed like an Aladdin's cave to him. With the various shapes and colours appealing, he knew some to be wine and others brandy. In addition, there was port and sherry and one of a curious green colour, the name of which eluded him. Sampling just enough of each so not to be noticed, he had, in the past, tasted them all. That was apart from the green one which he had never found tempting enough - it being, to a youth, the colour of pee. Glancing down to the floor, his peripheral vision had caught sight of a small, glass tube which had nestled itself against the cabinet leg. Bending down to retrieve it, he noticed the cork holding the liquid within and thought that this must be a very rare drink to come in such a small bottle. No-one would notice it gone, he'd thought, so he had secreted it within his pocket for later.

Now, laying his toy soldiers on the grass beside him, he delved deep and pulled it free. Looking down at the vial, once again he thought on how special it must be.

He would have to sample it and see.

*

Dabbing the damp cloth to his swollen cheek, Frederick winced once again as Rosie continued her rants.

"Serves you bloody right."

Her tirade ceaseless since the previous night, she had allowed him very little opportunity to utter a word by way of explanation. On the rare occasion that she did, had resulted in the rapidly blackening eye he now nursed. He had obviously said something that was not to her liking which, at present, did not appear to be too hard a task in achieving. Being well aware of her excessive mood swings and the extremes she could go to when in the midst of one, he now took the easy option and remained silent. With his elbows resting on the kitchen table, he watched her circle around it once again.

"Who does that bitch think she is?"

He sighed. She must have repeated that same phrase over a dozen times now.

"And you."

Coming from behind, he felt her hand slap the side of his head, pushing his fist hard against his inflamed eye. "Ouch!"
"I'll 'ouch' you." She slapped again. "How dare you embarrass me like that."
Cowering with his arms bent over his head, he leant to the side, fearful of further assault. But, with an obvious lull in the battle, he lowered them after a few seconds. Rosie, all fifteen stone of her, moved to the kitchen window, where she now stood wavering and muttering under her breath, "Bloody bitch."
Reluctantly, he attempted to appease her through apologetic discourse, "It meant nothing to me Rosie." He bit his lip.
"What!" She turned on her feet and within seconds had approached and was bent over the table, her face inches from his. "Meant nothing to you, meant nothing to you. Christ, Frederick, you came over her fucking face."
Over her face! A slight exaggeration he thought. "Yes, but..."
"'Yes but', nothing. She hadn't even started and you blew off."
What could he say? Not a word could he utter in the least that would placate her. She was right. He had been under Madeline's spell since the moment she had first knelt down in front of him... and what man wouldn't! Staring into her deep, black eyes he had lost complete control as she continued to tease him. He could feel himself harden even now thinking about it.
Rosie straightened up. "And do you think I've told the girls that?"
Why she would feel compelled to tell the girls anything about it he couldn't think. But his opinion in this apparently of little consequence, she continued without answer.
"Well if anyone asks, you say she was no good at it."
"What?"
"Tell them she was no good."
"Tell who? Who's going to ask?"
Rosie pulled a chair in behind her and sat opposite. Unconsciously picking up a small kitchen knife, she sat tapping its hilt on the table. "Listen, Frederick, I don't want it getting out that this..." Pausing, she closed her eyes tight to calm herself. "...this, this bloody Madeline..."
Frederick could see she was struggling. "Rosie." He made ways to stretch his hand out to hold hers but aware of the lethal weapon she held within her grasp, thought better of it. "Rosie."
Her temper at boiling point, she raised the knife up to face height before bringing its point down at speed and embedding it in the wooden table. "Fuck."
Frederick recoiled with fright. "Mon Dieu, Rosie." He'd seen her temper on numerous occasions in the past but even this was something new to him.
Leaning back, Rosie held her hands out, palms facing him. "Listen, listen. If word gets out that this bitch is, without doubt, the best cock-sucker here, then where does that leave the rest of us? They'll be queuing up for her."
"Yes, but she didn't..." He cut himself short.
"Exactly, she didn't bloody need to."

Frederick watched as she pushed back the chair, stood up and circled her way round the table yet again. Following her with his head, he countered, "But who's to know that? Just don't say anything to anyone."
She stopped in her tracts to face him. "How can I do that? They all knew what we were in there to do in the first place."
Yes, he knew alright, she couldn't stop herself talking about it, could she. "Okay, so what did you tell the girls, after I left I mean, because I certainly didn't hear you mention it while I was there?" Meaning the taverne where they had met them the previous night, he was curious to hear her account of the events.
"I told them she almost puked."
"What?"
Rosie looked pleased with herself. "That she was a hopeless case, that she gagged and choked and that Monique was not happy with her efforts."
It was a good job for Rosie that the kitchen door opened when it did. He had felt compelled to set her right. As much as he knew he loved her, which since the previous night had diminished dramatically, he felt a compulsion to come to Madeline's defense. Why should she ruin the life of another through envy or jealousy? Rosie, herself, had even admitted to him that she was very diverse in her trade and that very little was beyond her in the ways of fulfillment. So why all of the panic over one girl - she couldn't service everyone? And, in addition, this wasn't every man's choice.
"Hello all."
Frederick, on seeing his least favourite of the girls entering the room, stood to leave. "I'd better be getting to work."
Sporting a dress of hideous green and juxtaposed against her red curled hair, Charlotte spoke out, "Oh that looks a sore one."
Lifting his fingers to his eye, he remembered the swelling. Damn. What would he tell them at work? He'd had to sneak into his room the night before in case his parents had seen it. And it hadn't swollen up as much then.
By way of explanation, Rosie came to his rescue, "Stupid bugger walked into the door last night."
Approximately the same size as Rosie, but sweat-ridden with it, Charlotte chortled out loud. Not present at the previous night's drinking, she hadn't seen Rosie hit Frederick in the face with her fist during her semi-drunken and enraged state. But she did know of Rosie's temper. "Oh yeah, and who do you think's going to believe that one. What's for eating?"
Leaving Charlotte to her search within the larder, Frederick removed his jacket from the back of his chair and headed for the door. He felt no inclination to kiss Rosie goodbye as he had always done and she noticed it.
"No kiss?"
He spied Charlotte peaking back over her shoulder to see his response. "Have you two fallen out again?"
Frederick ignored her remark and looked down into Rosie's face. "I'll see you later."

Closing the door behind him, he heard the instant buzz of their chat. Madeline this and Madeline that, he'd bet. He wanted none of it. What he did want was sustenance. Feeling the emptiness within and his stomach churning, he now wished he had taken the proffered breakfast earlier. Unfortunately his appetite had dulled somewhat since his arrival twenty minutes hence and with Rosie's endless rants off-putting, he had broken his fasting on milk alone. Knowing himself to be way early for work, he decided he would stop off somewhere en route, a café perhaps. As the whereabouts to the possible places known to him mulled in his mind, he noticed the door ahead to his left open up.
He stopped in his tracts.
Wearing a loose fitting dress of summer lilac, Madeline exited from the room in time to meet him face on. As their eyes met, an all too brief hush descended upon them both as Madeline stood staring up at his face, astonished.
"Frederick."
He returned her acknowledgement with a nod. "Miss."
"No, Frederick." Shaking her head. "I wasn't saying hello, I meant your eye. What happened to you? And it's Madeline."
He removed his cap and nodded once again. "Yes, Miss... I mean Madeline." Impatient with his silence and the fidgeting of his hat within his hands, she pushed further, "Frederick, your eye."
"Eh, yeah, sorry Miss." Sensing Rosie's excuse to Charlotte somewhat implausible, he decided that walking into a door would not sound convincing enough for Madeline and, in addition to this, he felt reluctant to lie to her. "I had an argument with Rosie."
Her eyes widened. "And she did that?"
"Yes, Miss." Like a stuttering child being scolded for misbehaving, he remained unmoving and had it not been for the cap doing cartwheels in his hands, he would have considered himself frozen to the spot. His previous night's shortcomings forgotten about, he stared into her eyes and at that moment knew he had fallen in love with her. She had been his very last thought before sleep and his first when he had woken. Now here she was standing before him, a picture of grace and as beautiful as he had remembered. "Yes, well, I have to be going now, work I'm afraid."
Madeline stood aside to let him pass. "You have work today, on Sunday?"
With effort he moved another part of his body, this being his head, with a curt nod. "Seven days, Miss."
"Please, Frederick, my name is Madeline; you are making me feel uncomfortable."
"Sorry, Miss, it was never my intention." He forced a smile. "Madeline it is then."

She returned one of her own. "That's better. So, you work every single day? You have, indeed, a strict employer that allows no time off for their employees."
Frederick felt his shoulders relax somewhat. He always took pride in speaking about his work. "It's voluntary, they don't force me to attend. I work at the infirmary on my own time."
"Very commendable, Frederick, I do so admire and respect anyone who has the natural propensity to tend to the sick and needy."
These words were a joy to his heart. "Madeline... about last night?"
He noticed her face shy to the side with embarrassment but after a second she looked up. "Do you do that voluntarily as well, Frederick? For Monique, I mean."
He didn't get a chance to reply. His empty stomach had done it for him. With one tremendous rumble, the emptiness within him let itself be known. Madeline's eyes widened with joyous surprise and he immediately apologised amidst their simultaneous outbursts of laughter. This merriment, apparently loud enough to be heard in the kitchen, had led the door to be quickly opened and standing there, with reddened face, was an enraged Rosie.
Frederick, in an instant, felt the use of his legs return. "Well, have to be going."
With no farewell to either, he made for the exit and within seconds was under the hot, morning sun and the relative safety of the outdoors.

The streets were crowded for such an early time of day, so, with intent, he meandered through their casual pace whilst narrowly avoiding several parasol spokes to the eye as he went. He could feel the sun beat down on his shoulders. It would be suffocating in the wards today, he thought.
As he walked, he chomped his way through the sausage and bread he had so eagerly purchased from a market vendor, and considered how dramatically his mind had changed in the last twelve hours. Meeting Madeline had put his life in a new perspective. In the past he had casually waded his way through the course of things, uncaring of the future and reckless in family values. To have a common whore, such as Rosie, as a partner would be thought of as unthinkable by his parents and he had dreaded them finding out. But he loved the excitement of it all. Rosie was adept in the most outrageous indulgences and he had sampled her various ways on numerous occasions. He rounded the corner and smiled to himself at the thought of several very unique and unusual experiences they'd shared together. But even these were getting repetitive and Rosie's volatile temperament was becoming wearisome. Unlike Madeline, who was something new and very special. So much so, as to merit him considering changing his ways and thoughts of the future.
Springing up the dilapidated steps two at a time until he had reached the entrance, he readily passed over the remains of his breakfast to a child

beggar sitting nearby and pushed open the heavy wooden door. The heat and the smell of the disinfectant took his breathe away as it always did on his initial entry. With his body acclimatising to its surroundings, he paced directly ahead in a fashion which was now, to him, routine.
"Hi, Frederick."
There was no need to stop and turn, the voice was familiar to him, so, raising an arm, he hollered back, "Hello, Michelle. How's the new baby?"
"Fine, my darling. How's Rosie?"
"Dead." He continued walking, and heard her shock.
"Dead!"
He smiled to himself. "Yeah, she choked on a carrot."
"A Carrot!" Finally realising she was being had, Michelle hollered back sending echoes around the open hallway, "Oh, you little shit. You had me going there."
No, he deliberated. The only place you're going is the morgue, sweetheart. Including two sets of twins, that was your thirteenth baby and you're only twenty eight - and not one, apart from the twins, having the same father.
"Hey, Freddy, my boy."
"Yes, Garcia, I know, I'll be there shortly." Veering to the right, he continued down the hall.
"Freddy, Freddy."
"I'll get back to you in a minute, Raul."
He reached his intended ward and gently edged the door open as he knew it would fall off, it having no hinge.
"Frederick, love; oh nice eye; would you mind getting me some fresh swathes from the storage room when you have a minute?"
"Be there soon." He beamed, 'and with pleasure my pretty, little nurse.'
He had something to do first.
Knowing the bed to be second from the end, he kept to the left-hand-side, fearful of further wants upon his time. He reached it successfully. "You're awake then?"
"Awake! What do you think? This place is a bloody madhouse. I'd rather be back teaching at the school."
Sitting on the edge of the bed, Frederick gently patted the closer of his swathed legs. "Well you would get yourself run over by a carriage, young brother."

*

Madeline 2

Chapter 5

Sunday, Sunday

Part 2

Monique squeezed her slender frame out from behind the heavy, mahogany wall panel, thankful that she had, in the past, kept herself in good shape. Flicking at her dark, velvet dress until satisfied she was dust free, she casually dropped the muck-ridden handkerchief in the corner and sallied, with cane in hand, to her fireside armchair. Smiling inwardly to herself, she nestled her way into its deep confines and considered the kitchen conversation she had just eaves-dropped upon. All was going as expected,

she thought. Ever-dependable Rosie had played into her hands yet again. Had it not been for her reliability in such matters, this and her willingness to participate in some of her clients' more outrageous requests, she would have gotten rid of the overweight sow a long time since. It had been apparent that Rosie and Frederick would have their differences but it wasn't until he had left the room that Rosie's conversation with Charlotte really brought to light her intentions. And, as predicted, it was not in Madeline's favour.
"We need to get rid of that bitch." She'd heard Rosie announce to Charlotte.
Monique had struggled at that point to hear Charlotte's reply and had assumed by the stifled tone that she had immersed herself within the larder in her daily ritual of emptying its contents.
"She's got her eye on my Frederick."
"You're taking this too personal, Rosie." Eventually hearing Charlotte's voice.
"Personal! I'll rip her fucking eyes out."
Monique remembered grinning at this point.
Between the constant chewing of her early morning feast, Charlotte's semi-audible replies continued, "There's plenty for everyone Rosie, we're as busy now as we've ever been. I'll say one thing for the old crow, she knows how to get the men through the door and that means coin for us all."
'Old crow' am I, thought Monique.
"That's not the point, Charlotte. This fucking Madeline's not doing her fair share but still getting all the good things."
"Good things. I guess by that you're still on about her getting to use the shiny bath?"
Even Monique had been stunned by Rosie's pettiness at this point.
"No, not just the washroom...it's her getting in with the old crow and getting the special treatment from her."
Pressing her head tighter towards the wall hole, Monique had fought hard to hear them over a constant tapping.
"Please put the knife down, Rosie."
And, as before, Monique heard it pierce hard into the table. The fat minx, this was her house furniture that she was abusing.
"I'm the only one that gets to have Frederick's cock in her mouth, not that old battleaxe and certainly not some young, bloody country girl. We'd done this plenty of times before, so why did she do this different last night?"
Monique had heard Charlotte cackle, "So this is what it's all about - Madeline with Frederick? Hah, I've heard of his size - you, yourself, even bragging about it. I'd be hard pushed to get that thing down my throat."
Hearing the moment's silence, Monique knew that the coin had dropped.
"Oh, I see now. Frederick enjoyed it, that's what's annoying you, isn't it? I bet you he shot his load... Madeline made him come, didn't she? And you don't like it."
Hearing the chair being aggressively pushed back, Monique had pressed closer.

"Of course he enjoyed it. She didn't even get the bloody thing in her mouth and he'd come."
Charlotte had chortled further, no words necessary.
"It's not funny, Charlotte. Monique is up to something with her. We're on our backs every night taking all sorts of abuse from these sick bastards while Madeline gets to sit in the front parlour drinking wine and getting paid for it. Did you see who she was with last night? Lady fucking Caroline, that's who. And you know what she's in to, don't you?"
Keep going Rosie, my dear, keep going, you're doing well.
"Well no more, I'm going to get my own back on her. And don't say a word of any of this to the girls, especially the cock-sucking part. I'm handling it."
"I wouldn't dream of it..." Monique had heard Charlotte pause in mid-sentence. "... Who's that laughing out there?"
The conversation now in an apparent hiatus, Monique had pulled herself free. She had heard all that she needed to know.
Rosie was doing her bidding well.

*

With Frederick making a hasty exit, Madeline turned to face Rosie. No words were mentioned, only a hard stare in her direction before the kitchen door was slammed shut. She thought that, having risen so early, she would have made it to the kitchen before anyone else was up but now that Rosie held sway over it, she would have to do without breakfast in the house. Madeline considered her options. Should she return to her room with an empty stomach or perhaps retrieve some money from her cache and eat alfresco in one of the nearby cafes? It was a beautiful day outside, she thought, so she opted for the latter.

Adjusting her parasol to suit the sun's glare, Madeline turned in her usual direction and, on making headway towards her favourite cafe, was cordially greeted by many a passer-by. Sporting one of the dresses that Ramone had bought for her, the soft cloth felt sufficiently loose about her body to keep her cool but still commanded the plunging neckline that she knew was a prerequisite for male attention. Attired as such and with her long, black hair tied back exposing her natural radiance, she noticed the looks she was receiving from many a casual pedestrian. Their gazes were equally from women as they were from men and Madeline considered this with slight scepticism. Was this in admiration of her beauty, she thought, or did they have alternative motives for their stares? Did they know? Did they know what she was, what she had become since arriving in Paris? Her first venture along this very street a few weeks ago had been an innocent perusal of her new surroundings. For a naïve, young girl to be in such a colossus as Paris, as opposed to her own home town, had felt exhilarating to her. This same city held her future but, ironically, a different one to when her intention was

that of finding a wealthy husband. Indeed, it had become a city which she was now unmistakably determined to make as her own, without the need for one.
Looking ahead, she saw the café waiter recognise her and with open arms and a hearty welcome, beckoned her near.
"Ah, Mademoiselle Madeline, you are like a breath of spring to these streets."
The consistency of his fussing over her had not diminished one bit during her frequent visits, she noticed. He was, without doubt, the most annoying but likable man she had ever met. And she loved to tease him.
"Merci, Jacques, you are too kind." She stood patiently waiting to be seated.
Jacques remained in his usual state of awe in her presence before realising his faux pas. "Oh forgive me, Mademoiselle, please, please."
Ushered to a seat in the shade with all haste, Jacques continued with his dallying. Flicking the already spotless seat with his towel, he pulled it free for her. "So early today, Mademoiselle?"
Madeline noticed that, as was the case with Frederick earlier, both appeared hesitant in calling her by her first name.
She accepted the proffered seat. 'Merci, Jacques."
Locating her folded parasol on the adjacent seat, she tilted her head up to face him. This was just in time to see his eyes avert quickly from her cleavage to meet hers.
Madeline graced him with a tender smile before teasing him, once again, like she always did. "Your eyes appeared to have wandered somewhat there, Jacques."
Madeline knew she was being cruel but, to her, it was a game and she felt it did no harm. She suspected that Jacques enjoyed it every bit as much as she did. In one previous occasion he had spilled the entire contents of his tray when she intentionally brushed her breast against his arm as she passed him by. And it certainly did not seem big-headed of her to imagine that he would, no doubt, spend countless nights in his bed thinking about her. To have even considered such thoughts, or to indulge in such deeds a few weeks back, would have been, to her, unthinkable. But she was a changed woman from back then when she had used Jacques and this café as a tester for her possible attractiveness to men.
Aware of his minor impropriety, Jacques eluded confrontation and embarrassment with a hurried request for her order. "Breakfast as usual - eggs, ham and bread?"
Madeline nodded with friendly affirmation, she could see his face redden slightly and felt reluctant to humiliate him further. "And coffee."
Returning the smile, he nodded back. "Coffee, but of course."
As he turned to go, Madeline called his name.
Standing at an awkward angle between tables, Jacques looked round at her. "Yes?"
"Thank you, Jacques."

Unsure of what she was thanking him for, Jacques remained still for a moment before turning and heading inside; returning momentarily with placements for two as was customary during her visits. He attentively assured that, although she always sat alone at the table and that this may appear unladylike to passers-by, he helped create the illusion that she was with escort. This was one of the reasons she had thanked him; and the fact he had always kept would-be nuisances at bay. She had noticed his reaction to Gaston talking to her on her initial visit and also when she had been here with Jacob. He had seemed a much happier person on subsequent occasions when she had dined alone.

Returning for the second time, he poured coffee for two as was normal, unless she dictated otherwise, and left her to her thoughts.

With it being such an early time of day, her usual people-watching pleasure was somewhat limited in this particular street, so, with very little to keep her attention, her mind wandered back to the previous night. In particular, Frederick, or to be more specific, she thought, a certain part of Frederick. Not exactly accomplishing the task that Monique had put in place for her, she had, herself, achieved satisfaction in the fact that she had brought Frederick to climax her own way. If she could do it for him, could she then assume that it would work for others? She had considered it very probable. But the fact still remained that she had not yet learned how to do it by herself - only by way of Rosie and Monique's example had she been tutored. But this would not do. She would have to learn herself but not with a paying customer as she would first have to be proficient. She would have to find a willing participant and one she could trust. Suddenly aware of Jacques by her side, she watched as he laid her breakfast on the table in front of her. A quick scan of his body from head to toe led her mind to the possibilities. She looked up to him and smiled.

Jacques' day, she thought, was about to get better.

*

Madeline 2

Chapter 6

Sunday, Sunday

Part 3

Gaston paced himself as he descended the all too precipitous staircase. Gripping hard to the banister, each step he took sent sharp waves of pain through his entire body to agonisingly reverberate around his throbbing head. Stepping down as nimble-footed as he felt possible, he eventually made it to the bottom and, with relief, stood still to get his bearings.
Where was everyone? Were they still breakfasting outside in the garden or was it time for the picnic? Unsure of the time as he had also misplaced his

timepiece, he was hopeful of either. Although he badly required some sort of powered pain relief, he needed to find the vial first, so made straight for the library. He must have dropped it there. Or at least someone had inadvertently dropped it there, namely Janis.

The blurred but painful memories of the previous night's drinking came flooding back to him as he entered the room. And with his eyes instantly drawn to the drinks' cabinet, he felt his stomach turn.

Never again!

On his hands and knees within seconds, he had the entire floor scoured within minutes. He repeated the process once again, just in case his fragile head had played tricks with him, but still the vial's whereabouts eluded him. Where was it?

He distinctly recalled sitting by the fire and a vague memory of Janis standing before him, refilling his glass. He had it with him then, of this he felt certain, but anything after that seemed to him indistinct, blurred. He approached the fire and sat down in the chair as he remembered, this in the hope that it would jaunt some recollection of what had followed. But as much as he tried to evoke a memory, his head remained empty, save the incessant pounding. What had given him such a headache as this anyway? Never before had he suffered such pain through a night of drinking brandy.

The brandy!

His head turned, once again, to the drinks' cabinet and although the very thought of brandy turned his stomach, he needed to be sure. He would have to test it. Removing the top, he put his nose straight to it and sniffed. The emptiness in his stomach erupted as a reaction and he felt the bile start to rise. His continuous retching lasted for several seconds but, as much as it smelled revolting to him at that very moment, all appeared normal. He sighed. He would have to taste some of it to be sure. This, he was not looking forward to. He retched once again before the bottle had even reached his mouth and continued to do so as the first drop touched his lips. Convinced that he would bring up the entire contents of his already empty stomach, he swirled it around in his mouth to try and capture its taste, its texture, its body. Anything at all that felt or tasted different from the norm. But enough was enough he thought, his body had taken enough torture. He would have to spit it out on to the floor and blame it on one of the staff. So, returning to the fireside chair, he reseated himself as before and leaned back.

More pain!

Not only did his head hurt but a subtle scratch to the front of his britches reminded him of the rawness of his skin. How could he endure the next few hours entertaining guests?

What in god's name had Janis done to him last night?

*

Madeline's appetite had diminished somewhat.

Having eaten only partial segments of the cold ham and a small corner of cheese, she pushed the thick, wooden platter away from her. In doing this, she knew that Jacques would be by her side within seconds as she was still his sole customer. This and the fact that she knew he would be watching her from inside as he had done on previous occasions.

Sipping at her coffee, she pondered over how she would approach Jacques on such a delicate subject as this. After all, it wasn't every day that a pretty, young woman requested the use of such a private part of their anatomy as she would. But she knew, deep down, that he would not refuse. She just had to figure out the best way to proceed.

Going on appearance alone, Madeline judged his age to be mid-thirties and that he was without wife; he didn't appear to her to be the 'marrying type' somehow, whatever the 'marrying type' happened to look like. She had never broached this subject before but, then again, why would she, until now it had been of little importance to her, as had he. And although he looked liked he enjoyed and worked hard at his job, his routine life, she thought, would no doubt end for the day with him going home alone to an empty house. A life of ennui, she thought, but one with which she could empathise. She, herself, had suffered such an existence in the past.

As was expected, Jacques was at her side. "Is the food not to your satisfaction?"

She looked up at him and shook her head. "No, Jacques, the food is fine, thank you. I do not seem to be as hungry as I first thought." And unconsciously pulling at the top of her dress to free the cloth from her skin, she finished, "Perhaps it's the heat."

On doing this, she had inadvertently revealed more of her cleavage than was usual and noticed that this had not escaped Jacques' attention either. He quickly averted his eyes, once again, for fear of further embarrassment.

"It is so hot, even sitting here in the shade," she expanded.

Jacques looked at the coffee cup in front of her and offered an alternative. "Perhaps some water?"

"Yes, that would be fine, Jacques." And finger-dabbing at her bare chest continued, "And perhaps a cold cloth?"

With her hand movements drawing his eyes down to her chest once again, he stumbled over his words before suggesting further, "We have a washroom inside, as much as it is, if you'd care to come in and freshen up?"

Just the invitation she was waiting for, she thought. "I'd appreciate that, Jacques, thank you." Retrieving her parasol, she rose from the table.

Pulling back her seat as she stood, Jacques courteously led the way with an inviting hand. "Please?"

Once inside, Madeline was surprised at how organised the interior was. Certainly not what she was expecting. "The owner, indeed, keeps a very tidy and orderly establishment." She looked around. "Where are the staff?"

Jacques laughed. "Hah, I am the staff; and thank you for the compliment, I try my best."

"You work alone?"
"On a Sunday anyway - cook, wait, clean, lock up, go home. Throughout the week I have someone else in to cook."
Madeline had mistakenly taken him to be just the waiter. "Forgive me, Jacques, but I was not aware that you owned the café. All this time and you have said anything."
He shrugged. "I thought it pointless."
"Oh?"
"To what purpose would it have served to say that I owned the café?"
Madeline knew exactly what he was thinking and furthermore what he was insinuating and hinting. She remained quiet with his clandestine question unanswered.
It was Jacques who broke the awkward silence. "Please, Madeline, this way." She noticed the familiar use of her first name. "The cloth will be fine, Jacques."
He moved towards her and led her to a nearby chair. "Then sit, please."
Seated where invited, Madeline looked around the room as Jacques exited through a further door to the back. Neatly packed shelves containing various food ingredients lined the walls, all of which she noticed were meticulously labeled accordingly. Sacks of flour and salt sat regimentally stacked side by side on the floor above which hung a heavy, wooden rack containing a combination of liquids. To the left lay a variety of crockery and cutlery, once again efficiently arranged within compartments over which hung an array of cooking pots spread across the entire wall. She had to admire his ordered life. Perhaps too ordered!
"How long have you had the café, Jacques?" she called, intentionally raising her voice as to be heard.
The increase in tone unnecessary, Jacques answered as he entered the room, "This one, let me see now. About seven years, I think, the others just under that."
Madeline had vastly underestimated this man. "The others?"
"Yes, I have four in all."
"Four!"
Jacques stood in front of her with the overly-damp cloth periodically dripping from his hand. "I had this one alone when I was married but after my wife died I bought the others... just to keep me occupied."
Madeline had gotten this man completely wrong. "I'm sorry to hear that, Jacques. How did she die?"
He shrugged as before. "Who knows, just one of these things. One moment she was alive and the next day she was dead, died in her sleep."
"Oh Jacques, how awful. Come, sit down." She suddenly realised that there was no other than the one she was sitting on.
Jacques noticed her dilemma. "It's OK, I'll stand. Here, take this, it's nice and cold."

Madeline looked up into his face. Gone was the stuttering and fidgeting waiter she had known in the past, replaced now with an effortlessly warm and considerate gentleman. There was no way that she could carry on as planned. She thought she would have had the upper hand with Jacques but he had unintentionally turned the tables on her. She would just have to see what developed. "Well if you are going to remain standing, Jacques. Would you do me the courtesy?"
Turning on the seat, Madeline raised her tied-back hair up from her neck as an invitation for him to dab the cloth on her exposed back.
She waited and, unaware of what was happening behind her, she continued to wait knowing his deliberation. Eventually feeling the first cold touch of the cloth on her skin, she arched her back slightly to wallow in its freshness. She let him continue the sweep across her skin without a word said, but felt the drips of water trickle all the way down her back.
"I'm afraid the water is making the top of your dress slightly wet. I should have wrung it out better," he apologised.
On hearing this, Madeline reached up with criss-crossed hands and lowered the shouldered sides of her dress down her arms. "Better?"
She felt the silence fill the room.
"Slightly better but it's still wet. Sorry about that. Is it still cold enough?"
"Not as cold as it first was, that's fine, thank you." She swung round on the seat to face him. Fully aware that her breasts were exposed above her corset, she noticed that Jacques' eyes were at once fixed firmly upon them.
She invited further, "Front?"
Jacques' eyes widened. "What?"
"The front, would you do the front for me please?"
Madeline noticed his sudden gulp and also the cloth in his hand tremble slightly. But most important of all was the unexpected twitch that appeared in the front of his britches. He stuttered, "I, I, don't …."
Madeline leant forward and taking hold of his hand, placed the now tepid cloth to her chest. "Jacques, the front please?"
She watched on as the twitch progressed to a slight bump.
Dabbing haphazardly at the top of her neck, Jacques' hand continued to shake.
"Lower down, Jacques."
Madeline suddenly sensed the random dabs change to a full sweeping motion and felt the cloth glide gently across her skin in a downward manner. She was also aware that Jacques was feeling her full shape and warmth underhand as he did it. And, as a result, his bitches now pointed firmly in her direction.
"Jacques."
In unison, both turned towards the outer door in the direction of the holler.
The voice repeated itself but sounded closer this time as if approaching, "Jacques. Are you opened today?"

Announcing his presence with shaking tone, Jacques hollered back, "One moment please, will be right with you."
Madeline looked at the full expanse of his swelling. "Jacques, you can't go out like that."
He turned to face her. "Like what?"
She pointed towards his britches. "Like that."
Jacques bowed over in mortification with hands clasped to his front. "Merde." And realising his expletive, apologised, "Sorry, I mean, I meant to say…"
Madeline didn't know what to do or say, she had never been in such a predicament. She looked around her and at once stood up and grabbed one of the large pans from the wall. "Here, take this and carry it in front of you."
Still bent forward in humiliation, Jacques hastily swapped the cloth for the cooking utensil and turned towards the door.
"And straighten up."
He did as instructed and was at the door within seconds. "I'm coming."
Or not, Madeline suddenly thought.
Seating herself, she squeezed the excess water from the drenched cloth onto the floor; and proceeded to wipe the residue from her skin. She squirmed. "Yuck." Her undergarments were soaking wet.
Satisfied that she had removed as much as possible, she raised the sides of her dress and smoothed herself down, the task completed in perfect time to see Jacques re-enter the room. Closing the door behind him, he stood with his back leaning against it, his breathing laboured. With the pan swinging down by his side and britches surprisingly still bulging, he announced his intentions, "That's it. I'm closed for the day."
Madeline had gathered that for herself. "Good, then lock the door, Jacques."
"With pleasure." Unaware of what Madeline had in mind for him, he bolted the door shut and walked towards her placing the pan on a nearby table. "That was a first."
Madeline smiled at him. "I'm sure it was but I see it hasn't dulled your senses any."
Confused, Jacques followed her eyes down to see the cause of her ridicule. His shoulders slumped. "Ooh."
Madeline reached out and placed her fingertips onto his swollen front. "Would you care to show me what you have hidden in there, Jacques?"

*

Madeline 2

Chapter 7

Sunday, Sunday

Part 4

"Where are the children?"
Janis spun on her chair and looked around the company, her eyes bobbing between the guests. "I think Bernadette may be indoors, you know how she so despises the heat. Sylvain, I haven't seen him for a while." She returned as before. "Off by himself again, no doubt, probably down by the stream."

Adjusting her bonnet to suit the shade, the mother tutted, "It isn't good for the boy to be on his own so much. I had to prize a conversation from him last night." Attired in black, yet again, despite the heat, she flicked the similarly coloured fan at her face. "And as for Bernadette, the least said the better."
Knowing full well that her mother had very little time for Bernadette, it had struck her odd a few weeks back when she had insisted that her granddaughter chaperone her to her sister's funeral. A funeral, indeed. With all the money she had, never once had she suggested a holiday for the children. A mother she had been and still was to her, but an amiable grand-mother she was not. Janis sat and listened to her continuing diatribe, "If it were not for Gaston's insistence that I remove them from the house last night, I would have gladly remained in my room. I have no time for children's theatre."
Janis sat for a moment, speechless. "Gaston asked you?"
"Yes, Gaston." It was the mother's turn to look around. "And where is he? Some of these people have travelled considerable distances to be here and he hasn't yet made any effort to greet them."
Her eyes followed her mother's. Was it any wonder? Not one would she gladly invite as a personal dinner guest, most being government officials and the others distant acquaintances of the same. "It is an informal picnic luncheon mother, nothing more. I'm sure he will be down presently. Gaston is fully aware of his occupational duties and the requisite socialising which accompanies it."
"Pah!"
"And you changed the subject there. Your memory is not as it once was, mother."
Insulted by innuendo, the mother retorted with grated tone, "What do you mean by that, young lady?"
Janis leaned forward out of earshot. "It was me who asked you to take the children out last night, not Gaston."
"Yes indeed you did, my rapidly infuriating daughter, but not before Gaston had asked me first."
Janis sat perplexed. Gaston had. "Why?"
Noticing her daughter's puzzlement, she matter-of-factly added to the mystery, "He didn't say why. He just did."
Janis wondered. Had he the same thing in mind as she - a night alone together? Was it too much to wish for that a husband should want to spend time with his wife? She dearly hoped so. But then again she had carried out what she had intended. Her plan had succeeded in every way. She just needed to see him, gauge his reaction and know where their future lay.
She smiled inwardly at her own audaciousness the previous evening.
Bereft of undergarments, save from her open front panniers which exposed her pubic hair, she had daringly strutted about the room like some blazing hussy; and had it not been for the stiffness of the stay beneath her dress raising her swollen stomach, she would have felt like the archetypal fallen woman. As part of the seduction she would have preferred to have worn a

thin chemise but this would have hidden nothing, knowing that Gaston mustn't suspect that she was with-child - not yet anyway. This charade had seemingly come natural to her, she now thought, and she had felt quite at ease in the luring of her husband... this and the addition of the two brandies she had consumed herself as an encourager. With her dress raised aloft and allowing his favourite scent that she had dabbed on her thighs earlier to permeate, she knew that Gaston could not resist the temptation of leaning forward and immersing his face within. And to her joy, he willingly did by clasping both hands to her rear and pulling her forward, his tongue instantaneously finding a home at her clitoris. She had felt the warmth fill her in an instant. Not only had he flicked at it with the gentle strokes that she'd always taken pleasure in, but he had intermittently altered to the rough upward pull that had stretched her skin to the extreme. This had been new to her and in response to this stimulus she had gripped at his hair, her body trembling in reaction. Furthermore, with him taking her skin tight between his closely bound lips, he'd gently pulled at it until he had teased her to breaking point. Pulling his head even closer to her, she had basked in the long, deep thrusts of his tongue as it probed in and around her; and not for three long years had she felt like a woman in the proper sense as she had then.

"Janis, Monsieur Lombarde is addressing you."
Had someone spoken there, she thought.
"It appears that Madame's mind is elsewhere." She heard further. Grudgingly released from her vacillation, Janis looked up from the table and was greeted by a smile from Gaston's closest friend.
"Pleasant thoughts as well, judging by the beam on your face," he continued.
How very astute of you to notice, she thought, if only you knew how pleasant. As the courteous hostess, she smiled and proffered her downward hand in salutation. "Alexis, it has been a while."
Returning the greeting by way of the obligatory kiss to its back, he straightened up. "A fine welcome by the lady of the house, for sure." And aimlessly looking about him, finished, "But I see no sign of our host. I gather he is about?"
"Oh, he is about somewhere. But, unfortunately, we cannot guarantee in what state he will appear."
Janis turned on her. "Mother!"
"Pah!"
Alexis laughed; and within the audible bounds of the table, he bent down closer. "Well, Saturday night is brandy night."
"We had an evening at home," Janis sternly justified.
Alexis shrugged his shoulders. "Since when has that bothered... oh, talk of the devil."
Both mother and Janis turned in response. Gaston was making his way across the lawn towards them, and he was not looking good.

With no consideration for either of them, as was the norm with him, Alexis moved forward and commandeered his company in an instant. With a convivial arm around Gaston's shoulder, he uttered his greetings with a mischievous undertone and indecorously led him away from the table.
Charming, Janis thought. She felt her mother raise herself from the table.
"Well, must mingle."
"Do you want your parasol?"
"No, I think my bonnet will be sufficient."
Janis stood with her. "Well, seeing as Alexis appears to have requisitioned the host for a while, then I consider it my duty to do the entertaining in his stead."
"By the looks of him he wouldn't be terribly good at it anyway."

With their first port of call being that of two elderly ladies with whom her mother was familiar, Janis positioned herself amongst them in such a way as to keep her eyes firmly fixed on Gaston. Alexis was one of the main instigators of their frequent drinking sessions; and as she watched on, his boyish behaviour, whenever in Gaston's company, came to the fore immediately. Gaston, she noticed, was not his usual participatory-self. He was swaying somewhat. And he looked pale.
As the monotonous chattering about the unrelenting heat continued, Janis stood bored, fidgeting on the grass and twirling her parasol within her fingers. With a cursory glance of her surroundings and with the guests apparently content in their merriment, her mind drifted back, once again, to the previous night's liaison with her husband.

Her legs had been trembling with the delights being bestowed upon her by Gaston's tongue, and to such an extent that she had felt herself giddy on her feet. This especially when he had, from behind, inserted what she had considered to be at least two of his fingers into her now moist-self. And with the continuing circular movements inside her, she had had to try her hardest to prevent herself from buckling under and collapsing in a heap on the floor. But, to her relief, it was Gaston who had released her from her torment and lowered her down. Aware of the impending lovemaking, she had to coerce him into taking her from behind as to conceal her bulging front; not that it would have taken much persuasion as she knew, from past experience, it to be his favourite position. So, as she lowered her arms to help him undo his britches, she had been pleasantly surprised when he leaned forward and with a passion she had not felt in so long a time, kissed her with opened mouth… and continued to do so through the hastily removal of his garments.
Looking down, she had seen him fully erect. Her entire body had weakened at the sight. Every inch of its hardness did she know in the merest of detail - from its feel to its warmth, its texture and its form, from minuscule mole to each engrossed vain and rippled skin, up to its bulbous head which she had always thought of as her *coup de grâce*. She had had every part of it in her in

days gone passed and she longed for it now. So, taking him in her right hand and feeling the instant warmth from his skin, she pulled him gently back and forth in the slow, rhythmic movements she knew to be his preference. She had so dearly wanted to bend down and place him in her mouth. To feel the supple, swollen gland slide slowly between her lips and fill her mouth with its warmth, and the full, uneven texture of his hardened-self push deep down into her throat. She wanted all of him, every last inch, pushing in hard and choking her, gagging her, making her fight for air until she eventually felt him explode and taste the warmth of his seed run freely inside her. She wanted his taste so badly but she knew if she had done so, then he may have been spent too prematurely. And this she did not want. She wanted him deep inside her, as every part of her exposed-self was aching for his hardness.

Taking his cue, as if prompted to do so, Gaston had shimmied her body to the left and in one continuous movement Janis had found herself bent over the fireside armchair, elbows resting on the cushion and her naked posterior raised out to him in the offering. And at once felt his hardness and its length slowly sliding its way into her, inch by, undeniably satisfying and fulfilling, inch. And with every part of him within her, she had felt as one.

"Are you alright, Janis?"
Once again, she had to pull herself from her thoughts.
"We thought you were about to faint there, my darling," the smaller of the two ladies commented.
Janis shook her head ."I'm fine. Really... I'm fine, thank you."
My goodness, she thought, what must she have looked like while thinking this? She looked over in Gaston's direction, once again, to find him surrounded by more of his drinking acquaintances but even from such a distance she could tell he was not focused in on their conversation. Facing back, she repeated her mother's thanks for their concern and bade her au revoir for the present time. Moving on to the next set of guests, she heard her mother comment beneath her breath, "Your thoughts are, indeed, elsewhere today, Janis. Am I to presume you are preoccupied by the previous evening's events?"
With no time to reply, greetings were underway with the next group and if the previous encounter had been dull, then this one was tedium in the extreme. Three Parliamentarians and their respective wives stood huddled together in such close proximity of each other that Janis was convinced that they were joined together with cord. And not one of them had a jest or merry quip to offer and lighten the mood on such a beautiful day - in its stead, a stale conversation of government workings. Gaston should be thankful to have Alexis appropriate him and save his mind from stagnating during the course of the afternoon, as her's was now.
Staring through both the face and the voice of the current speaker, Janis, like on the previous two occasions, let her mind drift once again.

She could feel the sensation in her loins even now. Gaston had pushed hard against her rear with each thrust made, but what she had enjoyed most was when he periodically paused and leaned across her back. Feeling the rigidity of his every inch deep within her, she'd felt him slowly rotate his lower half as it pressed hard against her. This she knew was to appreciate the feeling of his loins next to her soft, tender rear while absorbing the sensation of its mass and shape. In addition, his hands had continually cupped both her, by then, fully exposed breasts, the nipples of which had been held tight within his finger and thumb. She could not remember it ever feeling this good, even in the early days of their marriage.

What was this powder that she had put in his brandy, she had remembered thinking? The guarantee from the supplier that there would be no side-effects, during or after, had her thinking now. Gaston had been sweating profusely. She had felt the drips of perspiration fall across her back. And looking over at him now, talking to Alexis, confirmed her suspicions - he looked simply dreadful. But what could she say? That she had drugged her husband into making love with her, this to win him back and possibly save a failing marriage. She thought not. How could she after what had transpired.

Releasing his grip and sliding his full length free from inside her, she had felt his hands place themselves upon either side of her rear and part them. She'd known then what would follow, them having, in the past, fully embraced this position as an enjoyable act for both giver and receiver. Feeling his face burrow its way into her, she felt his tongue do as before, except that this rear position made for easier and deeper penetration of his tongue. But, after only a few brief seconds of such pleasure, his mouth had begun to rise slowly and stopped at her anus. She had tensed slightly as she felt his tongue dart in and around her before driving it's curled up state inside her. This she now knew was to prepare her for penetration of a more delicate part of his anatomy. But beforehand, she had felt his moist finger enter as a vanguard, closely followed by a second. This particular method of lovemaking had never interested Gaston before or if it had, then he had never inquired as to her possible participation in it. But she prepared herself for the inevitable and gripped the cushioned sides and waited, knowing that his full length and girth would be twice that of his twinned fingers. But if this was what her husband wished, then as the dutiful wife she would oblige wholeheartedly. She would give him all he desired and more...
...Much more.

"I quite agree, Janis... Janis?"
"Yes, yes. I'd love to, that would be fine."
She looked around at the bewildered faces. What had she just answered to?

"It was her mother who came to her aid. "Janis, darling, Monsieur DeVane was asking after your health. He said you were not looking too well. Your face was contorting."
Janis felt like a fool. She had played out the scene in her head and her face had reacted in a similar fashion. What could she possibly say as an excuse - that she had been thinking of her husband penetrating her rear-end with his manhood? She thought not, although the idea of injecting a shock into their humdrum conversation made her smile inwardly. "It's the sun, I think. Perhaps a moment in the shade."
As paltry an excuse as this was, it was accepted by all who, out of courtesy, let her take her leave.
"Perhaps an hour in the shade would be more appropriate," she heard her mother aside as the walked back towards their sheltered table. Reseated, both sipped at their respective drinks. Once again it was the mother who spoke first, "May I speak frankly now that we are without company?"
Did her mother ever speak anything else, Janis thought? "Of course, mother." She looked around, and finished, "We are quite alone."
"You did take appropriate steps last night? I mean, you did not overdo it?"
Overdo what, Janis thought, the seduction of her husband? If that was the case, then perhaps, yes, in retrospect she maybe had done so, but she was unsure if this is what her mother was referring to. "In respect of what?"
Her mother leaned forward. "The powder, of course. You had the instructions for its use, did you not?" I assume you used it in its accordance."
Well, perhaps not, she reflected. She had poured in the amount required but, possibly in her resolve to ensure its desired effect, she had placed in a little extra and, in addition to this, something else. Something her mother knew nothing about. She noticed her mother's concern, apparently as a reaction to that shown on her own face.
"Oh no, you haven't, have you?" She sighed. "It's hardly any wonder Gaston is looking like he does."
Both looked over in his direction. He was leaning with hand on Alexis' shoulder, wavering. Janis closed her eyes and wrestled with her conscience. What had she done?

*

Madeline 2

Chapter 8

Sunday, Sunday

Part 5

Jacques sat half on, half off the table, his free leg swinging loose. "What kind of game are you playing with me here, Madeline?"
"I am playing no such game with you, Jacques. I merely enquired as to the contents of your britches." Madeline sat momentarily stunned with herself, astonished that she could have, so nonchalantly, announced this to a relative stranger such as him. She had to consider where all this audaciousness had

come from all of a sudden. Had it lay dormant within her all this time or was it now her predetermined goal to assert herself more freely in her quest? Her rumination brief, Jacques had interrupted her in mid-thought.
"I have had no other woman since my wife passed on, Madeline." His shoulders shrugged of their own accord. "Then suddenly, like a bolt of lightning, this happens to me. You must surely understand my misgivings in this."
Madeline sat silent for a moment, preoccupied. She hadn't really thought this through. She was toying with Jacques' emotions in her pursuit of knowledge, with total disregard about how he would have felt before, during and after the event. If she had carried out her plans then what would have ensued? Would he have considered himself the injured and abused party or would he have misconstrued this as the start of a relationship between them. She could not be so callous in her mistreatment of him. She stood to leave. "I'm sorry, Jacques, I shouldn't have said that. I'll go now."
Jacques edged from the table. "Madeline."
Unfaltering, she continued, "If you would be so kind as to unlock the door for me."
She only made it to the end of the table before Jacques reached his arm out for her. "Madeline, please."
Turning on the spot to face him. "No, Jacques, I have to go now."
With a firm grip on both shoulders, he held her at bay. "Madeline, what is it that you want from me? I'd like to think of myself as a friend to you."
She shrunk her head down in shame. "And does a friend ask from another such a thing as I have?"
Confused and enraged, he released his grip. "I don't even know what it is that you have asked of me. Please make it clear as I am at a loss?"
Slightly taken aback at his raised tone, and without thinking, Madeline blurted it out, "I seek an education in things." Time stood still as her mind was suddenly propelled back to her coach journey to Paris when, through naivety, she had sought to deceive an old woman the very same way. Only then it had been a falsehood in an attempt to cover the fact that she had absconded from her home, whereas now her true search for knowledge was a precondition for her future. She continued, "Certain things."
Jacques walked towards her and, with suspicion, stared deep into her eyes. "Certain things?"
Madeline remained silent and aloof in the hope that he would understand without her having to explain further. He did not let her down. He twigged immediately.
"And the contents of my britches are the education you seek?"
With a slight nod, Madeline smiled up at him. "Yes, Jacques, it is."
He sighed.
Madeline was unsure whether it was one of relief at solving the riddle or, as she had hoped, because he now found himself to be in such a fortunate position as to be asked to participate with her in such an intimate act.

Adjusting himself to the situation, Jacques turned and paced. "Okay. Okay." Madeline reseated herself as before and watched him pace the room, hands clasped behind his back and nodding profusely. "Okay, okay."
As he bent down to needlessly rearrange the position of a large bag of salt, Madeline interrupted his vacillation, "Jacques, it need only be tuition, nothing more."
He looked over in her direction. "No involvement?"
"No involvement." Her assurance resolute.
"Very well." He rose. "In that case, and although the hour is still early, I think I need something stronger to drink than coffee."
Madeline sat forward in anticipation. "So we can begin straight away?"
"Ah, the impetuosity of youth. Yes, yes, if you so desire, my sweet Madeline, if you so desire."
"Then what is it that I need do first?"
Ignoring the impulsiveness of her request, Jacques reached up to an overhead shelf and retrieved a dusted bottle. "I've had this here for a long time now, never thought I'd have the occasion to drink it."
Madeline, also realising his lack of response, pushed further, "Jacques, what must I do?"
Without turning, he put paid to her question. "You can be patient. You're chosen profession dictates it."
"My..." Shocked at the possibility of him knowing, she remained silent.
With his back to her, Jacques blew free the dust from the bottle and uncorked it. "Does it surprise you?"
Feigning ignorance, Madeline responded accordingly, "I know not of what you speak, Jacques."
He poured the thick, dark liquid into a glass. "You don't?"
Aware of her hands clasped tightly together, Madeline continued the façade. "No."
"I maybe only a café owner in your eyes, Madeline, but I am not a fool, so please do not treat me as one." He turned to face her, raising the glass as an invitation.
Where had she heard that uttered recently, she wondered?
Madeline looked at the glass. Whatever it was, she didn't want any. She shook her head in refusal. "Thank you, no. You perhaps have me mistaken for someone else of your acquaintance?"
He nodded. "That may very well be the case." Lifting the glass to his mouth, he drank slowly, letting Madeline ponder the connotations of his remark before finishing, "You are certainly not the young woman who innocently graced my café a few weeks ago, that is for sure."
Had she changed so much? On the outside that was. She certainly felt different within but did she now display such an altered personality as to be so noticeable? "I am unsure to what you allude, Jacques."
"Very well, Madeline, if that's the way you want to play it, then so be it." He pointed his glass in her direction. "But be warned, if there is no trust between

tutor and student, then..." He raised his shoulders in doubt. "...What is there to gain?"

"Whatever you may think of me, Jacques, and what you think I am are of little consequence. I only ask this of you as a favour to me. If you require payment for such services then I will oblige." She knew instantly that she had gone too far.

"What!"

Why didn't she learn to keep her mouth shut? She watched him approach her, his drink spilling from the glass. "You want me to prostitute myself like you do?"

Madeline pulled herself back into the seat in defense. "No, I did not mean that. I mean, what I meant to say..." Her excuse was useless.

His face now several inches from hers, he appeared to spew forth venom as he spoke in coarse tone, "You think I'm a fool. You think yourself smart, rubbing yourself against me." She felt him grab hold of her breast with his free hand and clasp it tight within his rapidly clenching fist. "And giving me eyefuls of these every time you come here?"

His grip tightened even further. "Please. Jacques, please, you're hurting me."

"You want to see what's hidden in my britches do you?" He threw the glass to the floor and wrenched at his belt. "I'll show you what's in my fucking britches."

*

As she watched Gaston waver further, Janis considered her actions the previous night.

If some lubricant or oil could have been close at hand, then she would have gladly used it. It hurt.

... At first.

Initially tensing, she had willed herself to relax and, on doing this, she was able to enjoy or at least take pleasure in this novel and unique experience. She was well used to the sensation of having him inside her but to feel him in a different part of her felt strange. His original entry had shot pain through her lower half and as he manoeuvred his way in she had felt the inexplicable urge to empty her bowels for some reason. But as she felt his stomach finally lay flat against her rear she knew his was fully in... and she felt every inch of him deep within her. Had his movements been slow, then she would have enjoyed this even better but with his fervency at its peak, his thrusts had been extreme and almost animalistic. But his conclusion had culminated in one last push into her, after which he had draped himself across her back. It had felt strange to feel him inside when he was spent, and his withdrawal felt, to her, like she had just relieved herself. When Gaston had slipped off to the side, she had immediately lifted herself from the chair and turned to see him sprawled across the floor. This was not to be the conclusion of their lovemaking, she had vowed then. So, bending down, she had gently kissed him on the mouth. She wanted him to feel the tender touch of her lips before she bestowed upon him their further delights. But as she had worked her way down his front to take him in her mouth, it had suddenly dawned on her in which part of her anatomy he had just been. She had hesitated, but her eyes had caught sight of Gaston's almost full brandy glass. Her outstretched hand had at once taken grip and had poured its contents over his genitals, and left just enough to fill her mouth. Gaston had been in such a semi-unconscious state he hadn't noticed the burning sensation that Janis knew would have been the case. So, with the strong alcohol spread evenly around him, she had slowly brought his form to life again. The frenzied movements of her mouth and hand would have rubbed the brandy deep into his pores and she was certain that the friction would result in his skin feeling raw. But it mattered not to her if he had been seeing another woman, she was certain that this part of his anatomy was going nowhere near another.

It had been everything she had wished it to be; and with the surge of his seed filling her mouth, she had tasted his passion once again. But as she removed him from her mouth, she saw the deep red marks on the full length of his skin and the rawness of the tip. He would, indeed, suffer in the morning, she had thought. Recalling his moans as she licked him dry, her eyes had caught sight of something on the floor, just by the drinks' cabinet.

- A little, glass tube.

She closed her eyes tight at the thought of what she had done. But the guilt did not have time to permeate her mind.
She had heard the girls' screams in the distance…
… And it was coming from the stream.

*

Madeline 2

Chapter 9

Sunday, Sunday

Part 6

Jacques regained consciousness. How long had he been out for, he thought? And hadn't anyone noticed him lying here?

Squinting, through swollen and cut eyes, at the pool of blood next to him, he added to it by spitting forth from his split lip.

'Bastard!' he thought. How could he have been so stupid? Café owner, indeed! Lying hurt and maimed upon the floor, like that of some wounded animal, he looked around the room. It was a mess. Not one thing did he see was in its place as it should have been. The bastard had made sure of that, he thought. The stock was in ruins and his livelihood in tatters. His sole consolation was that the building still remained standing after his threat of burning it to the ground…with him in it. He looked at his right hand. It was still shaking violently of its own accord. In his fit of rage at Madeline, he had attempted to force himself upon her. He could remember her plea to him even now.

"No, Jacques, please, no."
With his britches at half-mast, he'd held his erection up to her mouth with one hand whilst the other had clenched her long, dark tresses pulling her forward. And following her as she had shied away from side to side to avoid it, he'd viciously pulled her head straight once again.
"Now get the fucking thing in your mouth."
It was the last thing he had remembered saying to her.
He'd heard a wood-splitting crash.
Seconds later he had been lifted from the floor by a colossal force unknown and found himself thrown across the room, colliding with the cooking utensils in the corner. Momentarily dazed and blinded by the impact, he'd felt himself, in an instant, the target of this mysterious entity once again, it being in the fashion of a violent kick to his face. Sensing his lip bursting open upon contact and several teeth loosen within their gums, he'd slouched forward and watched the thin, red liquid freely flow from his mouth onto his exposed, pale legs. But within seconds of this happening, he had been dragged by his feet to the middle of the floor and made to sit facing up towards Madeline. Still seated as before, she had wept with hands to her face but, until now, the assailant had not made himself known to him.
"Big man with the girls, are we?" He'd remembered hearing, being rasped in rough tone. The voice had come from behind but as he'd turned his head to catch sight of him, he had felt the tremendous open-handed blow to his ear.
"Sit still."
Sit still? He couldn't have moved if he'd tried. Such was the impact, the reverberation of it had echoed around his head and he'd felt himself at once stupefied and with it, the need to vomit. It had taken what had felt like a lifetime for the pain to cease within him. He'd then smelled the stale breath on his face as his aggressor leant down and whispered in his other ear, "Don't fucking move."
"Missy."
All was silent but for her sobbing.
The harsh voice called again, "Missy."

Through watered eyes, he'd seen her look up beyond his shoulder to the voice behind.
It demanded further, "Outside, now, and wait for me there."
Madeline had sat stunned and appeared shocked by the extraordinary sight in front of her. Who, or what, in god's name was behind him, he'd thought.
Doing as instructed, she had hastily gathered her things together and, with minimum eye contact, had headed straight for the now broken lock door. Out of sight and out of earshot, he'd then feared the worst. And the worst had been still to come.
All was silent yet again.
Through the indistinct hearing of his injured ear and that of his good one, he was positive that he had heard the uncorking of his vintage wine from earlier. This closely followed with the avariciousness of its consumption and the thunderous burp thereafter, complete with the sound of spitting to the floor.
"You like to play games with young girls, do you?" the coarse voice had growled, repeating its accusation from earlier.
His peripheral vision to the right had seen an oversize leg come into view and as his eyes had slowly raised themselves up to a neck- breaking position, a giant behemoth had gradually come into full view of him. With the bottle of wine in his left hand, he'd smiled a black-toothed grin as he'd stretched his free hand behind him and withdrew from beneath his heavy, cloth coat a long, ragged-edged knife, the blade of which had shimmered in the bright light cascading from the window.
"Well, let's see if you can play with the girls without balls."
He'd felt the floor beneath him moisten as his bladder emptied. And as the pale, brown liquid trickled in front of him, he'd dipped his head in both shame and the fear of what was to come.
The cold tip of the blade had, without warning, been placed beneath his chin and the upward pressure raised his head to face him straight on. He'd also heard the faint piercing as the tip broke the skin and felt the blood run down his front. Finding no words to say as apology, he had sat quietly and waited on the inevitable.
Kneeling before him, the stark, staring eyes had bored their way right through him and with his face a mere six inches from his own, the smell from his body had made him wretch.
"Got no stomach for this kind of thing, have you?"
It was all he could do but to shake his head in affirmation.
"And that little missy out there, you think she has?"
Repeating the same gesture as reply, he'd felt his lips tremble like a child, this being due to the fact that two things had just happened. He had felt the man-odorous giant take hold of his right hand and had clenched both his index and middle finger in his tight grasp. And twisting to the side, his arm had locked back hard against the shoulder joint. Second, and worse of the two, the blade had found its way down to his testicles.
The rancid breath had spoken further, "Balls or fingers?"

"Wh..wh..what?"
The backward pressure on his hand had increased, the two digits stretched back to extreme.
The deep voice had repeated itself, this time closer into his face, "Balls... or... fingers?"
With each pause between words, both the blade had driven deeper into his scrotum and the fingers pulled back even further. He had felt the streaks of pain shoot straight through his body. "No..no..no...please...no..." He'd been in agony, but eventually....
Snap!
"Too late! Fingers it is."
Releasing his grip on the hand, he'd let the broken fingers flop freely to the side. Meanwhile, the blade remained motionless.
"You bastard, you bastard." He'd remembered screaming in agony at him as he'd tentatively caressed his lame hand to his stomach.
 "Right, you've had your fun. Now fuck off."
"Oh, no, no, no." He had taken another swig of the wine with his newly free hand and on wiping the residue on his sleeve, continued, "Did you think that was a choice there? No. no, no, that, my friend, was to see what came first... balls... or... fingers."
"Please, please. Look I have money. I have coin in multitude at home. Please take it, it's yours, please?"
"You have nothing, no coins, you wait on tables. You can fool missy there but not me. And when I've burned this place to the ground with you nailed to the floor, you'll have even less."
"Please, don't?"
Both had heard Madeline's voice and both heads had turned towards the door in unison.
"I said for you to stay outside, young missy. This is not for your eyes."
"Please, Monsieur, it was a misunderstanding. Hurt him no more, I beg of you."
His eyes had turned to look at the giant once more and, with pleading in them, had uttered concord, "She's right. It was a great misunderstanding and I apologise for it."
Madeline had inched forward. "Please, Monsieur."
He'd heard the giant mumble beneath his breath and had eventually spoken out, "Okay. You step outside and wait by the tables."
With relief, he had sighed.
The giant had turned to face him again and, after a second, had withdrawn the blade only to place it at his throat. And, once again, he'd moved forward and whispered in his ear. It had been the last thing he remembered, save the hilt of the knife coming down hard upon his head.

He was out of a job for sure. He couldn't hope to have the place back to normal by the morrow, especially with broken fingers. The giant had

obviously spent his remaining time ransacking the café as the mess about him reconfirmed. But to his bewilderment, he could not fathom out the last thing he had uttered into his ear. Something about his warning to him never to go near his girl again or he would, indeed, take his manhood from him but, for the life of him, he couldn't understand....
....Who the hell was Rosalind?

Madeline 2

Chapter 10

Sunday, Sunday

Part 7

Gaston had also heard the screams and with natural concern for his guests, looked around for its source. With his mind in confusion, he had stood restless these last ten minutes in a daze, their conversation going over his fevered head, but the severity of the female shrieks had pulled him momentarily from his delirium. Janis was by his side in an instant. Both

heads turned to follow the sound as the cries continued. Running up the grassed slope from the stream were two young girls unknown to him – daughters of some guests, no doubt – but it was the look of terror on their faces that alarmed him. With an instant clear head, he at once made in their direction. Grabbing the arm of the first one he reached, he stopped her in mid-dash, while the other made straight for her mother. The young girl's frightened state took some seconds to placate but she eventually explained, through sobbing and stuttering words, the cause of her alarm, "It's Sylvain." Gaston's head turned to the stream. "Oh, no!"
With Janis and other guests running in his wake, he darted at full speed down the incline, his body struggling to keep up with his tremulous legs. 'How many times had he warned his son about the water, how many times', continually blaming himself in mid-run, 'how many times?' He felt his breath labouring with each hurried step taken and the perspiration develop once again on his face. By the time he had reached the water's edge he was exhausted. He was not the first to arrive on the scene. With body arched forward and hands on his knees, Gaston tried in vain to catch his breath. But there, lying wide-eyed and motionless on the grass was his son, with pallid face and his jaw drawn to the side. Gaston's heart sunk at the sight of this and he feared the worst.
He knew then that his son was dead.

*

Choosing a relatively soil-free table in the corner, Rubin, with natural survival instinct, opted for the stool by the wall enabling him to face inwards. It wasn't wise or safe to have your back turned to anyone, he'd learned through the years, and certainly not with those who frequented this taverne. This was one of the district's toughest establishments and even with his renown and his capability of taking care of himself, it was always prudent to watch your back.
Seated at an angle to him, Madeline stared directly at his scarred face and watched his eyes take stock of his surroundings and its inhabitants. If she felt safe with anyone, anywhere, then she felt safe with him now. He was enormous and powerfully built. It had not been any wonder that he had been able to catapult Jacques across the room with ease. But his sadistic nature thereafter, during the torture, had made her cringe in revulsion. But there was a softer side to this man, she'd noticed. She had seen this in an instant, the moment he had exited from the café. Seated at the outside table as he had instructed, he had placed his gargantuan hand on her shoulder. It could have crushed her bone like soft fruit but, in its stead, he had gripped her gently as reassurance – like that of a father tending his child.
With his circumspective vigil complete, his eyes moved around and met hers. "You alright?

"Yes, thank you." It was all she could say, her not knowing how to start a conversation in a place such as this.

She saw the hesitance in his speech also but after a second of deliberation, he eventually spoke, "You've drank before?"

"Yes, I have. May I have Armagnac please?" Remembering the drink that Ramone had bought her.

Rubin opened up, his now usual self. "Hah, you'll not find anything like that here, missy, its wine or nothing – but a choice of three types mind you. The head-splitting; the gut-rotting; and the one that gives you the shi…" He hesitated. "Makes you do runners to…" He looked away in awkwardness – not with his choice of wording, nor the correction thereof, but rather the fact that this child-like woman had made him feel foolish in having done so.

Madeline giggled and finished it for him, "… To make toilet."

He nodded, and muttered under his breath, "If you can make it that quick." He, himself, hadn't on one such occasion.

Madeline leaned forward and with an elbow on the table, rested her chin on her upturned hand. "Why do you call me 'missy'?"

Rubin shrugged his shoulders. "Good a name as any, I guess."

"My name is Madeline. May I ask yours… kind sir?"

Rubin was ignorant to the written meaning but he did ☐ealized☐ irony in her question. He tilted his head back slightly and looked on at her mischievous, beaming face. He smiled inwardly. He liked her. He liked her innocence. "I know."

"You do? How?"

He shook his head. "No matter."

Madeline didn't push further. "Well?"

"Well what?"

"Your name. You do have one, I gather?" Still beaming.

"Rubin."

"Rubin. That's a fine name but not French, I fear?"

"No, not French."

Without the need to order, wine had automatically arrived at their table interrupting their stilted conversation and served to them by the owner, herself, Sally. Placing the bottle and two goblets between them, she stood waiting payment, her eyes all the time staring at Madeline, who had resumed her upright position on her arrival.

Rubin looked up at Sally. "My credit no good here?"

Madeline ☐ealized at once the predicament he was in, after all it was she that had suggested they come in here. She had noticed his hesitance beforehand but had assumed that this was because of its vicinity and the choice patrons within. She dug into her purse. "Oh, I nearly forgot, Rubin, here is my share of the carriage fare I owe you."

Rubin turned to her with surprise but knew in an instant what she was doing. Saving his face. He looked back at Sally. "Just leave the bottle."

Turning on her feet, she left without payment. "When do I ever not?"

He looked at the coins proffered in Madeline's palm. "Keep it. She'll get her money. And I'd get that purse of yours out of sight and tight against you." With a ealized d g head tilt, he finished, "Some of these bastards would slice your belly open just for what you've got in your hand."
Shocked, Madeline did as she was told and wrapped the clothed purse tightly to her front. She ignored his expletive.
Rubin looked at the two goblets. This was this first time Sally had ever brought anything other than the bottle to his table, with him always preferring to drink straight from it. So, contrary to his usual way of doing things, he uncorked it and poured two full goblets.
"It is so warm in here, Rubin. If I turn to face you and the wall, may I remove the cape please?"
This was an article of clothing that Rubin had so casually commandeered for her from an unsuspecting pedestrian prior to their entrance into the taverne. Suggesting to him outside the café that she felt the need for more than just coffee to help with the shock, she had skillfully persuaded him against his initial proposal to return her home safely but instead to take her somewhere close-by. He'd mentioned Sally's place first – it being just ten minutes walk away, with him knowing the short cuts – but looking down at her apparel and the plunging neckline, he'd thought better of it. But with further sweet-talking influence, as was now her way, she had cornered him by her innocent allure. He'd advised her that she needed to be covered up to some extent first.
His eyes scanned the room and then back to her. "Sure, go ahead."
By the time she had it unwrapped from her shoulders and arranged it loose upon her arms, Rubin had emptied his goblet. He sighed in appreciation of its taste and set the goblet back down on the table. His eyes, in an instant, had focused on her breasts, in particular her left one – the rapidly bruising one. He nodded to it. "He do that?"
Madeline raised her right hand and laid her fingers softly on the tender points. She nodded. "It still hurts so."
Rubin shook his head and stopped himself from further swearing. Instead, he reached out for the bottle. "You let yourself get into some dangerous situations, young missy."
Madeline sat confused by his statement and watched in silence as he refilled his wine but her curiosity soon got the better of her voice. "What situations?" With his goblet raised halfway to his mouth, Rubin held it in mid- swing. He looked at her quizzically, as if her question needed answering.
She repeated it just the same.
If she couldn't ealized the obvious, then he wasn't going to explain it to her. Finishing half the goblet, he laid it as before. He also felt the need to burp but refrained from doing so.
Madeline looked at her own goblet but thought better of drinking from it as it appeared to have a strange, sticky residue on its side. "You still haven't explained to me how you knew what was happening."

"Instinct."
His one word reply answered nothing. "Were you just passing the café and…" She thought. "…No, you couldn't have seen us or heard anything as to alarm you." Her thought's still aloud, she continued, "I hadn't called out. Or at least I don't remember calling out."
He stopped her train of thought. "I'd been watching you from across the street."
Madeline felt alarmed. "Watching me? When, why? Had you been following me?"
"Since you left the house. I work for Monique." He raised his goblet once again. "If you can call it work."
"She has you following me? Why, and since when?"
"More or less since you arrived or a day or so after. I don't know for sure. A couple of weeks now anyway, for your own protection."
He'd emptied his goblet in a second and it was obvious to Madeline that he had either not intended or had not been permitted to divulge this information to her. She slid her own goblet across to him. "You have been following me for weeks now and yet I have never laid eyes upon you until today."
He took the wine from her. "Good. I wouldn't be doing my job right if you had."
"Well I have much to thank you for then, Rubin, and I am, indeed, grateful to you and deeply in your debt but you mentioned situations in the plural. Today was one instance, what others were you alluding to?"
Ignorant to her penultimate word's meaning, he got the gist of what she was asking. He'd revealed to her far more than he had intended - the wine in his empty stomach apparently loosening his tongue, so why not go the whole way, he thought. "Old limp dick."
Madeline was lost to his words. "What, who?"
"Monsieur Leone."
"Ramone?" Madeline smiled at his connotation when she eventually worked out what he had meant but this was short-lived. A recalling in her mind of the incident with the attacker prompted her next question. "Are you talking about the scene with the knife? If you are, then Ramone saved my life that day."
Rubin's head had turned, his attention had been drawn to the general direction of the bar, where he noticed a heated debate had started over a spilled drink. "Did he now?"
Madeline followed his gaze but quickly returned it when she saw nothing of interest. "Yes, he did, he defended me against some brigand wanting to, wanting to…" 'What had he wanted?' she now thought. This question had never, until now, entered her head. Had it been her or her money or Ramone's? It had all happened so fast.
"What exactly did you see, Rubin? My mind is a blur as to what had actually taken place that day? I think I fainted… Rubin."
Pulling back to face her, he uttered out, "Huh!"

"I asked you what you had seen that day. If you had, as you stated earlier, been following me then you would have witnessed something of that day's event. You have me curious now."
"Do I?"
She leaned forward and rested her arms on the table. "Yes, you do."
"Oh."
"Rubin, you are either evading the question or answering my questions with other questions." Her head when up. "Brief as they are."
"Am I?"
She widened her eyes at him in child-like frustration. "Yes, and you are doing it once again. This is serious."
He knew it was serious but he liked toying with her. "So, Monsieur Lim… I mean Ramone, he saved your life did he?"
This was like pulling teeth, she thought. "Yes, Rubin, we have already agreed on that."
Rubin shook his head. "I've agreed on nothing."
Madeline's shoulders lowered and her head tilted to the side. "Then what did you see then?" Her voice clearly aggravated with his disinclination to divulge further.
Rubin finished Madeline's wine off with one fell swoop, after which he burped, albeit under his breath. He didn't feel the need to apologise though, it having been uncontrolled this time. "The old man shit himself."
Once again Madeline ignored his choice of words, knowing now that this language came natural to him. She did, however, ealize he had not meant it literally. "Yes, but surely such an act would have been in response to the situation. After all, he had a dagger to his throat."
"Stiletto."
"Sorry?"
"It was a stiletto, there's a difference." Rubin having been in the army for so long a time that he knew his weapons well. "And both are used for stabbing, not cutting."
Madeline sat upright once more. "If you ealized d the difference in such, then you must have been close enough at hand to have done so?" She felt she was gaining a little ground now.
Rubin felt himself cornered once again. What was it with the young girl that could manipulate his tongue so? "Your man must have some way with the authorities. Not one of them had noticed that the weapon, that was supposedly used, had no edge. Well, not one keen enough to slice through skin anyway. Or if it had, it would have taken a bit more than one quick slash." Once again his eyes were drawn to the bar, where the debate had developed into a full blown argument. He knew trouble was brewing.
Madeline stretched out her hand and laid it on top of his in an attempt to pull back his attention. "How do you know these things?"
Her ploy had worked. His eyes were at once drawn back in response at the physical contact. He sat staring with stunned gaze at the diminutive, feminine

hand placed on top of his grime-infested one. In an instant it was withdrawn through embarrassment in search of his goblet which, on tilting up towards him, he noticed was empty. Madeline lifted the bottle and emptied the remaining contents into it.
She let him imbibe before pressing further, "Rubin, please. Will you not tell me how you know these things?"
With a full bottle now inside him and in so short a time, plus what he had drunk of Jacques' earlier, he let his tongue wag once again. "It was my knife that opened the bastard's throat."
Madeline sat shocked with mouth agape.
Rubin leant forward to but a foot from her face and out of earshot. "But you keep your mouth closed about this. I value my head and want it to stay on my neck. You hear now?" He sat back.
No words could express what she felt inside. Of course he was referring to the axeman; and anyone having so violently murdered and without due cause would have certainly been sent there. But this was not what concerned her, it was this sudden announcement with the unexpected supplanting of her saviour. It had be he, and not Ramone, who had saved her that day.
Rubin continued, "He was in no fit state to look after you, so I stepped in. It was my job."
Eventually finding her voice, Madeline uttered through trembling voice, "You made everyone think it had been Ramone?"
"No-one seen me put the blade in his hand, not even him, he was out like a tot by that time." The wine inside him let loose some self- praise. "I know these streets well enough not to be noticed."
Madeline felt the dizziness in her head, so she closed her eyes tight to take it all in. She heard his voice continue.
"You alright?"
Madeline nodded with eyes still shut. "Yes, thanks. Can you take me home now please?"
Rubin looked up to the bar just in time to see the first blow being struck and the first knife to be unsheathed. "Perfect timing, missy."

*

Janis had arrived by his side within seconds and, on seeing Sylvain lying as he was, made frantic headway to get to her son. Gaston, at once, clasped her shoulders and drew her body close to him. As much as he had wanted to do the same himself, he consoled her as best he could. "Janis, please, let the physician have time with him."
A crowd of guests had now gathered about the scene and as the mutterings of such became overly loud in their concern, Gaston called for silence so as to allow the physician to do his work.
On his bended knees upon the grass, a diminutive, grey-haired septuagenarian teetered over the body. As ashen a face as the one he was

examining, it now lay pressed hard against Sylvain's front checking for any signs of life. Gaston could easily tell he was struggling to hear a beat as his face was contorted in concentration. It had been fortunate for them that such a person as this was one of the guests and luckier even still that he had been in close proximity to the stream. He felt Janis's grip upon him tighten as they watched him move round for closer examination. Unfastening the top of Sylvain's garments, the old man bent over and pressed down again, continually adjusting the position of his ear as he probed further. As Gaston's heart pounded relentlessly within his own chest, his attention was drawn to the grass by the left of the physician's knees. There, strewn about the ground, lay Sylvain's toy soldiers, as still and unmoving as his own son was now. But there was something else, something not quite right about them. His eyes focused in, then widened. Amidst the figurines, and to his utter astonishment, lay, what appeared to him to be, the vial – his vial, the vial of which contained the poison. Or rather should have, he thought. Upon closer scrutiny, he now noticed that it lay uncorked and bereft of liquid. It was empty. His eyes looked at once to his son's face, then back to the empty vial and instantly felt the blood drain from his face 'Oh, no. Please, no.'

Sensing his legs collapsing beneath him, he unconsciously slumped to the left 'Oh my god, no. Please, please, god, please don't let it be so.' His entire weight shifted to the side and had he not been clutching Janis, he would undoubtedly have fallen to the ground. He felt her grip on his arm as well as another to his right in an attempt to keep him from collapsing.

"Steady yourself, Gaston. Luke's a fine physician and he'll do all he can for him," a reassuring but misunderstood voice uttered to his right as he held him straight. The same voice spoke again but closer to his ear, "Be strong now, my lad. I know it's hard but do it for Janis's sake."

'Strong... strong... you fool, I've just poisoned my son and you're telling me to be fucking strong?'

He lunged forward in an attempt to reach his son – to hold him, to grip him tightly, to tell him he was sorry – but both on either side of him held him at bay. He also felt the nausea return and, with it, the intense pain in his head as he now realized the dire consequences of his actions. He had unwittingly murdered his own son and in paying for this he would meet the executioner's block. He fought to free himself from their hold, to get to his son and, more importantly now, to get to the vial. Pulling himself easily loose from Janis's feeble grasp, he wrestled with the grip on his right, where, with forceful effort, he finally freed himself and at once sprung forward. Grasping hold of the vial in his left hand during his feigned stumble to the ground, he now lay at an angle just several inches from his son's face. This, he now noticed, being the same distance as the physician's, who had remained calm and professional during the entire fracas. Gaston watched him proceed with the examination knowing full well that it was a hopeless exercise. His son was dead and no treatment would bring him back. The old man lowered his face further to an inch of Sylvain's mouth. Gaston assumed that this was him checking for a sign of breathing but was taken aback when the old man began to sniff. A strange way to check if someone was still alive, Gaston thought. The physician turned his face and stared directly at him with quizzical look. He followed the old man's eyes as they slowly moved their way along his body to the vial in his hand. It was no good, Gaston now acknowledged. The guilt he felt was too overwhelming – he had committed the crime therefore he should accept whatever punishment the system would deem fit. He dipped his head in shame and let the physician take it from his now opened palm. The old man had at least done this out of sight of the company and for this he was thankful. They would grieve their son's loss now - the humiliation and disgrace could come later.

Gaston saw Janis move forward and kneel down on the other side of Sylvain. She took hold of his hand and clasped it tightly to her breast. "My son, my son."

Gaston's head was fit to bursting, he felt sick to his stomach; and with Sylvain now dead, he saw his whole world crumble about him. And yet with their son dead, all that Janis could say was this. Did she feel nothing like he, himself, felt at his passing?

The physician turned to Janis. "Madame, your son is quite fine."

A hushed silence fell over the entire crowd. Both Gaston and Janis looked in his direction. Placing his nose to the vial he sniffed at its edge then, tipping it up, let the residue drip on to his fingertip whereafter he raised it to his tongue. He smiled. "Just as I thought."

He turned and placed his right hand onto Sylvain's cheek. Then to everyone's amazement, pulled it back and drew it hard across his face. The boy cried out in an instant and with it came the childlike sobs. He turned to Janis. "Madame, your son is inebriated."

Gaston sat stunned and also relieved at this news. But inebriated, how?

It was Janis who asked the question, "Drunk, my son is drunk?"

The physician nodded. "Oui, Madame, with brandy."

Gaston's eyes looked over at the vial in the physician's hand. "Brandy!"

He had blurted it out without thinking. But his mind was in confusion. His hands raised themselves to his head and as both sets of fingers combed their way back through his hair, he looked to the ground and tried to make sense of it all. His head shook at the absurdity of it. How could it possibly be, he thought. He raised his head to see Janis staring directly at him, and heard her speak.

"Yes, my dearest... brandy."

*

Madeline 2

Chapter 11

Day's End

Frederick had finished for the day. He had worked over and beyond his usual voluntary call of duty and felt exhausted. He was tired, hungry and certainly did not want to indulge in another night's quarrelling with Rosie. He just wanted home, home to his bed. Sitting by Jacob's bedside, he rolled up the leg of his britches.

His last duty of the day had been in the assistance of a leg amputation and this tedious operation had taken its toll on him. And without the aid of the relatively new nitrous oxide, the poor man had had to endure it with just the rudiments of the wooden stick between his teeth. Frederick's main and only duty had been to pin the tortured individual down by his shoulders and keep him there while his screams resonated around the room. This was one of the many chores that he disliked about his work, it being the suffering of the poor and needy while having very little in the way of anesthesia. He had held his eyes tightly shut but still heard the sawing of the bone and the eventual singing of skin as it was cauterised. But as was prevalent in a high number of cases in such a run-down infirmary as this, the man had died within minutes - the pain inevitably too much for his body and mind to withstand. So, reluctantly, he'd had to transport both his corpse and the severed limb down to the morgue, his least favourite place in the building.
If the whole infirmary stunk to high heaven, then the morgue was ten times worse. He had gagged repeatedly each time he had been there in the past and was confident that the soup he'd shared for lunch with his brother earlier would be brought up in an instant. But, much to his relief, that didn't happen. As he'd pushed open the door in expectation of the rancid smell filling his lungs, he'd stood momentarily shocked at the normality of it. With the faint light from the outside corridor extending into the room, he had been just able to see within. In lieu of the usual half-rotting cadavers and severed limbs strewn haphazardly about the room, it was, to his surprise, bereft of both. Bending down he'd grabbed his load and on dragging it inside, had barely reached its middle when his foot had tripped over the recently cleansed floor's sole item - a spade.
Now, in preparation of his leaving for the night, he dabbed at the cut on his leg he'd received from its ragged, sharp edge. Between this and his blackened eye, he felt himself at home in the infirmary but his realist mind instantly put pay to the superstitious belief that these things generally came in threes. By this time he couldn't care less whether they did or not. He just felt exhausted.
Jacob reconfirmed this. "Looks like it's been a long day."
Sitting by his bedside, Frederick teetered on a three-legged stool taken from the nurse's room. "That could very well be the understatement of the year, brother."
"Well things could be worse. Look at me! Another four weeks, they say, before I can get any way near to moving. I can't even feed myself, let alone toilet."
Frederick knew this to be true - he, himself, had fed him the hospital's insipid soup at lunchtime, but the 'toilet matter' brought a smile to his face. "It isn't everyone that gets a pretty nurse to hold him while he pees, is it?"
Jacob adjusted his position for better comfort. "Not funny, Frederick. Not funny at all. It's embarrassing having to defecate into a pot and have some female stranger wipe your derriere for you. And this bloody bed, it's rife

with bugs. Can't they get iron-framed ones? These wooden ones attract them."

Frederick ignored his rants and tightened the cloth around his leg. "That should do it."

"Don't you think you should get that seen to? After all, you are surrounded by nurses!"

Frederick stood. "I've worked here long enough to know how to treat a cut." He nodded down. "You okay for the night?"

"Yes, yes, just lying here in anticipation of this evening's gastronomic delights. I'll be half my own weight when I leave here, you just wait and see if I'm not."

Frederick thought of his own stomach - it was in dire need of food as well. He knew only too well that, with himself being a volunteer, he could of course eat here for free with the patients and staff but he'd had the honour in the past of once visiting the so-called kitchen and it had not been to his liking. One solitary pot had hung over an open flame and whatever meagre ingredients happened to have made up that day's meal was combined together therein. In a word, mush. He thought better of it. A hearty meal would be waiting for him on his arrival back home, hopefully.

"I'll see you tomorrow then, brother. I'll be sure to tell our parents that you are in high spirits." He knew this would rile Jacob further but he had meant it in jest only.

"Hold on." Jacob tried his hardest to sit further up. "You still haven't finished telling me what's happening with you and Rosie yet."

Frederick sighed.

Reseating himself as before, he prepared himself to continue their lunchtime talk. Whilst spoon-feeding Jacob his soup, he had inadvertently, during the course of their conversation, mentioned the trouble he was having with Rosie. Furthermore, he had, with loosened tongue, let it slip that he now had eyes for another. But at this early juncture in the relationship, he was hesitant to volunteer her name or who she was. If, indeed, there was a relationship already between him and Madeline. This being all in his own mind to be true but he had hoped, with careful tactics, he would win her over. She had mentioned her admiration of his voluntary work here at the infirmary which he'd considered to be a good beginning at least. But before Jacob had time to probe further, Frederick had been called away to an emergency concerning a burned patient. Now, with their unfinished conversation resurrected, he could see only subterfuge in his explanation. "We just don't seem to blend well together as we once did."

"Yes, but who is this other?"

Frederick shook his head and shuffled about on the splintered stool. "It's too early to say yet, we've only just met."

"Does Rosie know her?"

Does Rosie know her, he thought, didn't she just? "Kind of."

"What do you mean 'kind of'? Either she does or she doesn't?"

Frederick was getting agitated, not only with the conversation but with his seating arrangement. "Bloody stool." Rising, he kicked it to the side and, without aim or forethought, slumped onto the edge of the bed...his arm unintentionally falling on Jacob's leg.
His shriek penetrated the very walls of the ward.
Frederick sat up immediately and recovered from his mishap. "Sorry, sorry." Jacob's discomfort was apparent to him and his expletives reinforced Frederick's assumptions. "Time I left for the night. Sorry again, brother."
Three nurses had, in an instant, answered Jacob's cry of distress - one by his side to tend him and the two others to pacify the other patients who, now roused from their respective trances, were on somnambulistic walkabouts around the ward.
Leaving the chaos he, himself, had created, Frederick shied from the room and made for the exit hallway.
"Hey, Freddy, my boy."
Frederick raised his hand in both salutation and farewell. "Yes... goodnight, Garcia."

Back in the ward, Jacob lay still in his bed as the nurses rounded up the other patients. Why he had chosen to stay there when he knew his parents could have afforded much better care for him, only he knew. But, over the course of the last few weeks, he had at times regretted his individualist and political stance against the bureaucratic health system. Why should only the rich have access to medical well-being he'd always proclaimed but, witnessing what he had during his stay here, his opinion had changed dramatically. Most of them didn't receive it, some didn't even deserve it, others didn't appreciate it when they got it, and the rest were ready to exploit it when they had it. The system was a mess. But his optimistic view of the future of France still remained in his heart....
...As did another.
He hadn't given up hope with regard to Madeline. She had captured his heart, and although with his thoughts being so muddled at the time as to have so casually walked in front of a carriage, his remediation and subsequent convalescing here had given him plenty of time to reassess the situation. His conclusion being that he would find her and insist upon further explanation of her unanticipated disassociation from him. It had been, as anticipated, a glorious day spent with her, so why, at its close, did she say that she did not wish to see him again? It just did not make sense to him.
He wanted the next four weeks over with quickly so he could put his plan into action. And perhaps, in some time to follow, with Frederick and his newly acquired female acquaintance, they could all four enjoy a pleasant evening together.

*

Madeline lay naked on top of her bed, her left arm bent to clasp her breast in her palm. Lightly tapping her fingers to the tender parts, she winced, once again, with the pain. Looking down upon a deep blue marking, her mind recalled the entire incident in a flash. Had Jacques not turned into the resemblance of an animal, she would have gladly performed the act that he had so viciously tried to impose upon her. After all, it had been her original intention to do so. But she had foolishly suggested payment and this had turned Jacques into the monster he had become. Although things had happened so quickly, and her constant head movements to avoid him, her fleeting glances of his manhood had, funnily enough, been to her liking. She would have willingly accommodated its size and shape and was convinced now that she would have learned from it. But as terrifying as the episode had been, she felt, once again, as she had done after the knife attack, strangely excited by it. So much so that she had unclasped her breast and now held its bud between finger and thumb. Was it her wish to have been taken by force? Was this the thrill of it? Surely such violent acts should not go hand in hand with the tender wants of a woman. Was she getting some sadistic pleasure from this? She apparently did, as she suddenly noticed that her right hand had inadvertently found its way down between her legs, whereupon contact with her interior with lightened finger, she found herself moist to the touch. Allowing her free spirit to succumb to her body's wants and needs, her fingers maneuvered their way, as before, to her preferred locale. As her mind and body glided her upwards to unlimited heights, she recalled the aftermath of her ordeal and the surprising revelation thereafter.

Rubin had saved her life. On two separate occasions he had come to her rescue and in the most vicious of situations imaginable to her. She had much to thank him for. And now, for the second time after such a violent act, her mind was reacting in a similar way to her body's need. Was there a connection here, she wondered. Would it always be this way? Her fingers quickened their pace as she recalled Jacques' grip upon her, his forceful movements and the pressing of his hardened sex to her face. She thought of the knife at Ramone's throat, and the splayed neck of the attacker. Then back to Jacques again, with him thrusting himself into her mouth and her gasping for breath, the tightness in her throat and her gasping for air.
With her eyes tightly closed, she had brought herself to orgasm once again. Her fingers not stilled from their slow rotation, she allowed herself to bask in the après delights of it as her entire body shook to conclusion. What must it be like to have a man do this to her, she thought? Would he know exactly what to do, would he know the correct method to bring her to, what she now knew to be, her predilection? Or was it only the woman, herself, that knew her own body and mind? She had no idea. All she knew was that she was learning how to pleasure the opposite sex. But would she, herself, ever be

allowed this satisfaction in return? She saw nothing of it in the short-term future but dearly hoped that one day she would.
She leaned over and blew out the candle sending her room into the darkness she craved. And hearing the voices outside in the street, let sleep take her.

With the weekend almost at a conclusion, the street below filled with the usual night time carousers. But with a new week beginning the following day, most were content to see the day off quietly.
Two friends meeting together after a brief absence nodded to each other.
"Well, Jean, what kind of weekend did you have?"
"Oh, quiet. Nothing much ever happens around here."

Meanwhile, two stories above them and immediately opposite Madeline's room, the gap in the curtains twitched once again.

*

Madeline 2

Chapter 12

A friend indeed!

Four black Percheron horses pulled the decorative carriage into the courtyard where the butler, upon grabbing the reins, relieved the driver of his duties. Stepping back towards the door, he pushed down on the brass handle and pulled it open.

Alighting gracefully, the woman stepped free of her spacious confines and, adjusting her dress accordingly, moved towards the house. Ascending the six steps two at a time, she passed between the ornately carved columns and entered the opened door. Once inside she immediately relieved herself of her bonnet and cape, letting both drop to the floor without her missing a step. By the time she had reached the bottom of the curved stairway, she had undone her over- corset and set it to rest like the other apparel. And on reaching the top, her gown had been strewn likewise. Her gait meaningful, she glided along the top hallway and removed both panniers and what underwear remained. By the time she had reached the door, she stood naked with only laced boots and fine lace stockings apparent.
She heard the joviality within, so, pushing the bed chamber door open, she stood at its entrance unmoving, looking in.
"Ah, my dear Caroline, we were all wondering when you would appear. We have missed you this weekend."
Her husband and three others filled the room, but what gender these others were was hard to define, so elaborate and excessive were their costumes. Moving towards her bed on which her husband lay naked, she looked down upon him. "I see the games have begun early this evening."
His eyes followed her gaze. There, strapped around the base of his erection, was a black, leather cord, and so tightly pulled in that his skin looked fit to bursting.
"Come, my darling, join us." His outstretched hand inviting her closer.
She turned to the left and immersed her fingers into a jar of gelled substance and without thought smeared it between her legs. "I have found another."
"Have you indeed?" He adjusted his frame for her easy accessibility.
Mounting the bed, she extended her right leg over his body and taking hold of him in her hand, slowly guided him in.
"She is a willing participant in such games?" this said with his hand now beckoning another to join them.
Caroline laid her palms upon his chest for balance and began her rise and descent on him. "Perhaps with a little encouragement."
Now joined by a third, standing by the bed's edge, this person stood half-attired as a woman, complete with heightened wig, whitened face and rouge in abundance upon the cheeks. It was only the flaccid five inches that lay hanging between his legs that gave way to his gender. She watched on as her husband lifted it horizontal and nonchalantly placed it in his mouth.
Caroline continued with her description, "Culs-terreux."
As quick as it had entered, its removal had been twice as fast. He turned to face her. "A country girl?"
This term was what the gentry had called the provincials or country folk, literally translated as 'dirty asses', a term which spoke of their low opinion of them.
Caroline quickened her pace as the thought of Madeline entered her head. "But no ordinary girl. This one is special; and she's one of Monique's."

His interest now lost on the third person, a flick of the wrist signalled him to leave. "Monique! Surely we have not lowered our standards in our search for new blood?"

"Indeed I would have stayed well clear of her house but it had been brought to my attention from a person of both our acquaintance, Madeline's existence."

"Madeline?" His repeated use of her name had been casual in his search about the disheveled bed cover. Eventually finding what he was looking for, he repeated it once again but more question-like.

Caroline curtailed the conversation momentarily while her husband leaned over to the dresser table. After immersing the pair of half-inch thick, ivory phalluses into the gel, he pulled himself back as before. "Ready?"

Caroline nodded and remained still.

Sitting forward he stretched his arm behind her and gently inserted one of them into her rear. She nodded again with barely an inch free and allowed her husband to raise himself from the bed to do likewise.

"So then, this Madeline?" he eventually asked with interest.

"Sixteen years of age and all woman. Monique has even prided herself upon finding her and, apparently, chaste with it."

His eyes widened in surprise. "A virgin, no less, how novel." This said loud enough for all to hear. "We shall have to do something about that then, won't we Jacqueline?"

A semi-naked brunette seated at close proximity and who had apparently taken over where Caroline's husband had left off, nodded with full mouth. "Mm-huh."

Caroline spoke in hushed tone, "I'd like her on my own for a while."

"Now, now, my dear, it isn't nice to be greedy. We'd all like some enjoyment with the new flesh."

"In time, darling, in time. I want my fun with her first."

*

Madeline 3

Madeline 3

Prologue

**Chateau d'Estelle,
18th Century France**

He stood silent by the cell door and waited.
Would she still be alive, he thought.
He hoped so, but the state she had arrived in twelve hours since, he feared the worst. Many a cruel and heartless act he'd had to carry out in the past in the course of his duties as assistant to the head jailer but to aid in the incarceration of this unfortunate woman the previous night had been, to him, pitiless in the extreme. His instructions had been exact and as compliant to his trade as ever, he had carried them out in a dutiful manner. As custodians to some of France's most vicious criminals; amongst others, his superior had, in the past, informed him of the nature of their crime upon arrival, the duration of their sentence and the allocation of their cells. This was where he dictated that his responsibility should end and his assistant's duties begin. He sought the easy life, devoid of all accountability of the inmates and only on their eventual freedom or death would he become involved in the finalisation of their sentence. Until then, the daily machination and general housekeeping of the jail was left to him alone to administer the periodic punishments as was deemed necessary. The more heinous the crime, the worse their time, had been his initial instructions; and he had performed this task with forthrightness. But last night had been different. Protocol had changed. He knew that the Chief had received the official paperwork in respect of her imprisonment but some caveats had been added, through implicit utterances, from the two men who had brought her here. No harsh treatment, no violation of her feminine rights and, most important of all, that she remain in constant isolation from the other inmates. Her identity was to remain secret. Solitary confinement was harsh enough, he thought; indeed, he had seen many inmates lose their sanity through years of isolation, but to have her in such a cell as the one she had been placed was, in his eyes, a travesty. What

her crime was, had not been revealed to him; and as for the child she carried within her, where lay its future, he thought... if any.

It had also been dictated that, in the event of her death, she would be buried in a secret place - it being, ideally, the sea that would consume her body. As a jailer now for almost twenty years, hadn't he, in the past, heard of such a tale as this - spoken under hushed tones about prison governor Bénigne d'Auvergne de Saint-Mars and the infamous *L'Homme au Masque de Fer* - a man imprisoned under similar circumstances. He thought it very strange.

Convinced by past experience that he would find her corpse lying where they had left her, he prepared to push the heavy key into the lock. This, to his dismay, was interrupted by an accented muttering from behind.

"Some grub fur the wee lady eh? Wit aboot us?"

He knew the voice well. Looking down to the stone floor, he slid the tray of food closer towards the door with his right boot. "Ta gueule, English pig."

The voice raised itself in retaliation. "'Ave told you before, Monsieur Froggie, am no Englishman, am Scottish."

The jailer grunted, "Scottish pig, then."

Gripping the iron bars tighter with grime-infested fingers, the heavy bearded Scot pulled his face closer to the foot-square gap in the door and spat. He laughed out loud at the sight of it.

Looking at his sleeve, the jailer saw the thin glob of saliva slowly drip from its edge. Merde! Raising the abused arm aloft, he placed the flaming torch into the wall-holder and with him knowing the geography of the corridor well, there was no need to turn round. In one, fluid movement, his now free hand reached for the handle of the tethered whip by his side and withdrew it. Lashing in a backwards manner, the thong unwrapped itself in mid-air in the direction of the Scotsman. And within seconds, its tip had sliced open the right middle finger to the bone. Screaming like a wounded animal, the startled prisoner retreated into the darkness of the cell amidst his continuous cries questioning the jailer's birth.

He should think himself lucky, thought the jailer. At least his cell faced inwards, whereas this one he was now entering looked west, out into the sea. Retrieving the torch, he pulled the collar of his thick, tattered coat up to his neck and resumed his key-turning duty. Picking the tray of food up from the floor, he pushed the door open with his right foot and walked in. He expected the worst.

The sub-zero gust hit his face immediately. He looked across at the window first. If she was still alive, he would try and fix the exposed part the best he could. He inched forward into the semi-dark. Alarmed by the light from the flickering torch, several brown rats scurried their way towards the inner wall in search of their respective holes within. Casually kicking at one to help it on its way, he crouched down to alleviate himself of his load onto the cold, stone floor. On bended knees, he drew the flame closer and looked in her direction. If memory served well, then she hadn't moved from where they'd

left her. He shook his head. More food for the fish, he thought. How many unclaimed bodies had he thrown into the sea in the past, he mused. Was her body to be, yet another, in the long line of stitched cloth bags so unceremoniously tipped into the crashing waves below? He looked at her deformed state and with outstretched hand, laid his upturned fingers to the exposed part of her pale blue cheek. It was like touching death itself. Poor cow! He removed his hand and nudged at her side... nothing. Lifting her left arm, he let it drop hard against the floor... nothing. Bending over, he placed an ear to her mouth and slapped at her cheek, he slapped again... nothing. Lifting himself from her, he sat crouched as before and stared at the half-exposed face. This being the extent of his medical know-all, he reconciled himself to the fact that she was dead for sure. This time he spoke out, "Poor cow!"
He stood up to make preparations for her nautical burial.

"Merde!"
He drew his finger to his mouth and sucked on the blood. It had been the third time he had pierced his skin with the thick boned needle in an attempt to stitch the heavy linen together. A seamster he'd never make, he thought. Sitting cross-legged on the floor, he continued sucking in an attempt to stop the flow.
On leaving the cell earlier, he had at once proceeded to the upper levels to inform the Chief of her demise. But on finding him drunk and lying unconscious on his bed, he had hastily gathered together the necessary items for the burial. He had also noticed the half- strewn purse of silver coins on the floor, the payment of which had been his silence in this matter. Not that he, himself, would have seen any of it with the Chief being as covetous with coin as was his norm. He could have easily bent over and helped himself to a few. In his current state of inebriation, the Chief wouldn't have noticed any missing and, if he had, assumed he had lost them. But he had thought better of it. Or had this been due to the fact that he wanted a quick return to the cell? He didn't ponder an answer.
He withdrew the finger from his mouth and after satisfactory inspection, cupped his hands together and blew some warmth into them. Adjusting himself on to the kneeling position once again, he continued with the stitching. Pulling the cat-gut tight as he progressed his way up the body, he eventually reached a point where he knew there were only three more required. These were needed to pull the flap over the head, connect to the neck and stitch into place across the face, the final one being the hardest, not only physically but mentally.
Whether it was an old sailors' seafaring tale or just nautical superstition, the final stitch always went clean through the dead man's nose. This was to ensure that death had, indeed, taken the individual. So, in this manner, as if he were at sea himself and dropping the body therein, he had repeated this procedure for all in his final care. She, he thought, would be no exception.

Holding the cloth tight together with his left hand, he pushed the needle in through at the neck and hauled the remaining eight inches of gut out to the side. But upon pulling the flap across from the right, found he had to use all his centred strength to thrust the tip through the now three pieces. Four times he repeated the fruitless task of pulling it though but, as hard as he could, his fingered grip on the needle kept slipping. With freezing hands, he could find no purchase on which to pull it through. So, with clenched fist, he pushed down hard at its base with his thumb and with so much pressure that his arm began to shake. The thumb slipped off and in an instant his clenched fist found its way, with great force, straight into her face. Once again he swore at himself and clenched his teeth. If she were not dead, then she would have certainly have felt that one, he thought. Giving up the process as a hopeless exercise, he retracted the needle. He considered the alternatives. Again, he adjusted himself accordingly and sat himself astride her body in preparation of the final stitch. Pressing the cloth tight against the face, he pinched at the nose bone to find an exact point of entry and, when satisfied, placed the tip of the boned-needle to the side. Pushing hard, he felt it pierce the skin and further in through the cartilage. But as he did so, he heard a faint mutter. Had he imagined it? Pushing at it again, the same muffled utterance was heard, and then a stifled whimper.

He pulled back the cloth to reveal her face. There was blood flowing from her nose.

"Oh Mon Dieu!"

She was still alive!

*

Madeline 3

Chapter 1

Correspondence

Paris, 18th Century France.
Some years earlier

Madeline seated herself in the armchair by the window of her bedroom and looked down at the two very dissimilar letters resting on her lap. She lifted them both and deliberated over each of their appearance and contents. In her left hand she held one of premium quality paper, handwritten with the finest script and had been delivered, complete with waxed seal, by official messenger. This, she had known at once to be from Ramone. The second, a far inferior, graying parchment containing text and irregular grammar which, on initial viewing, appeared to her could quite possibly have been penned by an infant, its scribbling indistinct. She tapped the letter on her leg and smiled to herself, except that no child could possibly have written such intimate wording as was held within the transcript.
The smile was short lived.
It had been surreptitiously slipped beneath her bedroom door either the previous night when she had retired for the evening or early this morning before she had risen - she was unsure. She had heard nothing. This one had come from Frederick and he had unquestionably written it in the infirmary during working hours as it had a peculiar smell of liniment about it. But who had delivered this letter? Had he himself sneaked upstairs or had he gotten someone else to do it for him? Apart from paying customers and the immediate house staff, Monique permitted no-one on the upper floor. But it was not these factors that made her apprehensive about their respective correspondence - what did worry her was the unexpected contents of them both.
Ramone had been suspicious by his absence of late and she could not understand why, after their friendship blossoming so quickly at the beginning, he had not visited her as often as he had once done. Granted, she now knew the truth about the knife incident that Rubin had imparted to her but Ramone was not aware that she knew this. Or perhaps now, did he,

himself, have reservations about meeting her and not wanting to look her in the eye through deceit? She could only speculate an answer. His unexpected but very welcome letter of invitation to dinner had arrived two days previous; and after seeking permission from Monique to join him, she had been granted the night off from entertaining clients. Her excitement with this news had been surpassed only with the relief that he was still in contact with her. But now, on the day of their dinner engagement, this missive had arrived canceling it. And with no reason other than he was fatigued from work. What work did he do anyway? She had always assumed, with him so proudly sporting his uniform that he was retired from the services and had always appeared to her to be a gentleman of leisure. This excuse was mere subterfuge for the real reason she concluded - but what was the real reason? She would have liked to ask him but with her not having an inkling as to where he resided in Paris she could, therefore, neither reply to his letter nor visit him directly to challenge him face to face. Neither this letter nor the previous one had bore an address for her to reply to. He had presumed that she would be available for dinner and had not asked for RSVP. She sighed. The plain and simple truth being she was missing her friend. Leaning back, she looked out over the rooftops across the street and up into the blue, cloudless sky beyond and sighed again.

But the moment was taken from her when she remembered the second letter. And on looking down at the thin, light paper which was Frederick's semi-indecipherable epistle, her mind was in a further quandary. He also wanted to meet her but the contents of his letter hinted at a more intimate liaison and not merely a late evening's repast. He implied love. She re-read it again in full.

Madeleine,

Positive beginning, she thought, he couldn't even spell her name correctly... or was it his handwriting? She continued.

Our first meeting was never what I would have planned if I had met you any other place but there and done what we had done because I wouldn't have.

This sentence, she thought, was not merely ambiguous but just plain did not make any sense at all. She could find no logic in it whichever way she tried to interpret it. She read on.

I didn't sleep that night or the next night and then the next one after that as well.

She closed her eyes momentarily and shook her head. Talk about over description. She refocused her sight once again.

The second time we seen each other in the hall after the first time was the last time I seen you but I want to see you again a third time.

She sighed in disbelief. Did this man have trouble with repetition or what? She could hardly believe this was written by anyone other than a child. The entire letter thus far had bordered on farce. A severe lesson in punctuation, grammar and syntax was dearly needed. She prepared herself for the next line as her initial shock at reading it the first time had left her lost for words.

Don't tell Rosie about this. It will have to be our secret and no-one must know about us. Well not yet anyway well. I don't love Rosie anymore because of you.
What secret? What mustn't they know? She had done nothing to elicit such feelings from him; and she certainly did not have the feelings for him that his words were implying. What had happened in Monique's front room had been purely professional and their chance meeting the following day was simply coincidental. She had spoken to him out of conviviality and concern about his swollen eye, nothing more. Was this to be yet another admirer she had to hold at bay? In such a short time in Paris she had unwittingly, in part, secured the attention of Jacob, which she had, on several occasions since, regretted ending the relationship. Then had come Gaston, who although being married and with family, appeared intent in spending his life with her; and now Frederick. She immediately dropped Jacques from her memory, the least thought about that incident the better. In truth, the only real person she could call a friend without wanting anything from her was Ramone. And why would she ever consider speaking to Rosie about this matter. She valued her life too much, she thought. She had witnessed Rosie's tempestuous outbursts on several occasions during her time here. She read on.
Meet me at the park gates opposite the church on rue de caselle at 4 at night tomorrow.
As clandestine as he was suggesting this appointment to be, she had presumed it would not be 4 o'clock in the morning and in addition to this, four in the afternoon was hardly night time. And since the letter was undated, the 'tomorrow' part also appeared unclear. Had he written this letter the previous night or had it been this morning? Had he been working overnight? Which tomorrow did he mean, yesterday's tomorrow which was today, or today's tomorrow? Goodness, she thought, she was beginning to sound like his letter. She continued.
Until then Madaline...
Still wrong!
... I will think of you as I remembered you the first time and the second time as well...
Oh please, don't start that again.
... and looking very much to seeing you the third time then.
Oh for pity's sake!
Frederick.
My eye is getting better now since the second time.
She looked up to the ceiling and shook her head.
"Aagghhhhh!"

Three-thirty had arrived; and as she topped and tailed herself from the porcelain basin, her eyes looked over towards the letter which she had left resting on her chair. She was still undecided as to whether she should chance the date of the meeting as today and walk to the park at, as Frederick had so

wrongfully requested, four o'clock tonight. But then, if she did, what would lie in store for her if today was, indeed, the intended day? Would Frederick declare an undying love for her? Where would that leave her? Or was she presuming too much of him, after all he just stated that he was not in love with Rosie anymore, not that he now loved her. Her introspective debate continued. What harm would it do to just meet him? Oh, but what if Rosie found out? No, she decided, she wouldn't go, her mind was made up. So, aimlessly throwing her wash cloth into the water, she hastily fastened up her dress and corset, resolute in her decision.
Ten minutes of pacing the room later, she had to admit that she was bored. With her original plans with Ramone now cancelled and leaving her with nothing to do, this now made her re-think her earlier decision. "Oh pooh!" She stopped in her tracts. Funny, she thought, she hadn't used that expression since arriving in Paris. All her life, as far as she could remember, she had inadvertently used that expression when dissatisfied with something and yet here she was using it again now. What had changed her and now, more importantly, what had made her use it again? She looked down and flattened her over-corset home with the palm of her hands. Who was she fooling? Here she was, attired for a formal, outdoor meeting boasting one of her best summer dresses. Of course she was going to meet him. She had unconsciously dressed for the occasion. So, with a spring in her step she crossed the room to retrieve her laced boots from her wardrobe.

"Five minutes to four, young lady, and my timepiece is accurate to the minute."
Not doubting his word, she thanked the old man with nod and a smile and carried on along the street. Five minutes to get there, she thought. Knowing where the park was situated, having visited there before with Ramone, she knew only too well that if she increased her pace then she would make the allotted time, the deadline.
Deadline indeed!
What was she thinking? One, she would not be seen walking at speed dressed as such; and two, she would not be hurried into making an appointment so accurate - if she was late then she was late, he would have to wait on her. So, with a woman's stubbornness, she slowed her pace to a casual amble. It could be a wasted journey anyway, she thought.
Nonchalantly looking behind her every so often as she walked, she tried in vain to catch sight of Rubin, knowing full well that he followed her wherever she went. This, as he had inadvertently explained to her on their first encounter, was for both her own protection but, more importantly, Monique's inquisitiveness. Since then, she had tried her hardest to catch him out - this more for her own amusement rather than testing his stealth and covert surveillance. Today would be no exception.
Selecting the busier side of the thoroughfare, she mingled with both the outdoor street vendors plying their wares to their would-be purveyors and the

constant stream of uninterested pedestrians eager to reach their destination. Her choice of shop doorway to duck into was that of a butcher and once in there, instantly regretted it. As she waited to see if Rubin would pass her by so she could leap out at him in jest, she stood squeezing her eyes together at what sounded to her like a pig being slaughtered inside, resounded her ears.
"Mind yourself, ma'am."
Pressing herself against the door's side panel, she allowed the young man, complete with leg of lamb slung over his shoulder, to pass her by and exit onto the street. She couldn't have picked a busier doorway. As one exited, two more entered, both arbitrarily laden with various cuts of meat which, she noticed, was leaving a trail of deep red on the ground in their wake. Madeline had to side-step quickly to avoid any of the blood making its way onto her dress. Yet another passed her on the way out. Leaning forward, she peered inside and immediately surmised that the pig she had heard previously was now available pork, as all was silent.
A guttered voice called from within, "Can I help you, ma'am?"
Madeline didn't have a chance to reply.
"Monique not feeding you?"
This new voice had come from behind her and she knew in an instant that it was Rubin.
"Or are you playing girly games with me, young missy?"
Turning on her feet, she had to bend her neck upwards to face him given his height. "Rubin. What a surprise."
"What are you up to here?"
"Oh, nothing." She shook her head. "Nothing at all."
He nodded inwards. "Well, if you value your stomach any then I wouldn't eat anything that old Jess had to sell."
Attempting subterfuge as to her real reason for being there, she sidled passed him. "I was just curious, that was all."
Once outdoors, she continued along in her original direction but adjusted her pace accordingly to allow Rubin to catch up with her.
He did. "What mischief are you intending me to get you out of today then?"
Madeline ignored the sarcasm in his question and replied with ingenuity, "I have no idea to what you are referring. I am merely out for an afternoon stroll."
His long legs languid with her dawdling, Rubin paced awkwardly alongside her, all the while a path was miraculously clearing in the oncoming traffic as they advanced. Few people, Madeline noticed, were not intimidated with Rubin's size and stature and were only too happy to give this haggard giant a wide berth.
"Doesn't look like that to me." He spat on the ground, much to the mortification of two elderly women who's tut-tutting in unison he ignored. "There's purpose in your walking."

"Very astute, Rubin, but has it not occurred to you that I may be strolling with destination in mind." And before she had reprimanded him for spitting, he had done it again.
Coughing up more of the same, he had repeated his assault on the ground. Or he would have done, had the expurgation not found a home on someone's shoe. Ignorant to this fact, both continued walking but heard an irate voice holler from behind, "Here here, man."
Rubin thought nothing of it but it was Madeline who turned to see who the caller was addressing. "I think that gentleman means us, Rubin."
He stopped with her but refrained from turning round. "Does he now." This was uttered in a casual and matter-of-fact manner rather than a question.
"Yes, you, the big brute."
Unaware of what Rubin had done and the impending discord, Madeline chuckled, "Yes, I'm positive now. He is looking in our direction and by process of elimination, as I am neither big nor brutish, then by all accounts, that leaves only you."
Madeline's smile continued as she watched the caller approach them. "Are you deaf as well as loutish?"
The beam on her face was soon replaced with one of surprise as she saw him repeatedly poke his walking cane into Rubin's back as he spoke out the words. Madeline squirmed. Oh please don't do that, she thought. She had witnessed Rubin's violent and vicious nature before with Jacques and could only pity this man as he taunted Rubin. She knew only too well of what he was capable.
He prodded further. "You up there."
For a man whose physique bordered on colossus, even Madeline was shocked at the speed at which Rubin spun on his feet. And before he had stopped, the cane was in his hand. "If you don't want this stick to become part of your arse, then I'd turn and walk away now."
"But look what you've done to my footwear."
Rubin looked down at the dainty, buckled and rather effeminate-looking, cream shoes and noticed the brown phlegm on the left one. He knew right away it was his own doing. As his eyes slowly rose up over this diminutive-looking dandy, he took stock of his frilled apparel. Overly tight-fitting britches, the same colour as his shoes, were tucked inside dark brown stockings of lace. And with his voluminous jacket a gentler shade of his stockings, he looked like the archetypal Parisian poseur. Ashen-faced with hair wig to match, Rubin noticed the little eye-glass spectacles perched on his nose. Raising his free hand, Rubin removed them from his face and with little effort, if any, crushed them in his grip. "There, you can't see it anymore." He let them drop to the ground and leaned down to an inch of him. "Now fuck off."
The dandy quickly followed his mangled eyewear to the ground as a result of Rubin driving the cane hard into his stomach. Madeline jumped back at the

speed and intensity of it all as Rubin threw the cane to the ground and turned to resume their pace. "Right, little missy, let's go."
Madeline looked down at the injured man and it was all she could do but quickly curtsy and bid him farewell as apology. "Au revoir, monsieur."
Etiquette forgotten, she hurriedly ran after Rubin until she had reached his side. "That outburst was a bit uncalled for, was it not? You needed only apologise to assuage the situation."
"I take it from that fancy talk you think the little shit didn't deserve it?"
"Well, I agree the provocation with the walking cane was undeserved and that he could have drawn your attention with further discourse but it seems to me, Rubin, that it is far easier for you to get yourself into mischief than I." She stopped walking in the hope that he would do so also.
He did stop and stood looking quizzically into her eyes. "Hmmm, you twist and use my own words against me, little missy."
"You were fortunate that it was not a knife he had at your back; I do believe you dropped your guard there for a time, Rubin."
Rubin tilted his head back an inch as if to refocus his eyes upon her. "You think so?"
"Yes, I do. Had that man been a brigand, he could have driven a knife into your back before you were aware of it. You stood still all the while giving him the opportunity to do so."
Rubin puckered his scarred lips in thought and nodded slightly. "Uh-huh, and what does a pretty little thing like you know about these things?"
Oblivious that they were blocking the flow of pedestrians as they stood talking, Madeline continued, "Rubin, one does not have to have experienced things to know that they can happen or that they are real. I only commented upon the possibility that you were caught unawares."
"You think so?"
Vexed at his repetitive question, she stamped her foot and snapped at him "Yes. And stop saying that, it's really annoying."
Rubin smiled inwardly. Like their previous conversation in the taverne, he enjoyed toying with her. There was something about this young woman he liked. Apart from Annie, to whom he could never freely volunteer his feelings, Madeline was the only person in his life, at present, that he felt entirely happy in the company of. "Okay then. First off, if he had been a brigand, he wouldn't have given me a chance, he'd have just stuck me, no talking. Next, I can tell the difference between a blade at my back and a blunt stick; and last, a little dandy like him would have used a woman's pistol, they don't have the balls to carry a knife or the know-how to use one."
Put in her place, Madeline smiled at him. "Sorry, Rubin, I should have known better. I shall not underestimate you again as you clearly know your business." She suddenly remembered her appointment with Frederick. "Oh, the time."
"You got to be somewhere?"

Reluctant to tell him with whom she was meeting or where she was going, her reply was short and uninformative, "Yes, but I don't know the time."
Without taking his eyes from her, Rubin outstretched his right arm and holding a startled pedestrian at bay with his giant hand pressed hard against his chest, blurted out, "Time?"
Shaken with the suddenness of it, the distressed individual wrestled with his timepiece in order to answer. "Eh, eh, four, eh, four twenty."
Rubin released his hold on him and refocused his attention back on Madeline. "What's twenty?"
"What?"
"How many eights are in twenty?"
Madeline looked stunned. "How many eights are in twenty?"
Rubin nodded. "How many?"
Madeline shook her head in disbelief. "Two. Why?"
"Two."
"Yes, two. With four remaining…Rubin…" She folded her arms and took her weight on her left leg. "…can you count?"
Never one to be embarrassed with his lack of education, Rubin answered with verve, "I've got my own way."
"In multiples of eight, I take it?"
"Sounds about right."
Her meeting with Frederick completely forgotten about, she quizzed him further. "Well if you add one to eight you would have nine wouldn't you, so why can't you count to at least nine?"
Rubin shrugged. "Never had the need to."
Agape in astonishment, it took her several seconds to respond, "Are you telling me that all through your life everything has revolved around the number eight?"
Rubin remained silent, the question to him requiring no answer. It had worked for him in the past and he needed nothing to the contrary.
"Excuse me, but you're blocking the way."
Rubin turned his head in the direction of the voice and with casual retort, told the pedestrian to go fuck himself.
Madeline noticed his reaction to Rubin's insult and quickly apologised in his stead. Taking his powerful arm in her hand she coaxed him away from the scene. "We do not need a repetition of your earlier antics, Rubin. Let's walk."

*

Madeline 3

Chapter 2

Thoughts on Retribution

Janis flipped over yet another leaf in her book and once again read very little, if anything, of what was written within. This had been the fourth consecutive page turn in just under thirty seconds and it had not gone un-noticed.
"Either you have become an extremely fast reader, my dear, or the story is not to your liking."
Janis looked up from the page and across the sitting room at her mother. "I have read this one before."
Seated at a tapestry board with her back to her, the mother pulled the thread out towards her. "Then choose another." She turned on her seat and peered over her half-rimmed spectacles. "I have spent the best part of my life collecting all manner of literature and building an extensive library, Janis. Repeat reads are not necessary."
Janis slammed the book shut. She rose from the padded couch and stood tapping it in her hand. "I'm bored, mother." She paced the room.
"Pah."
She snapped back, "I happen to be missing my husband." The book found itself tossed, with complete indifference to its first edition value, onto the couch.
The mother noticed this but bit her lip, her concern for her daughter more important. "He's only been gone a few days. Surely that cannot be too much of a hardship?"
Janis picked up her part-finished embroidery and stood fidgeting with it in her hands. "Yes, but for how long?"
"As long as it takes, I suppose. He is on government business."
Picking at the loose ends of the material, Janis's tirade continued, "He lives in Paris, mother. He deals with *this* city's affairs. What has he got to do with Salon? It is at the other end of the country for heaven's sake."
The mother secured her needle safely at the side of her board and rose to meet her daughter. "Yes, but the entire ministerial ruling of France is run from here. Any city, town, village in France is under its jurisdiction. He was

obviously the correct man for the job or his superiors would not have commissioned him with such a task outwith Paris."
Like the book, her embroidery was tossed aside without care and missed her sewing basket completely. "Yes, but Salon. It may as well be the moon." Reaching her goal, the mother bent down and retrieved the cloth and placing it in the basket, secured the cover. "It has never bothered you this much in the past?"
Janis knew she was right. It hadn't. But things were different now. She had a commission of her own, one of her own appointing. She wanted her husband back. And not just back home from Salon but back in her arms, back in her bed and back in their marriage. She intended to have them all. The seduction of her husband some nights previous had rewarded her with knowledge that now gave her an advantage and she meant to make full use of it. She had an inkling of her husband's intention that night and reacted to it. The vial she had found in the library did not originally contain brandy as all had thought the following day. But before she had any chance to act on this, Gaston had left on the Monday afternoon for Salon de Provence. Now she would have to await his return and this, to her, was frustrating. She stamped her foot in rage.
"You cannot afford to get yourself so upset, Janis. Not in your condition."
Again she snapped, "Oh for goodness sake, mother, I am with child but a few months, not about to give birth."
"Yes, but still"
"But still, nothing, I am very well, thank you. I just want my husband home."

*

Gaston sighed.
For four hours he had sat listening to them ramble on incessantly. He fidgeted once again on the hard, wooden chair and adjusted his seating position in an attempt to get some life back into his posterior. More importantly, to try and alleviate the irritation that still came from his front, with the rawness of his skin still tender to the touch. Stretching his right hand out, he inspected his nails for the umpteenth time in so many minutes.
"Are we to assume that the authorities will not act upon this concern?"
He hadn't heard the question, assuming that it wasn't directed at him alone. Or if he had, it had exited one ear as quickly as it had entered the other.
"Monsieur, do we have your attention?" barked another.
Lifting his eyes from his cuticles, he looked around the table to see seven other pairs staring directly at him. He feigned vigilance. "Indeed, yes, you have my fullest attention, gentlemen. But until I hear something of the merest import, I will refrain from answering." He stood. "You have dragged me all the way from Paris, on one of the most arduous journeys I have ever had the displeasure of taking I may add, only to hear petty squabbles from town administrators concerning ghosts, goblins and red death."

He watched as the smaller of the two Church officials on his left rose to his feet. "But Monsieur, these are not petty squabbles, as you put it, but facts. This town of Salon and the surrounding countryside have endured, for many years now, the scourge of this demon red spectre. I assure you, it is real."

Gaston wished, as he had done on the previous day, that the long, narrow room in which they now sat had more furnishings or floored fabric of a sort as to absorb the sound. With it being devoid of these fittings, it made every raised voice resonate in the room and into his fragile and aching head, his postprandial over-indulgence with the local brandy the previous evenings being the cause. "And what, pray tell, are you expecting from Paris...an exorcism?"

"May not be a bad idea." He heard one murmur. "Bravo, Francis." Agreed a second.

Gaston made steps around the table, this to exert some authority as to his position and also to get some blood flowing back into his legs. "Oh come now, gentlemen, surely the days of witchcraft and sorcery have long passed us, Loudon and Aix-en-Provence trials lost to our memory."

"This is no mere witch or sorcerer. This is the very devil himself that plagues us."

Gaston had heard all these arguments and counter-arguments the previous day. They were repeating the same thing over and over. "And you still blame Monsieur Notredame?"

"His curse is well known," another spouted.

A curse! What had he gotten himself involved with here, he asked himself. This renowned apothecary and seer of a sort, Michel de Notredame, or later to be called just Nostradamus, had resided and died in this town, then entombed within the vaults of the Church of the Cordeliers...over two centuries ago. And yet these so-called men of authority were blaming this dead man for a sickness or plague which now ravaged their town. How on earth was he to come to a satisfactory decision on this farcical situation? He would have to send word to his superiors in Paris. This would, unfortunately, prolong his stay here as he would have to wait for their response and then act on their decision. As much as he resented the idea of being away from Paris and, in particular, not seeing Madeline, it would give him more time to prepare and organise what he had part-arranged the previous night. He looked across the table and eyed the accomplice in his scheme. This man had given him fresh hope for the future. Given that he had failed dismally in his attempt to poison his mother-in-law and, in addition, Janis's suspicions, he was left with no choice but to get rid of them both. He needed his inheritance to marry Madeline but, furthermore, he needed to be free to do so. Two birds with one stone would do the trick. But first he needed to appease this now, rabble. "Gentlemen, gentlemen, I can see no satisfactory conclusion to this argument, so I, therefore, propose that I inform Paris of the situation. I, myself, freely admit am not the best or qualified person to make this decision. So, in conclusion, I call this meeting to a close."

With murmurs abound, they eventually agreed.
Thank goodness, he thought. He needed the hair of the dog.

Corruption in authority was to be found from its nadir to the highest level in any governing body. Gaston knew this for a fact having risen through the ranks of government, albeit quickly, and seeing it for himself at each level, his superiors being the worst exponents of it. But the man who sat before him was something new to him - a man of the cloth. Was not even the church to be spared dishonesty with coin? It appeared to be a way of life to most now, he suspected.
Raising his glass, he allowed it to be refilled. "Merci."
He eyed, with suspicion, the elderly man who, with a non- participatory brandy himself, sat down opposite. Apparently this man did not imbibe, which in itself would be commendable considering his vocation, but would have been far more worthy of Godly praise had he not been involved with what they were discussing now... the murder of his wife and mother-in-law.
"Then it is agreed. The body will be moved."
Gaston nodded in reassurance. He would make sure of it. "But I still do not see what good it will do. It seemed well protected within the vault as far as I could see."
"Michel was revered many years ago but this new 'curse' has had many wish the body removed from its sepulcher and burned."
Gaston sipped at his brandy. It was very much to his taste and he had committed himself already to taking as much back of this local produce as he could on his return to Paris. "I will not concern myself with where you will take it to be re-interred but only authorise its removal. This is a Church affair anyway, my presence here as government official is not necessary. My request to Paris you know, of course, was mere subterfuge, the reason for which is obvious with our current discussion. Is this your only request?"
"I am out for no financial gain to myself, only to do whatever is necessary to protect Michel's body from harm, but perhaps a contribution to the Church."
The Church! Yes, sure, the Church. Gaston crossed his legs, determined to figure this man out. "But you are advocating murder here, isn't that against your principles, you being a man of God?"
He shook his head. "I am not advocating it, merely pointing you in the direction of one who can assist you."
"Yes, but by association you are still a guilty party."
"Then I will have to justify my actions to the almighty when my time comes... until then."
Until then, you become a rich man. You are fooling on-one, you old codger. But it was worth it. This man was to provide him with a solution to his problem. And what better alibi could he have than to be in Salon, when a person from Salon was visiting Paris and doing the nasty on his behalf. Perfect, he thought.
He finished his brandy... and took another in celebration.

Madeline 3

Chapter 3

Enlightenment from a friend

Madeline watched a small, brown squirrel eagerly gather its forage and make its way back to its home in a beech tree. Her eyes followed it up the side of the trunk, leap from branch to branch before disappearing from view. Seated on the park bench, she waited on Rubin to swallow what was left of his wine before speaking again. He had accompanied her to the park gates where, upon their arrival, Frederick was nowhere to be seen. Either he had given her up as a lost cause after being over thirty minutes late or, like she had considered earlier, it was today's tomorrow. There had been no need to inform Rubin of whom she was meeting. If Fredrick had been there, then she would have thought of something on the spur of the moment. She also had mixed feelings about his non-attendance but before she could contemplate them further, Rubin spoke out.
"We seem to be getting a lot of looks here."
Madeline was only too aware of this - she didn't need him to tell her. Here she was, dressed as such on a pleasant summer's evening, in the company of a battle-scarred, stubble grey-headed, oversized, shabbily dressed individual drinking cheap wine from a casket bottle and spitting indiscriminately onto the ground. Was it any wonder that courting couples and families out for an evening stroll should look upon with amazement at this odd-looking pair seated thus. But somehow Madeline didn't care what they thought, she liked Rubin. Not only was he a guardian of a sort, he was becoming a friend. She turned her head to face him and smiled. "You think so?"
Half-choking in mid-swallow, Rubin stemmed the flow of wine and wiped the residue from his stubble with his coat sleeve. Resting the bottle on the lap of his outstretched legs, he nodded his head as confirmation of her mimicking him. "Hmm, I wonder where I've heard that one before." Changing the subject somewhat, he caught Madeline off guard. "How late were you?"
Without thinking, she replied, "Thirty minutes."
Madeline watched him deliberate over the number.

"Thirty," she repeated. Her shoulders automatically lowered themselves as she sighed. "Oh for goodness sake…eight, eight, eight and six… Rubin, are you sure you can't see past this number? It seems very odd."
He shook his head. "No, it isn't."
Madeline twisted her entire body round on the seat to face him. "Rubin, I can assure you, it is."
"No, it's not. It's even. Eight's an even number."
"Oh, ha-ha, very funny." With a joggle, she resumed her forward facing position and, needlessly adjusting the front of her dress, continued, "And who's to say that I was late for anything anyway?"
"*You* just did."
Oh yes, so she had, 'pooh'. Inwardly kicking herself, she graciously admitted defeat. "Well, it is his loss." Then kicked herself again as she had just revealed the intended meeting was with a man.
Rubin picked up on it straight away. "He?"
Why she was being so elusive or, upon reflection now, her inadvertent lack of it when she knew that Rubin would have seen Frederick if she hadn't stopped in the shop doorway. Whether it had been today or today's tomorrow. "Yes, a 'he', Rubin. Am I to be allowed no privacy in this city?"
Rubin, after taking another swig from his bottle, attempted to placate her. "Monique likes to keep a tight grip on her girls but it's plain to me that you're something special to her. She doesn't have me chasing any of the others around Paris. It would make life more easy for the both of us if you told me where you were going each time you went out, that way we could come to some agreement. As long as I know where you are and who you are with, I can let you have a bit more leeway." He straightened up. "Who was he, do I know him?"
"That would be difficult to tell, Rubin, as I am not entirely familiar with whom you are acquainted."
"You know what I meant. Who is he? Is it old limp… Ramone?"
Madeline remained silent but her head movement indicated to him that he was wrong.
"OK, it's not important. I can't tell Monique what I don't know."
"Frederick. His name is Frederick."
Rubin sat up straight. "Not Rosie's Frederick?" Already knowing the answer. Madeline nodded.
Rubin emptied his bottle and tossed it over his shoulder. "You're not making a lot of friends in this city, little missy. Rosie! Even I would think twice about messin' with that one." Slouching down in the seat, he straightened his legs again and stretched his arms up behind his head. "Got some temper on her she has, our Rosie. I'd be careful with that one. Already doesn't like you."
"'Our Rosie'! How long have you worked for Monique? And I am fully aware of Rosie's dislike for me. She is no different towards me than the others."

Rubin sat unmoving, save suppressing a burp from escaping too loud. "Well?"
He inched his head round. "Well, what?"
"How long have you worked for Monique?"
Breathing inwardly through puckered lips, he pondered her question. How long had it been, he wondered. It seemed a long time now since he had left the army, so, on and off, probably a few years. No, it was more than that he was sure. He leaned to the side and pulled a second bottle from his right-hand pocket and uncorked it. "Longer than I'd want to if I had any choice."
Again she watched him drink and waited until he had finished. She wondered if he ever ate. "Is it because she is a bad employer or is it because you can find no other work?"
"Good or bad, it doesn't matter. Fair or unfair, it doesn't matter either." He raised the bottle. "Her wages keep me in this, that's all. And it's best you don't know what else I do to earn a crust."
"There was no answer in your vague reply, Rubin, about Monique I mean. You can tell me in all assurance that it will go no further than this bench. After all, you know my secrets and I would consider myself a true confidante to a friend."
"You speak some real fancy words for a young'en, missy. Most of the time I don't even know what you're talking about." He drank again. "Hah, I just nod… and I'm your friend now am I…ha-ha."
Madeline noticed he was getting tipsy. "Of course you are my friend, Rubin. You have saved my life on two occasions that I know of and you are still protecting me from harm as we speak. And friends speak to each other."
Rubin sat grinning with the inane look on his face of which only inebriated drunks were capable, but said nothing in response.
"Are you listening to me, Rubin?"
An indistinct muttering came forth from under his breathe, "You're not the first one she's had working for her like you."
Madeline could only make out a few words in his sentence. "You'll have to speak louder and clearer, Rubin, I could make no sense out of what you said there."
Adjusting his seating accordingly in an attempt to make himself more audible to her, he leaned to the side and, bending his free arm back, wrestled to withdraw his sheathed knife from the back of his britches. Resting it on his lap, he sidled in closer. "You're not the first."
Madeline looked down but didn't comment on it. "I'm not the first what, Rubin, first of what?" She now felt that she had to repeat everything to ensure he understood what she was saying. She was also aware of the further attention they were drawing from passers-by, his huge knife being as intimidating as it was.
"Put something in her drink and pilfered the money."
Madeline closed her eyes tightly together in recognition of hearing this. This time she had understood his words perfectly, both auditory and meaning.

And with it, her mind drifted back to her first night in Paris. Had Monique done the same to her? Was this what had made her collapse on the stairway and her money just simply vanish from her cache within the curtain the following day? She presumed so.

Rubin noticed in an instant that this news had struck a chord. "Made her plans well with you, young missy, Monique has. But I don't want to see happen to you what happened to the other one."

Madeline had to sit silent for a moment to take all this in. Her mind worked at speed to see how easily she had been manipulated into Monique's plan. But then again, where would she be now had it not been for this scheme of Monique's coming to fruition? At that time, she had only met Jacob. Her plans to meet and marry a wealthy gentleman had hardly begun when all this had happened. And so easily had she been duped into the life she was leading now. But what of this other that Rubin had spoken of. "Who was this other girl you mentioned? What happened to her?"

As if preparing to relate a person's entire life, Rubin rested on his elbow. "Few years back now. I wasn't doing as much for her, Monique that is, as I do now, just a few errands and the like, and some rowdy customers whose heads needed bashing, that sort of thing. Anyways, little missy appears on the scene, just like you - pretty, young thing from the sticks, some coin but nowhere to stay. Well, Monique ploughs her way right in, doesn't she, gives her a room, the room you're in now, and gets to work on her."

Madeline waited in anticipation as he took another swig from the bottle. This was followed by a burp that was loud enough for all to hear... and react to. He ignored their rants.

"I heard bits of this from the other girls, as well as the ones I seen with my own eyes. What coin this little missy had went right into Monique's box. Left her flat broke." He sat staring at the ground as if trying to remember the rest of the tale.

Madeline grew impatient. "What happened to her, Rubin?"

"Hmm?"

"I asked you what happened to her - the girl?"

Roused from thought, he continued, "Doing what you're doing now. But not with the ones she's got you in tow with, oh no, little missy; got the ones the other girls wouldn't touch. Made a lot of money out of her by all ears, that before…"

"Before, before what, Rubin?"

He sat up and swigged again. "Ah, I shouldn't be telling you this kinda thing." He turned to face her full on. "What is it with you anyway that gets all this out of me?"

Madeline forced a smile and tilted her head to the side. "Friendship."

Rubin could see that she was playing games with him but he knew deep in his heart that she was also taking this information very seriously and wanted to hear more. "She died."

Madeline's head straightened; and the smile was gone. "Died. Died how?"

"You don't need to know that bit, just make sure you don't turn on Monique. You've got yourself in with her now, she's not going to let go of you."

"You can't just leave it like that, Rubin. I need to know how she died... am I in danger?"

Finishing the contents of his second bottle, it found its way in a backwards motion through the air to join its partner on the grass. "Like I said before, be careful of Rosie. Monique can twist a lot of people round to her way of doing things and she doesn't have to do anything. She gets others to it for her. And that means me as well."

"You?"

"Yes, me. Who do you think got rid of the girl's body?" Damn, he thought. She'd led him again. He'd said too much already. Hadn't he silenced Sach for the same thing?

"Why did you have to get rid of the body, Rubin? Wasn't she buried?"

Oh yes, she was buried alright, he thought, buried out of sight of everyone. No mourners at this young girl's funeral. He'd been paid to make sure there wasn't. His mind drifted back to the cold, winter night of her death.

Drinking with Sach at Sally's place, he had just emptied his pocket and finished off the last of their wage on a further bottle. Laying the wine on the table, Sally took the proffered money from him and, looking down at her palm, thanked him for the gratuity and left them to it.

Rubin sighed. "Well, that's the last of it."

Sach lifted the bottle from the table and pulled the cork. "Fuck, that didn't last long. I hope you're not holding out on me, my friend." He filled his glass to the brim.

Rubin leaned across the table and took the bottle from him. "You got your share, and more, so think yourself lucky for what you got." He drunk from the bottle.

"Hey, hey, I trust you. I was kidding, my friend, I was kidding." He raised his glass in friendly salute.

Rubin stretched over to clink the side of the glass with the bottom of his bottle. "More fool you then."

They both laughed.

"A time with Annie, a hot meal each and a few bottles. Not much to show for two day's work is it?"

Rubin shrugged. "If you find anything better, then let me know." He leaned back against the wall and rested his feet on the table. "Fuck, I miss the army, Sach."

"Oh, were you in the army, were you?" He'd heard this from Rubin every day for as long as he'd known him.

Rubin knew the tone. "I know, I've said it before. But at least you knew where you were in the army. Just drifting from day to day like we do now is no good... picking up work here and there. We need a break, something to give us a head start."

Sach emptied his glass and pushed it along the table for a refill. "Like what? Who in this fucking city is going to give us a break? Look at us. We rob, pillage and get all the shit nobody else wants to do. Look at that doctor, what kind of sick bastard is he we work for?"

Rubin obliged with the wine and pushed the glass back, spilling some. His eyes scanned across the room and took in the scene. Most of the patrons were drunk, many of whom were similar to himself and Sach, just drifting from day to day, earning a coin by whichever means they could and squandering their spoils on cheap wine and women. Others, now incapable of application through bloated livers and other alcohol-related illnesses, were content to let their remaining days on earth consist of accepting free drink from their younger counterparts, safe in the knowledge that they had imparted to them all there was to know about city life as a non-entity. All in all, a future with very little hope of change, Rubin thought. You lived hard and you died young, this was life and nothing would change it. He turned and spat on the floor. He was well and truly part of it.

Sach nudged his foot. "Ain't that the young lass from Monique's?"

Rubin, pulled from thought, scanned the room not knowing what he was looking for. His eyes stopped at the entrance. There, leaning half in and half out at the doorway, stood Bella, the young maid to Monique. Waving her hand frantically inwards, she beckoned him over.

"Looks like she's after you," Sach added, "And a pretty young thing with it; you've done well there, my friend."

"Shut up." Rubin stood and made for the door, knowing full well that Bella would not even consider entering.

She made a short curtsy on his arrival. "Forgive me, monsieur, but I have been asked by Madame if you would come to the house at once."

"Why, what's wrong?"

Bella shook her head. "Please, monsieur, she did not tell me, but said to tell you that it was a matter of great concern."

"Uh-huh." Rubin turned and with a curt nod to Sach, bade him adieu. He noticed the wry smirk on his face in recognition that he now had the remainder of the wine to himself and by raising the bottle aloft, Sach sent the message home to him.

'Bastard'.

The ferocity of the winter's night cut into their faces as they negotiated their way through the howling wind and snow; and after fifteen minutes of bitter cold they eventually reached the warm haven of Monique's house.

They stood in the hallway, soaked. "There's no need, Bella, I know the way."

With a further curtsy, she hastily headed for the kitchen, removing her damp over-garments on the way. Rubin stamped his feet and shook down his own snow-covered coat. He noticed the mess he was leaving on the floor. 'Fuck it', he thought. Heading along the narrow hall towards Monique's sitting

room, he had only reached mid-point before the door was pushed open. It was Monique.
"Rubin. Good, you've arrived."
He nodded in salutation "Yes ma'am. But what's all the worry?"
She brushed passed him towards the stairway. "This goes no further than here, Rubin. You understand?"
He shrugged. "Sure, but…" He assumed she wanted him to follow her as she turned and rushed up the stairs "…what's the matter?"
"Hush now."
He remained silent as he followed her up to the second floor and along the hall towards the last door at the end. He sniffed. The potent smell of eau de toilette and other herbal scents filled the air, and was enough to make his unaccustomed eyes sting.
Monique stood at the door and with a stern face, which Rubin had very rarely seen on her, spoke out, "You will be paid handsomely for this, Rubin. I trust I can hold you to your word that what you see and do will never be repeated to anyone?"
Rubin stood speechless. Not many people in this world asked him to keep his word let alone consider him worthy of having one to keep. He nodded. "Sure."
She opened the door... and immediately held her kerchief to her face.
Rubin, in an instant, could tell why. The smell was nauseating. He understood now the need for the scent in the hallway, it was to disguise what lay within the room. The odour of death and human waste filled his nostrils and he watched as Monique wretched repeatedly in reaction to this. But to Rubin this was nothing new, he had smelled this many times before. His eyes were drawn at once to the bed and the blood-covered body that lay spread out upon it. He knew now what was required of him. Taking charge of the situation, he pulled Monique in and closed the door behind them. "We need to get some air in here." With haste, he crossed the room and pulled open the window to full extent and let the cutting wind blast its way into the room. As a result, it extinguished the bedside candle and with it being the room's solitary source of light, now plunged them into darkness. With a faint illumination from the street, Rubin could just see his way across the room and approached Monique. "Go downstairs. I'll do what's needed. You don't have to see this."
Monique nodded. "Thank you, Rubin. I'll…"
Rubin knew what she was about to say. "We'll talk about that later. Now go."
Monique thanked him again and, on opening the door, peaked out. Satisfied that no-one was about, she exited.
Left to his own devices, Rubin pulled the collar of his coat up and walked towards the bed. Holding the sides together at his neck, he squinted down through the semi-darkness and grimaced. Where once lay a youthful smile upon a woman's face, there was now the look of sheer terror. She had been

tortured before death he was sure. With one eye having been unceremoniously removed from its socket and placed on the pillow beside her, the remaining one appeared to be staring out into the vast nothingness of space. Her entire face had twisted in agony. He released the grip on his collar and bent down to untie the blood-soaked gag from her mouth. This, he surmised, had been placed there to suppress her screams. But as he pulled it loose, three of her teeth came with it, them being stuck within a thick brown mess he knew in an instant to be faeces.
"Wow!"
He pulled back in shock.
'Jeezus, this was one sick fuck,' he thought. 'She must have choked to death on the bastard's own shit.'
He'd seen a lot of cruel things in his life but this was the sign of a madman. No-one got sexual pleasure from this kind of thing. His thoughts on this were reinforced when his eyes ran down the length of her naked body. Her breasts had been hacked at by a sharp blade, he noticed, and as he continued on down, he stopped at her thighs. There, protruding from the girl's middle passage, stuck the hilt of a knife which was similar in size to the one he, himself, owned; and, aware of its length, knew exactly how many inches of blade lay penetrated within. Between this and choking to death, this young missy, he thought, must have died in agony.
But he was thinking too much, he needed to act fast. He had a job to do. Monique wanted rid of the body and it was his job to do so. And like she had said, she would pay him well for this service... and his silence. Her place of trade was well known to the authorities but through her cunning and deceit and with corrupt officials never in short supply, it remained unscathed by the system. But a body, especially one in such condition as this, would bring too much unwanted attention to her business which, over the years, she had striven to remain elite to the privileged few. He was also aware of the fact that whoever had done this was one of standing and he would, in the course of things, be paying Monique for her silence and cover up. It riled him how the upper class appeared immune to the penal system when the low life would immediately have been sent for the chop. He set himself to task but found it hard work given the lack of light. He would miss something, he was sure. So, raising himself, he made for the window, and crouching down for fear of being seen, pushed it shut and drew the curtains. Using his old army tinderbox, he re-lit the candle by the bed.
… And recoiled with a start.
What he had seen in the dim light before had been bad enough but to see it in full light made his eyes widen. The entire bed, in the body's immediate vicinity, was soaked in deep red and the sheets soiled with the young woman having emptied both bowels and bladder during her struggle. He shook his head. How in the name of god was he to get rid of all this lot without been noticed? Where to begin? He looked at the knife. That would be a good start, he thought - the sight of it vexed him.

Gripping the handle, he slowly pulled it from her but as hard as he tried to prevent it, the blade's honed-edge caused further lacerations as it slid free. Using a clean part of the sheet, he wiped it free of blood and sat studying it for a moment. Although not an uncommon blade, he did notice some unique features about it. Little things that the untrained eye would miss, a distinguishing mark here and there that would make it stand out amongst others. But he did not have time for further scrutiny, so he laid it on the bedside cabinet. He would give it a more detailed examination later. The knife was the least of his worries. Looking at the mess around him, he pondered his next move, which was the body. He suddenly remembered the curtains that he had just drawn.

Pulling the thick, tie-back cords from both, he would utilise these for binding the body once he had wrapped it up in the sheets. At least that way he would have more control over it when lugging it down through the house and into the street. He stretched to pull the further end of the sheet over her body but then noticed the eye. What would he do with this? What could he do with it? Try and stick it back into the eyehole. He certainly did not savour the thought of that and even as hardened an ex-soldier as he was, he had always had an aversion with anything to do with eyes, especially his own. It normally took him all his time just to clear a piece of dust from his own, flinching even at the sense of his finger nearing it. But his quandary was short-lived when he looked at the empty socket once again. He leaned closer. He hadn't noticed it before but there appeared to be some sort of clear, whitish fluid at its base... and then it struck him... it was of a consistency known only too well to every male.

He pulled back.

"Fuck, surely not." Was this the reason he had removed the eye? Jeezus. Hadn't this sick bastard been content with the holy trinity of holes like any normal man? He, himself, in the past had committed a lot of vicious crimes, particularly in his army days when torturing the enemy for information, but to do this to a woman for pleasure was even beyond his understanding. Plus, there was something else here that didn't sit right with him, something about the whole twisted face that seemed wrong somehow, but he couldn't put his finger on it. His eyes scanned every detail of her face and injuries again and as he reached her neck, it dawned on him. He leaned closer, and there it was…a small cut. Insignificant compared to her horrendous others but a cut just the same and deep enough to cause permanent scarring. He was proficient enough to know knife injuries, having carried one for so long and done serious damage before with the same, but this was no blood-letting cut, there was another reason for this. He sat up and considered this fact.

During a particularly ferocious battle in Spain, he had been fortunate enough to witness a rather unorthodox procedure of saving a man's life. As this soldier lay choking on his own blood, a physician of sort had placed the tip of his knife to the man's throat and pushed hard. The resulting hole in his windpipe letting the man breathe. Later, a hot iron sealed the wound and the

man lived to fight another battle. But this surely could not be the case here. Why would anyone gag a person and cut a hole in their neck to allow them to breathe when they could still use their nose. It made no sense. That was until he thought of the alternative. The physician had explained this to him. Along with the windpipe allowing a person to breathe, within the throat was a passage allowing words to come out from the mouth. A carefully selected point at the throat could prevent this. 'One wrong placement of the knife could cause a fatal mistake This would not allow the person to breathe but rather take their voice from them for good,' he remembered him saying. Was this the reason then, to stop her from calling out, take her voice from her? If so, then why gag her? His mind came to no conclusion and, along with the knife, would be thought about later. He still had to get rid of the body.
He looked at the eye again. Fuck it, he thought. Grabbing it, he shoved it into his coat pocket. He'd dump it later with the rest of her.

Madeline nudged his side. "What's so funny, Rubin?"
"Ummm!" He opened his eyes and shook life back into his head.
"You were smiling to yourself and then laughed out."
Searching on his person for his wine, he remembered he'd finished it.
Madeline confirmed this. "You have finished off both bottles, Rubin. That is, unless you have a wine cellar in your pocket."
His pocket, ah yes. He remembered now, that's why he had laughed out. Getting the body down the stairs had been no easy task, so, given that the snow on the ground was several inches deep, he had chosen the easy option. He had used one of the curtains to wrap her body in, so, dropping it from the window, he'd known that the padding of the fresh snow would cushion its fall. And given that no sane person would be outdoors in such inclement weather, there would be hopefully no witnesses to see him do this. Even if there were, he doubted that anyone would have taken the time to ponder what it was, instead running for shelter. It had only taken him an hour to reach his chosen spot, dig the grave and return to the house. He'd cleaned up the mess and returned the room back to its every day look, after which Monique had filled both his hands with coin.
Returning to Sally's place, he had been surprised to see Sach still there, considering they had spent all their money earlier. What had made him laugh out was remembering that he'd forgotten about the eye in his pocket. Later on in the evening when they were both drunk, he had dropped it into to Sach's drink when he wasn't looking. He laughed out loud again, remembering his reaction.
"It is, indeed, a mirthful thought you are thinking, Rubin. Would you care to share what you find so humorous about me asking why you had to get rid of her body?"
In retrospect, it wasn't funny, he thought. The young girl had suffered badly and at the hands of a vicious, cold-blooded murderer. One, who had escaped punishment for their act and who was still free to do so again. He knew

Annie was always at risk with her customers and he had sought to protect her from harm but he couldn't be with her all the time. It was one of the hazards of the thrust-upon-her profession. And as were true of the young woman who now sat beside him. "Just the wine, little missy." He burped. "Just the wine."

*

Madeline 3

Chapter 4

Concerns

"Why are you back here so soon anyway? You said you had the afternoon off, that you were meeting someone."
Frederick remained silent, deep in thought.
Adjusting his bed sheet, Jacob attentively smoothed it down. "Not that I'm complaining mind you, the days drag in here without company." He looked around the ward. "And this lot, huh, I've had better conversations with a cabbage."
Frederick couldn't hear his brother speak, there was voice, yes, but his words were lost to him, his mind elsewhere.
"One of which you, yourself, appear to be doing a good impression."
With his sole reaction to this semi-mordant insult being to lean forward and scratch at his leg, his mind and voice were still unresponsive.
Jacob sighed. "Riveting company, I must say." He lifted his book and left him to it.
Frederick's mind pondered the earlier scenario. Why had Rubin been with her? He had repeated this same question in his mind during his wandering of the streets and his eventual return to the hospital. Surely he had made it clear to Madeline in his letter that their meeting was to remain secret. If Rubin knew about it then other people would have found out too. He had specifically selected that particular park as it was a place where he knew that they could blend in with the crowd and, more importantly, a place where Rosie and the other girls very seldom, if at all, frequented. He had waited with impatience and baited breath for a full half hour after their arranged time. And in addition to this, with him arriving thirty minutes beforehand, he had spent one of the longest hours of his life preparing his dialogue. He had felt himself a nervous wreck. How do you tell one of the most beautiful women in Paris that you had fallen in love with them after just a few days? If this had not been bad enough, he feared the worst with her reaction? He scratched at himself once again.

Lifting his eyes from the page, Jacob commented, "Is that where you cut your leg?"
This time Frederick did hear him. "Yeah, it's as itchy as hell."
Jacob rested the opened book on his lap. "Is that a sign of it healing or, considering that you treated it yourself, an infection spreading?"
Knowing only too well that he should have had it tended to by one of the staff, in his obstinacy he had treated it himself thinking it was trivial. But in the last twenty-four hours he had found himself limping. His stubbornness shone through once again. "It'll be alright."
"For goodness sakes, Frederick, you're in a hospital here. At least get it seen to." He looked around him once again. "Mind you, considering what maladies we are in the midst of here, it's a true miracle I am still lying here with only the broken bones I arrived with as an ailment."
"Who's being pigheaded now? You don't have to stay here. You and your bloody principles, you know father can afford much better care for you if you'd let him."
Slipping his page marker between the pages, Jacob closed the book. "I am not going down that road with you again, brother. All I am saying is that you should get the cut looked at."
"Okay, okay. Just let it rest, will you?"
Jacob sat up. "What is the matter with you? You appeared earlier today wearing your best suit of clothes, all full of worldly cheer and you return here hours later as if that same world had chewed you up and spat you out."
Frederick blurted out, "You fucking know why."
A passing nurse overheard. "Frederick!"
He put his hand up in apology. "Sorr..eee."
Jacob had surmised as much but had said nothing. "Have you fallen out with your little woman, is that it?"
Frederick shook his head. "We didn't even meet to fall out; she didn't turn up." Which was in part lie, he knew.
"Oh!"
"Yes, oh. Perhaps now you know the reason for my mood." This more statement than question.
"I can understand your disappointment but I assume she would have a plausible reason for her not appearing. I take it you were exact on the time and place of your meeting?" This in return being more a question rather than a declaration of his brother's stupidity.
"Yes. Four o'clock... at night."
"At night?"
"Yes. At night...four o'clock. Today."
"Frederick, no-one says four o'clock at night, well not unless you are a complete fool, its four o'clock in the afternoon."
Raising the leg of his britches, he scratched again. "What bloody difference does it make? I'm not meaning four in the morning when it's dark at night, am I? I mean four at night when it's light in the day."

Jacob shook his head. "Frederick, I really wonder about you sometimes."
"Why, what do you mean?"
"With a statement like that, I'm not surprised she didn't appear."
"Well she did, alright." Damn it!
"What do you mean, she did?
He had foolishly let that one slip. "She didn't see me. I was hiding."
"This gets better all the time. You arranged to meet a woman at four o'clock at night and then hide from her?"
"She was late, okay."
"That doesn't mean to say that you hide from her, just because she's late. What kind of stupid thing was that to do?"
Frederick shrugged. Not wanting Jacob to know the whole truth, he'd rather appear the fool than give a whole explanation as to his reasons.
"And?"
"And what?"
"What did you do?"
"I left, came back here."
"You just left her there, wherever... and you expect her to see you again after that, do you? I bloody wouldn't."
"Yes, well you're not her, are you? She'll see me again."
"Too right I'm not, and wouldn't want to. What will you do the next time, wear a disguise?"
"Okay, I've had enough of this." As he wrestled to raise himself from the three-legged stood, Frederick buckled to the left and collapsed to the floor. Jacob had noticed that it was his injured leg that had given way under him. "Nurse!"

It was fortunate for Fredrick that the occupant of the bed next to Jacob had died the previous night thus allowing the nurses to lift him on to it. As he stretched over with his own restrictions, Jacob vied for a better vantage point through the gap of the two who attended him. "Check out his leg, he cut it some time back."
With one of them crossing to the opposite side, he could see better now. "The fool treated it himself. He was complaining about it itching." Aware of the sibling concern, the senior of the two replied with reassurance, "Right, Jacob, we hear you. Let's just remove these and see what we've got, shall we."
With her unbuckling his britches' belt, Frederick was having none of it. "Get off, there's nothing wrong with me, I just slipped."
"Let me be the judge of that, Frederick. Now be a good boy and lay still." This, to others, may have sounded patronising but Jacob knew it was through concern as Frederick was much liked amongst the nursing staff.
Giving up, Frederick let them remove his britches and once off both nurses looked down at the amateur swathing. It should have appeared an off-white colour but it was stained jet black.

"Oh dear, that's not good."

*

"All dolled up to the nines 'e was. Best bid and tucker."
Rosie climbed into her frightful orange-coloured dress and hauled it up over her enormous frame. Pushing her mammoth breasts into the top, she joggled them home. "My Frederick?"
Charlotte, seated on the edge of Rosie's bed with a plate of food on her lap, tore at the bread. "Never seen him looking so well dressed."
"Why the hell would he be all dressed up working at the hospital?"
Charlotte shook her head, her mouth now too full of bread and ham to answer.
"Strange."
"Mm-hm." Forcing her words out in mid-mastication from the corner of her packed mouth, Charlotte spat half the food in mid-speech. "Got himself a limp as well." Casually picking a weevil from her tooth, she nodded at Rosie. "Your doing, was it?"
"What do you mean, my doing? I haven't seen him for a few days now."
"Just thought... after the eye you gave 'im."
Rosie sat down next to her and fastened up her boots. "Unless he was visiting someone."
"He works in the damn place, so he could see whoever he wants all day long."
Rosie nodded in agreement. "Yeah, but maybe someone died. You dress up for that, don't you?"
Ramming more food into her already bulging mouth, Charlotte retorted, "Hah! In that place, where more people die than come out alive? He'd be dressed like that all the time then."
Rosie sat up and helped herself to a piece of ham from the plate. "Well, what do you think he was doing then?"
Charlotte stuck her hand into her plunging neckline and pulled out a thin, tin flask. "Open your eyes, Rosie. What do you think?"
Rosie watched as Charlotte uncapped the top and drank from it. "You'll get hell for that if she finds out. You know Monique doesn't like us to drink while working."
"Fuck Monique." She recapped the top and placed it on the bed. "What other reason do men get themselves all dollied up for?"
Rosie replied with the most obvious answer she could think of. "Courting."
"Exactly."
"But I haven't seen him today. He knows I'm working tonight."
"He was leaving the place when I was going in to see Michelle and the new one. That was hours ago. If he was coming here to see you then he would have been here by now, wouldn't he?"
"Then where was he going?"

Totally out of character, Charlotte laid an unfinished meal to the side of the bed. "Look, Rosie, you're my best friend and I don't want to see you hurt, but …"
Rosie rose to her feet in temper. "Don't say it, don't even fucking say it."
"I know what you're thinking…"
"It's that fucking bitch, Madeline, isn't it?"
"Now I didn't say that, only…"
Rosie grabbed the flask from the bed and undid the top. "You don't have to say it, I know." Breaking the house rules, she drank her fill. "He's changed since he met her. He hardly comes near me now." She drank again.
Charlotte leaned forward and took it from her. "Well, we have been busy."
"Not that busy. We don't work all day."
Stuffing the flask back into her dress, Charlotte lifted the plate and resumed its rightful place on her lap. "We work all night and you sleep most of the day, so when is he meant to see you, when he's at work?"
"That's never stopped us in the past." Stamping her foot down hard, Rosie stood with crossed arms. "Fucking Madeline. And I can't get near to the little cow."
Chewing at the bread again, Charlotte spat out more of the offending black beetles onto the floor. "There's more bugs in this thing than bread." Raising the plate, she offered Rosie the remainder of the ham.
Rosie looked at it and shook her head.
It was gone in one bite. "Didn't think you'd want to get near to her anyway."
Rosie had suspected Frederick herself and had promised that she would get back at Madeline the best way she could. 'Pretty thing, was she?' Well, she would have that prettiness taken from her. The only thing standing in her way was Rubin. He followed her everywhere. So until he was out of the way for a while, her counterpart in her scheme would have to bide his time. "Not me, someone else."
"Oh, Rosie, what are you up to?"
There was no time for Rosie to answer. The bedroom door was pushed opened and there, leaning half-drunk against the side panel, stood a portly, middle-aged man of both their acquaintance. "Rosie, Rosie."
Her first customer of the night, Rosie lowered her head and sighed.
Charlotte nudged her side. "Well, I'll leave you to it."
Noticing her raise herself from the bed to leave, Rosie's client approached her while unbuckling his belt. "Stay, Charlotte. Stay with us and watch." He freed a hand and tapped at the money purse hanging from his side. "Plenty of coin for both."
Charlotte met him midway into the room and, without stopping, raised her hand to pat his cheek. "Got cock of my own to take care of, sweetie." She raised her arm as she exited the door. "Have fun."
Retracing his steps, he back-heeled the door shut. "Looks like it's just the two of us then, Rosie."

She leaned over and pulled a soiled cloth from the dresser. She threw it across the room at him. "Well clean yourself first. I'm not putting that fucking thing in my mouth again if it's as bad as the last time."

*

Madeline 3

Chapter 5

Duties of Employment

In complete contrast to many of the bedrooms upstairs, Monique sat in the plush surroundings and comfort of her sitting room. Seated in her favourite armchair, she looked on at the young woman standing half-dressed before her. "Okay, that looks fine. Now remove the rest."
With her partiality towards women rather than men, Monique always savoured the moments when she inspected a new girl that had come into her fold. This was no exception. Tall, slender and dark-haired, she was satisfied that this new one would increase her income even more. And she needed new girls. Business had never been so good and she was not about to let possible custom slip through her hands. Supply and demand had been her motto for many a time now. Picking her teacup up from the side table, she gracefully sipped at its edge as she watched her latest acquisition undress. And when fully naked, she now stood upright, unashamedly baring all.
"Hmmm." As with a high percentage of women theses days, she thought, they looked better figured with the tight restrictions of clothes upon them. Once unclad, then nature appeared to take its true course and let all wilt freely to the floor. What had looked like full upright breasts within her corset, now looked like twinned wine bags hanging from a mule. Her sagging belly gave signs of childbirth. "You have been with child before?"
She nodded. "I have two children. Yes."
The feeding of her offspring explained her breasts but this was not what bothered Monique, what did was her concern for her tightness down below. Men needed a firm hold around them when inside the woman and she knew only too well that this could be a liability in this woman's case. But being only eighteen, she may have resumed her natural form. She would have to check for herself. Replacing the cup on the table, Monique beckoned her nearer. "Turn around."
With her posterior on show, Monique gave further instruction. "Lean forward."

Dipping her middle and index finger into her tepid tea, she flicked off the residue. Then, having pulled the left buttock cheek to the side and slowly inserting both fingers into the young girl, she was pleasantly surprised with the tight grip upon them. She smiled to herself. Satisfied with the outcome, she remained unmoving for an instant, basking in the moment. But not wanting to appear appreciative of the delights she had just enjoyed at this woman's expense, she withdrew. "Bravo, my dear. Not so many women regain themselves thus after childbirth."
Turning around, the young woman thanked her. "Merci, Madame."
Monique tilted her head to the side. "What is this?" She hadn't noticed it before but there was a scar on her right side just above the thigh.
She bowed her head in shame. "A bad man."
Monique knew what she meant. These were the dangers of life on the street in their profession. "Very well, but you need not worry about that here, this place is quite safe."
Smiling in the recognition that she had just been accepted to work in the house, she thanked her now new employer once again.
Monique returned the smile. "You can put your clothes on now."
In the midst of dressing, Monique explained to her the rules of the house and, most importantly, the remittance expected from her labours. "As you have lodgings of your own outwith this house, a resident room will not be required. But the daily rental of one used in the course of your duties will be deducted from your wage, as will all amenities available to you for everyday use. I, and I alone, receive the payments from the clients and you will be paid accordingly. Any additional payments offered by them during the course of your service will not be permitted. If they require further indulgence on what had originally been agreed, then the negotiations of such will be done by me and me alone. Is that understood? There will be no deviations from this rule and if broken, you will be removed from the premises never to return."
Her dressing complete, the young woman sat opposite where told. Remaining silent and subservient, she nodded in acceptance.
Without prelude, Monique got straight to business. "Now, what can you do; what have you done; what have you allowed to be done to you; and, most importantly, what are you now prepared to do to earn your wage here?" Monique needed specifics if she was to offer an array of services to her clients and she categorised each of her girls according to her proficiency. From the norm to the utterly sublime, she catered for all tastes.
"I will do whatever is needed to feed my children, Madame."
"Hmm, these children of yours, my dear, the unwanted results from your past labours I presume?" Monique had, in the past, lost a number of her girls through unwanted pregnancy but, as was expected, they had returned to her soon thereafter. Indeed, one had actually stayed on until her time, this to cater for several of her clients who took pleasure in the form of a mother-to-be.
"Both have the same father."

Monique eyed her with suspicion. She had deliberated over a very straightforward question, she thought, her reply ambiguous. It was either yes or no. She pushed for clarity. "It was lax of you to allow yourself to fall pregnant, or indeed unfortunate, but to repeat the mistake with the same individual was plain foolhardiness. Precautions have to be taken, my dear."
Once again, as before, she bowed her head. But it remained as it was. "It was not of my own doing, Madame."
"Come, come, my dear, surely you have to know when a man has reached his zenith? These men pay for your body, the consequences of which are of no concern to them. It is your responsibility to prevent this from happening." Why she was lecturing this young woman on things that in her profession she should know, was beyond her, having in the past neither cared whether any of her girls got pregnant nor concerned for their well-being afterwards. She would just replace them or accept them back on their return. But this tall, dark-haired beauty was hiding something. "How old are your children?"
Surprised with Monique's concern, she looked up and, without thought, replied, "Four and two."
Monique sat back and considered the odds. A two year gap between men and this same person was the father to both children. Hardly likely she thought. "Tell me, my dear, where exactly did you ply your trade prior to coming here?"
Silence.
"Come, come, now."
Yet again, her head looked to the floor. "Please, Madame. I have no trade." She fidgeted with her hands. "The father of my children..."
Monique sat forward. "Yes. Go on."
"The father of my children is ..." She raised a clenched fist to her lips.
"... my own father."

Having explained to Monique that her father had repeatedly raped her from an early age and that the wound on her side was where he had held the knife as he did so, she went further as to describe his demise. She had pierced his heart with the very same blade. Furthermore, with her mother dying several years previous, it had left only herself and her older sister at the farm. After burying his body, they had hastily gathered what belongings they could and travelled to Paris to elude capture. Fortunate for them, their father had just collected payment for his produce and although it being just a small holding, they had sufficient funds to find lodgings. But with four mouths to feed, their money was now running low, forcing her to do what she was doing now... attempting to find work at Monique's house.
"Please forgive me, Madame, I did not mean to deceive you. I have not had the experience of men for payment but my father forced me to do many things to him. These things I can do now for other men. That is, if you would still allow me the chance to prove myself."

Never the sentimentalist for a sob story, as she had heard them all before, Monique was a business woman and if she had taken on board everyone's troubles then she would be poor herself. But, business was business. She saw no reason why this woman shouldn't work for her. Granted she had, through cunning, wormed her way in but good for her, she thought, it showed initiative. Not that she wished this virtue instilled in any of her employees, she liked them acquiescent to her demands alone. Plus, this was a mother who was desperate. If she refused, she knew this woman would find her way onto the streets and that would be a great loss to her own clients. Like Madeline, she was of country stock and therefore needed to be tailored into Parisian fashion. With a little rouge on her face and proper clothing, she would be a welcome addition to her now ever-increasing stock. She didn't have many girls with her height, so variety had been expanded upon. But first, she needed more information on her family.

"What of your sister. Did your father not prey upon her also?"

With immodest retort, she shook her head, "No. My father only liked the pretty ones."

This woman had confidence in her own self as well. "She will tend to the children when you are here?"

"Oui, Madame, this will never interfere with my work. I promise."

And she appeared to have all the right answers. "Very well, but I want you attired more befitting your trade. I do not want my customers thinking I was giving them a dairy maid as an outlet for their lust."

She beamed. "Madame, if I work for you I will not need many clothes."

Monique saw the funny side of her intentional but respectful pun, and laughed aloud. "Bravo, my dear, bravo."

But this was short lived when she asked the young woman's name.

Her new employee smiled back at her.

"My name is Monique."

*

Not anymore it isn't.

'Monique', indeed!

This was her own name alone and no-one else's. Taken for herself on her initial arrival in Paris many years back, she had chosen this name from the Greek *monos* meaning 'one' because she had been determined to reach the top. And her aspirations to be *Madame* to the French elite, its Latin equivalent *moneo* meaning 'advisor', set in place her aim. She would oversee, advise upon and run her own house with others doing the work for her. And she had achieved all that she had set out to do. So it was hardly likely that she was going to share her name with a common whore from the country. This young woman had been told in no uncertain terms that, during her time at the house, she was to be called Monica. This, she thought, had been a fair compromise considering she could have demanded that she work under a different name. Enquiring as to her financial position, Monica had explained her circumstances, stating that the four had enough money to survive but she would be struggling to have the money to buy some new clothes, as was required. Therefore, an advance on her wage had been presented after Monique had taken note of her lodgings' address. She was to begin a life on her back the following evening.

There was a light tap on the door and, upon it opening slightly, she saw, to her delight, Madeline's face peak round its edge. "Bonjour…" Looking to see that she was alone, she continued, "…Monique. Peux-je entrer?" Monique beckoned her in. "Oui, bien sûr."

Assuming that the invitation to enter included sitting, she seated herself opposite Monique. "It is a beautiful evening outside, far too nice to be sat indoors, Madame."

"Oh, you have just arrived? I presumed you were leaving for your appointment with Ramone."

"He cancelled our dinner arrangement. He is poorly I think."

Monique had presumed as much when she saw Madeline leave the house earlier that afternoon alone. Too early for an evening's repast, she had thought, plus she knew that Ramone would have collected her by carriage and not merely arranged to meet her somewhere. She had been unable to confirm this until now as Ramone's wax seal had prevented her from opening his letter. But Bella had also given her Fredrick's note. He had stupidly entrusted her housemaid to slip the note under Madeline's door but having strict instructions that any missives addressed to Madeline come directly to her first, she had read it beforehand. This Frederick was, indeed, the fool she had always taken him to be; his writing immature, his intentions, although admirable, pie in the sky. Who did he think he was to even consider himself an aspirant for Madeline's affections? She was preening Madeline for much better things than a marriage to a mere casual worker. And although she knew his family to be of middle class, this still did not prevent her from such match-making. Her goal was to procure a great sum of money with Madeline and her plans, thus far, had gone well. She had isolated her from the other girls by showing far her too much attention and appearing to give her free rein. This may have appeared the case to others but she was manipulating Madeline's life for her own gain. And Rosie was fulfilling all her wishful thinking as well. It would only be a matter of time before she found out about their romantic tryst.

"Then what have you done with yourself in its stead?" She was curious to see what answer she would reply.

"I went for a long walk to the park at the edge of the city, the one towards the palace. The air is far more breathable there. The city, I fear, is now worse than I remember when I first arrived."

And was getting worse by the day, Monique thought. The population of Paris had increased ten-fold since her own arrival in Paris many years back. This now meant ten times more human waste for the streets to devour and the

same amount of corpses to fill the very few cemeteries of the city. Thus, the Seine and the very streets that the people walked upon were strewn with small pox, syphilis and typhoid-ridden bodies. It was hardly any wonder the air was so fetid. Furthermore, the tannery on the opposite end emitted smells which had the local residents dropping like flies. And with the animal entrails being, with casual indifference, thrown into the river, this added more stench and decay. The Seine was Paris's only source of water and people were expected to drink from it. A high percentage tried to refrain from this, preferring wine or ale as a substitute for their daily intake of liquids. But water was free, whereas wine and ale wasn't; and coin was not easily available to most, therefore crimes had to be committed to gain some. The entire city was on a downward spiral and it was for this reason that she very seldom ventured outdoors, preferring her comforts within. She knew that it was only a matter of time before the people of the city revolted against these conditions, when just outside the city boundary sat the splendour of *Chateau de Versailles* - a palace where they knew their King held sway over his crumbling city and his decadence and wastefulness widely known to them. It was to this end that she needed now to act quickly. Given this occurrence, her wealth and property would be stripped from her and this she was not prepared to give up lightly. She had worked too hard for it. Her plans were in motion and Madeline had a large part to play in them. She had already introduced her to Caroline and thus one more rung on the aristocratic ladder had been attained. Aware of her extravagant orgies, having participated in several in the past herself, she knew that Caroline and, in particular, her husband, Denig, would pay a King's ransom for such a delightful creature as Madeline. With their predilection for the deflowering of the chaste known only too well to her, she knew her demands would be met unconditionally. This, after she had informed Caroline that Madeline had not yet started to bleed. Her curiosity in this matter had clenched the deal. In addition to this, a certain acquaintance of all would be in their midst beforehand, if not already, and she was certain, if all went as she thought, then more coin would be making its way to her very soon. Patience had always been one of her virtues, so she just had to sit back and await the outcome of her scheming. In the meantime, she had Madeline's charming company all to herself and her mind had drifted off the subject somewhat.
"As you have the night free, and the girls are to their duties, would you care to join me in a glass of wine? I have recently obtained a new one which has just arrived from *Champagne*, and I, myself, have not yet partaken of it. Perhaps we may share the experience together?"
Madeline smiled. "Merci, Monique, but I have not, as yet, eaten, the cancelled appointment with Ramone having put pay to this."
"Splendid. Then we shall have an aperitif and dine together here." With her initial invitation to join her for a drink now transferred into an insistence they share food, Monique rose from her chair to fetch the wine.

"Please, Monique." Madeline leaned forward and placed her hand on Monique's lap. "Allow me."
As she watched the graceful movement of Madeline's body move toward the drinks' cabinet, Monique sat in awe of her demeanor. Oh, if only, if only? If only she had her youth again and if only Madeline cared about her in the way she did for her, heaven would have, indeed, opened its doors to her. That simple touch of her hand on her lap had meant everything to her, bringing rivers of joy into her very being.
The wine having been decanted beforehand by one of the staff, it took Madeline little effort but to pour out two glasses. "Please, Monique. Have you someone new working for you?"
"Why, my dear, what makes you ask that?"
Madeline made her way towards the chair and proffered the wine. "Oh nothing, it's just that I met a woman leaving the house as I was coming in. And she smiled at me."
"She smiled?"
Madeline reseated herself as before. "I know that may sound silly to you but none of the others have done that to me before. I was pleasantly surprised. She looked nice."
She would find out soon enough so there was little point in keeping it from her. "She starts tomorrow."
Madeline sipped at her wine. "May I ask her name?"
"Monica."
"Oh."
Monique watched as Madeline deliberated over the similarities in name; and eventually speak out.
"It is very…"
"I am aware of that, my dear, but I assure you they are worlds apart." Madeline grinned. "I meant nothing by…"
"I am sure you did not, my dear. Now hush and savour your wine."
Madeline sipped again but having the youthful impatience with silence, spoke out again, "Does she have a room here?"
Monique tried hard to quash her sentiment. Knowing that having isolated Madeline from the other girls, she was desperate for female friendship. With Ramone, and now possibly Frederick, being her only allies in Paris, save Caroline perhaps, it was only natural that Madeline craved the companionship of someone her own sex and age. Her mixed feelings towards this young woman had her mind in a spin. And not for so many years now had she been in such a dilemma. She could see the anticipation of an affirmative reply in Madeline's face. "No, my dear, she has lodging elsewhere."
Madeline shrugged. "Oh well, but we can still be friends I'm sure."
Taken on the chin with such gusto, Monique was surprised with her reaction. "You are not disappointed?"

"This day has been full of disappointments. Why should I let another upset me."

"Your dinner with Ramone, you mean?"

"Well, that and amongst other things."

Her meeting Frederick, she assumed. She would find out more from Rubin tomorrow.

Madeline sat upright. "Monique."

This was said in such a fashion that she knew a question was to follow. "Yes."

"What are your plans for me? I mean, for the future."

Monique sat stunned. Had this girl just read her mind? If she had so, then she wouldn't be seated opposite asking her, she would be out the door within minutes. "Haven't I made this clear to you already?"

"Yes, but I seem to be making little if any headway in the direction that you described when we first spoke about it."

"In which respect my dear?"

"Satisfying men. Like the other girls."

Monique had just recovered from the first shock when she was hit with this one. "You have been satisfying men in your own way. I can assure you that the gentlemen you have been entertaining have commented upon this. Some men enjoy the company of a pretty woman and there is not always the need for physical contact. I have specifically chosen these individuals for this reason. I want you familiar with and at ease in a variety of company. The education of which is your adaptability to different circumstances. It is a far more pleasurable way to earn your payments than what the others have to go through to earn theirs, you can take my word for that."

Madeline rolled her wine glass between her clasped hands. "Yes, but apart from my lesson with Frederick and Rosie, I have learned nothing more. Apart from, of course, having watched Monsieur Renault."

"A lesson then in its self, is it not?" Aware that the gentleman in question preferred his own indulgence rather than the touch of a woman, she knew that Madeline had, on two occasions, sat in the very seat she was now and watched him bring himself to climax.

"But he did it upon himself and would not allow my hand to touch."

"Some men enjoy the thrill of someone watching as they do it, others, I suppose, feel that they know themselves better than anyone else. You have to remember, my dear, that no-one knows their own body better than they do themselves. Of course, it is our business to know every part of the man's body and what makes him tick, so to speak, but the sensitive parts take a great deal of time to learn about. Did you, for example, notice and take into account which parts of himself he favoured to touch most, how he held himself within his grasp, his pace, did he perhaps use his other hand to aid in this? These factors combined all add up to their enjoyment of the experience. If you had watched, taken note, then you would have, indeed, learned something from it."

Madeline had sat wide-mouthed upon her every word and eventually spoke out, "I did. I watched him very closely. Only, I felt myself redundant. If he had allowed me to even assist, then I would have learned more, would I not?"

"Redundant! Not at all. You had served your purpose well by just being there and allowing yourself to be made to watch. That was his pleasure. And by watching, you have learned." Raising the glass to her mouth, she emptied it. "A palatable wine, I must say. Another?"

Madeline, in her haste to follow suit with her mentor, did likewise. "Merci."

Rising from her chair, Monique made her way to the cabinet. On taking Madeline's empty glass from her as she passed, she noticed that she was still deep in thought about what had been discussed. "You may think you are learning nothing, my dear, but take it from me, you are."

Madeline's head followed her. "But very little."

"You are to be Paris's finest escort, my dear, not some little tramp to lie on her back for just anyone. When the time comes for you to, as you put it, 'bring pleasure to the man' in the way that you wish, I will make you aware of it. Until then, you sit, look pretty... take note and learn."

*

Madeline 3

Chapter 6

A Fool's Game

Ramone sat upright in his bed and looked down into the bowl of rich mutton consommé that Claudia, his maid, had prepared for him. With his spoon swirling the liquid into ever-decreasing circles, he had played with it for the last ten minutes until it had gone cold. It didn't matter anyway, he thought, he had no appetite for it. Indeed, he had fasted for several days now and knew within himself that his ageing body was weakening rapidly as a result. But this was also of little concern to him. With his breathing laboured, he knew he wasn't long for this world now. The life and soul had been taken from him and he had remained in his room since his return from the chateau. With all forthcoming appointments not merely postponed but cancelled outright, he wished to see no-one or be seen. This had even included his dinner engagement with Madeline several days ago. And this was, to him, the worst of all as he missed her company so badly. Without doubt, she was the one true person who he knew cared about him for what he was and not what he could give her. But he had been humiliated beyond measure and could face no-one. Not even his Madeline.

It had been exactly a week ago.
He had arrived at the chateau just several minutes short of the invitational time and had been heartily greeted by both Denig and Caroline. Clad accordingly for this so-called informal occasion, he knew it would just be a matter of time before the excess of their indulgences began and their respective costumes donned. But as was usual, he'd seen from afar, Jacqueline with her impatience with the time constraints laid upon her, had at once began mingling amongst the guests with her gargantuan breasts already bared and on show for all to see and touch. The prominent nipples of which, he'd noticed, having been smeared beforehand with her customary bright rouge. Accepting the waiter's proffered Armagnac, he had been congenially left to mingle as his hosts extolled further salutary greetings upon others during their arrival. He'd known most in the company anyway and had

nodded to several of them in recognition, but had chosen to remain uncommunicative as his attention had been at once drawn to the far right wall. His eyes had widened in appreciation of the large painting which adorned it. Approaching with mouth agape, he had stood several feet from it, transfixed by its brilliance.

"I am also in reverence of its charm. A fine artist, is he not?"

The voice had come from behind but he didn't recognise its tenor.

"It is called *Le Serment des Horaces*." The feminine tone volunteered further, now reaching his side.

He turned to be greeted by the smiling face of a lady he took to be only a few years younger than his own aging-self. And contrary to looking down into peoples faces, he found himself merely tilting his head. With he, himself, standing a few inches taller than six feet, this female stranger stood a mere several below eye level. "Forgive me, Madame, I am not familiar with this particular artist or, indeed, the style in which he paints."

"Jacques-Louis David, one of a new breed of these so-called 'Neoclassical' painters. But, alas, I doubt very much this technique will be widely accepted by the masses, other than those with a keen eye for art, of course, but if this were to happen then it would be a great loss to the art world, would you not agree?"

An avid art lover himself, Ramone countered with gusto, "I am, myself, a keen admirer of the Rococo style." He smiled and turned towards the painting again. "The romanticism it exudes. But I do agree with you about this, there is something about it, a certain something, yes, something deeply profound."

Enamoured with both the countering of her explanation and viewpoint with that of his own, she pushed further, "Surely in this 'Age of Enlightenment' with philosophical thoughts in abundance, these ideas should make themselves known to us mere mortals through the mind and hand of an artist, should they not?"

"Oh without doubt, yes, without doubt." His mind still engrossed within the artwork.

"Otherwise, why would we be here tonight if not for our gratification in such pleasures?"

He turned again to face her and looked quizzically into her eyes. He pondered her conciliatory question. Had she been talking about the painting or had she alluded to the main reason for their gathering? She was a stranger to him, he had not laid eyes on her before and although at his age he still appreciated the no-holds-barred attitude of his hosts, he had to wonder to what extent her own excesses limited themselves. Denig and Caroline's parties were considered legendary within libertine circles and were certainly not for the lily-livered, he could not imagine this genteel lady indulging in such outrageous extremes as was normal after the imbibition of drink and the inhalation of opium. He looked down at her daintily clasped hands. "Oh, you are without refreshment. Would you permit me the honour of remedying this?"

This was done wholly to take stock of her physique with his peripheral vision. His previous contemplation of her now reinforced by her garments, he stood perplexed. Had it not been for the overly-tight corset pushing up so high what little bosom she had, he would have considered her a retired schoolteacher. As scrawny a neck as he had ever seen, it sat perfectly in line with the skeletal form she so boldly exhibited within the confines of her tight-fitting, lack-lustre dress.

Alert to his eyes scanning her body, she curtly refused. "Thank you, but that will not be necessary. I care not for the taste of strong drink."

Conscious of her awareness to this and, furthermore, to her terse reply, Ramone countered, "I, myself, am." Emptying the glass in one go, he then drew, in turn and with mocking tone, a curled index finger across both sides of his thick, grey moustache. "Another, I think."

"Am I to take it from your attitude that you do not approve of what you see?"

Ramone answered in a matter-of-fact fashion while looking for the waiter, "In what respect, Madame?" Catching his eye, he raised his empty glass aloft and resumed his look on her face. "A cursory glance to your hand to see it bereft of glass can hardly lead a man to judge a lady's taste now, can it?"

"I was not referring to the emptiness of my hand, as you well know, but rather to your scrutiny of my entire-self."

Exchanging the empty glass for a full one, he let the waiter take his leave before replying. "I was admiring your height, Madame, as graceful a stature as I have ever seen," he lied.

It was her turn to do the scrutinising. Her eyes looked him over from head to toe. "You are the permanently uniformed one they call Monsieur Leone, are you not?"

While this was uttered in a way that a few would consider condescending, he stood unmoving, taken aback at her sudden outburst, and somewhat confused, as her smiling face spoke to him otherwise. "I am he, as you rightly put it." His head curtly nodded. "And at your service, Madame. But I fear you have me at a disadvantage?"

"Do I now?"

"Indeed, you have, Madame. If I have offended you in any way with my earlier reproach, then please feel free to seek redress from me with a gentleman of your own choosing."

She shook her head. "Please, dispense with the theatrics. What is it with men and their duals? And you will please refrain from addressing me as 'Madame'."

Ramone shrugged his shoulders in surprise. "Then what am I to call you?"

It had been Caroline who'd answered his question on her approach. "A Comtesse. I see you have met Ramone, a dear and beloved friend of the family."

He had felt like a fool. As he did now, lying in his undergarments within a dimly, lit room and cocooned in a home completely devoid of all cheer. What kind of life had he led these past ten years? A sham, an existence full of pretense and make-believe, an aging artifact living a younger man's dream. A retired soldier, indeed! This affectation had made him look like the decrepit fool he was. And if it had been spoken of through hushed tone, even within the company of his closet friends, then it had never hit home as hard as it had done during the course of that evening.

He had consumed far too much drink in so short a time, he now remembered. And whilst Caroline had led the Comtesse away for further introductions, he had noticed on his occasional glances across the room at her, she was returning his gaze each time. She appeared to be isolating him from the rest of the crowd. The pairing of couples for the night had, in the past, been very rare with most participants being hedonistic enough to prefer indulgence in orgiastic playing, but he had known right from the start that she had singled him for herself. If this was truly the case, then did she know of his affliction? Did she know that, through no fault of himself, he could not satisfy her in the proper sense? Perhaps, he had hoped, in a declaration of her intention to Caroline, her hostess may have imparted the truth about his inability to obtain an erection, thus alleviating him of the embarrassment later. The regular attendees were used to his exhibition with open britches; and a few, both female and male, had tried in the past to assist in its raising but, to date, no-one had succeeded in their task. So, on accepting his seventh drink from the waiter's tray he looked over once again, just in time to see Caroline rejoin her. He noticed her follow the Comtesse's gaze towards him and at once turned to whisper in her ear. Whatever had been uttered resulted in child-like giggles from them both, quickly followed by a warm embrace and culminating in a passionate meeting of their lips.
"Caroline has found her fun with the new flesh it seems."
Knowing full well who it was by the voice, he felt no need to take his eyes from the sight of the two women, the older of which, he noticed, was now stepping free of her dress which Caroline was helping to remove. "Your use of the word 'new', Denig, is hardly an apt description, she is by the far the oldest reveler to attend these games, is she not?"
"Would this be discounting your good-self, my dear friend?"
Ramone turned to meet his eyes or would have done had they not been drawn down to the hooded figure to Denig's left. With black cloaked head, a young nubile and dark-skinned female was on her knees before him. He, at once, caught sight of her small, pointed breasts and the hooks clasped tightly through each of the nipples. Attached to these were thick, brown-leathered cords which met in the middle and tailed up as one, travelling the four feet or so to Denig's clasped hand. Aware of Ramone's eyes upon her, Denig tugged at the cord to stretch the nipples outwards and as a reaction to this, as if on cue, the woman barked out like that of a dutiful cur.

"Excuse me, Ramone, my pet needs feeding."
Attired for the evening as a Roman soldier, Denig parted the loose fabric strips of his Pteruges and on clasping his flaccid penis, guided it through the two inch gap in the hood. "Yes, as you were saying. I agree, the Comtesse is of an age where life should be at a slow and graceful ebbing, but she has a reputation in the south you know."
Ramone sipped at his drink knowing full well he need not enquire as to why. Denig would furnish him with the answer and after only a few seconds of silence, as was expected, he expanded further, albeit concise, "Three husbands."
Ramone shook his head. "And?"
"All dead." Leaning closer, he finished in a whisper, "Died in their beds."
Ramone's shoulders raised themselves in response. "A pleasant way to meet your maker, I have to admit."
"No, No." With incredulity, he shook his head. "Not dead in their sleep but in *her* bed." He winked.
Denig remained silent waiting a response but Ramone's attention had been drawn to the laughter coming from across the room. With eyes fixed firmly upon the Comtesse who, by now, was standing completely naked, he watched her clutch at Caroline's hair as she knelt before her with face buried deep between the top of her long, slender legs.
"Did you hear me there, Ramone?"
Pulled from thought, Ramone faced him again. "Sorry, what?"
"She fucked them to death."
There was little chance of her ever doing that to him, thought Ramone, but his curiosity was rampant. "She is new to the city, I gather, for her face is not known to me. How did you come to meet her or better still, who is she?"
Deep now in conversation, Denig quickly lost interest in the pleasure being bestowed upon him so, withdrawing himself, he allowed the hooded-maiden to squat by his feet. "Comtesse d'Armagnac."
Ramone erupted with laughter and looked to his glass. "You are jesting with me, my dear friend." He raised his drink. "d'Armagnac?"
"Yes, as you say, the very drink you are enjoying. And she holds court at the highest level." Leaning closer once more, he finished with excited tone, "With *Madame Déficit* no less."
Ramone's eyes widened but immediately nodded down to Denig's feet.
"We are quite safe, Ramone, she is from the black continent and speaks no French."
Ramone's eyes turned once more to fix hard upon the Comtesse. He was familiar with Denig's derogatory term for the Queen of France, this stemming from her so-called involvement in a scandalous fraud against the crown jewellers regarding a diamond necklace of which she had been later proved wholly innocent. But the people of France had marred their profligate Queen, *Madame Déficit,* and it had stuck. To all others, she was simply known as Marie Antoinette.

"The Dauphine?"

"Yes, the Austrian jackal to our own King Louis. And if the Comtesse is anything like our beloved Dauphine, then this country of ours will soon have a revolution on its hands. Mark my words if it doesn't."

Ramone was well aware of the state of unrest amongst the commoners of France and he knew, only too well, that Denig was correct in his assumptions. The outcome of such an uprising would see an end to the aristocracy and their wealth, but he, himself, was at an age that it mattered very little to him. Even so, on such an eventuality arising, he had already made his plans and formulated a strategy of losing himself within the system. Both his wealth and his very being would be safe from harm. Few others, he knew, were in the same position as he was to be able to do such a thing or, indeed, had the foresight or ingenuity to do so. And a high percentage preferred instead to remain in a permanent state of naivety or ignorance thinking it would never happen. "Perhaps so, but I doubt very much that a Comtesse's everyday lifestyle would sway or influence the thoughts of the people en masse."

"Not directly, no, but a woman such as she can influence the everyday lifestyle of The Dauphine."

"She has the Queen's favour?"

"Very much so, I've heard." He changed the subject. "She was asking after you earlier."

"She was?" Ramone watched Caroline raise herself up and embrace the Comtesse once again. But over her shoulder, her eyes were fixed upon him. And within seconds she was making her way across the room in his direction, her tall, slender body swaying from side to sensual side.

Denig noticed this too and taking it as a signal to leave them, he bade Ramone au revoir for the moment and tugged on the cord. His pet responded with yet another yap and followed on in his wake.

Ramone nodded on her arrival. "Comtesse." And instantly felt her hand clutch at his front.

She feigned a frown. "You are not open as I expected. Is there something wrong tonight?"

Her opening gambit and deed was a shock to him as he knew fine well she was referring to his usually bared-self. But, of late, he had not pandered to his normal wants. Since meeting Madeline several weeks back and her reinventing his game with her own rules, he had not felt the inclination to repeat what, for years now, had been commonplace in such company. "Perhaps later." His eyes lowered to her naked body. "You are without costume?"

She tilted her head to the side and repeated his reply, "Perhaps later."

Ramone felt her static hand clutch tighter and begin a slow, circular movement. "Our host has informed me that this has not been in working order for some considerable time now."

He raised his glass and smiled. "Well that all depends on which of its roles you consider may not be functioning properly. Your very good health, Comtesse, I not only drink to you but also your name."
She watched him finish. "Please, Ramone, it's Jeanette. I fear we may have gotten off to a wrong start earlier."
"That, I assure you, was far from my thoughts... Jeanette."
He looked down again at her bared form. The transformation was astonishing. Whether it was the brandy working in his system or with indistinct vision from the same, but her skin had smoothed out akin to that of a younger woman. The dress she had worn on arrival had not done her body shape justice one bit. He felt himself smile.
"Do I take it from the beam on your face that I am now acceptable to your eyes?"
His stare now firmly on her shapely exposed breasts, he replied without thought, "You are that, Madame." He shook himself. "My apologies, Comtesse, I mean, Jeanette."
"Then shall we join the others in the fun or is your role here merely observational?" Lifting his free hand with hers, she guided it up towards her left breast and on cupping its entirety, held it in place. "Or perhaps your enjoyment in the proceedings is limited to drink alone?"
He sighed. "In days past I would have gladly indulged in all manner of games, Jeanette, but alas, I cannot fulfill the needs of a woman as, no doubt, Caroline has explained."
"But surely you can have appreciation in mind if not in body? After all, one can still value fine art without having the natural ability to paint."
His smile broadened. "A fine way of putting it, I'm sure, but the fact still remains I have not had the pleasure in that way for many a year, although I have to admit that there is a certain stimulus in what you are doing at present."
"Then let us expand on it. Come, join the fun."
Leading him by his free hand, Jeanette guided their way through the crowd and found vacant for them a heavy, padded seat of deep red. Exchanging his empty glass for a full one en route, Ramone now sat next to her with drink in hand. Looking around the spacious room, he saw the gathering was in full swing. Thirty or so participants now in various states of undress and excessive costume, indulged in whatever pleasure was their want. Jacqueline, as ever, being the centre of attraction. On all fours, she displayed her natural talent of allowing a semi-naked dwarf to insert a tapered candle into her rear end in an attempt to beat her own record, with most cheering her on, inch by inch. Others, not enamoured with her exhibitionism, were content to drift into oblivion with the smoking of opium while deep in the thrusts of carnal abyss. One such partaker of this substance, he noticed, was Denig - at ease to lie upon the cushioned floor surrounded by four skin-painted women, one of which appeared to be happy to have her head rested upon his thigh, unmoving, but with filled mouth. His pet, meanwhile, sat nearby waiting

further commands. His eyes drifted across the room and caught sight of Caroline in the corner. On bended knees, she congenially squatted two feet over the head of an obese parliamentarian, who was rejoicing in the fact that she was emptying her bladder onto his red, bulbous face.
"A joy to behold, is it not?"
"Our hosts certainly know how to entertain their guests," Ramone retorted with glee.
"Would you allow me to undress you, Ramone? I think it unfair for me to sit as such with you dressed thus." She pulled at his jacket. "Or do you tease me?"
Ramone ran a curled finger along the inside of his stiff-necked collar. "Well it is rather warm, perhaps just the jacket."
Jeanette smiled. "Then stand."
But such was her allure and persuasion, he found himself completely devoid of apparel within minutes, his uniform scattered to the floor around them. And with her seductive overture immediate, she took hold of his penis within her fingers. "Shall we see if we can't convince this soldier to stand to attention?"
Ramone shook his head in dismay. "As I have already commented upon, Jeanette, this soldier, as you put it, has long since abandoned his post."
Shaking him freely from side to side between her light-fingered grasp, she elaborated, "Ah, but perhaps this combatant has not been treated with the due respect it deserves. After all, one assumes it has been dutiful and loyal to its General in the past."
Ramone laughed at her wordplay and seemed content to continue in a similar vein. "Its participatory role in many a battle has seen it triumph one hundred per cent. But alas, victorious battles are of little consequence if one ends up losing the war."
"Then we shall begin a new one. Make a plan of action and attack with full force." She released her hold on him and made way to stand. "We shall release the beast."
Ramone had now lost his grip on the conversation and had to sit still to hear what the Comtesse intended. With gusto, she had at once risen from the seat and centred the floor, her attention-seeking claps announcing her proclamation, "Friends, friends, friends."
Rather odd, thought Ramone, considering she knew little, if any, in attendance, save her hosts, but sat in awe of her brazenness and curious as to what she had in mind. Even Jacqueline, who now having easily beaten her previous record, sat up to attention, the soiled, tapered candle twirling nonchalantly in her fingers.
Strutting unashamedly naked around the floor, the Comtesse appeared at ease with public oration, her commanding tone exacting the ears of all. "When Joshua crossed the river Jordan and led his Israelites into the land of Canaan, he encountered the vast city of Jericho, the walls of which he knew had endured many a siege. He could see no way of defeating his enemy thus

heavily fortified." She paused and, on raising her right hand aloft, pointed upward with index finger. "But!" She paused again for dramatic effect. "Joshua had God on his side." Resuming her casual stride, she scanned the room and with her gaze fixed firmly on each set of eyes on her passing, continued, "And as instructed by the almighty, he and his army for six arduous days did circle the city but on the seventh, and with the deafening blast from their ram horns, did the walls crumble down before their very eyes."

Not exactly the way he remembered reading it in the bible, thought Ramone, but he congratulatory nodded in appreciation of her rendition of the story, that and her accompanying theatrics which appeared to have captured the attention of her audience. Even Denig's pet, who spoke no French, sat mesmerised and was following her every move. But Ramone was at a loss as to what she was getting at, as was the company, who now sat in silence awaiting explanation.

In the meantime, he emptied his glass and before he had raised it, was offered another from a very attentive waiter clad as Egyptian.

"Now, depending on whether you believe this story matters not," she continued, "For my quandary here is not whether it is so easy for a strong and robust structure to collapse under the force of nature or rather if you take it from the scriptures, the power of belief. I prefer to contemplate this tale from another point of view."

With all around perplexed as to her meaning, the silence continued unabated. Ramone considered whether this was the respect due to her title or, like him, they were just plain baffled by her ramblings. To him, she was talking in riddles; or perhaps it was the copious amount of drink he had consumed dulling his senses. He was unsure. He also felt himself sway somewhat.

"It is so easy to destroy something already established but the real task is to create something from the remnants of what has been destroyed or even damaged beyond repair."

Some uttering came forth from a scattered few, as this statement at least made the mind ponder an answer to the problem. If, indeed, this was her intention. They, like Ramone, awaited further erudition.

"Think not of a collapsing wall but rather that of a monument that had, in the past, stood proud." And, as before, pointed her index finger upwards. "Is it not safe to say that the very same harbinger of destruction used in the Lord's name can be equally utilised for the purpose of good, for one of rebuilding. Is not God the creator rather than the destroyer of all things?"

A unanimous murmur of affirmation was heard from a predominantly Catholic attendance, Ramone noted, but he, himself, remained aloof as he had an inkling of where she was heading. And he did not like it. Not one bit.

As if this whole fiasco had been rehearsed, the Comtesse had reached Caroline during her speech and accepted from her the object she now raised high above her head. Unfortunately, she did not get the reaction as was intended, this being due to the fact that very few people could make out what

she held in her hand. Unperturbed by this, she quickly made amends by placing it to her lips and blowing. All became clear.
- A ram's horn.
Their realisation of this was immediate and their reactions were instantaneous. Cheers were abundant.
Now receiving the response she craved, she swaggered around the room, teasing them further by intermittently rubbing the horn seductively between her legs amid her sharp, high-pitched blows.
Jacqueline, as if prompted, cried out above the blare, "Try rebuilding Ramone's cock."
"Now that would be a miracle," cried another.
Further calls of encouragement followed on, "Come on, Comtesse, raise the dead." and "Put some life back into the old rascal."
The Comtesse, awaiting this reaction, spun on her feet and stood facing Ramone, the pendulous motion of the horn between her finger and thumb taunting her audience further. "What say you, Monsieur Leone, do you think God's instrument of destruction can be used for resurrection?"
Without noticing her approach from the left, Ramone suddenly felt Caroline's hand clasp his and, cajoling him gently from his seat, led him towards the middle of the floor - all this to the riotous applause and further cheering from the onlookers.
Ordinarily he would have felt at ease at this function, positioned with open britches, but to stand as the centre of attention and being taunted so, made him feel like a fool. A staggering fool, he could hardly keep himself upright. Had it not been for Caroline by his side, he would, undoubtedly, have keeled over.
The Comtesse inched forward in his direction, her swaying body movements like that of mocking stealth. "But first, let my own body juices mix with the instrument of revivification and that of the recipient."
Standing a mere three feet from him, Ramone looked down to see her slowly insert the smaller end of the curled horn round and deep between her legs and in one fluid movement, kneel down before him. Extending her hands to take grip of his waist, she leant forward and parted her lips slightly, thus allowing the tip of her tongue to raise his manhood horizontal. Then opening her mouth further, she pushed forward letting his entirety slide fully in. With her lips pressed hard against his abdomen, she stared up at him, her tongue all the while probing and exploring his every detail. Ramone gazed on her with unfocused eyes, now realising that the drink had, indeed, taken its toll upon him for he felt the need to vomit. But to do so would have garnished further derision from the crowd. He just wanted out of the room and away from these people as quickly as possible but his legs felt useless, unable to carry him. And within seconds they had given up the task. He collapsed and fell to the floor but, to his surprise, the Comtesse still remained attached, her controlled fall keeping her grip upon him with both hands and mouth.
The cheering continued.

- And then the pain.
With her front teeth, the Comtesse had dug deep. His stomach muscles automatically clenched to absorb the shock of it. Like a rabid dog with lockjaw, she clung hard to the base and even with his attempts to pull away, her teeth clenched tighter.
What in God's name had he done to this woman to warrant such a vile act, he thought, as he fought hard to free himself from her.
But her heinous action was short lived. Releasing him from the pain, the Comtesse knelt down before him and withdrew the horn from her body. Then, placing the larger opened end over the tip of his aching penis, she blew down its length once again.
- The resurrection process had begun.
As if attempting to inflate the flaccid skin within its hold, she continued with the now muffled tone and with each blow came further cheers of encouragement.
But to no avail, Ramone remained as he had been for so many years.
Hoping that she and the others would now give this preposterous façade up as a lost cause, he threw his silver drinking goblet, which he miraculously had still clutched in his grasp, to the side. He barked, "Enough of this nonsense... now."
But the Comtesse was having none of it, she had only just begun. Lifting herself erect, she hollered out above the crowd, "Then we shall release the beast." Repeating her words from earlier.
All was silent in an instant as the twinned main doors were parted and every head in the room turned in their direction. Entering first as vanguard to a parade of eight naked women of various genus, were four outrageously decorated minstrels announcing their entrance with horns blasting. Splitting into two columns, they arched their way round the room and proceeded directly towards the centre of attention.
- Ramone.
His eyes widened at the sight. Immediately behind them was the beast in question. Jacqueline's participant from earlier - the hideously deformed dwarf - now entered the room with spring in his step and with hearty laughter, leapt his way into and around this now sordid arena holding a leash, the end of which held a single-horned goat.
The Comtesse announced its arrival, "If not the horn, then the very beast from whence it came."
Ramone fought hard to get to his feet and escape this outrage but felt hands of strength upon his shoulders keeping him at bay. The ram meanwhile was being lead in his direction with the Comtesse beckoning it to them. Whereupon its arrival, and from nowhere, she produced a hand filled with a brown glutinous gel which she proceeded to smear, with delight, over his genitals. The smell, like that of rancid food, made Ramone's already delicate stomach erupt and in one tremendous retch, promptly emptied its entire contents up onto his lap. And as was expected, the riotous laughter exploded

to ear-shattering proportions. His eyes and nasal passages began to sting with the rapid expulsion of the raw alcohol and stomach acid seeping forth from each orifice. With continued coughing, his breath became laboured as his chest tightened and he could only watch through watered eyes, as the goat consumed the nauseating mixture which now covered him.

The Comtesse meanwhile had continued her shrieks from the horn encouraging the entire company to stand to their feet and applaud his humiliation.

And as if his aching-self had not endured enough pain with the Contesse's bite on him, he now felt the ragged edges of the ram's teeth bear down and into his raw, pained flesh.

It was the last thing of the evening he could remember. Assuming he had passed out with the drink, he had awakened some time later within his own carriage. His eyes tightened together at the thought. The shame of being carried out naked through the courtyard and led into his home by the house staff had been unbearable. Not once had he ever let himself be seen in such a disgraceful state as he had been in then. He had not left his bed chamber since.

What had led this to be done to him? He had never met the Comtesse before, he was certain of it. In his now numerous retrospective thoughts on this during the passed week, his conclusions had been minimal. It had certainly been prearranged, of this he was sure. But for Caroline and Denig to be party to it, this he could not find good reason. To him, they had appeared friends for many years now, so why commit themselves to his humiliation. What, if anything, had he done to Jeanette to warrant this? And what was he now in the eyes of all present...?

... A damned fool, that was what.

In a fit of rage, his right hand upended the food tray sending it crashing to the floor. He felt the gripping pain.

And with this, the same hand clutched tightly at his chest.

*

Madeline 3

Chapter 7

An unknown history

Caroline waited for her servant girl to finish pouring the hot water from the ewer before speaking out. Soaking naked within the sunken oval bath of her chateau, she watched Jeanette, seated opposite, kill time by deliberating over which of the various peeled fruits to pick. Selecting a single, dark-skinned grape from the floating salver to her side, she popped it in her mouth and returned Caroline's stare. Jeanette shrugged. "So what if he does die. Wasn't that our intention?"
With outstretched arms along the bath's edge, Caroline leaned back letting her breasts bob on the surface of the water while her right leg waved beneath to spread evenly the newly added warmth. "Perhaps your aim, but he has been a good friend to us for a long time now."
With no consideration for her fellow bather, Jeanette spat the pips into the heavily scented water. "Hardly a friend I am sure. Do not friends know about each others secrets?"
Caroline showed concern. "He hasn't been seen out for days now. Just sits alone in his bed chamber by all accounts."
Abruptly sitting up from her slouched position, Jeanette sent ripples across the water. She stretched for her wine. "Then our task is almost complete."
"To what end? I have only been given snippets of information regarding your knowledge of Ramone and, for that matter, your full intention towards him."
"Money, of course, we know that... and revenge."
Jeanette sipped at her wine, allowing her remark to sink its way into Caroline's head. And by the look on her face, it had.
"Revenge?"
"For me, yes. And for you, the money... badly needed money, I may add."
Caroline had assumed from the beginning that it was for this sole purpose that they were doing what they were doing. To live the frivolous life in the fashion they were accustomed to, took money, but to be able to continue this lifestyle it had to be available to them in the first place to have to spend. In most cases these days, this was not the case. France was in a state of

financial chaos at present and although nobility were excused from paying taxes, if your outgoings exceeded your income ad infinitum, then pauperism was inevitable. Even their King was hard pushed in recent years to find money to survive, she knew. It had become dog eat dog in Parisian circles now and it was widely known about Ramone's wealth. How he had come by it, whether by birthright, hard toil or just plain booty from his army days, was unknown. If, indeed, he had been in the army. Ramone's life, to most, was a mystery. Except, of course, for the Comtesse, who appeared to know more about him than many others. Her original scheming had been for financial gain only and this was what had attracted Caroline to her plot. How Jeanette would eventually attain his money had not yet been made clear to her. She had merely been an abettor in the ruse, with her hosting the party. But revenge - revenge for what?

Caroline raised her empty glass as an instruction for it to be refilled. "You made no mention of this before. I assumed you had arrived in Paris to seek wealth through deception and dishonesty like all others."

The servant girl having obliged with the wine, made her way round the perimeter to do likewise with Jeanette's, who, upon receiving it, eyed her up intently. "This part is no concern of yours. Ramone and I have some unfinished business to take care of."

"I was not aware you had known him previously but only of his existence through word of mouth upon your arrival."

Jeanette refaced her. "I did not know him before, only of him."

Caroline looked surprised. "Ramone is a known figure outwith Paris?"

The Comtesse shook her head. "No, only to a select few who know him as such."

Caroline gave up with the questions. The more the reply, the darker the riddle became. "Then what do we do next?"

As if bored with the conversation and without warning, the Comtesse rose from the water and climbed the three marble steps in the direction of the servant. "We let nature take its course."

Raising her arms aloft, she allowed the waiting towel to envelop her and the hand maiden to dry her down. Once complete, the young, long-haired brunette stood before her awaiting further duty. Jeanette gazed deep into her eyes then lowered them slowly to take account of her body. Pulling the loose fabric of the girl's top to the side, she looked down at the exposed breast. Having cupped it in her hand to take note of its form, she tentatively rolled the deep brown nipple between her fingers. She turned to face Caroline. "I will dine alone in my bed chamber tonight but I'd like this one to join me later in the evening if you would oblige."

It was all Caroline could do but to nod in consent. "Of course."

It had taken only a moment after the Comtesse had closed the door behind her before Denig appeared through the side panel in the wall.

"Another one? Is there any of our staff left who she hasn't had bury their face in her glory hole?"
"Now husband, we agreed. This is a means to an end."
Denig picked up the Comtesse's unfinished wine and, on sitting at the bath's edge next to his wife, let his feet dangle in the water. "It had better be. Fucking bitch is bleeding us dry."
Caroline sipped at her own wine. "It is, indeed, bad times when it comes to this, is it not - cheating on a friend to gain coin? I feel for Ramone."
"Fuck him." He looked around the room. "You think this place runs on its own? We can hardly pay the house staff as it is and she's bedding every one of them. We'll wake up one morning to find them gone. They'll only take so much, you know. They're not paid to fuck her."
She looked up and smiled at him. "Just us?"
Denig saw the funny side and smiled back. "Yes, just us."
"Anyway, you worry too much, my darling. Work is hard to come by these days. They have a roof over their heads and a full belly when going to sleep at night. Not many have that; and having a wage is to them but a bonus."
"Yes, well letting nature take its course could prove costly for us. It's okay for her, she is living here gratis. We still have the running costs to cover. And that fucking party was a fortune. Most of which was on credit. Not once has she offered to pay for anything."
Caroline slouched down further into the water to absorb the heat from the oils. "It still puzzles me though how she is going to get access to Ramone's money. She is very elusive when it comes to that part."
Denig kicked at the water. "She's been very elusive since she came here. How the hell we ever got entangled with her I don't know. A Comtesse who has had three husbands, all of which died and left her money and yet she comes to Paris seeking to dupe a man out of his wealth...hmm. And especially now with this revenge part, where did that spring from all of a sudden? There is a hell of a lot she isn't telling us. We are maybe being played for fools here."
Caroline patted his leg. "Perhaps so, darling, but it is a chance we have to take. We have no choice."
Reciprocating her affection, Denig threaded his fingers through her hair. "I know. I just preferred our life before she arrived. Which reminds me, what of the new flesh you mentioned before, this...Madeline, whatever, the country girl?"
Caroline finished her wine and placed the empty glass by Denig's side. "This one is special, my darling. I am waiting for the Comtesse to leave and when we have our share of Ramone's money, I will send for her. I am not willing to share this particular one with anyone. I want her to myself."
"She must, indeed, be something special."
"She is but, until then, we have more important matters to deal with." She rose from the water. "I'd better make ready myself for dinner."
"Am I to presume we are dining alone?"

"We are." She bent to kiss the top of his head. "And the next time you wish to share my bath, have the common decency to undress first."

Denig looked down at his sodden britches. "Shit."

*

Madeline 3

Chapter 8

Pending Departure

With hesitance, Madeline inched her way along the hallway towards her bedroom. She had used the excuse of dining with Monique as a way of getting some much needed wine inside her. In truth, she was afraid to come upstairs immediately on her arrival back from the park, fearful of entering the room that she had so adored since she first arrived in Paris. A room which had a history and that history was a young girl, similar to her, who had lived in it previously and died there. Was she to share the same fate? After the warnings from Rubin about Monique and Rosie, she now feared for her life and as much as he had reassured her of his protectiveness towards her, she still felt vulnerable. He couldn't be with her twenty four hours of the day. She had tried her hardest before and after dinner to coax further information from Monique with regards to her plans for the future. But being her usual vague-self, she had simply mentioned the heights she wished to reach with her. Madeline had always assumed she had meant meeting and entertaining the nobility, which was her own original plan before leaving home anyway, but Monique's unwillingness to let her participate in the more intimate side with customers made her wary of this. Surely she couldn't just continue to sit in the company of men without actual physical contact forthcoming day in day out. When was she to be taught these so-called trade secrets that Monique so brazenly described but carefully guarded? She needed advice from someone. Someone she could trust... someone who would listen.

Reaching the hallway's end, she undid the lock and opened her door. She heard, in an instant, the outside revelry from the street through her opened window. At least this brought a little comfort to her. She knew the room well enough to make straight for her bedside candle and, once lit, she sat on her bed's edge, hands clasped upon her lap. Her eyes looked down at them, the unconscious fidgeting at once taking her back to her time in the carriage travelling to Paris. She had been wary of her own decision-making back then and that same feeling now showed through as to her decision whether to remain. Was all this so important to her as to endanger her very life? Was it worth it? But what was the alternative - to return home? And if so, what would be waiting for her there; what would her future be in a town which would already know of her absconding? She had left as a child but would return as a woman, but for what purpose? What would her future hold there? Questions, questions and more questions... but she had no answers. All she could do was sit like the frightened child she was, alone in a dimly lit room within the unforgiving and hostile city of Paris.

She jumped.
The hard knock had come from her door.
… And then again. Someone was impatient.
"Un moment, s'il vous plait." She held her hands together tighter and looked towards the door. Who would be calling for her at this time? Monique had said she was retiring for the night when she left her earlier, so it could not be her. One of the girls, no, definitely no, not one of them had ever come near her room before. And it would certainly not be a customer without Monique's knowledge…or her payment.
It came again. Only this time she heard a voice accompanying it. "Madeline."
Between the outside cheer and the muffled tone through the door, Madeline did not recognise the voice of this solitary word.
It called again, followed by more rapping. "Madeline. It's Monique."
With such a sigh of relief that it almost emptied her chest, Madeline rose from the bed and headed for the door. She had only just turned the lock when the door was pushed open, almost sending her into a spin. Monique was in the room within seconds.
"Madeline, my dear, get dressed quick…oh, you are dressed. Good girl. Collect your apparel and make yourself presentable within five minutes."
Madeline stood in the middle of the room perplexed at her outburst. "Please, Monique…" She quickly looked to the opened door. "…Madame."
"Oh, there's no time for that now, quickly, my dear, quickly, there is a carriage waiting for you outside."
Being ushered towards her wardrobe to collect her cape, Madeline turned to counter. "But Monique, where is it I am going?"
"Going, going? You are going to see Ramone."
"Ramone?"
It was a pleasure to hear, she had to admit. It had been the answer to her prayer. If anyone would know the answer to her dilemma then he would - but why at this late hour?
Monique steadied herself. She saw the look of concern on Madeline's face. "Ramone is ill, quite, quite ill. And he has asked for you."
Shocked at the news, Madeline fell back, seat first onto her bed where she sat bent over trying to take this in. "Ramone is ill?"
"Yes, my dear. Now hurry yourself. There may not be much time."
Madeline looked up. "You mean he may die?"

Monique, having been informed of the gravity of the situation by Ramone's driver, nodded. "I'll get your cape."

Periodically peering out from behind the carriage blind, Madeline had recognised the streets and had known her whereabouts for the first five minutes of the journey but she was now heading into unfamiliar territory. The rocking of the carriage had subdued somewhat from the rough, muck-encrusted streets to a more stable ride the further they travelled. They appeared to be heading out of the city and as they passed through one of the boundary tolls, this confirmed it. Seated alone, she clutched at her purse bag and thought of Ramone. Had this been why he had cancelled their dinner engagement? Or had he been ill for long or perhaps his malady had just occurred. Monique had been as vague as ever, even in a serious situation as this - or perhaps she was not privy to such from the driver. She could only hope that her presence would help him through his sickness, whatever the circumstances.
The carriage drew to a halt and, within seconds, the driver had dismounted and pulled the door open. With impatience, she did not wait for the steps to be lowered for her. She leapt out onto the thin gravel...and immediately looked up.
A grand a set of apartments as she had ever seen stood before her. The fascia of which was marble smooth with tall, glass windows inset within. Situated behind a row of various evergreens, it was idyllic. Ramone did, indeed, reside in luxury. Guided towards the entrance by the driver, Madeline was met at the bottom of the stairs by a mid to elderly woman she took to be the housekeeper.
"Monsieur Leone is waiting." With an inviting arm, she bade her to follow.
Madeline nodded. "Merci."
Following on with identical pace as she dawdled up the six wide steps, Madeline grew anxious at her seemingly lax movement. Passing between two carved pillars she noticed they were imbedded with what looked like a family crest. If she hadn't been in such a hurry she would have stopped and admired the workmanship. She grew annoyed. This woman had no speed to her at all but, not wanting to appear rude, she remained silent but intolerant to her pace. However, her usual impatience got the better of her.
"May I ask what ails Monsieur?" Madeline did not want to sound overly familiar by using his first name.
Without turning, the housekeeper muttered under her breath, "He is an old man, age comes to us all."
Hardly a descriptive answer, Madeline thought. She decided not to push her further, she would find out for herself soon enough... if they ever got there.
Eventually making the hallway, they turned to the right and passed through an opened door which led to yet another hallway. Further stairs took them to another level and finally a door which looked like a bed chamber. The

housekeeper led Madeline in and announced her arrival. And there, lying on the opposite side of the room in his bed, was Ramone.
With no restrictions upon her pace now, Madeline raced across the room. ... And with opened arms, embraced him.

Ramone looked nothing like the proud man she had met on their first meeting. His face, now sallow and drawn, bore no smile with which she had always associated him, and his normally brilliant white eyes, lack-lustre. His embrace upon her had even lacked the strength to hold her with any effect and she realised in an instant that he was, indeed, truly ill. He had aged at least ten years since she had last seen him.
Seating herself on the edge of the bed, Madeline laid her purse bag down in front of her and took hold of his hand. "You have a fine house here, Ramone. I would dearly like to visit you again and perhaps you could show me the place in better detail."
Ramone forced a weak smile. "That is very kind of you to say so, Madeline, but I'm afraid that option will not be open to me."
Aware of the housekeeper's presence, Madeline tried to keep her conversation light and on a positive note. She noticed the untouched soup on the bedside dresser. "Well if you don't eat, then you will not have the strength to. Was it not you, yourself, who told me that food was life?"
The housekeeper was by her side. "May I take your cape and bag, Mademoiselle?"
Madeline nodded. "Oui, merci." She undid the top and handed it to her. "I'll keep my bag with me."
Draping it over her arm, the housekeeper made moves to remove the food tray from the dresser.
Madeline held out her arm. "Is it still warm?" She did not wait for an answer. "Leave it here. And that will be all for this evening, we will not need you further, I will tend to Monsieur."
Taken aback with her brazen assertiveness, the housekeeper looked to Ramone for instruction.
He nodded. "Thank you, Regina, Madeline will see to me. And please make ready one of the guest rooms, it is too late an hour for her to return to the city tonight."
Madeline remained quiet. She watched Regina nod in compliance and leave the room.
At ease now with her gone, Madeline sprung from the bed.
She noticed the chicken pieces in the soup and touched the side of the bowl. No matter. She lifted the tray and stood in front of him. "It's cold I'm afraid, but I will make a deal with you, Ramone. I will eat a spoonful each time you do. We will make a game of it. See who wins."
Ramone looked away from her. "I have no appetite, Madeline."
"At least some bread then?"
He shook his head.

Madeline returned the tray to its place and reseated as before. She took the same hand in hers. "What is wrong with you, Ramone? Have you been seen by a physician?"
Once again, his head movement indicated no.
"Why? How are you meant to know what ails you if you don't?"
Ramone gripped her hand as tight as he could in reassurance. "I am old and weary of this world now, Madeline. There is no cure for that."
Madeline returned the grip and looked deep into his sorrow-filled eyes. "Please, Ramone... don't leave me."
His faint smile returned. "My dearest, dearest Madeline, these past few weeks knowing you have been amongst the happiest of my life. It has been a great pleasure getting to know you and our times together. But it must end."
Madeline noticed the beads of sweat on his forehead. She leaned over to retrieve the cloth by his pillow and while dabbing his skin dry with her right hand, she let her left hand fingers brush at his forelock. "You are a very valued friend to me, Ramone, and I do not wish that friendship to end before it blossoms fully. You cannot leave me alone. You have to stay with me, look after me. There is so much more in Paris for us to enjoy together."
"That is very sweet of you but when an old man's time has come, he has to take it as best he can. That is why I wished, of all people, you alone to be with me at the end."
Madeline felt the tears build up in her eyes but she had to be strong, not let him win. She had to fight for him if he wouldn't. In a fury, she looked behind her. "Is it any wonder you are so hot."
She stood up and marched straight towards the fire which was in full blaze. Pulling the fireguard through temper, she hauled its weight in front of the flames, thus hoping the heat would go directly up and lower the temperature. She pulled at her stay. "I can hardly breathe myself."
Unbuttoning it during her return to the bed, she let the corset drop to floor before she reached its side. Before resuming her seat as before, she had to move her bag further along the top. He was still sweating. "We will have to cool you down a bit here, Ramone. Please?"
Lifting his arms slightly, she pulled the top of the bed cover down from his chest and folded it over just above his waist. She noticed the pools of sweat there also. "My goodness, Ramone, you are burning up."
As she wiped his chest and stomach dry, she felt him wheeze several times before coughing. Sitting him up slightly to allow easy access as it continued unabated, she incessantly patted his back to assist in the clearing of his airways. And finally, to her relief, it did.
Laying him down as before, Madeline took hold of his hand once again but this time more for her own gain than his. "You frightened me there, Ramone."
Releasing her grip on his hand, he raised it to her cheek. "This would never have been my intention."
She covered his hand with hers and pulled it closer. "Then stay with me."

"This choice is taken from me now, Madeline. Had I been fortunate to have met you with two score years from my age, then Paris would have, indeed, been at our mercy. But alas..."
... "Alas nothing, just have the will to live. Please. Do it for me, do it for a very dear friend."
His wheezing continued. "I am not the man I used to be, Madeline. Not for a long time now as you know." He paused. "... And of late more than ever. But I am dying and wish to do so with some dignity. Here, away from all."
By 'of late' she assumed he was talking about his illness, so did not enquire further. "You will always be a man in my eyes, Ramone, a true man and a gentleman through and through. You do not have to die, be the man you are and live through it."
His eyes grew heavy as his breath laboured. "It's too late."
Infuriated at his unwillingness to fight on, she stood up in temper. "It isn't too late, it isn't. If you feel as if you cannot continue to live because you do not feel like a man, then I will make you feel like one again."
She unbuttoned her dress.

*

Monique leaned over and relit her bedside candle.
If anything ever kept her from her sleep, it was the thought of money. Not money worries like most these days but coin still to be earned. Ramone was dying and, in doing so, she would gain from it. Pulling her shawl up around her shoulders, she leaned back against her headboard and considered the facts.
Caroline had heard from Ramone of Madeline's existence - supposedly telling her how wonderful she was and proud of the fact that he alone had stolen her eye. Which was in part true, she knew, but not in the way he had described it to Caroline. He was a father figure to her, a friend, and that alone. But she knew Caroline's curiosity would have gotten the better of her, hence the need to visit Monique's house in order to see Madeline for herself. Her constant search for 'new flesh' as she put it, was known to many in her circle of friends, past and present. To this end, Monique was in favour of introduction. She would be the profiteer from Madeline's participation in their sordid affairs and she would not come cheap. This was her first rung on the Parisian nobility ladder. But something new had happened since... Jeanette.
This Comtesse was unknown to her but her reputation as libertine extraordinaire had gathered momentum within a week of her arrival. And on hearing about Madeline, had in turn heard about Ramone and this had pricked her interest. A scheme had been hatched to remove Ramone's wealth from him and in a way, she knew, would hurt him the most... his pride.
Satisfied that her participation in this would see a return, she leaned over and blew out the candle.

She could sleep easy now having finally convinced herself that she had made money on the deal.

*

Madeline climbed on top of the bed and laid herself, full length alongside him. Having unloosened the top of her dress enough for Ramone to see beneath, she placed her hand on his chest. He may have given up the fight as a lost cause, she thought, but she had not. She was determined to pull him through this, one way or another. He would either live on as the man she knew him to be or if he was determined to die, then she would make sure he did so as one.
Ramone's failing eyes at once fell upon the delights before him. "Please, Madeline, don't."
She raised her index finger to his lips and hushed him. "Shhh…" Facing into him, she lowered her hand and let the back of her fingers run down the full length of his exposed chest; and on reaching the cover's top at his waist, she reversed them so the tips ran all the way up through his thick, greying hair. She looked at his physique.
"You still have a fine figure for a man of your age, Ramone."
Being the recipient of such a compliment several weeks back would have been accepted in the manner in which it was given but Ramone felt emaciated through his lack of eating. He forced his words out between heavy breaths. "Please, don't tease me."
"I am not teasing you, Ramone. I am simply doing and saying what pleases me to do so…" Reaching across for his left hand, she pulled it towards her. Slipping it into her opened dress, she placed the full extent of his palm over her breast. "… as does this." She squeezed tighter so that his grip within hers would feel her full shape and the heat from her smooth, silky skin beneath. "And pleases you also I hope."
He could utter no words, only to nod slowly in agreement.
Madeline noticed the perspiration return to his forehead but knew, on this occasion, it was not the heat from the fire. Releasing her grip on his hand, she felt happy when he retained his hold on her. Her own hand, meanwhile, had found its way back to his body where she resumed her previous strokes.
Her mind in an instant was pulled back to the two occasions when she had held Gaston in her hands. In both instances she had simply done what was asked of her, with him manipulating her hand movements and the pace of his favoured strokes. In addition to this, Monsieur Renault's self-indulgence with her as spectator had, in no uncertain terms, given her further explication of a man's preferred method of bringing himself to climax. Contrary to what she had led Monique to believe earlier in the evening, she had watched him intently, eyeing up his every move and taking note of all. Could she possibly combine these experiences and observations to do her own bidding now? It only remained for her to try.

As her hand slowly worked its way down to his waist again, it did not stop and return as before. She allowed it to continue on and slip beneath the sheet.

*

Rosie had dropped the coins one by one into his hand as she issued him with his instructions.
"I don't want her dead. I just want that pretty fucking face of hers messed up, okay. So do what you have to."
This had been days ago now, he thought, but the time had eventually come when she was by herself. She had left Monique's house alone by carriage and without Rubin in her tracks. He was convinced of this. As well as following on horseback, he had also made certain that he wasn't being followed himself. This was his chance. He just had to wait patiently until she appeared back outside and he would make his move. Having done his reconnaissance of the place, he was satisfied it would be an easy task. He would take care of the coach driver if need be. This had been his plan anyway, until the waiting carriage had unexpectedly left fifteen minutes later without her. So, crouched within the undergrowth opposite, he pulled his collar up and prepared himself for what could be a long wait.

*

Madeline could see his lips tremble as she clasped his entirety in her hand. A pitiful sight now in contrast to the strapping, uniformed soldier she had first met, his stomach had jerked up in reaction to her first touch on him. She remained unmoving for a few seconds to gauge his reaction and, to her delight, she saw a glimmer of a smile appear on his face. If she could continue in this vein, she thought, then she would be half way there. And, in addition, he still hadn't removed his hand from her breast. In fact, she was convinced now that she could feel his grasp upon it tighten.
Preferring to look into his eyes, rather than see what her hand was doing out of sight, she returned what she thought was his smile and leaned closer towards him. She placed her lips softly against his and kissed him. And as she began to move her hand beneath the sheet, she simultaneously whispered to him, "My man."
Like a child, his lips trembled further as her movements about him increased. Madeline imagined in her minds eye what she held within her grasp and what she could do to bring additional pleasure to him. From the heel of her hand to the base of her fingers she felt the soft roll of his manhood. With her fingertips and thumb on either side, she sensed the loose-skinned sack of which she knew held the twin, delicate orbs from where the man's seed flowed. She was aware of the fragility of these, so was careful not to hold

them too tightly. Instead, she focused what lay in her palm. Lifting it free from its nestling state, she clasped it fully in the grip of her small, delicate fingers and, once entwined, turned her clenched hand to rest on Ramone's stomach. Feeling the heat emanate from within, she pulled her hand back and with it, gently drew the loose fold of skin to expose what she also knew to be his most intricate part. Madeline felt the identical jerk from him, as before, in reaction to this stimulus. Feeling good within herself, she gave another feather-light kiss to his lips and smiled again but this was no contented smile, it was a smile that beamed silently to him that this was only a precursor of the further delights to follow.

Remembering what she had seen done by both Gaston and Renault, she pulled the skin forward again and then back. It had seemed awkward at first as she found it difficult to negotiate, with competence, the globular tip. She was fearful of hurting him. But as he had not appeared to be in any discomfort with her doing it, save his malady, she tried again. On repeated attempts, she found that, as well as her grip around him, if she held the skin higher up with both thumb and index finger, she could get over this hurdle with confidence. So, with continued trial and error, she finally had her strokes upon him mastered, as the tightened grip on her breast confirmed and the faint whimpers under Ramone's breath acknowledged.

She was learning.

But she wasn't going to stop there, she thought. Her task had only just begun. She was determined to make Ramone the man he once was.

Her eye contact with him was only broken when she leaned forward to place her lips on his chest. But beforehand, and to maximise his view, Madeline had pulled her hair to the side so her full face was visible to him. She wanted him to miss nothing of what she was doing or about to do.

With a soft kiss through his thick, chest hair, she could feel the hot sweat from his skin on her lips. She kissed again, and with each one more gentle than the next, she inched her way down his body. Adjusting her own position when required, she continued with her hand movements on him; and by the time she had reached his stomach, the hair had thinned to such a degree that she could taste the salt on his skin. Eventually reaching the sheet top, she shifted her arm in such a way as to lower it without stopping what she was doing.

And there before her lay her goal.

Held daintily within her grasp, her hand enveloped him fully with only the rounded tip visible. Adjusting her grip immediately, Madeline now held him with only fingertips and thumb wanting it more on view to her. But it looked to her, for some reason, red and raw as if maltreated in some way. Ramone had shown no discomfort with what she had been doing, so she proceeded with her intentions unperturbed.

Once again, her thoughts were of Renault, Gaston and now Monique. They had all paid particular attention to the part connecting the outer skin to the

head, in particular Monique during her lesson with Fredrick. She would do likewise to see Ramone's reaction.
Tilting her head slightly for him to see, she leaned over and placed the tip of her tongue on the very same point. His body shuddered on contact. Indeed, his entire lower half had automatically raised itself from the bed an inch in response. And she could have sworn that she felt movement within her grasp. Smiling at him through eye contact, Madeline let her tongue move freely around the tip and was pleasantly shocked to find herself at ease doing so. Were things beginning to come clear to her now, she thought, her impulses natural without planning? Her hand had automatically begun its slow rhythmic strokes again and, surprisingly, her tongue had adapted to her movement, their timing now as one.
She felt it again. And then again... movement in her hand but it was not her strokes - it had come from within.
Ramone was stirring.
Madeline could feel growth within her hand, she was convinced of it. And staring directly up at him, she could see that he had gripped both sides of the bed, his hands shaking and his knuckles white with tension. His face had the same intensity about it, but there was something else, something that saddened her. There were tears in his eyes. But not the tears of pain though, nor sorrow, nor emptiness, but ones of happiness... ones of fulfillment. A slight whimper came forth and a faint groan of pleasure. And an utterance of her name, repeatedly through his constant search for air within his lungs. Madeline did not have to look to her hand to see what she now held, she felt it. Her grip, in accommodating his enlargement, had widened somewhat but her strokes on him had not changed, only more freedom to allow the fold on his skin to roll more freely back and forth, which she continued to do.
She immediately compared his size with the time she had held Frederick. There was no way then that she could have done to him what she was about to do now but she was convinced that Ramone was of a size she could manage with confidence. All she need do now was to repeat Monique's procedure. So, pulling the skin fully back on his now fully hard six inches, she beheld the purple globe which would be her first undertaking. With her tongue slowly circulating its perimeter and making certain Ramone's eyes were upon her, she leaned forward and let it slip between her lips. It was a unique experience, she had to admit, the initial feel and texture was something new; and as she let more slide into her mouth she felt certain that she would be able to complete her task with ease.

Ramone had repeatedly uttered her name amidst his groans of pleasure but when she had taken him into her mouth his body had convulsed in ecstasy and continued to do so. His entire body was shaking and his grip tightened at the bed even more. And with almost his entire being within the mouth of an angel sent from heaven, he felt then that he was at that very place himself. Not in so many years had he felt like this, never had he felt the passion of such a woman, the feel of her, the touch of her hand, the softness of her hair as it brushed along his skin. Her entire being was like that of a goddess. And she had brought his mortality to the fore one last time before he made his final journey to where all mortals went. Once again, this young woman had played the game by her own rules, he thought. His eyes filled further and he felt the tears of joy roll on his cheeks. Releasing his grip on the bed, he laid his right hand gently on her shoulder, feeling the softness of her skin and touching his angel one last time.

He cried further... and felt the explosion of his very-self erupt in one last powerful jolt of his body and his seed run free... the seed of life which in turn was taking his own from him.

He called out her name one last time before he closed his eyes forever.

*

Madeline 3

Chapter 9

A Dear Friend Lost

Madeline cried further.
Sitting cross-legged at the top of the bed, she held Ramone's head in her arms and sobbed like a child. Like a child that had just lost its favourite toy. Rocking him in her arms, she let her tears fall freely from her face onto his; and knowing that he had, in fact, not uttered such a thing, she continually chastised him for leaving her. "You promised me, you promised."
Still the tears fell.
She had lost her best friend. "And friends don't break their promises to each other," she continued.
Madeline had done what she had set out to do but she felt cheated. In doing so, she had taken the life from him and now here she was, alone, with the only person in Paris that she had felt confident to seek advice from, dead in her arms. With Rubin's earlier warnings of possible threats to her well-being and now with her allies rapidly diminishing, in respect that she had just lost a valued confidante, her mind was made up in an instant. She would return home.

Accompanied by Regina, who held a lantern out before her, Madeline descended the steps towards the waiting carriage. The physician having being called to the house an hour earlier had, indeed, pronounced him dead. Cause of death, a simple weakening of the heart. But before calling on Regina, Madeline had made certain to resume the bed and sheet to its former organised state, and have Ramone situated in such a position as to have them make believe he had simply passed on with her holding his hand. In addition, she had had to smooth out his facial muscles to show a look that would reinforce this front. Then, having redressed and rinsed her face from his wash basin, she had made herself look as before upon arrival.
They stopped at the bottom of the steps. It was Regina who broke the awkward silence. "I will inform you of the funeral arrangements in due

course. I am led to believe that Monsieur has requested a burial outwith the city but I am uncertain as to its exact location."

Madeline nodded in acknowledgement. "Merci, Regina."

She turned towards the carriage and then paused. "Oh, pardon. I almost forgot." She turned around and handed Regina a handkerchief. In the midst of her earlier sobbing during the physician's visit, Regina had kindly enough handed Madeline a fresh one of finest silk. She remembered at the time feeling gauche with the idea of staining such a beautiful cloth with her tears, and also using it for its main design.

Regina accepted its return. "Thank you. It was a present from Monsieur on my birthday."

Madeline smiled. "He was a true and considerate man."

Regina returned the smile but said nothing, her heart also broken with the loss of her employer.

"Well, au revoir."

But before she could turn, both their attentions were drawn to the dimly lit undergrowth opposite. A darkened figure had appeared but as suddenly as it had come into view, it disappeared just as quickly. Regina raised the lantern out in front of her. Both saw nothing.

"Probably just an animal."

Madeline stared on - she was not so sure.

She yawned.

Suddenly realising the hour and that she had not slept since early light the previous day, Madeline stifled another.

The uniform rocking of the carriage and the darkness within was enough to send her heavy eyes to close, but the sudden reminder of the night's events sent her melancholy once again. Her thoughts were of Ramone and their first meeting, their trips around Paris and the shopping sprees where his generosity had showed no bounds, with him insisting in outfitting her entire wardrobe to Parisian fashion. She smiled but with it came the tears. It was not only these material things that made him the man he was, it was his loving and caring nature. His easy ear had been made available to her when she needed advice and reassurance. Who now did she have?

She cried once again. And in the total darkness of the carriage, she tried in vain to search for her own handkerchief within her bag. But something was preventing her from doing so. Wiping her eyes clear of the moisture with her hand, she sniffed in to clear herself. Opening it fully, she peered in, but seeing nothing in the darkness, rummaged again. Something foreign lay within, something she knew should not be in there. She pulled it free. And felt its shape.

It was a letter.

… A heavy letter and cumbersome to boot. How on earth had this gotten into her bag, she wondered. She knew its contents well and had not left it with anyone since she, herself, arranged it the previous morning. Then she

considered earlier. In Ramone's bed chamber. When she had been at the fire, she had returned and sat on the bed. But it had not occurred to her that her bag was in a different position. She had to move it further along so as to reseat as before. Had Ramone placed it in her bag then? It seemed the only logical explanation. Frustrated with the lack of light, her fingers probed the outside. She felt what she thought to be the wax seal of Ramone on the back but something heavier than just a letter was inside.

To her delight, they approached the city boundary and with it came a faint source of light. She raised the coach blind a few inches and leaned the letter into the faint shaft of illumination. Breaking the seal on its back, she unfolded the paper but on doing so she heard a small thud on the floor. Something had fallen out. Leaning forward, her hand groped blindly about the floor until she felt what she was looking for. She raised it to the light. ... Two keys.

One of silver the size of her thumb, the other much more robust and made from iron were clasped inside a ringed coil. Madeline sat staring at them in her opened palm. "Keys." Strange, she thought. "Keys to what?"

Pulling the letter fully opened, Madeline hurriedly read the contents in case the light was lost. She sat with mouth agape. Re-reading it again, she lowered it to her lap and leaned back... the sly, old fox.

She smiled... she would not be returning home after all.

*

News of Ramone's death had reached Caroline just after sunrise and in turn, as was instructed, the Comtesse was informed immediately.

Jeanette smiled and nodded her head. "Good. That is excellent news. Then our plan is in motion."

Caroline, standing half-undressed by Jeanette's bed, looked down at her. "What plans? You have told us nothing of this scheme of yours."

Jeanette casually dismissed the naked servant girl from her bed. And once she had gathered her clothes together and left the room, only then did the Comtesse continue. "I will have the house searched today."

"Which house? Ramone's?"

Jeanette rose from her bed and walked naked towards the dresser. "Of course, Ramone's house. Which house do you think I mean?"

Caroline followed her. "What are we looking for - his money?"

Lifting the brush from the top, Jeanette sat in front of the mirror and tugged at her knots. "That and amongst other things."

Caroline knew she was being vague, yet again, but as long as the main objective was the money, then she was satisfied with that. "Who will do the searching may I ask? You know persons of such a nature in Paris?"

Jeanette turned on her seat and faced up at her. "This plan has been long in the making. Do you think I would leave it to chance that some common criminals of the city could do my bidding? No, I arrived with two individuals

of my choosing. Both adept, I may add, in this kind of foul play. With their help I will accomplish all I set out to do. The first part is complete - Ramone is dead. Now we await the outcome.
Caroline nodded in compliance. "Very well."
Jeanette raised her right hand to the middle of Caroline's chest on which she laid the tip of her index finger. And on slowly running its way down her centre, she finished, "Until then, we can indulge in some pre-breakfast delights."

*

Madeline 4

Madeline 4

Prologue

**Chateau d'Estelle,
18th Century France**

She should have died the previous night.
How she had survived the bitter cold was lost to him. The harsh conditions of the cell would have had the most hardened of criminals fight for existence and where others of less resilience would have succumbed to death through hypothermia, she had fought through it with grit. She had clung to life with such determination and a strong will to survive that he could only ponder her incentive to do so. For body and mind to wrestle with death's grasp under such circumstances and triumph over it was the true miracle of human endurance. Or could it perhaps have been that her knowing if she were to perish, then the same fate would await the little one that was growing within her, this being the absolute epitome of the bond that existed between mother and unborn child. He could only wonder. Lowering his eyes from the pitiful face before him, he stared at the dressed wound on her neck. He deliberated over the reason for it. He of course knew its effect; it had taken her voice from her, but who would do such a thing and more importantly, for what reason. Her isolation within the cell would have been enough to secure her silence as he as the sole jailor would have been the only person she would be in contact with. His only conclusion was that it had been to prevent her from

revealing her identity, but then again, if she could write, what was to stop her from using the written word as communication. He lowered his eyes further. And as for her chest, what was that this abomination? He appeared to have more questions than he had answers, but before he had time to consider further some possible explanations, she had stirred.

The benevolent act of trying to pad the hard wooden pallet on which she now lay with whatever fresh straw he could muster was immediately overshadowed with the heinous, but unintentional wound he had inflicted upon her during her almost premature burial.

Her right hand immediately made for her nose. She flinched in pain. This being where he had tried hard to drive the needle through, he squirmed with embarrassment. Hadn't she endured enough without him adding to her injuries? "My doing I'm afraid. I thought you were dead."

Showing no reaction to his apology by way of explanation, he watched her look around the cell and take stock of her situation. Her eyes fixed directly on the opened window.

He followed her gaze and returned it in an instant. "Don't even think about it. It's too much of a drop to the rocks below."

Ignoring him for the second time, she pulled her tattered, loose fitting top, tight against her chest.

On realizing his faux par; that of her thinking it a possible escape route, he knew now that she was alluding to the cold wind blowing in through the gap. And although it was not as cold as it was the previous night this did not prevent a constant breeze coming in from the sea. "I'll try and fix that up as best I can. Unfortunately I'm stuck for what we have here." But within seconds of saying it he smiled to himself. He knew exactly where he would get what he needed and it would give him great pleasure in taking it from where it was now, the adjacent cell. He would use the Scotsman's pallet. 'Fuck it...' he thought '...he can lie on the floor, she was more important."

She looked quizzically at his lips and he recognized her quandary. His mischievous smile did not go hand in hand with her squalid surroundings he sensed from her, but could think of nothing to appease the situation save to explain to her where she was. He thought better of it though as this information could wait until later. He was in no hurry to tell this young woman that the cell in which she now sat was her home for the rest of her life. He remembered the food by his feet and nodded down to his left. "I've got some soup here if you can swallow it?"

Referring to her neck dressing, he reached out to touch it but watched as she pulled away in fright, her right hand defensively raise itself and clutch at her throat. She made efforts to speak out but all that came forth was a coarse rasp. The pain of which was evident to him, as her reactions showed, with three consecutive dry coughs.

"I didn't mean you any harm. It was only out of concern, not with harsh intent. My name is Oswald. I am...I am...I am keeper of this place."

Her eyes once again looked about the cell, but this time more slowly, taking in all the details, as much as they were. Apart from the pallet on which she lay, the only other thing of consequence was a wooden bucket in the corner which she immediately took to be her toilet. All else was bare, with the hard stone floor blending in with four walls of similar matter, the outer one of which had a constant stream of foul smelling water running down its full length and was clearly the cause of the damp smell. Several rat holes were evident at each base which meant that she would have frequent visitors during the night. The heavy wooden door she noticed had a hatch at the bottom, presumably to slide her food through. She would at least have a view she thought as she heard bird sounds coming from the open window.

Raising her body from the pallet, she sidled to the left and let her feet rest upon a hard stone floor. Now facing Oswald straight on, her head titled to the right like some lost pup, her mind searching for answers.

"You're in the Chateau d'Estelle.

Her eyes squeezed in tight, seeking further information from him.

"I've no idea who brought you here or why but I'll do all I can to help you." He nodded to her neck. "Can you swallow?" Without waiting for an answer by way of a tilt or a shake of the head, he pointed at her belly and finished with a reason for her to try. "You're having a young 'en."

Being more of a statement than a question, she took it as the later and on pulling her bent knees up tight to her chest she clasped her arms about them and nodded.

"Then that's all the more reason for you to eat then."

Oswald tilted his head back to admire his handiwork. Having secured the window with some minor adjustments to the Scotsman's pallet, he had stuffed strips of torn cloth in between the slats thus hoping it would at least prevent the worst of the cold wind from penetrating her cell. Stepping down from the three legged stood which he had brought temporarily from his own room, he turned just in time to see her jostle with her undergarments and adjust her clothing after having relieved herself in the corner bucket. He pulled his head away until she had finished. "That should keep the worst of it out I think."

On hearing her resume her place back on the pallet, he turned to face her again. His eyes were drawn directly to the unfinished soup. "I know it was sore to swallow but you'll have to eat more than that if you are to live. Can you manage some more?"

She shook her head and once again clasped at her throat.

"Do you mind if I have a look at it? The head fixed it up when you first got here but if the dressing isn't changed it might get infected."

Her only response was to exchange her hand from one wound to another, notably her nose. Her middle and index finger rested on the outside in an attempt to alleviate some of the pain.

Squatting down in front of her, Oswald made further explanation. "It was a boned needle. When you think of it, it was lucky that I did it or else you'd be in the sea by now. You weren't showing any signs of life...I thought you'd had it." Upon reflection, perhaps a quick death would have been more of a godsend to her rather than to live out her life in this hell hole he thought.

They sat in silence for what seemed to him like an eternity. With casual conversation never having come natural to him in the past, this one sided discussion was torturous to him, so he decided he would leave her for a while. Standing, he reached for his stool and made for the door. He looked down at the unfinished soup. "Try and eat some more. I'll be back later."

Oswald would not return later that day as he had promised. Not until the next morning would he make an appearance. She would lie on the pallet unmoving and eyes fixed straight ahead at the trickling water. And as the day blended into dusk and dusk into night she stared at the wall through the thick black void...and eventually heard her night visitors make their appearance in the dark.

Cold, shivering and alone, she cried herself to sleep.

*

Madeline 4

Chapter 1

Avarice

Paris, France
Some time earlier

As the sun tried, in all earnest, to split apart the haze of the permanently polluted Parisian clouds, a privileged few rose from a quiet slumber to greet the morning, and with outstretched arms, yawn in anticipation of what this new day would bring them. Breaking an overnight fasting on eggs, meat and bread could be commonplace to the select, but others not as fortunate would greet the same rays of sunlight wondering where their next crust would come from just to survive the day. And although the entire populace; irrespective of class, breathed in the same contaminated air and contracted indiscriminately incurable diseases, it was the capital division that would eventually not only be the city, but the entire country's downfall. In Paris, money was everything. Revolution was imminent and if both divisions were unprepared for it then they would pay the price and miss out. The rich would have their wealth taken from them and the poor would lose out on gaining coin through theft or deceit. It was an opportunists' world to those that had nothing, but to them that had coin, then the love of it would inculcate plots to gain even more. Like most places the world over, money meant power, but no more so than in Paris, where people, rich or poor, would do anything to get it.

Jeanette woke with one such plot deep in mind.

Within seconds of opening her eyes she had smiled. And not because she felt the soft skin of the two young women lying naked in bed beside her, but rather safe in the knowledge that Ramone was now finally dead. She had planned this from the very moment his whereabouts had become known to her. She would not only gain wealth from his passing but more importantly, the revenge she had sought after for some time now. With his sublimation from commoner to nobility being the deception which had him elude her for years now, it had taken almost a decade to track him down. Resolute in her determination to avenge the death of her loved one and to take back the money stolen, she had been heartless in her approach. She had metamorphosed from a genteel woman to that of a callous monster. A cold hearted bitch she now considered herself to be...and she had chosen her company accordingly.

Raul and Raul had assisted her in the more delicate matters when it had come to persuasion. The chances of her finding her prey by herself would have been minimal and had it not been for their influential approach to investigation through interrogation she would still be going round in circles now. The authorities had done very little to discover his whereabouts, with them understandably reluctant to believe that simple Luis could have committed such a crime, preferring to concentrate their efforts on a more obvious suspect...mainly her. But with the passing of each week, their investigation appeared to have been working its way down the bottom of the pile and eventually with no leads to go on or evidence to convict anyone, the case had been closed.

But not to her it hadn't. As the authorities had investigated her, she had taken matters into her own hands and had simultaneously commissioned an investigation of her own.

On his hasty departure from town on the night of the murder, Luis had stolen a wagon and headed east. This was where the trail had ended and all that she had had to go on. Her monthly endeavours to send men after him and to seek out his whereabouts had been fruitless and all had returned with little or no information. It was as if he had vanished into thin air. This had not deterred her and even though her own resources had been spent in doing so, she had gained additional financial support to fund future searches by marrying into money. And when her husband's resources had diminished she had resorted to extreme measures by instigating an early widowhood. Conducted through cunning and clever planning, she had never at any time been suspected of murder and as a widow had been free to marry once again. And thus she had readily done just two weeks later, to Henri, who although had not been as wealthy as her previous husband, had still been a manipulative enough individual for her to drain the family account until exhausted. To enable her to marry a third time, another hole in the ground had been required and three weeks later her husband's body fitted comfortably six feet down in it. And yet again, suspicion had never once fallen upon her. As an ardent lover that night, she had sent her second husband to meet his maker with a smile on his face. Cause of death, exhaustion to the heart through excessive strain...amongst other parts she remembered. Meanwhile Luis' whereabouts still evaded her and in dire need of money she had hit gold the third time when she married Sebastian.

A mystery to her from the beginning, Sebastian appeared to play out a role which was not entirely true to life. And similar to Luis who would later adopt the alias Ramone and reinvent himself as nobility, she found the thrill of the subterfuge addictive and was happy to take on the title Comtesse in lieu of plain old Jeanette. In light of this, she now wondered if anyone in France was actually who they claimed to be and how easy it was to dupe people when you had coin to back up the façade. And to such an extent that no-one had even questioned her titled name which Sebastian had cheekily taken from his favourite drink. His easily accommodating nature; and wealth to back it up, had enabled her to continue her search for Luis and with her husband being well connected with some less-than-savoury characters, he had engaged Raul and Raul to do her bidding. Sebastian had assured her of their loyalty and although using some rather viscous and unorthodox methods in their work, they had always produced results when they had been employed by him in the past. Sebastian was not wrong in that respect she remembered. Within seven months they had found Luis living in Paris under the guise of an ex-Italian army officer named Senior Ramone Leone. They had also left a trial of blood in their wake when doing so. But this had mattered little to her as, by then, she was used to using unscrupulous methods herself and had became immune to such trivialities. It came with the job. Their news was what she had been waiting to hear for years and she had set her planned revenge in motion immediately. Thanks to Sebastian she had found her prey, but she also found herself no longer in need of a husband...

...Sebastian was buried four days later.

*

Denig was first to waken.

Pulling his heavy bloodshot eyes opened, he looked around the room in an attempt to gauge the time by its brightness. It was still early.

As was the norm at this time in the morning and especially after a heavy night of drinking, he found him-self fully erect. And as was customary; with his wife Caroline's naked posterior just inches from him beneath the covers, he turned on his side and nuzzled into her back. With his penis still tender from the previous night's love making, he quietly spat into the palm of his right hand and lubricated the tip of it with the saliva. Parting the cheeks of her rear slightly for easier access, he gently guided himself between the two and released his hold. He allowed the grip of her thighs to keep him in place as he pushed forward just enough to let his skin unfold between.

"You won't come Denig, you need to piss first."

He knew his wife to be right in her assumption and that the stiffness was the result of a full bladder. "Oh, I didn't know you were awake."
Caroline pushed back slightly. "How can I sleep with this thing between my legs?" She tensed and with a pelvic grip on him, wriggled back "and when have I ever been asleep when you've fucked me…even when it's a dry one?"
Denig smiled and nestled closer, kissing at her neck "Only because you hate to miss out on things my darling."
Caroline's face joined him in a smile and she pulled his arm closer around her "You know me so well my husband."
Jostling forward in mischievous manner, he pushed his lower stomach tight against her back "Then open up for me, bitch."
Wide awake now and laughing at his boisterous behaviour, Caroline turned abruptly on her back loosening her grip at the last moment.
Wrestling himself out from beneath her, Denig clutched at his tender skin "Fuck sake Caroline, you almost had the bastard off there."
Still laughing, her hand stretched out to add comfort and rested it on his as he gripped at its base. She leaned forward. "Would I be so stupid to let that happen?" She kissed its tip and looked up into Denig's eyes. "Now go and empty yourself."
Having risen from the bed with a drunken stagger, Denig positioned himself a mere two feet from it and on pointing down at an awkward angle befitting his erection, began filling the chamber pot. "Well, what are the plans for today then?"
Caroline noticed the speed at which he was urinating due to the build up of pressure and in particular the resulting splashes which were making their way onto the carpeted floor. She reprimanded him at once. She also noted the gradual deflation of his aroused state.
Adjusting his stance as commanded, he answered his own question. "Entertaining miss-fucking-lady-fucking-comtesse along the hall again no doubt." He shook himself dry and fell onto the bed, head resting on Caroline's lap. He looked up. "She had two along there with her last night you know, heard them at it when I passed the door. Fuck knows what she was doing with them. I'm telling you Caroline, this had better be worth it."
Caroline brushed the tip of his forelock with her fingers. She had her own doubts about what had been promised to them by Jeanette in payment for their efforts. But nothing had been mentioned about Ramone's death for several days now. Reluctant to push the matter further as the Comtesse had assured her that things were in hand, she found herself having to sit tight and wait what was coming to them, whatever that was. Denig, with the patience of a spoilt child, was less tolerant then herself to Jeanette taking over their house and her constant demands, and not only from them but the staff included. Two had left their service already, with them unwilling to submit to Jeanette's extreme wants, no matter what the payment was. Both she and Denig were renowned for their own libertine lifestyle but even Jacqueline had commented upon Jeanette's excessive behaviour, stating that she had

enquired of her the possibility of procuring a large dog. And dog as in a male dog, the reasons for which had been obvious to her. Jeanette's invitation to join her had left Jacqueline speechless. But as a means to an end, Caroline now felt obliged; nay compelled to see the whole thing through to the end. They needed the money and the Comtesse had promised it in abundance.

"You have your own doubts now I see." Commenting on her silence and the deliberation on her face, Denig had reached up to place a reassuring hand on her cheek.

Caroline clasped it in hers and smiled. "We have no choice but to carry on. We shall just have to put up with it all a little bit longer."

Denig sighed and shook his head. "Then we'll be destitute before we are rich." Rolling over on his back, he clasped his hands behind his head and lay staring at the ceiling. "Assuming she is good to her word that is. I am still not fully convinced about how she would gain from Ramone's death. She still hasn't made it clear to us how she knows him, and for that matter, why she wanted him dead."

Caroline followed suit and lay on her side, threading her fingers through Denig's chest hair. "Does it really matter? Is it so important that we know and not just be content with what we gain from it?"

"Gain from it…gain. It has cost us thousands so far Caroline. Thousands that we cannot afford, nor have at present to lose. If we do not get a grand return from this investment in the Comtesse then we are finished good and proper. I mean it Caroline, you can kiss this house goodbye. And then where would we be?

Caroline sat up straight. "Are things that bad?"

"My dear, I have three loans taken out against this house already, and some part repayments are due. I have been putting them off in the hope that this scheme of hers will clear our debt entirely."

Caroline tried to calculate the expenditure in her head. "Where has it all gone, surely she hasn't cost us that much?"

"If it has been available to her then she has either bought it or hired it, paid by with our money on my credit with suppliers. Clothes, perfumes, jewellery, carriage hire, eating out, wine of the highest quality, it all mounts up you know…" he paused and looked to his left "…speaking of which." Stretching over for a half filled wine glass, he unwittingly changed the subject. "Imagine me falling asleep without finishing this last night."

"A bit early is it not?"

Sitting up, he leaned against the back bed panel and lifted the glass to his lips. "Hah, better make the most of it my darling because this could be our last." He swallowed it in one go and stared at the empty glass in his hand. "Ah, a liquid breakfast, the best kind."

Caroline looked passed him to where the wine decanter sat on the bedside table. It was still near full. She smiled at Denig. "Then I may as well join you. Forget our troubles for a while and lie here all day."

Denig sat up further and bent down to kiss the top of her head. "That's my girl, yes, let's have a day in bed, get drunk and fuck our brains out and the only person we will see today is when someone brings us wine and then more wine." He grabbed at the decanter.
Caroline looked down at his penis and took it in her hand. "Is this up for it today, it looks tender and sore to the touch?"
Denig laughed as he poured wine into a fresh glass for her. "I know, either my cock is getting bigger or your arse is getting tighter."
She elbowed his side.
Denig handed her a glass and began filling his own. "You've seen what a dog does when it has a wound haven't you?"
Caroline sipped at its edge and nodded. "Yes, it licks it until better."
With a clink of his glass edge against hers, he raised it in salute and continued. "That is because there is healing power in the spit from its tongue. It is a common fact that my darling."
Caroline shrugged her shoulders perplexed.
"Well, you're my bitch aren't you?" He nodded down to his red coloured penis. "So get licking."
Caroline smiled and leaned over to kiss his cheek, and with puckered lips, whispered in his ear...
"Woof!"

*

Jeanette slapped at the face for a second time.
"Stupid bitch, how dare she fucking die on me?" She slapped again "and in my own fucking bed as well."
The second of the two young girls sat naked, cowering on the corner of the bed. Shaking for fear of reprisals upon her, her stark, staring eyes followed Jeanette as she walked round the bed in her direction.
"Please Comtesse, it was not of my doing."
Jeanette screamed out at her in hushed tone. "So then you are saying that I was the cause of it?"
The young girl looked over at her dead friend and the red marking on her neck, and lower down to the dark bruising on her inner thighs. Then beyond to the nearby chair where the broad eight inch ivory phalanx sat. She turned with pleading eyes to Jeanette and shook her head. "No Comtesse. I did not say that. Only..."
"Only what?" Jeanette stood in front of her, unashamedly naked with hands on hips and yelled at her again "only fucking what?"
The girl covered her ears as if to block out the sound, and with it came her tears. "You hurt her. You hurt both of us."
Unmoved by mock tears and sentiment, Jeanette drew her right hand hard across the girls face, and with it, the back of her chunky gold ring found a home in her left eye. The scream was deafening.

*

Caroline almost choked.
Pulling her mouth free from Denig, she looked up. "What the…"
Unconcerned, Denig stared at the unfinished business still grasped in her hand and sipped at his wine. "She's started early, just like us."
Her task forgotten about, Caroline spoke out with apprehension. "Oh my God, what is going on along there, what is she doing to them?"
The screams continued and with no introduction by way of a knock, their bed chamber door flew open. It was Jacqueline. Indifferent to the scene before her; that of Denig's erection clasped within Caroline's hand, she moved forward with fear on her face. "You'll have to come quickly. One of the maids is dead and that bitch looks like she has another in mind."
For the second time in so short a space, Denig shrunk again, this time in Caroline's hand. "Are you joking…dead?"
Jacqueline shook her head "I wished I was Denig, I wished I was."
Caroline leapt free from the bed and grabbed her robe. Slipping it on in mid pace, she followed Jacqueline through the door. Denig meantime; having trouble locating his, spilled his wine on the sheets.
Heading at speed along the hallway, Jacqueline tried to explain what she had found earlier, just to give Caroline a head start prior to entering the Comtesse's room. But before she had finished, they had reached the opened door.
The first thing Caroline noticed upon entering was the motionless, naked body of the young maid on the bed. It was Clara. But before she had a chance to take this in, the scene to her left took her eyes from it in an instant. There, hovering over a frightened, cowering girl stood an equally naked Comtesse, violently beating the maid with what she considered to be an onyx ornament. On closer inspection of it; as she inched forward, she could identify it with clarity. She had used a similar device before on herself, but the enormity of this one was overwhelming. How indeed, could anyone fit this item inside them, she found herself inexplicably asking. The screaming continued. In her attempt to evade the deadly blows, the young girl had shielded her face with her arms but the constant pounding had taken its toll on them. In lieu of her normal looking limbs, there now hung from her shoulders, two disjointed pieces of broken flesh and bone. Caroline felt herself transfixed to the spot and unable to move. She sensed Denig by her side. Standing with glass in one hand and decanter in the other he stood as motionless and shocked at the scene as she was.
"Fuck me. What the hell is that she's hitting her with?"
"We have to do something Denig." It felt a stupid thing to say under the circumstances, as if this had been an everyday occurrence, but fearing Jeanette's temper could turn on her, she felt hesitant in moving forwards. It was Jacqueline who took the initiative.

Waiting for the upward swing of the phalanx, Jacqueline grabbed at the object and pulled Jeanette off balance. As both fell to the floor, Jacqueline's clenched fist found its way at speed into the Jeanette's face. It was enough to momentarily stun her and Caroline took advantage of the lull. She made her move to restrain Jeanette further but Jacqueline had it under control. With her full weight upon Jeanette's chest, she had both arms pinned to the ground.
Denig turned and looked at the bed. "Fucking great...
...now we've got a body to get rid of."

*

They had not been the only ones to have risen early.
Several miles across Paris, Monique sat, fully dressed at her breakfast table and as always, contemplative of her money making schemes. With Madeline's future set out in her mind, this additional venture with Caroline and Denig would see further coin make its way into her already bulging coffer. The accumulative wealth which had amassed itself over the years of her hard labour was one she now furtively guarded, secreted at close quarters, and easily accessible to her given any eventuality, namely the imminent uprising of the masses. She knew her days as Madame were numbered in Paris but had made plans accordingly. In fact, in retrospect, it had been none other than Ramone that had advised her to do so, saying that he himself had done something similar. His plans, she now thought, had been pointless. He would certainly not have envisaged his untimely death or the circumstances which would drive him to it. Of late, he had become more of an acquaintance to her rather than a client and over the years had unconsciously volunteered to her several snippets of information about himself that was not known to others. Indeed, she had pieced together a reality far a field to that of him living out the life of a retired officer and gentleman. But this reality had inconsistence at its core as well. Aquitaine had figured prominently in his life she was certain; Toulouse to be exact, but to what extent she was unsure. Had he been born there, had he family? The existence of a wife had been a possibility, but Ramone being more of an enigma than a mystery, had contradicted this later by mentioning a single life in Lyon. These two possibilities were not in line with the life he had portrayed to others, that of being Genoese. Never having heard him utter a word in the Italian language save the few phrases which could have been picked up by anyone, he had always spoken in the French tongue, the idiom of which had given way to the fact that this had come natural to him and was no secondary language. Whether or not others had picked up on this or had simply chosen to ignore it as irrelevant she was uncertain. When you are solvent; as indeed Ramone clearly had been, these trivialities were more often than not overlooked. Monique was fully aware that money could have such an overwhelming effect on peoples' sensibility and that being affluent

could mask a thousand irregularities in one's life. At what point in the social ladder of things did you become eccentric rather than being odd, she thought, or the transition of being assassinated rather than being murdered for that matter. Her own accent in this ladder was developing nicely and with some of Ramone's wealth soon to make its way to her, she smiled as she cracked open her second egg.

But the appetite was taken from her as she considered it further. Her head tilted up to the ceiling, and looking through the various floors above in her mind's eye, she thought of Madeline. Ramone's death had taken a lot from her, as she was certainly not the young girl she knew and had grown to love. Ignoring the constant asides and whispers from the other girls under her employ, she had permitted Madeline once again some respite in her duties. How long she would allow her to mourn was undecided but at present she was content just to have her in attendance at night with clients. Madeline was still earning money for her in this respect but it could not go on ad infinitum. There was coin to be made from her and Caroline had been the one that would get her further up the ladder she so craved to climb. She rose, and with coffee cup in hand, made her way gingerly towards her favourite armchair content in her thinking…

…but her plans for Madeline were about to take a dramatic twist.

*

Madeline 4

Chapter 2

Tasks in Hand

Madeline woke to find her pillow wet once again.
For three consecutive nights she had unconsciously cried in her sleep and had woken in the morning with damp and swollen eyes. She was missing Ramone dreadfully. And having received no correspondence from the staff at the house with regards to his funeral, this had upset her even more. Should it take so long to arrange such things she wondered? Having only attended one interment in the past; that of her uncle when she was thirteen and which had been a simple town affair, she could only ponder on what was so difficult and time consuming about ordering a casket and placing it in a hole in the ground. In her naivety, she was lost to the possible pomp and ceremony that could accompany one of stature and which the aristocracy within the city was known for. Even in death, such libertine extravagance could prevail upon them, assuming they had the money to do so. Therefore the preparation of such could take time, especially if mourners were travelling from further a field than the city walls. Raising her head from the damp pillow, she reversed it in search of unsoiled cloth then lay back with her head facing up towards the ceiling and thought further on the days following her friend's death...one of which she herself had assisted in.
Monique had been such a considerate and understanding employee that it could have almost been believed to be a genuine friendship concern. Upon her return from Ramone's house that morning, it was she who had informed Monique of his passing. But there had been something curious about her

reaction to the news. It was as if she already knew. This, Madeline considered, could have possibly been put down to the fact that Ramone's carriage driver had requested haste in his return journey the previous night, them expecting the worst, but she thought otherwise. It was as if her news was not only expected, but welcomed. She also knew that both Monique and Ramone had known each other for a considerably long time; albeit in a more professional capacity, but surely she would have nothing to gain from his demise, indeed she would be losing a loyal paying customer. But most welcoming of all was Monique's insistence in the relaxation of her entertaining duties for a few days. So, further to the time she had received after the first knife attack, her tasks had been curtailed to a minimum and limited to assisting Monique in attending to some of the less adventurous guests...the ones without the need for physical contact. The mere sitting in attendance and the serving of drinks was her sole function. This respite she had gladly accepted as her experience with Ramone was still fresh in her memory. The only drawback to this was the reaction of the other girls who knew only too well of her preferential treatment. But if things went as she had planned, then she would not have to endure their snide remarks for a while. She needed only await the return of Rubin to see her plan of action take shape.

Ramone's letter to her had included some very intricate wording and if she were to follow his instructions then she needed someone like Rubin to assist her. In the short time that she had known him, she had placed her trust in him on many an occasion and as yet he had not failed her. And although his appearance to some would undoubtedly draw mistrust, Madeline knew deep within herself that he would not let her down. It was a strange relationship for sure, but there appeared to be some invisible bond between them and with them being so different in every way, she had yet to fathom the link.

Rubin had not been privy to the letter's full contents, just the parts that she thought he needed to know, for the time being anyway. She was still not one hundred percent sure of what Ramone's plan for her was or what his legacy entailed. Only that the two keys bestowed to her would open up an inheritance of a sort. But the letter made no mention of what was held within the vault in question....a vault that was hundreds of miles away from Paris. One thing was for certain though. They had a long journey ahead of them.

*

For two hours Rubin had lay in the bushes watching the house and as yet, not one person had shown themselves. Highly unusual considering there was meant to be preparations for a funeral underway he thought. Furthermore, he was fed up as he had left the city without a bottle in his pocket. He needed a drink.

It had been Madeline who had sent him on this errand. Unable to remember the route she had taken previously, she had, the previous evening, promised him she would not leave the house if he were to use his connections and find out where Ramone lived, then to come here and reconnoitre on her behalf. He knew that it was not the funeral that she hankered to attend so much as her reluctance to start their journey until it was over. She wanted to pay her respects before leaving. As it was, this had not been necessary. He had visited Ramone's house on a previous occasion, but there was no need for her to know about this. Lying in the undergrowth though was not to his suiting as he was a man of action and needed to be where he could find things out for himself. He rose and headed for the main entrance.

*

Both Denig and Caroline sat in silence as the Comtesse laid out instructions regarding the disposal of the body. Fully dressed now and sitting in the main parlour, they listened intently as she calmly explained the course of action.
"I have sent for two who will assist us in this matter, they are to be trusted, you have my word on that. As for the other one, she will be tended to and taken care of with payment in lieu."
Payment in lieu, thought Denig, for breaking her arms out of all recognition. That was her livelihood in service lost, so what possible payment could be a substitute for her losing the use of the tools that earned her living. And who would be making this payment to her, he wondered, him, no doubt? He looked over to Caroline to judge her reaction, but she had sat motionless the whole time, hands clasped firmly on her lap and deep in shock with the whole scenario.
The Comtesse continued. "It is indeed unfortunate, but alas, casualties are inevitable with the games we play."
Denig could not believe his ears. His mind raced. The games we play? Clara's snatch had been powdered black and blue, plus the marks on her neck signaled some extreme asphyxiation during their so-called games. He could not condone this. And how in the name of goodness were they to make a body simply disappear? Clara had family. They would notice her disappearance, and with her being in their employ, it would be the first place the authorities would look.
Reading his thoughts, the Comtesse explained further. "Everything will be taken care of, I assure you of this." She stood and as if dismissing an unruly child, finished. "Now, if you would be so kind as to let me attend to breakfast, we can speak later. Tell the cook I want my eggs poached, and in clean water. You will inform me immediately the moment they arrive."
'They' being the 'two' she had mentioned earlier Denig presumed and not her eggs.

Dabbing her lips with the napkin, Jeanette finished her breakfast just in time to hear the knock on the door. Permitting entry, she was informed by the maid of Raul and Raul's arrival.

As immaculately dressed as ever she had seen them, both entered the room and doffed their hats. Remaining silent until spoken to, they stood awaiting instructions.

By way of an upward hand, Jeanette offered them a seat opposite.

"Gentleman..." Gentleman indeed, she thought, if people only knew. These two men were amongst the cruelest people in France. Their guise was a veneer for brutal and cold hearted murderers who took extreme pleasure in their work. "...before you furnish me with an update, I wish to inform you of another task I would like of you."

With one sharp tilt of the head, both nodded in unison.

"I find myself in the awkward position of having a dead girl on my hands." She paused to see their reaction.

As expected, none came. With their faces as lifeless and solemn as the black suits they both donned, the two sat unmoved by her news.

"Yes, well. You see my predicament." Clutching at the gold pendant that hung from her neck, she toyed with it in her hand, letting this sink in before proceeding to her next request. "There is also a young girl who has just recently arrived at the infirmary. She bears wounds to her arms. I do not wish to hear of her existence again. Am I understood?"

Clearly she was. Only this time a wry smile accompanied their nod.

"Very well." Reaching to her side, she pulled a leather pouch from her dress and tossed it across to the larger of the two. In one swift movement, the coins were caught in his hat. He nodded with thanks.

"Now, moving on to more pressing business."

Taking this statement as a question, the recipient of the cash pouch who she knew to be the more loquacious of the two, spoke out. "We could not find the whereabouts of the keys."

This was not what she wanted to hear. "And the house staff?"

"They could tell us nothing."

Jeanette could only imagine what in what state they had left them.

*

With his eyes on constant lookout about him, Rubin approached the outside stairway and started his slow ascent. All seemed normal around him, but as he reached the halfway mark and with his towering height he could look over the final step towards the doorway. Even from such a distance away he could estimate the door to be ajar approximately six to seven inches. Strange he thought. No housekeeper or butler would leave a door opened thus. Unconsciously adjusting the knife at his back he inched forward.

Peering through the gap he could see nothing more than the highly polished marble floor and further on towards the side wall. But on it hung an eight foot mirror and within its reflection was the entire hallway to the opposite side. All appeared normal and was still. He pushed the door's edge and with a well set of oiled hinges as he had ever heard, it opened without a sound.

He hesitated for a moment. If he took one more step in then this would be construed as breaking and entering. Did he really want to take that chance, especially with the young Missy's task in hand? He would be no use to her banged up in jail. 'Fuck'…where was his bottle when he needed it?

But he needed to know, Missy needed to know. What could he say on his return if he didn't go in, that no-one was at the house? This would not do, not one bit would it do. No information was useless information. He had a job and he would see it through…like he always did and always had done.

Before he entered, he hollered out. His voice resonated around the hall and beyond. Before the echo had died he had hollered a second time but there came no response to his calls. Surely if anyone was at home they would have heard his booming voice. Before he knew it, he was in the centre of the hallway, but being unfamiliar with the layout of the house he found himself in four minds in which direction to head first. He opted for the right and made tracks towards the door there. This too was opened and before he entered he could tell that something was amiss. Fragments of a shattered statue lay strewn across the door entrance and when he had opened the door fully he could see the room had been ransacked. Even the very paintings which had adorned the walls had been pulled free of their locations and the canvas ripped. Tables and chairs were upturned, all of which had the upholstery torn and shredded. This had been no random act of vandalism he concluded, someone or some ones had been looking for something here, and to such an extent that even the soft fabric cushions had been ripped apart for contents inspection. Satisfied that no person lay within the room, he turned and left, leaving the door opened as he found it. He headed across the hallway to the door on the left hand side. This he could see was also opened and he approached this one as similarly furtive as the first. Like a mirror image of the previous one this room lay in ruin as well. It appeared to Rubin to be a library of a sort but it now had every one of its books lying on the floor. But not in a haphazard fashion he noticed, it appeared to Rubin that each book had been individually removed from the shelf and checked. The near ordered piles along the floor reinforced his thinking. Whoever had done this was obviously a professional and had a patient temperament to go through as many volumes as were now sitting before him. It would have taken time to do it. And this was what worried him. Either none of the house staff had been around to disturb them or worse case scenario, they had been prevented from doing so, which would undoubtedly have meant either restraint…or death.

He would have to investigate further.

Having checked the third room on the lower floor and finding it the same, he climbed the stairs to the upper level. Upon reaching the top, he had unsheathed his knife and hollered again. But the silence was deafening. He moved along the carpeted hallway and the first door he came to on his left was, once again, wide open. He could tell in an instant that the same fate had befallen this room. Only, there was something new here. He saw a spray of deep red across the door and the nearer he edged into the room he could see why.

The room was an explosion of violence.

Ramone was there. Or rather what was left of him…someone had taken the head from his body. Suspended in midair, it hung ungraciously from the chandelier by a thin chord which had been tied to his hair. Its grey sallow face with sunken eyes looked straight at him and Rubin knew whoever had done this had sliced off the eyelids to enable it. If someone was making a statement here, then he was certainly getting the message. They most definitely hadn't been the best of friends. And if young Missy was to attend his funeral then some stitching would be in order. Assuming, that was, he could find the rest of the body. As he moved further in it wasn't long before he did. With arms and legs extended to the extreme, Ramone's naked body had been nailed to the wall directly above the bed. And if this hadn't been satisfactory enough for them to send a signal home to whomever, they had congenially removed his genitals and manhood adding insult to injury. His eyes scanned the rest of the room. The thick sticky mess of congealed blood was everywhere, so much so that he thought it highly unlikely to have come from Ramone's body alone. He was correct in his assumptions. When his eyes had reached the corner of the room he pulled back in astonishment. He had seen a lot of brutal things in his army life including the harsh treatment lashed out at enemy prisoners under interrogation, but this took the proverbial biscuit. Pulling an upended armchair from the floor, he corrected it and sat down for closer inspection of this bizarre sight before him. Two individuals; both naked, were strapped together face to body with a strip of leather. The man, seated upright on a wooden chair and whose emaciated body was clearly devoid of all blood had his bent legs pulled wide apart. The woman, who was on her knees in front of him, had her face pressed hard against his genitals and bound there, unable to move. Both were dead and it was easy for Rubin to work out how each of them had died. Leaning forward, he used the keen edge of his blade to cut the strap and with a heave of his foot pushed the woman to the side. As her bloated body fell to the floor, an eruption of blood spewed from her mouth.

…Just as he had thought. With the tip of the man's penis removed, he had bled to death, but the woman who had been forced to place the bleeding stump in her mouth and with her head strapped into place, she had choked to death on his constant blood flow. It was apparent that neither of them had known the answer to the question they had been asked by their interrogator. Furthermore, as Rubin leaned to the side to see what had just caught his eye; it being the mass of blood at the woman's posterior, he had just found the missing parts of Ramone, crammed deep into her back passage.

*

Having not questioned their experience in these matters, Jeanette had had to take their news as fact. She had been convinced that his housemaid would have known, after all, she had been in his service for years, been his bed partner on frequent occasions, and most importantly, had known him as Luis all these years ago. Having come from the same town as they had, Regina had been party to his new life as Ramone and as she had found out, a true confidante. What woman would not be, to a man she had been in love with? But the voluble Raul had given her hope.
"There is one possibility." She remembered him saying. "There was a young girl. She had visited him the night of his death and was apparently at his side when he died."
This revelation had been a godsend to her, and at once given them instructions to find out who she was and where she lived.
She repeated the girl's name over in her head.
'Madeline, Madeline. Where had she heard that name before?'

*

Rubin had thought better of telling her what he had found. He had felt it wise to let her know that Ramone had been buried without her knowledge. At least this way they could make plans for their journey. But he could see the disappointment on her face.
Seated at the back of a café two streets from her room, Madeline sat in silence for a moment. Regina had seemed a reliable enough house keeper to have kept to her word, so why would she not have informed her of Ramone's funeral? She felt saddened, but now had to resign herself to the fact that she would have to pay her respects at his graveside upon her return. She looked up from the table. "Then we shall set off tomorrow. I want to start as soon as possible."
The flow of wine that was making its way down Rubin's throat was abruptly halted. He sat with a motionless glass an inch from his lips. "You don't mess about young missy."
"I see no reason to tarry Rubin. Tell me it is possible."
"Hah!" He drained the glass and placed it on the table. "I've lived the best part of my life able to move anywhere, at anytime, at the drop of a hat. But you, this journey we're taking, it has to be planned out. We'll be making our way across a lot of country you know."
Unperturbed, Madeline continued. "I understand that, but I travelled to Paris on my own remember, I am quite prepared for another trip in excess of that one."
Rubin shook his head. "It's not just a matter of being able to do it, we need money, provisions and how are you going to explain to Monique where you are?"
Madeline inched herself closer across the table. "I've thought about that. I will tell her that I have had news from home, that my father is ill. Together

with that and my grieving the loss of Ramone, I think she will understand and let me go for a few days, perhaps a week."
"It'll take longer than a week."
"Then if it does, it does, I can make my excuses on my return." She moved her hands across the table and unconsciously began rolling Rubin's glass in her palms. "So, can you arrange provisions and perhaps some mode of transport by tomorrow? You can purchase them with my money." She paused. "You still have it don't you?"
With complete indifference to her insinuation, Rubin grinned. "Course I do. It's in a safe place. Somewhere I can't even get at it."
Ever since Rubin's story; that of Monique robbing the previous girl of her savings and later, her own cache on her second day in Paris, she had thought wise of having her newly earned money out-with that of Monique's grasp, so she had given it to Rubin to look after. "I did not mean that the way it sounded Rubin. I apologise."
He uncoiled his glass from her hands and began refilling it. "No need to. It's not a lot of people who would trust me with their coin." He hadn't even trusted himself not to spend it and had given it to Annie for safe keeping. He lifted his glass and reassured her once again. "It's in safe hands so don't worry, this wine was paid with my own money. A friend came up with some coin he was owed to me."
Not doubting his word or how he had acquired the money being of little concern to her, Madeline resumed her talk of the task in hand. "Then we can proceed?"
Rubin leaned back on his chair and grinned "I'm ready when you are little missy."
Madeline smiled back at him. "Good."

*

Madeline 4

Chapter 3

Deception

Monique was not fully convinced with Madeline's explanation, but she had no choice in the matter other than to let her return home for a spell. After all, she could not keep her prisoner within the house and if she wanted to leave then she would do so eventually no matter how tight a rein was held on her via Rubin. No missive had arrived to inform Madeline of her father's illness, of that she was certain, if there had been then she would have known about it. She had just put this down to a young girl trying to deal with a loss and perhaps with her family about her this would help. But Monique was long past trying to figure out the emotions of others and dealing with them. This sentiment, she thought, had been lost to her a long time since as she had learned over the years that it could be a liability, the burden of which could make you lose sight of your goals. And yet her love for Madeline tweaked at her heart when she least expected it and she now found herself cow tailing to her wants on a whim. To protect her interests, though, and her investment in Madeline's future, she had called for Rubin and explained the situation. With expenses for his travel, he was to follow her home without her knowing. She wanted Madeline kept safe and for him to deal with any situation, should it arise, in a way he saw fit. He had taken this assignment on with verve, especially when he had seen the pouch of coins in her hand. With her now safe in the knowledge that he was looking after her interests, she could concentrate on her other money making schemes, mainly exploiting this new girl Monica. Thus far she had kept to her word and had been as hard working as her other girls, if not more. With her height and looks, she had proved as popular with her clients as she had hoped for and decided there and then that she should use Madeline's room in her absence. It was one of the finest bedrooms in her house so she did not want it to go to waste. Monica could do her entertaining there before returning home to her children at night. This way she could charge her more for the rental of a better room, whether she wanted it or not. Meanwhile she had seen Madeline off to her carriage at the station convinced in her mind that she was in control of the whole situation and all was going as planned, they way she wanted it.

This could have not been further from the truth. Events were about to transpire in which she would have no control over…

…and everything she had worked for could be in jeopardy.

As Madeline had packed her travelling bag earlier, the curtains across the street from her room had twitched once again. And behind them; crouching forward on a three legged stool, had sat an individual who would be a participant in such connivance. With laboured breath, the movement of his clasped hand around his erection had gathered such momentum that he finally climaxed while watching her and repeating her name aloud. He had to have her, he would have her…in time he would have her.

*

At a prearranged location, Madeline stopped the carriage two miles from the city boundary as Rubin had instructed. With astonished looks from the other passengers, she disembarked at a remote spot next to a wooded copse. Making her way through to a clearing, she eventually saw the private carriage she had hired earlier to meet her and had part paid in advance. Travelling six miles in the opposite direction and around the city perimeter she finally reached the spot where Rubin had planned to meet her. She paid the driver and with an extra payment to guarantee his silence made for their tryst. It only took a few minutes before she saw Rubin in the distance, wiping the sweat down from a brown horse. She smiled. Placing her bag on the grass edge, she walked in his direction "A very good choice Rubin."

As a veteran soldier, Rubin had heard her approach before she had spoken out, so didn't need to turn around to know it was her. He could tell by her gait and the way the crisp, dry twigs snapped beneath her light footing. "Everything go well with Monique?"

Madeline stood in front of the horse and patted its front. "She thinks that I am on my way home to visit my family just as we had arranged. She was very good about it."

Rubin grinned. "Yeah, so am I." He continued the job in hand leaving his statement to her cryptic.

"I don't understand Rubin."

With one final wipe down, Rubin threw the damp cloth to the ground. He looked into her face as he passed her by. "You don't need to." Changing the subject, he nodded to a nearby rock. "Got a musket as well, and it hasn't cost us a thing so far. You're money is still in tact young missy. You want it now?"

Madeline shook her head. "No, it is safer in your hands I think." She ran her hand along the side of the animal's frame feeling the muscle texture beneath. "He is a fine horse Rubin. What is his name?"

Rubin shrugged. "Horse."

Madeline turned to face him. "You named your horse, Horse?"

"I haven't called him anything, he's a horse. You don't give a name to something you might have to eat." He slapped its rear on passing.

With the size of Rubin's hand hard on its rump, Madeline had to pull on the reins to calm it down. Patting its front again, she soothed it with calm voice. "Then I will name him."

Rubin threw the frayed edged blanket across its back. "Do what you want. But if I've got one of its legs roasting over a camp fire one night, then I don't want you howling over it."

Madeline tutt-tutted. "Pay no heed to him Felix."

Rubin stretched his head round to the front. "Felix?"

Madeline nodded. "And what is wrong with that? My friend at home had a horse called Felix. I rode him once."

Rubin shook his head and bent down to pick up the makeshift saddle. Heaving it onto its back, he proceeded to fasten it home, tight against the blanket. "Felix the horse eh, sounds like a story for kids."

Madeline ignored his ribbing. "Where did you get him?"

Rubin pulled at the leather strap and lowered the stirrup. He paused. "Um...from a friend."

"You have very generous friends Rubin. Would that be the same friend that gave you the gun?"

Rubin looked over at the musket. "Eh, yeah, same one." He screwed his face up knowing that his lie was pitiful. He awaited her retort.

As expected, Madeline peered round Felix's head. "Rubin?"

He remained silent for a moment as he strapped their rolled up bed blankets onto Felix's back. "Okay, not the same one."

"Rubin?"

Walking away from her towards the musket, he picked it up and sat down on the jagged rock. "Had one just like it in the army." He raised it to his shoulder and looked down the sight. "It'll do for us just fine. Hah, if I can remember how to shoot it, that is."

Madeline released her hold on Felix and let him graze. She followed Rubin to the rock. "A horse and a musket Rubin, only just the other day you had barely enough money to buy wine, and now this?"

Once again, Rubin shrugged. "Things change."

She sat beside him. "Then it was fortunate, was it not, that these 'things' just happened to come into you possession exactly at the time we needed them. Coincidence?"

Rubin continued with the examination of the weapon. "Seems so." He had answered without knowing what the last word of her sentence had meant.

"Rubin, if we are to undertake this journey together and I have put all my trust in you, would you at least reciprocate to a degree and tell me the truth about certain things?"

Rubin rested the musket on his lap. How could he tell her where he had got them from? Did she not have enough to think about without knowing that he had saved her life once again? That the owner of these items was the very same man who had lay in wait within the shrubbery outside Ramone's house. His intentions clear.

He had known something was wrong that night when he had heard of Ramone's carriage arriving at Monique's house. He had been there himself. After seeing Madeline safely back from the park, he had went to the back door where Bella had let him in. She often fed him from the kitchen and they would sometimes sit and talk for hours. But not knowing where Ramone lived, nor having any transport to follow them, his only option left had been to ride along with them. Luckily for him, Ramone's carriage was of such luxury, that the underside held enough space for him to crawl beneath. And once wedged between the wheel axels, he had used his britches belt to strap himself up and take his weight. It had been a painful journey, but one he was now glad he had taken. He had also known within minutes of the journey that they were being followed. And after their arrival, it had only taken ten minutes to find the lurking place of her would-be assailant. He had sat all night only feet from him. And he hadn't noticed. The man had been an amateur. Once the carriage had reappeared to take her home he had made his move…only to have Rubin's knife pushed into his neck.

There had been no need to return home by the same means in which he had arrived. He was by then, the proud owner of a horse, and along with it, a musket that had been strapped to its side. And after rummaging through the dead man's pockets before he hid the body in the undergrowth, he had found not only cartridges but a handful of coins as well. It had been a profitable night all round.

Now, carrying the remains of the spoil, plus Monique's payment and the young missy's money, this had been the most coin he had been in possession of for a long time. There was many things he could do with it if were all his, he thought. He looked about him to make sure they were still alone and decided that the time had come to do what he had planned to do.

"There's a lot of things in life you don't need to know about young missy…" He stood and laid the musket as before. "…and them's one of them." Pulling his knife from the back of his britches, he unsheathed it and let the scabbard fall to the ground. Holding the lethal blade just inches from her face, he demanded that she stand.
Madeline looked up with fear on her face. "Rubin!"

*

The previous day's misfortune with the two young girls forgotten about, Jeanette had demanded a male companion in her bed for the night. Denig had obliged, but not with one of the staff. He had procured the services of a friend who was known for providing such youth for the pleasure of the gentry. And as the young man passed her by on his way out the door, Caroline looked at his face. He had obviously endured an ordeal with Jeanette she thought. His face was lack lustre and devoid of mood, but to her relief, he was still in tact and even better, still alive. She continued across the hallway in the direction of her dining room.
On entry, she noticed that Jeanette had just finished a late breakfast, or given the hour and what she was eating, an early lunch. She was also aware of the two men seated to her right.
"Ah, Caroline, permit me to introduce two associates of mine."
Caroline recognized them as the two who had visited the previous day and knew that is was them who had obliged Jeanette by removing Clara from the house later in the day. She felt ill at ease in their presence and on hearing their identical names avoided the formal introductory protocol by way of a simple nod. "Messieurs."
It was noticed by all but it mattered little to her as neither of the Rauls had risen from their chairs upon her entry. She seated herself at the opposite side of the table and waited for Jeanette to continue.
"It appears Caroline that we have; residing here in Paris, an acquaintance of a mutual acquaintance."
Again, Caroline remained silent, awaiting expansion on her vague statement. She sat forward in the pretence of looking interested.
"You are familiar with a young woman called Madeline?"
Caroline's silence was now one of shock. Was there anything happening in this city that this woman did not know about? It had never been her intention to deliberately prevent the Comtesse from knowing of Madeline's existence; although recent events had made her glad that she hadn't, but had wanted to keep this girl for her and Denig's indulgence alone. She had never met a woman such as Madeline before and one who had captivated her from the very first minute of their meeting. To introduce Madeline to the Comtesse now would be a travesty as it would be a squandering of something very unique. But what part in the scheme of all things did this girl have to play she wondered. Had it not been for the presence of Raul and Raul, then Caroline

could have put it down to the Comtesse seeking new blood. But this was not the case, she was sure of it. This had something to do with her plan against Ramone. Her question had not simply been her asking if she knew Madeline or not, but insinuating that she did. What answer could she give without involving her?
Jeanette pushed further. "She has a room with Monique and is in her employ. You have met her. Monique has informed us of this."
What could she say but to agree, these men had apparently questioned Monique on the subject. She now felt intimidated in her own home. "She sat in attendance for me one evening, yes."
"We know this already. She also knew Ramone. To such an extent that she was with him the night he died."
This was a revelation to her. But not with Madeline having known Ramone; with him being a frequenter at Monique's house she would have, but rather the fact that she had been the last person to see him alive. She could see now where all this was leading. "You think she may have knowledge of Ramone's fortune?"
Jeanette played with her pendant again, as was the norm when she was deep in thought. "It is a possibility, and is being looked into."
Caroline hated having to ask the next question, but felt compelled to do so, if only to be assured of Madeline's well being. "Have you questioned her about it? Did she say anything?"
"We would have, only she has disappeared, apparently to return home to deal with an ailing parent. Unfortunately no-one knows where this home is. We were hoping she may have afforded you this information during your lengthy talk with her that night."
Caroline shook her head. "She spoke briefly of her family but I cannot recall her mentioning where they lived. Sorry." It was obvious that in questioning her, they were at a loss as to when exactly she had left Paris. And with so many carriages leaving for different parts of the country in any given day, they would have a hard time trying to trace her movements. She could see their predicament. And even though she had no knowledge to impart to them, she found herself asking if she had, would she have given it.
Jeanette turned her attention to Raul and Raul. "Then with that gentleman, it appears you have a difficult task in front of you."
Both remained seated as if expecting something in addition from her.
"Ah, my apologies gentleman, forgive the memory of an aging woman. Whose turn is it to have their cock in my mouth this time?"
The smaller of the two rose to his feet and undid his belt buckle.
Taking it as a cue to leave, Caroline headed for the door.

*

Madeline stood up as commanded and immediately felt herself taken from the ground. With a hand under each arm Rubin had gently hoisted her onto

the rock where she now teetered, and with her face at eye level with his, he spoke out. "We need to get you sorted."
Madeline had chosen one of her own lightweight summer dresses from home to travel in, but even this to Rubin was too prim for his liking. Taking hold of its edge, he pulled it tight and let the knife slice into it just below her knees. The keen edge of the blade ran easily round the perimeter and within seconds, the bottom half of her dress had fallen to her feet.
"Rubin!"
"Stand still." Slicing at the remaining cloth, he cut in such a way as to feign a worn and tattered look. He leaned back a few inches to admire his handiwork. "Hmmm..." Flicking the knife so as the blade stuck into the ground, he opened his right hand and spat into his palm. Bending down, he grabbed a handful of dust dry soil and rubbed it into his left. Encircling Madeline's left leg approximately six inches above the ragged hemline, he drew his hands straight down to her ankles. He repeated this procedure with the other.
"Oh, Rubin, that's disgusting."
He stood to be greeted by an irate child. He grinned. "Shut up."
He spat again, and with the muck mixture in his hands, proceeded to haphazardly wipe them on and about what remained of her dress. When reaching her breasts, he was still dabbing randomly and smearing it on her exposed chest and neck when he looked up. "Don't worry missy, I'm not getting anything from this."
Madeline stood with quizzed look. "I gathered that."
He nodded. "Good." The remainder was used on her face.
"Oh, Rubin, I'm going to be sick."
He stepped back a pace and looked her top to bottom. Her soft leather sandals looked too new, he thought, but they would weather on the road. "That should do for now. Till you get some real travelling dust on you that is."
Madeline held her dress out to the side. "Look at the state of me."
Rubin nodded towards her bulging cleavage. "And get them out of sight." He leaned over and pulled his knife free. Re-sheathing it, he grabbed the musket and walked towards Felix. "Do something with your hair as well, mess it up a bit, we can find a hat along the way."
Madeline jumped from the rock. "Is all this really necessary?"
Without turning to answer, Rubin fastened the musket into his makeshift holder on Felix's side. "We've a long road ahead of us, and through bad lands, so I don't want to be spending *my* time with mens folk wanting to spend *their* time with you. I don't want any heads turning, for you or thinking we've got anything worth taking." He slapped Felix on the rump again before turning. "'part from Felix the horse here."
Madeline approached him carrying her travel bag. "I look terrible."
"Good." He nodded at her hand. "What's in there?"
"My clothes, and, well...personal things."

"Ditch them." He nodded towards a fallen tree trunk. "Stick it behind that and cover it with leaves 'n stuff."

"But Rubin, I'll need a change of clothes." She tugged at her dress with her free hand. "I can't wear this all the time. I look terrible."

"Good, I want you to. Means we're worth nothing. Now ditch it."

Madeline looked at the loose bag hanging from Felix's side. "You have one with you."

"That's things we need for the road. Not clothes and the likes."

Madeline stretched her hand out and patted its side. She heard the faint clink from within. "Oh, essentials is it?"

Rubin leaned forward and once again, nodded in the direction of the tree trunk.

Madeline's shoulders sunk. Turning on her feet, she headed where directed. "Great, you get to load us down with wine and I can't even have a spare dress to take with me."

Rubin grinned at her sulking and turned to face Felix again. Pulling a two inch wide strip of leather free, he slid its length through the back of his knife's scabbard. Fixing it diagonally across his chest, he fastened the iron buckle at the front, thus enabling the eight inch blade to sit at such an angle on his back that he could pull it free in an instant. Its smaller twin was already tucked down the side of his right boot. Bending down, he lifted his coat from the ground and pulled it on. He dug deep into the pockets. A few musket cartridges and tinder box in one, and in the other, a few more delicate items he'd need for the journey. The rest was in the bag. He spat on the ground and looked up to see Madeline approach yet again. This time with a cape clasped about her top.

"Will this do, to cover me up?" her sulking still apparent to him.

He unclasped it from her neck and dropped it to the ground. Standing on it with his right foot, he crushed it underfoot and kicked it about a bit. Bending down to pick it up, he flicked the residue free and handed it back to her. He spat again.

"It does now."

*

Madeline 4

Chapter 4

A Deceptive Appearance

Janis grabbed the letter from the tray and at once broke the seal. She had recognized Gaston's handwriting immediately. It was the first piece of correspondence she had received from her husband since his departure to Salon, which to her had seemed like weeks ago now.
Excusing her daughter's impoliteness, her mother thanked the maid and allowed her leave to resume her duties. She sat opposite and with cutting knife in hand, began to peel an apple. "It is not wise to let your feelings show themselves in front of the staff Janis."
Oblivious to her chastisement, Janis unfolded the parchment and hurriedly read through its contents. With the occasional muttering, the mother knew she was scan reading in the hope that the date of his return to Paris was indicated. When finished, she did what others automatically did, turn the letter over and foolishly think that additional wording was contained overleaf where the address was.
Janis let it rest on her lap for a moment before raising it again to reread it, this time more slowly.
Allowing her daughter the time to fully absorb the contents, she continued to peel the red skin from its pulp in the hope that she could make it in one

continuous strip. It being her favourite part of eating fruit, she had accomplished this more often than not. This time she didn't.

"Pah!"

Janis folded the letter and clasped it in her hands. "He will not be returning in the foreseeable future. He has to remain in Salon awaiting word from his superiors, here in Paris."

The mother lifted the strip from her lap and dropped it into the small wicker basket at her side. "It comes with the position I'm afraid. He is young and it is inevitable that this will happen again in the future."

Janis pondered this remark in her head. Assuming she still had a marriage left when he did finally come home for him to do it again, that was. She knew deep in her heart that nothing had been resolved before he had left, so everything that had happened previously had not been discussed or clarified. What his intentions had been the night of their lovemaking had never truly come to light, but she knew she had some sort of hold on him. She had substituted the contents of the vial with brandy in the hope that its eventual whereabouts would lead her to his intended goal. She certainly did not envisage their son swallowing it, but in retrospect she was glad he had. Gaston's reaction when he found that Sylvain was still alive had spoken millions to her. She just needed to be sure.

Aware of her mother staring at her, she uttered the words of a pining wife. "I just miss him so much. As do the children. They ask for him each night as I put them to bed. 'When is Papa coming home?'"

With her grandchildren of little interest to her, the mother spoke further of her son-in-law. "Absence does in fact make the heart grow fonder. You will have to get used to it Janis. As I did."

Janis shook her head. "You don't understand mother."

Piercing the apple with the knife, the silver haired woman laid them both to the side and leaned forward. "I had a husband once myself if you would care to remember. With diplomatic duty, your father had responsibilities that took him away from me on many occasion. With France appearing to be at constant war with some other country or other, these trips could be far in excess of your numbered days missing Gaston." She settled back and continued. "But the times apart made the times together all that more special to us. Our intimate moments together could not have been matched by any other and these memories kept us going during our times apart. So do not lecture me on not being able to comprehend the feeling of missing someone dear to me. I loved your father as much as any woman could love a husband and it is for that reason that I never remarried after his death. No-one could ever come close to him. I counted the days of his absence from me at the beginning, but had to grow to accept it as you will have to do now. I was carrying you when your father was in Spain as you are now with Gaston in Salon. It may be hard, but it is the price we have to pay to remain in the luxury that so surrounds us now."

Janis sat with mouth agape. Never in all her life, had she heard her mother speak so openly about her father. Not in this fashion anyway.
"It is very seldom you speak about such things to me mother, I am glad I have you here with me at this time." She clutched at her stomach and imagined their child within. "It will be alright mother?"
Leaning forward again she placed her hand on Janis' knee. "It will my dear, I assure you it will. Gaston at this very moment will be missing you every bit as you are missing him."

*

With a brandy bottle in one hand and a firm grip of the brunette's left buttock in the other, Gaston pushed himself deeper inside her.
With one single vision in his mind's eye, he focused in with clarity on this solitary picture until he could think of nothing else. And so impregnated was it in his vision, that he could almost smell her, taste her. With each thrust, Madeline's sweet face drew closer until she was only inches from his and he could feel her soft breath on his lips. In rapturous thought, he withdrew himself slightly from the brunette's grip and arched his back. Changing the scene in his head, he substituted the moisture from the body he was immersed in, into that of Madeline's lips. Pushing forward slowly, the thought of him sliding into her mouth sent waves of pleasure around his whole body that his entire self shuddered uncontrollably. He knew his climax was imminent, so taking another swig from the bottle, he clasped the brunette's other buttock with what remained of his free fingers and pushed forward again. He imagined Madeline's hand about him, pulling in deeper, further down her throat, her encouraging groans willing him on and to fill her mouth with his seed. "Fuck!"
With several more thrusts, he felt himself explode within and with continuous jerks, emptied himself in spasm, until he was spent.
"Fuck!"
His voice resonated around the room until he shuddered to a stop.
"Fuck!"
He blew out through puckered lips and laboured breath.
Wiping his sweated forehead with the back of his free hand, he took another drink from the bottle and pulled himself free of her. With a gradual turn in midair, he fell back on top of the floor. "Fuck!"

*

Preferring to sit on Felix in front of Rubin rather than permanently cling to his back, Madeline was enjoying the first leg of their journey. It felt good to smell the fresh country air again. As much as she adored living in Paris, she hadn't realized how much she had missed the open countryside. "Can you smell that Rubin?"

Rubin sniffed at the air. "It's probably Felix."

She back elbowed his stomach. "No silly. I meant the fresh air."

Rubin had known what she meant. He just didn't like to miss a chance of ribbing her at any given chance. He looked around at the ground below. "Yeah, not a dead body in sight."

He felt the elbow deeper this time.

After only four hours of casual gait, it seemed as if Felix had taken them from Paris into a different world. The meadow footpath took them through lush, overhanging trees on either side of them. To their left, a steep incline ran down to a rippling stream below. It was a joy to behold the various coloured fauna, to see the wildlife run free about them and was in complete contrast to the grime and filth of the city they had just left. Madeline looked up as mid-afternoon sun split its rays through the trees and breathed in deep again. "I would like to have my own house in the countryside one day."

Steering Felix to the right, Rubin led him away from the steep edge of the bank. "Ain't that where you're from?"

Madeline looked at her blossoming surrounds. "In the country yes, but not like this. I lived in a town, very different."

At a fork in the path, Rubin veered up to the right and headed towards the open country beyond. "What's the difference?"

"Hmmm, well I expect that out-with a large city like Paris, a town would, to you, be the country, but a town to me is not my idea of the countryside." She nodded towards a solitary building in the distance. "Some remote place like that farmhouse there. Now that would be the countryside to me I suppose, being isolated and far away, surrounded by fields and meadows, and flowers and trees."

"A farm eh, good." Rubin gee'd Felix further to the right and headed uphill. It was what he had planned and hoped for, to get provisions along the way and not be laden down with food. "Well let's visit this little country farm of yours. Show me what you're dreaming of."

"Rubin, we don't have time to visit a farm, I was only daydreaming about it. I thought you said we would be on a time schedule?"

"I did, and we are. You any grub on you?"

Madeline peered back over her shoulder. "No, I do not have a bag with me, remember. It's sitting under a tree."

"Uh-huh, did you bring any to start with?"

She looked forward abruptly. "You know fine well I didn't."

"Well I can't be sure that we'll find much to shoot at for food as we go on or even if my aim is still true enough to kill it even if we do. I ain't shot a musket in a while. So we'd better get something to keep us going, for today anyway." He grinned. "You don't want to be chomping down on old Felix here, do you?"

He felt her elbow hard in the solar plexus this time.

Felix cantered up the slight incline and when they had reached semi-level ground, Rubin slowed him to a trot. "Right young missy, get to the back of me."
"What?"
Guiding her arm with his right hand, He lifted her up slightly. "I want you behind me. I need my hands free."
Jostled round in one swift movement, she reseated and clung to his back. "You are too big to get my arms fully around you Rubin. I can't get a hold on you properly. I'll fall off."
"It's not me that's too big. Hah, it's you that's got short arms and big titties." He laughed out loud and spat to the ground. "Yee-haw" Heeling into his side, he gee'd Felix to a gallop.
Immediately thrown backwards, Madeline grappled at his coat.
"Rubin...."

Still laughing at her constant attempts to keep a grip on him, he eventually slowed Felix down as they approached the farmhouse. Madeline tried to adjust her seating and fix her disheveled hair as they trotted at pace through the farm gate. She punched at his arm.
"That's far enough."
The coarse instruction had been hollered from the front door as it was kicked opened and out with it came the barrel of an aged gun. The holder of the weapon followed out soon after. "Keep your hands away from that shooter you got there." He limped forward a pace.
It was plain to Rubin that this old man was referring to his musket, which being strapped to Felix, was in open view. It was also clear that this half crippled individual; with his lank tresses and loose hanging beard casually blowing about his face was nervous. And shaking hands had loose fingers.
"Calm yourself old man. We just need some food, and we've coin to pay for it." Lowering his right hand, he undid the pouch on his belt. He tossed it towards the farmer, who, upon releasing his grip on the barrel caught it in a downward snatch.
The old man's reflexes didn't go un-noticed by Rubin either. There was still life in this old dog, as he had continued to hold the ancient arquebus level with one hand. He watched him jiggle the pouch to judge its contents and then nod up at Madeline. "Who's that you got there with you, your daughter?"
Madeline made moves to speak out, but it was her turn to feel Rubin's elbow in her stomach out of view of the old man. "Yeah, she is that...and hungry with it."
Rubin sat motionless, returning the old man's stare as his aged eyes tried their hardest to determine this stranger's character, and then switch to Madeline, where they remained fixed for several seconds.
Even with the muck on her face, her beauty shone through. He looked back at Rubin and his battle scarred face. "Got her looks from her mother then."

Rubin knew it was more a humorous jibe than a question and he liked the old man's spirit. He nodded. "That she did, for sure."
The old man stood silent for a moment deliberating, and on finally lowering his weapon, tossed the pouch back to Rubin. "The name's Pacard." He nodded to the right. "You can hitch your horse over yonder. There's feed there." He turned on his feet and limped towards the door.
Rubin led Felix in the direction indicated. "Well, looks like we've just been asked to eat."

Having tethered and tended to Felix with loose hay, both walked across the yard towards the door. Madeline dawdled behind and tried best to make her appearance more presentable to their host. She rubbed at her chest, neck and face hoping to remove at least some of the grime Rubin had rubbed on to her. "For heaven's sake Rubin, look at me."
Rubin kept walking. "You're fine."
Madeline ran to catch him up. "Can't I at least wash before we eat?"
"That depends on what we're eating." Uttered without thought, Rubin's mind was on other things. They had reached the door which stood ajar several inches. Holding Madeline at bay with his right, he slowly pushed it opened with his left. Peering cautiously in as the gap opened up, he heard a female voice usher them in. Rubin pushed the door fully opened and both were hit with the smell of fresh stew and vegetables cooking on the stove.
Madeline crawled under his arched arm. "Mmm…smells lovely."
She was in before he knew it.

*

Gaston woke to find himself lying naked on a bed with a thin sheet partly over him and the brandy bottle still in his hand. It was empty, as was the room he now found himself in. Apart from the damp sheeted bed he was lying on and a half broken window there was nothing but a door on the far side. He released his grip on the bottle and threaded his fingers through his hair. His head was pounding. 'Fuck!'
He squinted at the glow from the window and going by its light guessed it to be late afternoon. Why was he so stupid to have started drinking so early in the day? But then, with little else to do while waiting on word from Paris, he had seen all that the town had to offer by way of its culture and its history. The truth of it all was that he was bored. Bored with having to wait here and impatient to return to Paris and the news he had been waiting to hear, that of the death of both wife and mother-in-law. This would pave the way ahead for his plans to wed Madeline, but the days were dragging on. To this end, he had risen early and after breakfasting alone at the inn, set out to wander the streets once again. By mid morning he had seen enough of the same old thing and had decided he would enter one of the so called drinking dens that he had been told by others to avoid. 'Fuck it' he had thought, a bit of risk in

one's life would alleviate some of the boredom…and this was when he had met Sylvia.
Having found it vaguely amusing that her name so resembled his own son, he had permitted her to join him at his table. It had been the beginning of a hard morning to afternoon drinking session. He closed his eyes and through blurred thought, recalled the event.

He hadn't noticed where Sylvia had been seated or who she had been sitting with on his entry into the taverne. He had simply made his way to the counter and ordered a brandy. The local brand he liked.
"Ah, you'd be the official here from Paris, would you not?"
With slight embarrassment Gaston smiled at the barman. "Yes, here to visit your picturesque town." He lied. He also noticed the moustache he was sporting. To say it was thick and bushy would have been an understatement. With it spreading an inch or so across each side of his face and hanging down over his mouth, Gaston could barely see the lips move beneath as he spoke.
"Honoured to have you in our humble abode sir, wouldn't have thought it to be you type of place, if you pardon me for saying so."
"No, not at all, happy to be here." He downed the brandy in one go and ordered another. A large one.
As he refilled the glass, Gaston noticed him look across the room and give a sharp nod. He followed the barman's eyes and turned in the direction of a table in the far side of the room.
"See you've taken to our local brew sir."
Not having time to take in who was seated at the table, he turned back to answer. "Yes, yes. Indeed it is. I have ordered a few cases to take back to Paris with me. Is there anything wrong?"
"What do you mean sir?" On realizing what Gaston meant, he added explanation. "No, no sir. Just some customers wanting refills, that's all. Now sir, would you be wanting anything in the way of food sir? We got nice mutton on today. Freshly cooked, no bugs."
Annoyed with his over use of the 'Sir', he declined the offer of food saying that he had not long breakfasted, but he would have another brandy in five minutes. "I'll be over there."
When he reached the table he had nodded to, he pulled the wooden chair free from its confines and seated himself, facing out. He scanned the room as he sipped at the glass edge. It wasn't that bad a place. But then, it was early. Even for him. He knew that even in Paris, the most peaceful of tavernes can by day metamorphose into something quite different by night. He was surprised however on the amount of patrons there was for such a time of the day. He smiled inwardly. Surely they all couldn't be as bored with the town as he was. His eyes took one table at a time. Two pipe smoking croons chatted idly at the first one, and with only one glass visible, Gaston assumed that both were sharing the same drink. At the next, four men of various

stature and age were deeply engrossed in some kind of gambling card game. The pot of which, he noticed, was hardly worth the bother of winning. His view of the next table was masked somewhat by a wooden pillar. It had been the one that the barman had nodded across to and going by his restricted view, there were at least three seated at the table. And one was a woman, of that he was sure. Her long brown hair was unmistakably feminine. He almost laughed aloud as his eyes went to the next. Seated alone, this man appeared to be trying to outstare the drink he had in front of him. Unmoving, he was leant over with folded arms across the table and with his face a mere four inches from the glass, sat with wide, unblinking eyes. And like most drinking establishments, many were content to stand while imbibing their favourite tipple. This place was no different. A dozen or so others were arbitrary spread out in small groups and it gave the impression that this taverne was a money earner even so early in the day. Not bad for a town with a population of around ten thousand, a high percentage of them being church goers. It reminded him of Paris in a way. And with Paris, came his thoughts of Madeline. 'Damn it'. He downed the brandy and without having to ask, the barman had acknowledged his earlier request and was by his side with the next one. But as he turned to leave, the view of him was replaced by a woman standing at his back.

"You are content to sit here and drink by yourself?"

The initial impact of the large brandy going down momentarily stunned him. He had to wait a second or so to the get his senses back. And before he could raise his eyes to see the face that had spoken to him, they were transfixed to a bulging cleavage, the surrounding breasts of which took on the shape of perfection in his mind. So sheer was her top that he thought he could actually see her dark brown nipples show through. He caught his breath and looked up. He recognized the hair of being that of the brunette from the table opposite and with no hesitation his opened hand beckoned her to sit. His foot nudged out the adjacent chair and pulled it closer to him. "Please, please sit. Would you care to join me in a brandy?"

Her head movement signaled a negative response, her verbal reply the same. "No thank you. It is a bit early for that, although I am partial to that particular type." She took the offered seat though.

It was one of Gaston's pet hates, sitting drinking when the other person was not. The conversation never appeared to run in parallel as only one got progressively drunk. But his disappointment was soon to be replaced with joy when she spoke again.

"I will take some wine though."

Great, he thought. He not only had a drinking partner, but one who was stunning. After days of ministerial who-hah, and being in the company of decrepit old fools with talk of witchcraft and red deaths, he finally had someone with whom he could pass the time of day with. After all, it was her who had approached him, not him seeking the quick services of a wench. He must have appeared interesting enough for her to leave the company she was

in to make a move on him. He leaned to the side and noticed that the table she had been sitting at was now empty. And yet he was convinced she was not selling her services. Looking into her face, it was not one of a common whore, but more genteel in nature. She had a kind face, a face you could trust. He was also aware of the barman by his side.
It was she who ordered. "Wine please, Max."
He remained still, awaiting further order. Gaston waved his hand at his brandy. "I'm fine at the moment, just the wine thanks."
Allowing Max to leave before speaking, it was she who spoke first. "I have seen you walking the streets for several days now." She smiled and continued "…like a little lost lamb in a large field."
Gaston laughed. "Have my wanderings been so obvious to all?"
"Only to those who take notice of such things, the people of Salon, for years now, have taken to treating strangers with suspicion."
"Ah, you mean this recent spate of so called sorcery and death." He paused. "Please, where are my manners, I have not yet introduced myself, nor indeed have I asked your name. Forgive me?"
She proffered her downward hand and introduced herself as Sylvia. And as Gaston took it in his, he kissed its delicate back and felt the soft tender skin beneath his lips and the subtle smell of her cologne fill his lungs. For what seemed an uncomfortable and un-necessary length of time, he remained still before releasing his grip. "Please, forgive me again. It has been a long time since I have felt the delicate touch and the perfumed smell of a true woman."
Her smile once again brought cheer to his heart. "Your apology is not necessary. It is me who feels the need to thank you."
Gaston lifted his brandy and swirled it. "Oh, in what way is that?"
"It makes a woman feel good within herself to receive such a compliment. Surely a man such as you would know that. I am just as pleased to be in your company as you apparently am in mine."
With further cheer, Gaston raised his glass. "Then, Sylvia, we are in agreement, your very good health Madam."
Raising hers in salute, their concord was sealed with the click of glass against glass and as both were emptied, another was ordered in their place. Within twenty minutes they had consumed two more until Gaston had told Max to leave the respective bottles on their table. He would fill them as required. It was the most pleasant time he'd had since arriving in Salon and in the course of their conversation his eyes, on a few occasions, had lowered to her breasts. He knew that Sylvia had been aware of this but she had not commented on it. She had just smiled as if reading his thoughts. But the more he drank, the more visible these thoughts were becoming. Although Madeline had entered his head during their talk, he had deliberately put her out of his mind. He knew he was in love with her, but felt that he was somehow betraying her by just being in Sylvia's company. But it would only be a one-off encounter, he convinced himself. He needed some relief from this hum-drum life and was content just to sit here in her company. What

harm could this possibly do? He leaned back into the chair and rested the glass on his leg. "And here was me thinking that today would be just another day in Salon."
"It is not often that I frequent this place. As luck would have it, a friend had asked me to meet him here to discuss some private business otherwise I doubt we would have met."
He raised his glass. "Then I drink a toast to your friend Sylvia."
She nodded in agreement. "I will join you in that Gaston…"
"…how else would we have got a chance to fuck?"

It had not been necessary to remain in the taverne after this revelation, he remembered. It had been clear to both, their mutual intentions and so having procured a full bottle of brandy he had accompanied Sylvia back to her house. He looked about the squalid room. As much as his head hurt, he was certain that this was not in line with the house she had led him to earlier. The smell from the bed he was lying on was one of stale urine and the place had a vile musky smell to it. There was no way on earth that she would have had a room like this in her house. He remembered commenting on her good taste on décor the moment he walked through the door. This had been said out of conviviality though, as interior decoration or the furnishings of any house held little interest to him. But compliments were compliments and it always stood you in good stead with any woman. You never knew where it would get you.

"A fine home you have here Sylvia."
She followed his eyes around the parlour. "My late husband was generous enough to have left everything to me, having no other family of his own. I am very fortunate in that respect."
Indeed she was, he thought. She would be a very good catch for any cash hungry rascal seeking a ready rich wife. But something was wrong with this setting, something he couldn't quite put his finger on. And as his eyes caught sight of the glass fronted drinks cabinet, it struck him odd that she had allowed him to buy the brandy at the taverne when the same type, plus an array of other drinks, filled its hold. There was something else though, something not quite right, but before he could think more of it, she had spoken again.
"I have been widowed for just over a year now." She offered him a chair in front of the unlit fire and took the one opposite. "Not that I miss him of course, it had been more of an arranged marriage from the beginning, the union of two families, so to speak."
Gaston sat with the bottle still in his clutch and considered her remark. This was something which was all too common these days, even with families on bordering countries trying to accumulate or to safeguard their wealth. "How long were you married?"

She hesitated somewhat, as if trying to count the years in her head. This while undoing the top buttons of her dress. "Thirteen years I think, it could be longer. You lose track of time through tedium."
It was clear that her marriage had not been all she had wished it to have been; this being the case with most arranged unions, but aware of what her fingers were doing, he made efforts to show no reaction and keep eye to eye contact. "I have a similar marriage."
With the buttons fully undone, she removed both sides of her dress from the shoulders in mid sentence. "Then you will appreciate what it is like when there is little or no activity in the bed chamber."
It had not always been the case, Gaston thought, his relationship with Janis at the beginning had been more than satisfactory. Things had changed though, but this was neither the time nor place to elucidate why. Present events were more worthy of consideration. He noticed that Sylvia's removal of her garments was in such a matter-of-fact fashion, that the suggestion of an impending sexual encounter, although not fully implied, was hinting at it. Her closing words in the taverne, he remembered, had indicated something similar. But if this was the games she liked to play, then he would willingly participate. "I agree with you there, a marriage can only survive if the bed chamber needs of both are fulfilled."
Sylvia stood up from the chair and let the dress fall to her ankles. She proceeded to unfasten her tight fitting corset as she explained further. "My needs alas were never fulfilled, my husband was neither the adventurous type, nor indeed was he equipped with anything worthy of a satisfying nature. I had to seek solace elsewhere." She stood still for a moment and stared down into his with her own feigned, sad eyes. "Was that naughty of me?"
Jeez. Was this woman a fucking tease or what, he thought? On watching the gradual undoing of her front laced corset and her breasts slowly come into view, he had felt the bulge in his britches fill the loose space. Now standing before him with only laced boots, panniers and both sides of her open corset tantalizingly hiding the full delights beneath, he sat transfixed as the brandy bottle shook in his hands. "No, no." He stammered. "If needs must."
She smiled. "I'm glad you agree." She released her grip and let the corset slip from her body.
Gaston almost erupted in his britches. If he had thought that her breasts looked perfect within the confines of her clothes, he now sat mouth agape when they fell free as nature had intended. Within the darkened surrounds of each deep brown and fully erect nipple lay small dimples spreading out a finger width. And with both being the epicenter of a bountiful and curvilinear holding, he could imagine feeling the weight and full profile of each in his hands. He sat speechless as he watched Sylvia remove her panniers and then stand naked, save her boots, in front of him.

Sylvia looked down at him once again and stared deep into his eyes. "I do so hope that you Gaston are in possession of something that would satisfy my needs?"

His eyes made their way down her body, and after a brief but pleasurable look upon her orbs-delight once again, continued down over her evenly toned stomach to the dark mass between her perfectly shaped thighs. He felt the sudden twinge in his britches. Too damned right I have, he thought. He looked up and nodded.

"Then isn't it time that introductions were made?"

Laying the brandy bottle to his side on the chair, he frantically made efforts to unbuckle his belt and pull down both britches and undergarments. When fully undone, and both resting at his ankles, he laid back into the chair with his erection pointing up in her direction. "Will this do?"

She smiled. "Now that, Gaston, is something that I could easily make full use of." Kneeling down in front of him, she clasped it fully in her right hand and gently pulled the skin back and forth as if determining its full mass and potential. She held the skin back and looking down at the swollen head, nodded. "Yes indeed it will." She leaned forward and allowed the tip of her tongue to run around its perimeter, concentrating her efforts on the underside.

Upon contact, Gaston's body had immediately tensed and remained so as he watched her lay her hands on either side of him and freely let her mouth take in his entirety. Pushing forward, she allowed him to unfold naturally as she glided his full seven inches down her throat and let her lips rest at his base. And slowly pulling him free until only the head remained in her mouth, she repeated this procedure several times and all the while to Gaston's delight.

He could have emptied himself there and then, but thought otherwise as he wanted this woman's body in his arms, to feel her skin against him and have the soft touch of her breasts in his hands. He would have to remain focused so as not to come too quickly for her.

But, as if in response to his predicament, Sylvia withdrew her mouth completely and looked up at him. And without saying a word, rose from the floor and turned to face the wall opposite. She titled her body forward slightly so as to expose her naked self a mere three inches from his face. "I want your cock inside me Gaston, but first, the brandy."

'Fuck the brandy', he thought. As much as he liked it, this was certainly not the time to be thinking about drinking it. He felt himself harden even further at the sight of the twinned globes before him. As perfectly rounded as two cheeks could be, he clasped one within each hand and felt the suppleness of her within his grip as he massaged them to full extent. In expectation of what lay within, he slowly pulled them apart and as he did, his eyes lit up as they beheld the pink moist skin which sat boldly as sentinel to the pathway to his heaven. He could only look upon this sight with reverence and as his face inched its way forward with exaltation, the scent of her femininity filled his nostrils. His lips automatically kissed out at the moist parting of her inner

self and he felt sucked in by its allure. With the supple skin on each side of his lips, he pressed inwards and with it, his tongue immersed to taste her womanhood. He remained motionless while his senses devoured its sweetness and as his tongue explored further within her, he felt her body spasm.
"The brandy Gaston, I want the brandy now."
What! He pulled his face free. What the fuck did she want with brandy at a time like this? It was the last thing on his mind. He was about to stand up and push his cock inside her and she wanted to stop for a fucking drink. He ignored her plea and rose to his feet.
"No Gaston, sit down please. I want the brandy in me."
Reluctantly, he reseated and looked to his right to find the bottle. And then it hit him…the bottle, the shape of the bottle.
Most of France's brandy came in short dumpy bottles, but Salon's local brew was bottled in glass with a prolonged neck. And it was this four inch long neck that she wanted inside her, not the contents. He understood now her need for a virgin bottle from the taverne. But, if she wanted this as a precursor to him inside of her, then he would willingly oblige. He found himself excited by the thought. So, lifting the bottle by it body, he placed the neck at the precise location of where his lips had been just moments before and with delicate manoeuvres, attempted to make its entrance into her as gentle as possible. He heard her speak again.
"Not there Gaston, that place is reserved for your cock…go up one."
Gaston sat still, stunned by this announcement. Had he heard her correctly? She wanted this bottle up her back passage, and as well as that, him inside her in the natural way…at the same time. He looked at the bottle neck and then to the orifice in which she had required it to be inserted. He blew out. With this kind of extreme pleasure new to him, he hesitated in his thinking, but decided there and then that he would play out his part in the game and do what was requested of him. But not with timidity though, he assured himself, he would be diligent, as if this was to him a common occurrence. He would surely have to moisten her first though, for easy access. But it was apparent that Sylvia was growing impatient with his deliberation. "Gaston, please?" She lowered herself onto all fours in front of him.
Following suit, Gaston kicked loose the garments from his ankles and knelt down behind her. With her rear on open show to him, he could have gladly just slid inside her at that very moment, but true to his word, he bent down and pushed his face in between her cheeks. Finding the would-be orifice immediately, he used all the spit he could muster to drive his curled tongue in and around as far as he could. But on doing so, he heard Sylvia's voice once again.
"There is no need for that Gaston. The pleasure is in the pain."
Rebuked for his consideration, Gaston sat up and reached for the bottle. If pain was what she wanted he thought, 'then fuck it', he would just push it home the way she wanted. It wouldn't be hurting him. So, parting the cheeks

slightly with his thumb and fore finger of his left hand, he held them at bay as he placed the tip to the entrance. With a little cajoling from left to right, he managed to squeeze the tip inside her. The first hurdle over, he thought, and although he had heard some utterances from her by way of a groan, he knew that it was not the sound of her wanting him to stop. He twisted further, from left to right, and with each slight turn, the bottle neck began to disappear from sight. He was amazed at how easy its penetration was, especially as the neck widened to the main body of the bottle. He had finally reached its limited. He could go no further. He leaned round to the side. "Is this alright for you?"
Sylvia let out a satisfactory sigh and nodded. "Yes, perfect, Gaston. Now get your cock inside me."

He remembered lying down on the floor and letting her squat over him. It had been somewhat difficult to enter her from behind with the restriction of the bottle but eventually he had managed it. It had certainly been a unique experience that was for sure, and when both were spent, it was Sylvia who then suggested that they open it. They had sat naked on the floor, drinking and talking, and with more than a few intermittent bouts of lovemaking, it had been an enjoyable afternoon. Sylvia appeared to have had some sort of fascination with his cock as it had found itself inside her mouth on three more occasions. It was the last two that stood out in his mind though. He had closed his eyes and thought of Madeline. This he thought would help alleviate the guilt he felt with being in Sylvia's company. Silly now, he thought. But where the hell was he?
He needed to get out from this foul smelling room, and fast, so flicking the thin sheet away from his unexposed left, he went to swing his legs to the right. But something was keeping him from doing so. His left leg was jammed somewhere. He looked down to his foot. "What the fuck?"
Manacled by a three inch wide shackle round his ankle, it was connected to the iron bed frame by a foot long chain. He shimmied himself along the sheet to the bottom of the bed and gripped at the clasped iron. As much as he pulled at it or tried to wangle his foot free it still remained tight. "Fuck, fuck, fuck."
He threw himself back onto the bed and screamed. "Fuck!"
He heard the door open.
Pushing himself up and with Sylvia's name on his lips to lambaste her, he was shocked to see three men enter the room. The last of which appeared to be carrying his clothes from the Inn. They were tossed unceremoniously onto the floor beside the others he had been wearing. As he left the room, the two remaining stood at the bottom of the bed, dressed in official apparel.
The taller of the two spoke out. "It is my duty to inform you that you are now officially a prisoner of the Peoples Revolutionary Forces of France. You will remain here under our care until a ransom is met to enable us to purchase armaments. Is there anything you wish to ask?"

Gaston could say nothing...
...just bury his aching head in his hands.

*

Madeline 4

Chapter 5

A Life Reinvented

It had been a hearty meal, and Madeline was full to the stomach.
While Rubin idly conversed with Pacard over a glass of cider, Madeline now sat perched on a hard wooden stool as his wife stitched additional cloth into her dress. This plump, gingered headed woman had jumped immediately at Rubin's request of her patching something in to cover her chest. And now, peeking down at her cleavage, Madeline noticed that the blending had been astonishing, if no-one had known about it, they would have assumed it was of original design. "You are a very fine seamstress Ma'am."
The elderly woman bent down and bit at the thread. "Merci Madeline. I have had many years experience." Packing her things into her sewing basket, she let it rest on her lap. And laying her clasped hands on top, she spoke further. "I'm afraid to say that if you are going to attempt to disguise your education through common tongue, you will have to do better than that. It does not compliment your appearance one bit."
Madeline knew exactly what she meant. By using Ma'am, she had assumed that this would be more in line with her masquerade as a commoner. But her pronunciation of it had been in total contrast to the rest of the sentence. She remained silent, as she had done during their meal. Rubin had given her strict instructions earlier in the day that she should divulge as little, if anything, of their mission to anyone. But she felt bad about this now, especially when

they had been so kind to them. She had hardly uttered a word in the last two hours and when asked something, had replied with one word answers, with Rubin doing most of the talking. This after he had found out that Pacard was an ex-soldier and a flagon of cider had been uncorked. And since it was too late in the evening to continue their journey, Rubin had taken him up on his offer of letting them sleep in the barn. Not that she minded that bit of course, it had been a long first day and she was tired. At least sleeping under a roof was a bonus. She just didn't like the idea of fooling this kind woman.
"I'm sorry Margaret."
"There is no need to be. I imagine you have good reason to be traveling incognito." She nodded towards Rubin. "And I gather that he isn't your father."
Madeline looked into her benevolent eyes and shook her head. "You have known all along, haven't you?"
Margaret smiled. "From the moment you walked through the door."
Madeline looked at her quizzically. She didn't need to ask how.
"Oh, come now. You are from better stock than the feigned ragged clothing you are wearing. I can make a dress from a fold of cloth and know my cutting well." She pulled at the hem of Madeline's dress. "And this is no natural fraying."
Madeline looked over in Rubin's direction as if to seek guidance on how she should proceed, but his hearty laughter led her to put trust in her own judgment. She heard Margaret speak further.
"I've also washed enough clothes in my time to realize that this is no everyday filth caked upon the cloth. Nor your skin, I may add."
Madeline had turned to face her again. "Is it so obvious?"
Margaret nodded. "I'm afraid so. If you can't fool a farmer's wife, who else are you hoping to deceive?"
Madeline twisted her lips with saddened thought and looked down at the tattered edge of her dress. "Hmm…"
Margaret laid her right hand on Madeline's knee. "But you're luck." She stood to her feet. "Follow me."

Without knowing it, they had found together in two battles, Pacard having served as a regular soldier in the infantry, whereas Rubin had been mercenary. The cider had continually flowed throughout their fighting talk to such an extent that both were now past the point of talking with clarity, each one of them congratulating the other on their description of an enemy kill. Two empty flagons now sat on the table next to them, and as Pacard pulled the cork on a third, an adjoining room door opened.
Both turned.
Rubin squinted across the room and focused on the doorway. "Hey Pacard, you didn't tell me you had a son."
Margaret shook her head. "No Rubin, we don't have one anymore…" She beamed back at him.

"...but you have."

Having led Madeline into the room, Margaret had instructed her to strip, totally. Pouring fresh stream water into a bowl, she had handed her a cloth and made her wipe herself down thoroughly. Meanwhile her would-be tailor set to work fashioning one of her old corsets to her specific design. Madeline had sat watching her professionalism in removing the stiff underlay and her raising the chest line further up by way of stitching in additional material. Thus when she pulled it tightly to Madeline's body, it did not push her breasts up as to present a cleavage, but rather cover them entirely and depress them evenly to the side. This had given the impression of a much smaller chest and not the more bountiful ones that Margaret had looked upon with pleasurable envy beforehand. But this had only been the first part. Having informed Madeline that her son had fought with her husband in battle, and that he had been killed and was buried in a grave further up the hill. He had worked on the farm beforehand and his working clothes still remained within the wardrobe untouched for years with neither of them wanting to change his room. The clothes were of a loose fit about Madeline, but this was to her advantage Margaret had informed her. The bagginess of the shirt top would hide further, her womanhood. Some minor adjustments to the waistline and the leg length had been called for, and within twenty minutes Margaret had brought about a semi made-to-measure outfit for her. With the substitution of her soft feminine sandals with her son's raised boots; which she had padded to make fit, this finished it off entirely. She had set at once to Madeline's face and hair thereafter. In lieu of the manufactured grime Rubin had placed on her, Margaret had taken the gleam from her face by smearing it with dull coloured oil. Finishing with a light powdering of black ash from the fire on her lower face, this gave the impression of an unshaved look. Madeline had winced with the pain as Margaret pulled back her hair and tightly at regular intervals pinned it fast against her head. With her son's hat soon to be placed on her head to finish it off, she had been reborn a man.

*

In contrast to the night time serenity of the country farm, it was at this point in the evening that Paris really came to life. It was safe to say that for those who preferred to remain indoors, they could at least be isolated from the debauchery of life on the streets. When frequenting such places, you took your own life in your hands.

Both Rosie and Charlotte knew the streets well and were ably equipped to counter any situation which could arise. They had been raised the hard way and with neither having any family to speak of they had fended for themselves all their lives. Prostitution may not have been the best way to earn a coin, but both had learned their trade well and were proficient enough to deal with any request from Monique's clients…no matter how sordid their wants.

With Rosie being attired in a tight fitting pale brown bodice over her dark brown dress, she could casually walk along the street side in harmony with her surroundings. But it was Charlotte who, incongruous in a bright green dress that stood out in the crowd. She preferred it that way. Having a friend who created the most outrageous pigments from lichens, Charlotte had him dye all her clothes for her. If this hadn't been enough to have her noticed, her girth certainly did. So between this and Rosie's chest heaving its way out from the top of her dress, the whistles and asides from male street-goes were inevitable. They both knew most of them anyway, so the shouts of 'Show us your tits Rosie, and 'Lets see your snatch Charlotte' were treated as routine. There was no malice in their words, they knew, it was just the way commoners spoke to each other as a way of acknowledging their presence, it being easier than having to stretch their limited vocabulary to consider a civil greeting.

With the occasional retort or middle finger being presented, they made their way through the bustle of the crowd towards the infirmary. With an hour's respite from the seemingly never-ending line of customers, they had decided it would be an ideal time to visit Frederick. It had not been good news.

"So would you still fuck a man with only one leg?"

Coming from anyone else, Rosie would have thought this question callous in nature, but she knew Charlotte spoke no other way but direct. "Course I would. I love him."

Narrowly avoiding a mess of dog excrement, Charlotte stepped to the side. "A one legged man and a whore, I've seen better matches."

Rosie stepped with her and pulled her dress up slightly. "Maybe so, but Frederick needs me more now than ever."

"Probably get a better chance now with Madeline out the picture."

Rosie stopped in her stride. "What?"

Turning to face her, Charlotte explained. "Well, with her gone."

"Oh! When? When did this happen? How do you know?"

Her mind was racing. She'd heard nothing back from the Salvatore after paying him the money. She had not wanted Madeline dead, only messed up a bit, just enough to make her repugnant to Frederick. But to have her dead, she was now an accomplice to murder. "When did this happen?"

"Slow down. Slow down." Aware that they were blocking the entrance to a taverne, Charlotte grabbed at Rosie's dress and pulled her to the side. This in time to miss the spray of vomit that one of the patron's had retched up on his hasty exit onto the street. Charlotte pushed at his shoulder and he stumbled to the ground. "Let's move."

They rounded a corner onto a less busy street where Rosie stopped once again a few feet along it. "Well are you going to tell me?"

There was a holler from across the street. "Hey Rosie, how about a feel of your…"

But before they had a chance to finish, she had turned. "Fuck off." She refaced Charlotte. "Well?"
"She's left the house for a while, gone back home for something or other." She shrugged. "No idea when she left, yesterday I think. That new girl Monica's got her room for a bit, while she's gone. I thought you knew all this, where the fuck have you been?"
Rosie made a sigh of relief. Not with the fact that Madeline had gone, but that she was still alive. As much as she hated her, she did not want her dead, just out the reach of her Frederick. But what had happened to Salvatore, had she just thrown away good money? Had he conned her? It mattered little now she thought, Madeline was out the way for a while and even if she wasn't, would Frederick have any chance now with his leg been taken from the knee down?
"Thought you'd be pleased with that news."
With a strained smile, Rosie nodded. "Yes, sure I am."
"Well, are we going to visit your dream man or not, see if he's hopping about the ward?"
Both laughed, but felt a presence by their side.
"How much?"
Realizing that they were standing close to the street corner, this stocky individual had mistakenly taken them as plying their trade.
He looked at both set of breasts before him. "…for the two of you."
Charlotte looked down at his feet and then up to his face, which she then gently patted. "Sorry sweetheart." She nodded her head in Rosie's direction. "…you've got too many legs for her liking."
They left him standing with mouth agape.

*

Frederick lay in bed and watched Jacob hobble across the ward on his crutches. Reaching the chair by his side, he felt into it.
"Well brother, how's the leg?"
Frederick sighed. "If I find out where it is, I'll ask it."
He ignored the pun and shuffled his still splintered leg to a comfortable position in front. "Oh come on, it's not all that bad."
"How can you say that Jacob, I've lost my leg?"
Placing the clutches on the floor, he adjusted himself to face him. "Well look at me. Look at the state I've been in and still am."
Frederick pulled himself up to a seating position. "The bones in your leg are only broken, they'll mend. Mine won't, it's gone for good."
"Yes, but I could have died in that accident. I'm still alive though, and for that I am grateful, as should you. If that infection had spread any further then you may not be sitting where you are now."
Unconvinced with his brother's reasoning, Frederick spoke further. "How am I meant to earn a living now with only one fucking leg?"

As much as he detested swearing; knowing that an expletive was a poor substitute for proper grammar, he allowed Frederick its use this time without rebuke, given the circumstances. "You'll still have your job here. Whether you believe it or not, you are very popular with both staff and patients. They all appreciate your hard work brother."

"That's not going to feed a wife and family is it?"

Jacob's head pulled back in disbelief. "I'm impressed Frederick. You have not only made plans to wed, but to have children as well."

"Well those plans have gone the way of my leg, down the shit hole."

Jacob bit his lip. "It would be different if you were a manual worker, in the fields or the like, then the lost of a limb would indeed be a hindrance, but you are young." He finger tapped his temple. "You have a brain in your head. Use it."

He faced his brother full on. "In what way?"

"In a way that befits your natural disposition." His head pointed around the ward. "Here, in the infirmary. Stop fluttering your life away with casual voluntary work and with the likes of Rosie and company as friends. Make something of yourself. Become a doctor, it's what you have the natural aptitude for. It's in your blood, otherwise why would you been working here in the first place. Father has subsidized it for years now. I'm sure he would be more than willing to carry on with the same arrangement knowing what the outcome would be. So why not speak to this little lady of yours; whatever her name is, and make plans. If she has any interest in you then she will wait."

Frederick considered everything that Jacob had said. But there was still one major drawback. "That is all very well, but my leg."

"Never mind your leg. Live with it and deal with it. You are a natural merrymaker, make light of it in her eyes. Don't let it be a burden to you both. Let her know you are still the same person."

"You think it will work?"

"Of course it will. Don't make the same mistake I did. Win her over. I myself have made plans. The moment I get out of here I am going in search of the woman I lost and I am determined to have her as my wife. This I have promised myself."

And he would have Madeline as hers, thought Frederick.

*

Madeline 4

Chapter 6

The Course Ahead

Rubin's jaw had dropped in response.
Steering Felix to the middle of the dirt track, Madeline smiled at the thought. The look on both the men's faces the previous night had been a treasure to behold. Margaret had worked wonders with her appearance and here she was now, comfortable in the knowledge that she was at least clean. Her only obstacle so far had been earlier when she had to negotiate the removal of this unfamiliar apparel during her need to relieve herself. She had struggled on how to position her body after the unbuckling and lowering of her britches, but she smiled further at the thought now.
She pushed back.
Rubin was a weight against her. Slumped half over her shoulder, he held a tight grip of the reins, but it was she who was doing the steering. His constant, intermittent grunts between falling asleep behind her were a steady reminder of his continued snoring the night before as they slept in the barn. She'd had to nudge him periodically to get him to roll over from his back, and furthermore, with his hourly, on the hour, visits outside, she was wakened with him. If it hadn't been for this, then she would have enjoyed her first sleep outside, wrapped tight within her blanket and the straw

beneath her which she had fully adjusted to the contours of her body. All in all, she had spent a happier night in the past.

And now this, she nudged again "Rubin, you're hurting my back."

Roused once again from his slumbering hangover, Rubin shook his head. "Eh. What?"

"I'm all crushed up here Rubin. You keep leaning on me."

Rubin sat up straight to stretch, and with a repeated cough and clearing of his throat, this culminated in his ungracious spitting to the ground.

Madeline cringed at the sound, especially when it was followed by a loud burp. "Oh. Yuck!"

"Got to get these things out little missy." He coughed again.

Madeline smiled to herself and spoke out. "That is one thing you will have to stop doing Rubin."

"What, coughing?"

She nudged at his stomach again. "No stupid, you calling me missy. I'm a boy now remember."

"Oh, yeah, right." It came flooding back to him, especially the cider part. He raised his hand to his head. Ouch. Focusing his blood shot and aching eyes, he looked around to get his bearings. "Where are we?"

He felt Madeline's shoulders rise on his chest. "I don't know. You just told me to keep on this trail. We have not reached a crossroads yet so I am still going in the right direction. I think."

With a squint in his eyes, Rubin looked up to the sun in an attempt to gauge the time. "Nearly mid-day, good."

Madeline looked to her right shoulder. "Good for what, are we making good time?"

"Means we've been on the go for five hours now and going by old Felix's pace here, I guess we've covered a good distance." He peered round Madeline's shoulder. "We haven't stopped have we?"

Madeline's replied in lowered tone. "Only for a minute or two."

"Why?"

"Rubin, I don't need to tell you why, we just did alright. I did."

It took a moment, but it finally dawned in his pounding head what she meant. "Oh, right." He thought more. "Where was I then?"

"You sat like a statue on Felix…snoring."

Rubin nodded. "Uh-huh, okay." He changed the subject. "So then, little missy, what do I call you now?"

Madeline sat in silence. This hadn't even occurred to her. She needed a new name. A boy's name, as she certainly couldn't be called Madeline. Not looking like this. "You mean you would actually call me by name?"

"Eh?"

"Rubin, I have never once heard you call me by my first name, it has always been missy. You do actually know that it is Madeline don't you?" She knew her sarcasm would not be wasted on him.

"Is it? Ouch! And stop that, unless you want a belly full of cider up over you."
Madeline cringed once again at the thought.

Their day had been as uneventful as Rubin had hoped for. Given that he had dozed on and off most of it, the times awake were given to quite contemplation and only when Madeline had spoken to him did he speak. But they had settled on a name.
Madeline had originally suggested Landis, after her eldest brother, but Rubin had considered the name uncomfortable and said that it did not flow easy from his tongue, so a variant had been agreed upon. Madeline was now called Lander.
This new identity had been given to her seven hours previously, and as they sat around their camp fire, Madeline could count on one hand the times he had inadvertently called her missy. And just as many on the other one as to the times he had just simply called her 'boy', with him forgetting her alias. She had tried to catch him out on several occasions, and thus far he had failed miserably. Content now that they had made even more progress with a full day's travel, she was relieved to be off Felix's back, with her rear end hurting from irritation within her britches. She sat quietly staring at the flames. Reheating more of Margaret's stew over a small fire, Madeline admired Rubin's cooking technique. Teetering from a twigged branch embedded at an angle in the ground, his old and stained pot hovered six inches above the flames, suspended by twisted and dampened twine. With intermittent stirring using a split wooden spoon, he looked quite at ease outdoors. The only thing wrong that she could see was that there was little heat coming from the flames.
"Can't we build a bigger fire Rubin, there is not much heat from it? And it's getting chilly."
Rubin shook his head. "This ain't a heating fire little mis…I mean …boy. It's a cooking fire."
"Can't you cook over a big fire?"
He shook his head once again. "There's fires' that can be seen from a distance and there's fires that can't. This one won't."
Madeline; sitting cross-legged on the ground, inched herself closer, and pulled her blanket tighter around her. "I don't understand."
"Yesterday and today was okay, quite safe, but we're now into bad territory, bandits and the likes. I don't want our whereabouts known to them. So I build a fire that can't be seen in the dark."
In addition to that, he was well aware that given what he had found in Ramone's home, they may not be the only ones after his fortune.
"You can do that?"
He winked at her. "Trust me?" He had intentionally picked the very spot they now sat for that self same purpose. He had learned well in the army. "Hand me your plate."

Doing as instructed, Madeline watched him dish out evenly, the remains of the stew and when done, pass her plate across to her. He sat himself down on a yard high rock opposite and in three consecutive swoops of his spoon, filled his mouth with more than plenty. She watched the now empty spoon in his hand keep time with his chewing until eventually he had swallowed enough to speak. "Good cook Margaret."
Astounded with the amount of food a person could force into their mouth at any one time, Madeline nodded. "Yes, you look like you are enjoying it." She knew he would be hungry as he had eaten little the previous night, preferring the cider instead. And he had not eaten a thing all day due to his hangover and delicate stomach. But now sober, he apparently had the appetite of a horse. She had only eaten two spoonfuls herself when Rubin had burped and thrown his empty plate to the ground. He wiped his mouth with his sleeve.
Madeline stretched over. "Here Rubin take mine."
He looked at the plate in her hand. "You not hungry?"
"No. I have being eating today when you haven't." She laid the plate on the ground and pushed it as far along towards him as she could. "Please Rubin, take it. I have eaten bread and cheese today. Margaret certainly packed a well stocked bag for us."
"Okay, if you're sure."
She nodded.
It took him just under thirty seconds to clear her plate and the empty receptacle to find a place on the ground next to its twin. He burped again. "Yeah, a fine cook, she is."
Madeline stared into the flames again. "They were very kind to us. All they had given us and would not take a single coin in payment."
Well not directly anyway, thought Rubin, as he picked at his teeth. He had left payment for it all on the fence where they had tied Felix to graze. He didn't like to be beholden to anyone, even a fellow soldier. Pacard would have found it by now. "Yeah, good people."
Madeline sprung to her feet. "An apple?"
Rubin looked up from the ground. "Eh?"
"An apple, for afters. There are some in the bag." Pulling her blanket in tighter, she walked towards Felix who Rubin had tethered to an old oak.
"Felix and I have had two today already, they're delicious."
"Nah, you two have 'em, I'll just have a bottle from the bag." He kneeled down by the fire and adjusted the burning embers, after which he carefully positioned more wood on top.
"Which bottle is that Rubin?"
Sitting cross legged in front of the fire to nurture its kindling, he answered without looking. "Any one, they're all the same."
Madeline turned from the bag. "Oh, the wine you mean. Sorry, I had to leave them all behind. We didn't have enough room for those, not with all the food Margaret had given us."

Rubin looked up from the fire. "What?"
Madeline fed Felix an apple, and with her hand peeking out of the blanket, crunched into one herself. "Are you sure you don't want one Rubin, they are really quite tasty?"
"No I don't want a fucking apple." He rose to his feet in temper. "Why did you leave my wine behind? We had plenty of room, we could have got another bag."
"Tutt-tutt now Rubin, are you sure you should be swearing in from of your young son?" She smiled at him.
"Fuck. It's not funny." He sat down as before and kicked into the fire. "I knew I should have checked the fucking things myself."
Madeline stood at the opposite side of the fire. "Rubin…"
He ignored her.
"Oh, Rubin. Ah-huh." With no response, she feigned another cough.
He eventually looked up…and on noticing her standing with a bottle of his wine swinging between finger and thumb, he jumped to his feet. "You little shit you."
On seeing him rise, Madeline doubled over with a surprised scream and as he made moves towards her, she ran around the fire with him hot on her heels. Amidst her laughter and his playful rants, she circled it within seconds after which she ran towards Felix to hide behind. Each way Rubin tried around Felix, Madeline went in the opposite direction until he eventually just stood straight and reached his arm over the top. His outstretched palm easily took the top of Madeline's head and he held her at bay. Her laughter had not abated, even when she was caught.
"Now give me the fucking wine…Lander."

Still she giggled.
"There was panic in your face there Rubin."
He had emptied half the bottle in just two swigs, and now with his back to the rock rather that sitting on it, Rubin rested the bottle on his outstretched legs. "If you *had* been my son, then my boot would have found a way to your arse for that."
Madeline, seated cross legged by the fire, burst out laughing. "Oh, I'm sorry Rubin, I just couldn't resist it. It was too good an opportunity to miss. And I wanted to get back at you for not allowing me to bring my own bag with me."
"Well you know the reason for that now. Boy."
Madeline nodded towards his bottle. "If there are bandits about here, is it wise for you to be drinking wine?"
Rubin looked down at his lap. "One bottle won't do any harm. I've eaten two plates of grub and it's nothing like that cider." He blew from puckered lips. "Ain't had anything that strong in a while."
Madeline smiled. "Yes, you looked awful." She bit her lip. "Sorry."
Rubin raised his eyes. "Hah, you mean worse than usual."

She knew he was referring to his scarred face and stitched lip. "How did you get the scar on your face?"
Rubin grinned. "You don't fuck about much do you, young missy."
Madeline apologized again.
"Nah, it's okay. Got it in battle, caught off guard and some bastard took a swipe at me with a sword."
Madeline's face lit up in amazement. "A sword?"
Rubin nodded.
"My goodness Rubin, he could have taken your entire face off."
Rubin laughed. "A whole face, hah, take a face off. How do you do that then?" He swigged again awaiting an answer.
Madeline pulled her blanket in tighter. "Oh, you know what I meant." She hesitated over her next question, but it blurted out just the same. "How many people have you killed? When you were a soldier I mean." She inched forwards in anticipation of his answer.
Rubin's eyes dropped and he watched himself roll the bottle in his palms. "Hmm…"
"That many you can't remember?"
His shoulders went up. "You don't stop to count when you kill 'em."
"Was it more than eight?" She tensed up after she said it.
He raised his eyes to be met by her smiling face. He grinned and nodded back. "Yeah, more than that."
With excitement, she inched closer. "Tell you what Rubin. Why don't I teach you to count?"
Rubin noticed her movement. "Little missy, if you get any closer to that fire, you'll be in the fucking thing."
She pulled herself back. "You're avoiding the question Rubin. Let me try. We do nothing but ride Felix all day, so it will keep us both occupied. And don't say you can count already. Counting all the way up to eight does not constitute being able to count."
Rubin said nothing, but his face to Madeline gave an indication of 'Why not, nothing to lose'.
"Good. We can start now." She looked about her for broken twigs to set out, but Rubin having cleared the campsite earlier with a leafed branch, had brushed most of them away.
Rubin laid the bottle to the side and rose to his feet. "Nope, we can start tomorrow." He grabbed hold of his musket. "Too late now, can't count on a full stomach."
Madeline's head followed his track as he walked round the fire. "Where are you going?"
He leaned down towards her and grinned. "You don't need to ask."
Madeline knew. "Oh."
With Rubin vanishing into the darkness of the bush to relieve himself, the camp now felt empty. Left alone with the silence save the crackling of the fire, Madeline looked about her. The dark irregular shapes of the bushes felt

threatening, closing in on her and the sinister twisted branches of the trees looked as if one would swoop down any moment and grab at her. She shivered and pulled her blanket tighter, more for safe reassurance rather than warmth. She fidgeted with her hands and eventually stood and walked towards Felix for comfort. Patting at his head, her own periodically looked round in the direction of where Rubin had walked. Where was he? Felix toyed with her hand. She looked again. 'Oh for goodness sakes Rubin, what's taking you so long?' With one final pat she bent closer and kissed Felix's to calm him as before. "Sshhh…"
Holding the blanket closer to her neck with her left hand, she turned and inched cautiously towards Rubin's egress. Standing at the edge of the camp, she stood nervously with her right hand pinching at her bottom lip. "Rubin." Peering into the pitch black, she senselessly tilted her head for a better view of the dark. She called again. "Rubin. Are you there?"
Growing impatient with his tardiness, she stamped her foot. "Rubin this isn't funny. You're scaring me."
She felt a hand on her shoulder.
Feeling like the skin had just left her body, she jolted in fright.
"Lost something?"
Madeline on recognizing his voice turned on her feet. "Fuck!"
Conscious of her expletive outburst, she quickly raised her hand to her mouth.
Rubin leaned closer. "Tutt-Tutt, you really think a son should be swearing in front of his father like that?"
He felt the side of her clenched fist on his chest.

"That wasn't funny."
It was funny to him, he thought. "Well, no harm done."
Madeline watched Rubin spread out his makeshift bed on the ground. "No harm done, you frightened the life out of me there."
Rubin, with his back to her, grinned, but remained silent.
"Where do I sleep?"
Rubin looked over his shoulder. "Where you are, but don't lie too close to the fire. Don't want you rolling over and burning."
Madeline looked at the dying flames. "Little chance of that."
Rubin followed her eyes. "Well, make the most of it. It's not getting built any more."
"Why? Can't we at least have some heat from it?"
"Nope. If anyone comes into our camp, I want them with the same problem as us, stuck in the dark."
Upon reflection, Madeline could see the logic in his thinking. If you can't see, then you can't be seen. It made perfect sense. But the night was cooling rapidly, and she would be freezing. Doing exactly the way Rubin had done, she flattened out a space with her feet. She shivered will the removal of her

blanket and once it was spread out on the ground, immediately lay down and pulled it across her. She shivered again.

Rubin stood over her. "You need to go, first?"

Madeline looked up.

He nodded across to where he had been earlier.

Her eyes followed his nod to the edge of the camp and the darkness beyond. She had always made it a rule to make water before retiring for the night, but on this occasion she thought, she would make an exception. It could be kept until morning. She shook her head.

When Rubin had kicked at the fire sending their camp into even darker surrounds, Madeline pulled herself into a fetal position and lay still. Facing away from him, she could hear Rubin cough, spit and make himself ready. And within a minute all was silent.

The faint light from the fire had dwindled to such a degree that Madeline wondered whether she had her eyes closed or not. She pulled up closer and shivered again. "Rubin, I'm freezing."

"Stick your head under the blanket. Your breath will heat you up."

Madeline did as instructed, but still her body remained cold. She pulled her head free. "Rubin, would we not get more heat from two blankets."

"We only got the one."

She turned around and resting on her elbow, peered into the dark. "Yes, but we have one each. If we were both under the two then we would be warmer."

Rubin remained silent..

"Did you hear me Rubin?"

"Okay, young missy, get yourself over."

Madeline smiled and sidled across in the direction of his voice. And once there, between them, they rearranged the blankets accordingly.

"You happy now?" He felt her nod on his back.

With the two blankets over her and Rubin's body heat, Madeline felt warmer as she snuggled into his back. With her arm across and over his powerful chest she felt cozy and safe. She pushed up slightly and kissed the back of his head.

Rubin looked over his shoulder. "What was that for?"

Madeline smiled. "Just a thank you, that's all."

"Oh, right…." Clutching the musket into his chest, he coughed and spat his final one of the day. "…ain't been kissed by a man before."

He felt it in the back of the knees this time.

*

Denig yawned.

He wasn't in the mood for this and could muster up no enthusiasm to participate. At the Comtesse's request, several friends and other guests had been invited to their home and as usual, he was footing the bill for the drinks and food. Even the smell of the burning opium was annoying him, he found it nauseating. Standing alone, and away from the main body of the company, he had nursed the same drink in his hand for over twenty minutes that the glass now felt warm to the touch. And he detested warm wine. He sighed. Scanning the room, his eyes fell upon Caroline. She appeared to be in the same frame of mind. He could tell, even from a distance and from the look on her face that her heart wasn't in her efforts. Half attired in a red laced corset, she was seated upright with legs apart and in the middle of which was Jeanette's face on all fours in front of her. But it was Caroline's actions with the man standing to her right that made him think of her lethargy. Content to just have his erection in her hand and to pull back on it, Denig knew that under normal circumstances his wife would have had it in her mouth while doing it. It was clear to him that she was bored with the proceedings as he was. Even the naked Jacqueline, who was making her way across the room towards him, seemed different. Renowned for her trademark rouge painted nipples it was clear that she had made little effort tonight. He looked down at her colossal breasts on her approach. "A bit brown looking tonight are we not Jacqueline. Have you exhausted the city's supply of colourant?"

She tugged at his sleeve. "I may ask the same of you, is it so cold in here as to warrant wearing full dress?"

He smiled at her and nodded, acknowledging what she had meant by her sardonic quip. "You as bored as I am?"

"Not the same tonight for some reason, is it?" She turned to stand by his side. "Look at her, acting as if nothing's happened."

Denig could only see the naked posterior in front of Caroline, but he knew Jacqueline was referring to Jeanette. "I see the mark on her face you gave her hasn't dulled her appetite much."

"I can assure you Denig, it gave me great pleasure in putting my fist into her face. I'm surprised though how easily she's forgiven me over it. She was alright at the start; when she first arrived, but now she's hard work and a pain in the rear end." Her head turned to face him. "Do you know she asked me to get her a hound? Huh, as fucking if. I may be bad, but not that bad, and wanted me in too."

Denig sighed once again. "I know what you mean. We've really fucked up here Jacqui. That bitch is bleeding me dry, I'm almost broke. Everything I had in the world is almost gone because of her. I just want things back to the way they were before." Through frustration, he lifted the glass to his mouth and immediately spat out its tepid contents. "Yuck."

His exasperation with Jeanette apparent, Jacqueline took the glass from him. "Come Denig, let me get you a fresh one. I have something I need to tell you, and not in view of her." Taking his arm in hers, they both side stepped their way through the variously situated bodies lying on the floor and crossed to the drinks cabinet.

Before she could ask, he had answered. "Brandy."

Exchanging his wine glass for one befitting his request, she filled it to within an inch. "Here, get that down you. Drown your sorrows."

Denig took it from her and held it up. "Fuck sake Jacqui, are you trying to bankrupt me as well."

"Just drink it."

He did, and handed her back the empty glass. "Satisfied?"

Jacqueline laughed. "Not yet, but the night's still young."

He smiled at her innuendo. "Thanks Jacqui, you're a good friend to me, to both of us."

Jacqueline knew that he meant Caroline. "You two are the best friends I have in the world Denig and it pains me to see you this way. Not many in life would have taken me under their wing the way you and Caroline have. I'd probably be dead by now."

Always the one to shy away from sentimental accolade, Denig changed the subject. "Right, that's given me the taste now, another?"

"You just can't take a compliment can you Denig? Never allow yourself to accept praise for any good deed done. It is a fine quality you have, one that makes you stand out amongst others. I'd do anything for you and Caroline, you know that don't you?"

"Enough Jacqui, just fill the glass."

While Denig had attempted to steer the course of the conversation away from maudlin, it was Jacqueline who would change the mood to that of gravity. "You'll need it for what I'm about to tell you."

"Great, that's what I need now, more bad news."

She handed him his refill. "It's worse than bad. Hannah is missing."

"Hannah?"

Jacqueline filled a fresh glass with wine for herself before continuing. "She was last seen in the infirmary. Since then, she hasn't been seen by anyone. I heard about it when I was out earlier. Her parents have informed the authorities so it's just a matter of time before they appear here, with her being in your employ."

If this wasn't news enough to make him drink, then nothing was. He swallowed half the glass. Thinking out loud, he muttered under his breath. "...and the state of her arms as well." He thought further of it then angled his head towards Jeanette. "You think she's got something to do with it?"

"I wouldn't be surprised if she had. She got those two weirdoes to get rid of Clara's body remember. After the beaten she gave poor Hannah, she might have thought herself exposed to trouble if she were to report it. She was also a witness to Clara's death remember, so I wouldn't put anything past that woman Denig, she's the kiss of death that one. And another thing, if she did arrange to get rid of Hannah because of this, then you, Caroline and me are also witnesses. So what next, do we all have to watch our backs?"

Denig rested his tilted forehead on his fingers. "Honestly Jacqui, what the fuck have I done to deserve all this, what the fuck have I ever done to anyone to get this shit on my doorstep?"

"It was easier enough with Clara, with her having no family living in Paris. Going missing could have been covered by a number of reasons. Gone back

home, ran away with a beau, a dozen reasons, but Hannah's different. She went home every night straight from working here. It was obvious she would be missed."
Denig raised his palm out. "That's it Jacqui, I don't want hear anymore. I must have rotted the inside of my stomach by now over this woman, the amount of brandy I've drunk with worry. I haven't got a sou to my name and now I'm party to two fucking murders."
The remaining brandy was downed in one swoop. What will Caroline think of all this when she hears about it? His mind raced.
Holding it steady with hers, Jacqueline refilled the glass in his shaking hand. "I'm with you all the way in this Denig, I assure you."
He looked into her eyes, they were deadly earnest. "I know that Jacqui and I appreciate it. Doesn't alter the fact though that if this goes pear shaped, then we're all for the chop."
Jacqueline remained silent for a moment before she spoke out again. "No, No. Wait a minute. Perhaps we're looking at this the wrong way. We've done nothing wrong, have we? It's Jeanette who's arranged all this not us. She's the one responsible for Clara's death. She was the one who arranged for the body to be removed. She, maybe, as we don't know for certain yet, got rid of Hannah, dead or not. Denig, we weren't even responsible for Ramone's death. Just having a laugh at his expense doesn't mean we had a part in it."
Before Denig had a chance to consider this and form an opinion, they were joined by a mutual friend at their side.
"Come, come, Jacqueline, has your persuasive powers diminished of late, you've being speaking to Denig for a good ten minutes now and still he remains fully clothed."
Not the favourite of their acquaintances, Elle stood facing up between them, and as ever, he had to furtively hold his breathe while she spoke. This middle aged woman's breath; even peripherally, was undoubtedly the worst he had ever smelled. He had always avoided her in the past during these gatherings, as he could not prevent himself from retching within a foot of her. She continued.
"If I can be of any assistance in this matter, then please allow me, or if Denig is unwilling tonight, perhaps we two Jacqueline could...."
She had taken Jacqueline's left breast in her hand and holding the weight of such in her palm spoke further.
Or she would have done had Jacqueline not interrupted her. "I had at the very moment of your arrival persuaded Denig to do just that Elle. He's promised me his cock before others tonight..." She removed Elle's hand and with a dismissal, finished. "...perhaps later."
She smiled. "I will look forward to that then Denig."
He watched her turn and walk towards another unsuspecting victim. He finished his brandy. "Like hell you will."

Jacqueline faced him full on and began to undo his tunic buttons. "Even I'd have to think twice about having that foul smelling mouth near my snatch." Both laughed.
To keep up the façade, Denig allowed her to continue, but wanted to resume their conversation. "So what were you hinting at earlier?"
"She's bled you dry Denig, so cut your losses."
Lifting his arms, he let her remove his top layers until bare-chested. "Cut my losses, do you know what that amounts to?"
She leaned forward to start on his britches. "Does it matter? Would you rather live penniless" She hauled at the stiff buckle. "... or go to the guillotine just as poor?"
His eyebrows raised, she had a point there he thought. "Here, I'll get those for you." Bending down to pull free his tight fitting boots, by the time he had straightened up, Jacqueline had both britches and linen drawers down over his stockings and at his ankles. He stepped out of them as she pulled them free. "That was quick, even faster than when I do it myself."
"Years of practice Denig, years of practice." To enhance their charade further, she stood up and took hold of his penis.
"Ooh!" As unexpected as this was, he let it remain there. "So what do you suggest we do now then? About our predicament, I mean."
"I knew what you meant Denig. Put your hand on my chest."
"Oh, right." He did as required and cupped the right one full on.
She looked down. "Is that it? What are you doing, holding it on?"
"Sorry, sorry." Grabbing as much of her mammoth breast as he could, he lifted it up slightly and squeezed.
"Denig, you're not picking a fucking melon at a market stall, at least make it look real."
"Okay, okay. Christ, I need another drink."
"Never mind the brandy just now. You have to report her before it goes any further. You'll be thought of by the law as keeping it quiet and then you'll be an accomplice. Fuck her, get her out of the house and let her stand on her own two feet."
"Then where would I be? She's used up all the money I had in the world. She'd promised us a part of what she would gain from Ramone after he was dead. I can't give all that up now."
"She's conning you Denig. I wouldn't be surprised if that title Comtesse of hers was made up. Who the hell's ever heard of a name like that anyway? Get out now while you still have a chance."
Without realizing it, Caroline was standing by their side. "Hello darling." She looked down at his flaccid penis in Jacqueline's hand. "Having trouble tonight are we?" She turned to face Jacqueline. "You losing your touch Jacqui? Not like you to keep a man down."
She made movements in her hand. "Oh, he's getting there Caroline."
Preoccupied with where Jeanette was, Denig looked over Caroline's shoulder to find her, but she was nowhere to be seen.

"Is anything wrong Denig?"

He refocused on her and with feigned ignorance to her question looked down at Jacqueline's hand. "No, no, nothing's wrong, getting there." He laughed to make light of the situation. "Don't worry. I remember what happened here to the last person who couldn't raise his cock."

*

Having been informed that Raul and Raul were waiting for her in the library, Jeanette casually walked naked across the marble hallway towards the door. With them calling at so late an hour, she was hoping that their news was worthy of its urgency. She entered, closed the door behind her and stood waiting on their report.

Without preamble and a complete indifference to her naked form, the taller spoke out. "She headed south from the city and got off the carriage a few miles out, at a desolate spot."

"South, that is understandable. Her destination is apparent is it not?"

"She was then met by a private carriage, the driver of which then took her to the opposite side of the city, to another isolated spot."

"North! Why would she be heading north? This is far too convoluted a ploy for a mere child. Who was there to meet her?"

"He didn't know. He saw no-one. He was paid and he left."

"You questioned him about this?"

He nodded. "Until he could speak no more."

"Very well gentleman, you will have to follow her trail. I will not see you again until your return. Go home and pack. You have a long journey ahead of you."

*

Madeline 4

Chapter 7

Alone

Madeline woke to find herself the sole occupant of their makeshift bed. Initially panic stricken, she only needed to raise her head three inches from her folded arm for Rubin to come into view. Relieved, she adjusted herself to watch him. He was shaving. Or, what she took to be shaving. Sitting cross legged in front of the fire, she saw him spit into his hand and rub the saliva into his chin and throat. Tilting his head to the side, he proceeded to drag his sharp edged knife from the neck upwards and over his bristles. Madeline cringed. She could hear the scraping sound from over six feet away. He repeated this procedure until done. With another spit; this time into the fire, he picked up a battered tin cup by his side and on tilting his head back, poured the contents over his face. Shaking his head, he wiped the dripping water off with his hand and used it to drag over his grey stubble hair.
Without turning, he spoke out. "You sleep okay?"
Shocked with this, Madeline sat up. She hadn't made a sound and he hadn't even looked over. "Oh, yes. Thank you."
"Good. I want to get an early start today. Cover as much ground in light as we can. Had a look at the map earlier, there's a town up ahead, a few hours ride from here. We'll stop there..." He nodded to the fire. "...can't live on this all the while."

Madeline hadn't noticed before, but over the fire on a spit were roasting two…what were they she wondered. They were small animals of a sort she presumed, but she was not familiar with their shape. "What is that Rubin?" Before he had a chance to answer, he raised his left hand in the air as if to silence her.
Madeline sat still and followed his gaze, she could see nothing. But in one swift movement, Rubin had lifted his knife from the ground and thrown it. Her eyes followed its rapid spin through the air and eventually find its way into the body of a brown squirrel. She looked back at the fire. Now she knew.
Rubin raised himself from the ground. "If the little bastards made it any easier for me, they'd be walking to the fire."

Madeline was happy.
The sun was shining down on her face and she had a full stomach. What meat there had been on the little creatures she had savoured, not having eaten squirrel before. But on reflection, it wasn't something she would repeat in a hurry. And with Rubin being sober, the day thus far had been to her liking. Apart from one incident that had upset her. The first hour had seen them leave the thick wooded area and in the distance ahead, had lay a vast expanse of open, level ground. As they had travelled further, the fields which should have been bountiful with wheat and the likes, had lay desolate with a low yield, this being the result of France's recent climate change. Where they should have being seeing carts full of produce passing them by, they had only seen one solitary person the entire journey. And he had been dead. Lying face down, naked upon the ground with the back of his head missing, he had been stripped of his belongings. The result of a bandit robbery Rubin had informed her. Apart from that, they had travelled for three hours without incident.
"This is a far more comfortable ride than yesterday."
"You think so?"
"Yes I do. I spent most of it bent over Felix."
Rubin leaned over to his left and spat.
"And would you please stop doing that. It turns my stomach each time. I can understand the need to do it when you cough and clear yourself, but it appears to me you just spit out of habit."
"You think so?" He felt her elbow again. "That's getting to be a habit of yours too."
Madeline smiled. It was true and he was right. She liked Rubin and was growing very fond of him. She knew that with each bodily connection; albeit a poke, a nudge or a punch at his chest in frustration, it was reassurance to her that he was still there, keeping her safe. But with feminine pride, she would not let him know it.
She changed the subject. "How long do you think now?"
"What, you mean to the town?"

"No. I meant until the end of our journey."
Rubin blew out in thought. "Long ways yet, got a good few days to go at least. We're going the long way round remember. Don't want to leave an obvious trial behind us." He leaned round at her. "Why, you getting bored?"
"No, I'm not bored. Ah, and that reminds me, you agreed last night to let me teach you how to count."
Rubin's face screwed up. He had hoped she'd forgotten about that.
"Well?"
"Well what?"
Madeline straightened up with tutorial prowess. "Count up to eight."
"I can count up to eight."
"I know you can Rubin, but just do it for me now. But when you reach eight, add the number nine at the end."
"Why?"
"Because nine follows eight, that's why. Now do it."
Madeline listened intently as Rubin laboured his way through the numerals and eventually finish with nine. "Good. Now count again, and after the number nine add ten to the end."
Once again, she listened to him slowly repeat the numbers and after pausing briefly at nine added ten to finish off. "Bravo Rubin. Already, that is a twenty-five percent increase in …I mean, two more numbers than you could count before."
Surprised with his sudden interest in the fact that he could count higher than before, he urged Madeline on. "Right, what comes next?"
Pleased with his enthusiasm, Madeline continued and within twenty minutes she had him count through the teens.
"Fifteen, sixteen, seventeen… eighteen…nineteen."
"Well done Rubin. Now it gets a bit tricky and changes somewhat."
"Tenteen."
"No, not tenteen Rubin, the teens are finished."
"Why?"
"Because they are, they only go up to nineteen. Numbers change in divisions of ten."
With the number eight having been stuck in his mind all these years, it was easy for him to take this away from ten. He thought further. "Well what happened to eleventeen and twelveteen?"
Madeline's shoulders lowered. Goodness this was hard work. "There is no eleventeen or twelveteen. These numbers stand alone by themselves, eleven and twelve."
"Why? What makes them different from the rest?"
"I don't know. I didn't invent the system, they just are."
"Seems silly to me, why not oneteen and twoteen like the rest, why change after that?"

Absurd as it was, Madeline thought, Rubin had a point, but her mind was too exhausted with her tuition. "Okay Rubin, I think that will be enough for today. We can start again tomorrow at twenty."
"Twentyteen?"
Madeline sighed. "Yes Rubin. Twentyteen."

They could see the town in the distance.
Billows of black smoke soured up from the outskirts and when they had reached it, they could see why. Unlike Paris, where pox ridden bodies lay rotting by the street edge, these townsfolk had the good sense to exhume the bodies on large pyres. The smell of burning flesh had Madeline retch repeatedly and even with her coat sleeve pressed hard to her face, the stench permeated through. Unperturbed by the smell, Rubin had slowed Felix down a steady pace as they passed. One of the men had lowered the cloth from his face and spoken out to him.
"Hope you've got good reason to be going into town?"
Rubin brought Felix to a halt. "Provisions, for the road." He nodded towards town. "How bad is it?"
The man stuck his spade into the ground and leant on it. "Bad enough. Seven more last night."
"Pox?"
"That, an' something else, something real bad. Been spreading through the town like hell's fire."
Rubin nodded in thought. "Can we get stuff sent out to us?"
The man removed his hat and scratched at his flea ridden head. "Don't think there's much left to be had."
Rubin looked about him. "Any farms nearby?"
He used his hat to wipe the sweat of toil from his face. "All around, but they won't have anything. Nothing growed this year, but they still have to pay the taxes. Just like us all, bloody money grabbing bastards…"
Rubin turned Felix around and headed back, leaving the man to his rants.
"Well I guess that's that."
"What will we do?"
Rubin grinned. "Squirrel?"

"What have we got left in the bag?"
Madeline rummaged through. "Not much I'm afraid."
Rubin pulled the rope tight and left Felix tethered to the tree. He walked toward her. "Thought you said she packed a full bag, apples and the like?"
Madeline, seated on a small rock looked up. "Sorry Rubin. That was part of the joke, with the wine I mean." She bit the inside of her lip. "There were only two apples."
"And you gave mine to old Felix there? Hah."
She contorted a smile. "Sorry…"

"Ah, no matter, hate the fucking things anyway, unless they're fermented." He squatted down beside her. "So, what *do* we have left?"
Madeline pulled the meagre contents from the bag and sat with an item in each hand.
Rubin looked at them. "Is that it, a piece of cheese and an edge of bread?" He sat down beside her. "Well the joke's certainly backfired on you little missy. I can go for days without food, but I know you can't."
Madeline looked around at the surrounding trees. "Isn't there anything here you can catch? More squirrels perhaps?"
Rubin grabbed the empty food bag and rose to his feet. "Nope. There's only one thing for it. I'll need to go into the town."
It had been his intention to do so anyway. Since they first turned from the pyre and rode off. But he certainly wasn't going to take her with him. He had ridden Felix for a few miles until he had found a spot where he could leave her. She would be too exposed in the open fields, even dressed as a boy, the dead man on the roadside earlier, his worry. This high piece of wooded ground had been an ideal choice and she could hide here quite comfortably.
Madeline rose with him. "You mean you're leaving me here. Alone?"
"I've no choice." He walked towards Felix. "I don't know what's in that town, so I'm not taking a chance with you."
She was hard on his heels. "But what if something happens to you?"
Rubin knew that she had asked this through concern for his well being and not the selfish act of what would become of her. "Don't worry ma boy. Nothin'll happen to your dear old papa."
"Very funny Rubin, but I mean it."
He un-strapped the blankets from Felix's back and in addition, his bag and the water pouches. There was no need to carry a load for no reason. He climbed on to Felix. "Be back in an hour. If you hear anything, hide in the thick bush over there. You hear?"
Madeline had no time to answer. He had turned and was gone.
She was alone.

*

Gaston had spent the entire night shivering beneath the single thin sheet. His clothes; which lay haphazardly about the floor had not been within reach. As much as he had stretched his arm out to get hold of at best, the shirt which lay closest, he could not manage it. The chain was too short. And he hadn't eaten or drank anything. After their proclamation that he was a prisoner of their so called revolutionary movement, the two men had left the room. And not since then had anyone entered, to explain further, or more importantly, bring him food or water. He hauled at his fettered ankle once again and winced. His skin was raw beneath the iron shackle and with each movement the pain became more pronounced. And having no spit through his dehydration, he could not moisten it somewhat to ease the friction it caused.

He looked at the window again, but did not have the energy to holler. He'd spent the first hour of the previous day shouting cries for help, but to no avail. It was this that led him to think that he was not within the town boundaries. If he had been, then he would have been gagged. They had obviously thought it un-necessary, so he had come to the conclusion that he must be in an isolated location. But where, and who would know where he was? Surely someone would have thought it suspicious to have them remove his clothes from the inn. At least one person must have noticed his absence? Having so many questions in his head, before he had given consideration to an answer, his mind had raced to the next. And what had been the pretense with Sylvia all about. Had she been in on it? If so, then why go through all the rigmorale of getting him drunk and seducing him. Couldn't they have just kidnapped him on the street, late at night, during the many occasions he had been too inebriated to fend for himself? He had repeatedly asked the same questions in his head and came up with no plausible explanations for their actions. He wasn't anything special. He was worth nothing to them in their fight for liberty or equality. What use was he to them and to whom would they be seeking this ransom money from? He considered it further. If they were to approach the authorities in Paris then it would be clear that there would be retributions. On the other hand, if they knew him to be affluent in personal circumstances, would they then have thought better to approach his family instead, namely, his wife.
If this were the case, then he was in deep trouble...
...Much deeper than he was in just now.
If what he had planned to happen, had occurred already and both Janis and her mother were be dead. Then where would that leave him? Shit! Where would the money come from?
But then again, this could be to his advantage. If they had indeed been murdered, then the authorities, knowing his whereabouts here in Salon would be obligated to send word, or better still, duty bound to send an envoy to inform him personally.
He kicked at his ankle once again and threw himself back on the bed. If not knowing anything was the worst thing he could think of, then not being able to do anything about it came a close second. All he could do now was to wait. He kicked at the ankle again.
Not that he had much choice in the matter.

*

Having hauled everything to the centre of a clearing, Madeline had spread one of the blankets out on the ground. Her thoughts were to make a little camp of her own as she may as well be comfortable in her wait. But she soon became bored. Now, seated on her small rock, she drew rough pictures in the dry dirt with a broken branch. A little cottage with a garden and a fence running round its perimeter had been the start. She added to it a tree to the

left and flowers, and then herself standing at the gate gazing out. Her little house in the country she thought. But there was something missing. She mused over it and then it finally came to her…a husband, a man to share her life with in this idyllic home. 'Hmm.' Or was she waiting at the gate for her husband's return from the fields? She smiled. Yes, that was it, this was a better scenario. She had just prepared dinner and was now looking out for him to join her. Drawing the sun in the top right corner to complete it, the branch was thrown to the ground. "One day perhaps."
She rose to her feet and sauntered about the clearing. An hour could pass you quickly by if you had something to occupy your mind with, she thought, but with nothing to do but wait, she would count every minute. With this and her constant worrying for Rubin's safety, she had to do something to take her mind from it. Having walked towards their belongings, she knelt down and took hold of the main ☐raveling bag. Knowing for sure, that as well as containing the utensils and equipment for their journey, it also held within, Rubin's personal things. She hesitated, but convinced herself after a few seconds of self persuasion that he wouldn't mind her looking. She hoped. And within a minute, all items were laid out before her. His cooking pot, two small battered cups, two plates in dire need of straightening out, two forks, one of which had a prong missing, two bent spoons which were heavily stained through use, a split wooden cooking stick, two bottles of wine, and a bag which on squeezing had an unfamiliar feel to it. She took this to be the cartridges for his musket. To these items she added the second blanket and two near empty water bags.
She felt guilty for her earlier chastising of him. Apart from the wine, Rubin had brought nothing of his own, not even a change of shirt. But then again, she had never seen him out of the clothes he was wearing now. He was obviously used to ☐raveling light, and apart from his musket and his knife which she noticed had been strapped to his back, he carried nothing else save the contents of his coat pockets. She was certain that, from all the men of Paris she couldn't have chosen a better person to help her on her quest. He was truly a one off and she was fond of him. So much so, that her concern for him was brought back to the fore. She tried to estimate the time he had been gone. "Oh, pooh!"
Rising to her feet again, she wandered aimlessly towards the edge of the clearing and on noticing a small pathway through the bushes, she followed its trial. Within seconds, she heard the faint sound of what she perceived was a babbling brook. Oh! Surprised that they were so close to running water, like a bee to a flower she headed in its direction. The trial ended abruptly and she stood upon a pebbled surface which ran eight feet to the water's edge. While not being a river as such, it was a stream nearing its size and as her eyes moved from its edge to the centre, the gradual disappearance of the stones beneath the surface of the clear water gave an indication of its depth. She looked to her left. The sound she had heard was the entrapment of the flowing water at a boulder's edge and it dropping several feet into the main

body again. Apart from this soothing sound, all around her was quiet. She thought of the water bags. She could refill them here, with fresh water. Turning on her feet, she returned to her camp and on emptying them of their tepid contents, carried the bags back to the water, happy in her mind now that she was doing something of purpose.

Squatting down next to the boulder, she laid the bags to her side and cupped her hand in the flowing water. Raising it to her lips she felt at once its coldness and when swallowed relished in its taste. It had been the first cold and fresh water she had drank since leaving home. She cupped again, and again and finally sat back in the heat of the mid-day sun. Her eyes were drawn to the slow flowing stream and her mind drifted back to her childhood when, with her brothers they would swim in water similar to this. And with her being the only girl; their over protectiveness of her was, she had felt at the time, perhaps too fervent for her, even then, independent nature. She had felt smothered by their attention on occasions like that, but then, at other times she had felt alone, distanced from them. There hadn't appeared to be consistency in her sibling relationship, the sole constant in her childhood upbringing being her father. Closing her eyes, she thought of him and his illness she had left him to endure. This had been the only thing she had felt guilty about when leaving home. On numerous occasions, since arriving in Paris had she tried to convince herself of her blamelessness in this. Not the fact that she could do anything to prevent it, but not being there for him if it finally took him. She made her mind up there and then, that when they had completed their mission, she would return home to see him.

Fidgeting on the ground within her britches and tugging through the sweat stained top to the tight corset beneath, she looked out at inviting coolness of the water before her. If only?

Apart from the woods behind her, her eyes could see nothing but miles of open tract across the water. Similar to this side, it rose at a slight pebbled incline to the fields beyond. To her left and right, the same, nothing. No-one was near her, she was alone, no-one would see. She bit her lip again. Should she risk it? Surely she could see in the distance a person's approach and duck for cover within the bushes. Her hand rose to her face. She would have to be careful not to remove the oil and black chinned soot. Even though Margaret had given her a small pouch of it to redo as required, she didn't want to risk it. Only for a minute or two, just to be clean, in and out in a moment. Unconscious of her own decision making, by the time she had made up her mind to do it, she had unbuckled her britches and they had dropped to her ankles.

*

Rubin noticed the arrival of a new cart. This man had a busy day ahead of him he thought. It was stacked high.

He shrugged as Rubin passed, this time speaking to him through the cloth at his face. "On your own head then."
He hadn't even noticed Madeline's absence. Or to him, what he would have considered to be Rubin's son. He just dragged a random body from the open end and threw it on to the flames.
Rubin heard the instant hiss of the searing flesh. He rode on.
Having taken Felix to full gallop on departure from the wood, he had him walk at a slow pace into town. A town, even he had reservations about entering. He had seen death in Paris through numerous causes, pox and syphilis that weren't a pretty sight, but this new scourge the man had mentioned had him wary. How contagious was it and what were the symptoms? Before death he meant. He pulled Felix to a halt. Recalling his army days and seeing so many battlefield medics doing their duty, Rubin pulled the knife from his back and leaned over. Slicing a long strip of blanket from beneath the saddle, he re-sheathed it as before and followed suit with the town-man. He tied it round his jaw, but not to cover the smell which pervaded in the air, this not bothering him in the least, but more to protect his lungs from whatever this town had within its midst.
Kicking his heels into Felix, he rode on.

*

Free from the restrictions of the corset, Madeline rubbed at her aching breasts. Now, standing naked, she bent down to pick up the one thing she wanted to launder, the linen cloth with which she wore beneath her britches. Drawers, she remembered Margaret calling them. They were soiled slightly and a quick rinse through and scrub with a stone would take but a minute. So, with her squatting down at the boulder, she rubbed the coarse stone over the moistened cloth, while looking up and around every few seconds. She knew the heat from the sun would have the cloth dried in no time, if she wrung it out properly and spread it on the rock. The outer garments she knew Rubin would still want to look worn and dirty. She looked about her one more time before standing. Satisfied that she had arranged it in such a position as to catch the full rays of the sun, she folded the rest of her clothes and after tucking them behind the same large boulder, walked towards the water.
In the course of living in Paris, Madeline had grown accustomed to her own nakedness, and the baring of her body to others was, to her, a necessity she had come to accept given her vocation in life. But the thought of strangers seeing her unclothed was the least of her concerns, what was, was the fact that she had to remain hidden from them, now. So with trepidation, she eased herself towards the river's edge, all the while being vigilant for prying eyes. And before she knew it, she was ankle deep in the cool water.

Yet another cart had been loaded and was heading towards him. The driver of which; whose face was also covered, nodded in passing.
Rubin nodded back but said or asked nothing. He kept going at pace.
The entrance to the town happened to be the main thoroughfare and as he made his way along its middle he could see on either side of him, further corpses lying in wait. In complete contrast to Paris, the road was relatively clean, with neither human nor animal filth on it. The various shop fronts with signs above, indicated to him a thriving town, where each purveyor's wears were obviously of such quality and in demand as to warrant them being there. And with the surrounding area being agriculturally productive, save the last year, Rubin considered this town to be a place where a person could live comfortably. But as it was now, the life had apparently been taken from it, with the sight of the three snarling curs hauling at a male cadaver for food. He could hear the woeful cries of female voices emanating from various houses, their grief apparent. The intermittent musket shots he heard, he knew to be some folks relieving the suffering of a loved one with a quick death. The stench of death and decay could still be smelled, even through his thick cloth. 'Fuck' he thought "what a hellhole'.
He pulled over to the right, just outside of what he took to be a food vendor, going by the symbol on the sign alone, as no produce was evident either outside or in the window. He would try here first. Dismounting, he pulled the musket and food bag free, but finding nothing to hitch Felix to, he looked into its eyes and gave muffled instruction. "You stay here. Okay." He gave one solitary pat to the side of his head and sticking one end of the food bag down the front of his britches, he turned to enter the shop.
With the musket already primed and loaded, he pulled the lock to full cock and with his finger on the trigger, edged the half opened door out further with his left foot. He peered in. The shop was in a mess, wooden boxes and cloth bags lay strewn about the floor and several areas where dogs had done their business. He looked behind the door and once satisfied, walked in. Little chance of finding anything here, he thought. There was a further door to the back, so negotiating his way through the filth, he inched forward. He could hear a slight murmur beyond, a whimpering of a sort. Focusing his ear to the sound, he couldn't make out whether it was sobbing or speech, or both. This door was closed, so freeing his left hand from gripping the barrel, but still holding the musket level, he reached over and turned the knob. He pushed it open an inch and when resuming the hand's place back in its position, kicked it open with his foot.
The occupant of the whimpering sound had become apparent at once. But on his entry he had heard an additional sound, one that had made him smile. Seated on the floor against the opposite wall with bent knees, was a fully naked man clutching a slatted wooden box in his folded arms, the contents of which was clear to Rubin by the sound. Oblivious to his presence, this man stared unerringly into a vacant space while rocking his body to the side in

time with the indistinct mutterings of a song. Rubin knew at once that he had gone mad. He had seen enough crazies in his life. New recruits driven to the point of madness by the horrors of battle, seeing their friends with heads and limbs severed from their bodies, or disemboweled by cannon shot. He edged in, and once again, after checking behind the door, scanned the room. He pulled back with the initial shock.

Rubin could see now why the man was in the state he was in. Seated to the man's left and upright upon a chair, was a body which Rubin took to be the man's wife. Her death had not been recent, that was clear to him. With sunken eyes and sallow gray skin, she must have been there for at least a week. The signs of decomposition were so advanced as to have Rubin wonder how the man could have suffered the smell from her. But on looking at him again, he wondered whether he could now comprehend anything. Rubin lowered his musket and moved towards him. He put up no resistance when Rubin removed the box from his hands, only to clutch his arms closer in and around himself. He hadn't missed a note in his song.

Rubin held it up in his left hand and shook it. The small chicken came to life once again. Rubin's eyes borrowed into it, checking for any signs of disease. Apart from being underfed and starving it appeared fine. He leaned the musket against the wall and pulled off a few slats, and after reaching in, dropped the box to the floor. In one quick tug of its neck, the body went into spasm, and as the bird twitched its way to death's door, Rubin stuffed it into the food bag. "That'll do for a start."

He looked around the room again, but it was no different to the previous one. If he were here to pillage, then he could have filled the bag with all sorts, but food was his only concern. Plus he wanted in and out quickly so as to get back within the hour. He heard the man behind him utter out in panic, apparently having realized the box was gone from his grasp. Rubin turned and grabbed his musket. The chicken was fine, but he wanted to check further on first, he needed more than just a solitary bird. Adjusting the musket to leave, he looked down at the pitiful sight before him. He paused for a moment, staring into the wide vacant eyes...

...then raised the barrel to the man's head.

*

She would normally have ducked beneath the surface during a swim or while bathing, but Madeline was aware of her need for the water to remain at shoulder level. And dearly would have loved to remove the tight pins from her hair, if only for a few minutes. Her head had never been so itchy. It was so tempting just to pull them out and duck below the water, but she could not take a chance on ruining her disguise. It was daring enough to do what she was doing now without Rubin being present. But, on reflection, these were slight inconveniences compared to the luxury of the cool water she was immersed in. And if she was in and out quick enough, then Rubin may never

know. Estimating she had been in for about five minutes, she allowed herself five more and by the time she had dried, dressed and filled the water bags then by her reckoning she would be back in camp before his return. Her eyes had never once left the open fields ahead, except for her frequent scans from left to right. This had taken in the full vista and as yet, she had seen no-one. So, on lifting her feet from the river bed once again, her wavering arms kept her afloat and apart from the continuous water falling at her boulder, all around was quite...
She heard the sound of feet upon pebbles coming from behind. Surprised, her own feet hit the bottom in reaction. 'Oh, Pooh' Rubin had returned sooner than expected. She cowered, waiting on his rebuff, but it never came. In its place was a sound she was unfamiliar with. She slowly turned her body round and did not see Rubin as was expected or even hoped for, just four other men in his place...and one had a musket pointed straight at her.

Madeline 4

Chapter 8

A Game of Nerves

Rubin had reloaded the musket after seeing the man off.
He guided Felix down the side of the street, pausing momentarily at each shop entrance and peering through the doorways in the hope that something of worth would catch his eye. But to no avail, the town's belongings had long since gone. As would its inhabitants he thought, after hearing yet another two musket shots fired. It wasn't until he had turned and walked almost the length of the opposite side that he saw a glimmer of hope. Having centered the street to give the rabid curs a wide berth, the third shop from the end appeared to him like a taverne. Or perhaps a café he hoped, as it had several tables and chairs situated at its front. It suddenly occurred to him that never in his entire life had he ever wished for a café over a taverne until this moment. With food now being more important than wine he found himself unselfishly thinking of another rather than that of his own wants or needs. This young missy had certainly changed his way of thinking.

Likewise to his previous excursion indoors, he gave Felix his instruction to remain still and approached the entrance with caution, musket at the ready. There was no need for him to push this particular door open as it had already been torn from its hinges and lay split on the floor several feet within the room, so he edged his way in over it. Similar in messed state to the others he had seen before, whatever fittings and fixtures still remained from the room's original decor lay smashed and broken. Moving in, he felt shattered glass underfoot and looked down. His earlier hopes of it being a taverne were confirmed. Looking closer, he sighed. Broken wine bottles, most of which were still corked and had been full when smashed had him grieving. To see the deep red contents of each one having stained the wooden floor made him curse under his breathe. What a waste. He casually kicked at a few as he moved further on.

"Got fuck all worth taking."

The voice had come from the bar counter and Rubin turned in an instant, with the musket facing it straight on. He inwardly kicked himself for having being caught unawares.

A head emerged, rising from behind. "Cept what I've got here."

Rubin remained silent, awaiting the man to come into full view.

He placed an opened bottle of brandy on the counter. "Join me?"

Rubin looked at the bottle and licked his lips. As much as he could do with one, he shook his head. "Who else is here?"

He casually refilled the glass in his hand. "Don't worry stranger, just me. Rest of 'em are dead, or at least getting there." He raised the glass. "Sure you won't?"

"Uh-uh. Just looking for food. Got coin to pay for it."

"Hah, your money's no good here stranger." He looked around. "There's nothing here to buy and no good to anyone anyhow. Them's that are dead are the lucky ones." He finished the drink in one. "Should burn the whole fucking town to the ground."

Convinced now that his continued search would be pointless, Rubin resigned himself to the fact that nothing else would be found. And unconcerned as to why this seemingly uninfected man wouldn't just leave town beforehand, Rubin nodded and bade him adieu.

With a grip on both food bag and musket, Rubin mounted Felix and steered him around. And as he rode out of town, he thought of what mischief little missy had got up to in his absence.

*

Madeline's peripheral vision had taken into account that there were three others, but her focus had been on the one pointing the musket. He taunted her with it and spoke out again, but his words were meaningless to her ears. It was a language that meant nothing to her.

"He wants you out of the water."

This new voice had come from the left, and had spoken in French. Seated on the boulder where her laundry had been spread, was a young man in a soldier's uniform. He was holding what appeared to be one of Rubin's wine bottles in his hand. She noticed the musket standing by the boulder at his side.

Another, of comparable age, to her right, called out soon after, also in French and with similar clothing. "Looks like we've scored here boys. Got ourselves a nice little clean 'en coz he sure don't look like he's in for a swim." He turned to face Madeline and hollered at her. "Now get yourself out here boy." With his musket in his left hand, he clutched at the front of his britches with his right and squeezed in on himself. "Coz I've got something real hard for you here."

The fourth, who was seated with knees bent and legs opened, upon the pebbles to her extreme right, had until now remained silent. But he laughed out at his friend's salacious remark and drank from the second of Rubin's bottles. He, like the one pointing the musket at her, was dressed in civilian clothes, and was also armed, his musket lying on the pebbles by his side.

All four had weapons, she thought. What chance would they have even if Rubin were to return now? Her entire body shook within the water and she jumped when hearing the third shout at her again.

"We ain't got all fuckin' day here boy, get your arse out of the water, now." He raised his musket and within seconds had fired a shot into the water just two feet to her right. Her natural, startled reaction was to pull her hands to her face, and with it came a high pitched shriek.

Rising to his feet and walking to the river's edge, the fourth cried out. "Hah, he squeals like a fuckin' girl."

The third grew impatient with Madeline's unwillingness to move. "He'll be squealing a lot more in a minute with my fuckin' cock up his arse." He threw his musket to the ground and as he walked towards her, began to undo his britches. "Now move it."

Number four meanwhile; having unbuckled his britches for an alternative reason, stood by the edge, urinating into the water. He laughed at his own boyish antics of arching and bending its flow through the air. "Emptying mine here boy, for seconds up."

The foreigner inched to the side to let the third advance, but still kept his aim firmly on Madeline, who by this time had began to move slowly forward, out of the water.

Having resigned to the fact that the moment these men had seen her for what she truly was, she would be subjected to all kinds of abuse. If they were so desperate in their need to relieve themselves with what they thought was a boy, what then would they do with someone like her? She thought it futile to try and conceal her gender from them, preferring to get what was coming to her over and done with as quickly as possible. With her arms gliding through the water to keep her footing balanced on the rocks below, she waded her way out until the water was just below waistline.

Number three had waded in to ankle deep to grab her, but stopped in his track. "Well just look what the fuck we've got here?"
Madeline watched his eyes as they followed the cool glimmering water on her pale skin run down freely over the curves of her breasts. And continue on, finding its own downward path over her slender waist and filled hips which extenuated her full feminine shape to them. She stood still, glistening in the sun, like some goddess having risen from the sea, waiting, and watching.
He stood motionless, transfixed to the spot with dropped jaw, staring down at the curves of her breasts but could say nothing else.
Madeline's eyes moved right to see number four who, through puckered lips, let his slow, descending whistle run in tandem with his rapidly decreasing arched urinary spray. She looked to her left, to the musket bearer. He too had succumbed to her allure, the weapon shaking in his hands. Her eyes moved passed the third's shoulder up towards her laundering stone to see the last of them, but he was nowhere to be seen. He had vanished...
...but in his place, she was sure she had caught a fleeting glance of a familiar and very welcome face.

*

Rubin had heard the musket shot and at once taken Felix to full gallop. On approach to the clearing, he had dismounted and after grabbing his musket, made for a concealed spot in which to take stock of the situation. He had seen it bare and apart from their belongings spread out on the ground, there was no-one in sight. It was then that he had heard the holler from beyond the bushes and thus signaling their whereabouts. He had found the path which he knew they would have taken, but not knowing where it led to, he had with stealth, worked his way around. He now sat, crouched down within the thick bush only a few feet away from a uniformed soldier sitting on a large rock. He noticed that the bottle in his hand was his. Bastard! He also took stock of the musket leaning by his side. Peering down to the scene below, he could see Madeline in the water and in front of her, a civilian pointing a musket straight at her and another soldier, the one who was doing most of the shouting. He leaned to the left. A further civilian was rising from the ground and making his way to the water's edge. Rubin noticed he had left his musket on the pebbles. That made four, he thought, but only one was armed. He could manage them fine. Pulling the small knife free from his boot, he edged his way forward.
With the three facing away from this one, Rubin knew he could knife him without drawing their attention, but he couldn't afford to let him cry out. He would normally have covered and gagged the victim's mouth with his left hand, then draw the blade clean across his throat with the other. But this man had the wine bottle clasped within his hand and periodically drank from it,

plus he was leant forward with elbow resting on his bent knee. He couldn't take the chance of not getting to his mouth, so he switched tactics.

With the sound of the water on the rock covering his approach, Rubin crawled up behind him and grabbed hold of his shoulder length hair and yanked it back. With his throat stretched back to extreme, Rubin had simultaneously plunged the knife deep into the side of his neck. As the blunt end scraped its way across the spine, the body of the blade blocked off his air passage preventing any sound to come from it. And with one tremendous push forward, Rubin let the keen edge drive its way out through the skin and open his throat completely. All this was done as he had pulled the body to the side and before they had both hit the ground, Rubin had turned to muffle their fall with his coat. He released the grip on his hair, and as the man's body convulsed on the ground beside him, Rubin covered his mouth while he plunged the knife hard into his belly and twisted.

Satisfied with his efforts, he released his grip and on looking down, noticed the bottle still gripped in his hand.

With the knife, his hand and most of the sleeve covered in the spray from the man's neck, Rubin pulled himself free from his coat. Plunging his hand and knife into the water, he flicked the residue off and returned the blade to his boot. He reached out for the man's musket and checked it. Good, he thought, it was already loaded. He now had two muskets at his disposal.

He peered over the tip of the rock just in time to see Madeline immerse from the water. No-one was moving. So deep in thought at the sight of her nakedness, that none were aware of his presence nor that their companion lay dead beside him. With the way they were situated, it only took him several seconds before his military mind worked out his plan of attack. He would have to drop the musket holder first, but at this angle, he was directly in front of Madeline. He couldn't be sure that from this distance he could drop him before the musket went off in his hand. He couldn't take that chance. He could drop another before he got to his weapon, and by his reckoning, could be down there before the last one reached his. But all this would have to be with Madeline's participation, she would have to move away from him in order to get a clear shot. He would have to risk her seeing him.

And without them noticing that she had.

It was him!
Rubin was there, she could see his face, just above the boulder.
Her face should have automatically lit up with surprise, but she tried her hardest to prevent herself from doing so and remain solemn. Should the elation she felt inside, show on her face, then his presence would be known to them in an instant. He was signaling to her, but she could not afford to take the chance of staring at him for too long or show any reaction. The arduous task of pulling her eyes from him was removed when number three hollered at her again.

"Out, now!"

Her attention was drawn directly to him, but not before she had inwardly acknowledged Rubin's hand signal telling her to move to her right, away from them. She had an inkling as to why and what was coming. If she had been nervous before, she now felt positively terrified. Her entire body was shaking.
Wading out of the water, she did as instructed and veered to her right, towards number four.
"Where the fuck do you think you're going?"
Number four barked his approval. "Hey, hey. She wants me first."
The third, evidently displeased with her decision making, sloshed his way through the water in her direction.
The musket bearer had kept his aim true on Madeline the entire time, but as she moved away from him, he back stepped his way out of the water. But, on doing so, he lost his footing on the wet rocks below.
It was then when Madeline heard the crack, the loud bang…
…and her face sprayed wet.

Rubin had originally intended a head shot to the musket bearer.
His plan had suddenly changed when he saw the weapon hit the water. Resting his own barrel along the top of the rock, he had had him in his sights all along. But with the intended victim having lost his balance and fall sideways into the water, Rubin had changed tactics. He switched to his left, took aim and fired.
The direct hit had taken the side of the man's face clean off. Within seconds, he was dead in the water.
He threw the discharged musket to the side and grabbed at the loaded one. It was not necessary to aim true along the sights with this shot. He stood, pointed towards number four's stomach and fired. He saw the deep red cavity appear and the body hit the pebbles. His eyes moved to the musket bearer who was frantically trying to stand and find where the shots had come from. And when he had finally caught sight of Rubin, splashed through the water in Madeline's direction.
Rubin pulled the knife from his boot and ran down to the waters edge. But before he had gotten there, he saw the blade held at Madeline's throat.
Knee deep in water, he pushed the edge hard against her skin and shouted.
Rubin understood his words. It was German. Or what he took to be German, but with a slant on the accent. He hollered back in the same tongue. "Your three friends are dead, as you soon will be."
The foreigner tightened his grip on Madeline's chest and pushed the blade further against her neck. "Then she'll die with me."
Rubin had known from the beginning that all four had been deserters and would have been trying to exist on the road by whatever means necessary. So to feign patriotism to their own Germanic heritage, and his obvious need for money, Rubin spoke back. "Ah, you're from better blood than that, as I am. What good would a French slut be to any of us if she was dead? You want to

fuck a stiff?" He pointed to the pouch at his side with his knife. "I've got coin here, her coin. Quite a bit in fact, took it from her earlier."
As expected, at the sound of the word coin, his eyes had lit up. He nodded at Rubin's hand. "Your knife, throw it in the water."
Rubin shrugged and did as instructed. "Means nothing to me, I was going to have her before you lot showed up. But I wasn't goin' to share her with four of you." He smiled at him. "Don't mind sharing her with you though, a fellow countryman. Soon as she takes all the shit off her face, that is. Want her looking like a woman."
He grinned back, at thought of both coin and her body. "How much you get from her?"
Again, as expected, this foreigner's thoughts were of coin first. Rubin reached down and pulled it free. "Full bag here, you count it."
He threw it towards him.
With no free hands to catch it, the money pouch hit off his stomach and dropped into the water. Without easing his grip on Madeline, he tilted his head forward to see where it had landed.
While his eyes were off him, Rubin switched his own to Madeline and titled his head to the left as a signal.
The foreigner looked up. "Hah, nice try."
Rubin held out both empty hands to the side. "What am I goin' to do, kick water at you?"
Fearing that this giant, even without weapon, was still too close for comfort, he nodded upwards. "Back up a bit, towards the bushes."
Rubin obliged. He raised his hands up to within an inch of his neck and began to back pace. He stopped after a few feet.
"Further back my friend, don't fuck with me."
Rubin took a few more and stopped. By his reckoning, they were about the right space apart, any more than this and he would be struggling for accuracy. But as luck would have it, the greed of the man outdid the need for his own safety. He released his grip on Madeline's chest and stretched down to retrieve the pouch.
It was the last thing he ever did.
Taking advantage of the moment, Rubin pulled the eight inch blade from his back and with true aim, sent it flying through the air the moment he had straightened up.

Madeline had been temporarily blinded in one eye by his blood.
As she attempted to wipe the remainder of the dead man's face from hers, she had stood motionless with the shock of it as his body dropped to the water. She had then heard the second shot and watched the man to her right fall with a stomach shot. Unable to move, she had stood, body trembling until she felt the grip on her chest and her neck pushed to the side. It was then that she had wet herself. As she watched Rubin approach the water's edge, she had felt her bladder empty and run down her legs. Her mind had

sped up. A hundred and one things had ran though her mind, all jumbled together and with no apparent structure. Her room in Paris, Ramone, her home town, her night at the farm with Margaret, her first meeting with Jacob, her time with Frederick, Rosie, Monique, the list had went on. All this while a language was been spoken in her ear that she could make no sense of. And as she watched the knife drop from Rubin's hand, a sense of impending doom had hit her and then the life slip from her as he edged his way back, leaving her to her death. She felt the tears within her grow, and a feeling of loss, emptiness and vulnerability, of being a child in a grown up world. As her mind had raced earlier, so now did her whole world slow down around her. She was alone, and the further Rubin backed away from her, step by slowly measured step, the lonelier she became, and distanced now from his protection of her. It was the end she was sure, the short life was soon to be taken from her and all that she was, would be no more. She could see through hazed vision, Rubin standing with hands aloft and with this she slowly closed her eyes and felt her head fall loose to the right.

But the grip around her was suddenly released and she heard the slow hollow sound of a thud and crack at her side. She warily opened her eyes and faced to the left. Her captor stared ahead with wide open eyes and mouth agape as his arm about her neck shuddered violently on her shoulder. Rubin's huge knife was embedded so deep into the man's forehead that only an inch of blade lay exposed near the hilt and as the head shook from side to side, she watched the blood stream down his face.

Her face contorted with a mixture of shock and relief, and with her mind having taken so much, the pressure had to be released somehow. As the startled body slumped down into the water she raised her arms to the side and let go a slow resonating shriek. "No!!!..."

As her body quivered, her wails turned to that of weeping aloud and as a continuous howling of emotion filled the air, she cried like a child.

"Missy."

She looked ahead to see Rubin's outline through her swollen eyes, his outstretched hand beckoning her to come to him. Her mind was delirious. She shook her head.

"Missy."

She heard his voice again, as if echoing in the distance and as indistinguishable to her as the tongue uttered earlier. She shook her head once again and stepped backwards, away from him.

Then silence. She took another step back, and then another. She heard his voice once more, this time softer.

"Madeline."

With her crying reduced to that of a sob, she stood trying to determine what she had just heard. She looked straight ahead and seen him again, with hand held out waiting to take hers. He called to her.

"Madeline."

With her mind refocusing and upon realization that Rubin had spoken out her name, the relief was too great. Released from her stupor, her legs thrashed through the water as she sped towards him with outstretched arms. "Rubin." She ran straight into his powerful chest and wrapped her arms around him. "Oh Rubin."

Unprepared for this, he stood like a dim-witted giant not knowing what to do. He hesitantly lifted his arms around her for consolation, but found contact too hard. He stood patting an inch aura around her frame. Looking down at her, she pulled her head free, and with side fisted punches pounding at his chest, each one was accompanied with a word bellowed from her mouth.
"Don't. Ever. Leave. Me. Like. That. Again. Rubin."
He let her vent her anger, and when sated she pushed herself against him once again. This time he held her tight. And he swore there and then that he would never leave this young woman's side again and that he would protect her always…even if he died doing it.

*

Madeline 4

Chapter 9

Shadow in the Dark

Monique climbed the steep ragged steps.
She could have seen this tryst far enough as it had been a long day and she was tired. She just wanted home to her bed and rest. But it had been prearranged some days previous and for her to receive her just rewards she needed to reveal what information she had accumulated.
As she ascended, the light became dimmer until she had reached a point where she was wary of her footing. Twice now she had slipped on the rough edge. And twice she had cursed this isolated spot at which to meet. But it was necessary. There was no way anyone could find out about it, they had too much to lose.
"Remain where you are."
Startled with the suddenness of the voice, she almost far back. But she recognized the voice and clutched at her chest. "You scared me there."
Unconcerned with her state, the voice continued. "Tell me what you know."
Having convinced herself that the information required was of such importance and secrecy, she knew she had to give what conclusive evidence

there was and not just rumours based on hearsay. Her questioning of others had been of such a nature as not to give away why she had been asking, rather that it appear within the context of a casual conversation. She wanted no-one but herself included in this one. This was where she would make her money. "It is near at hand, this is for certain. She guards the secret very well and trusts no-one. She has, over the years sought one who would bring her the wealth she seeks. She has found it here in Paris. She keeps no money where she resides at present, preferring to live off others for everyday expenses, but she does secrete the remainder. I will find out where in time."

Her revelations uncommented upon, the voice in the shadows remained silent. But a pouch flew out from the dark.

Monique was caught unaware, but bent down to pick it up from the ground. She felt its swelling and as she went to speak, her 'merci' was cut short.

"You have done well so far Monique. We shall meet again in one week's time."

This time she did get a chance to say thank you, but finished. "And my name is not Monique anymore…

…she has called me Monica."

*

Madeline 5

Madeline 5

Prologue

**Chateau d'Estelle,
18th Century France**

Oswald looked down at the body and kicked its side once again.
He was dead for sure. But for how long had he lain like this was uncertain.
His eyes caught sight of the half eaten food dish further along the stone floor.

Under twelve hours anyway, he surmised, it was the meal he had brought to him the previous night. But the body had not yet succumbed to full rigor, he was sure of that, the sunken eyes and disfigurement of the jaw a direct giveaway.

He squatted down and pulled the man's head to the side and noticed the reddish-purple discolouration on the neck. Hmm, perhaps under three hours, he figured. He had seen enough cadavers in the course of his duties to know the time line of such. This poor creature had been a prisoner in the same cell for the eight years he had been jailer here. He was certain he had been a resident for at least a further ten before that. It was a wonder he had lasted so long. Human endurance had always amazed him. He pushed his bended knees straight and stood. Another one gone in the night, he thought. They were dropping like flies these days.

Part of his duties now was to inform the Head of this man's death and then pack the body for an unceremonious burial at sea. So, collecting the wooden bowl and spoon together, he made for the corner to pick up the toilet bucket. He winced at its smell on approach. Peering down into the mixture of pale coloured urine and thin defecation, he noticed the thick, clotted blood floating on its surface. His lips stretched to the side, it wasn't the best part of his work. He dug into his right pocket and pulled out a piece of ragged cloth. It was wrapped around his hand before he lifted the bucket by its soiled handle and then with nothing left to collect, made for the door. Its contents slopped to the side and splashed onto his britches.

"Fuck!" Great start to the morning.

With fresh britches on, he descended the stone steps to the lower cells carrying the canvas sacking and cord in one hand and the flaming torch on the other. He wanted rid of the body as quickly as possible. Stitching up a stinking corpse was not a task he favoured. But as he made his way along the passage he stopped for a moment outside one of the cells. It was the little lady's. He stared at it for a moment before a voice from behind drew him from vacillation.

"We gittin' fuckin' breakfust the day or wit?"

Oswald could make out only one word of this Scotsman's tongue, that being his variation on the word breakfast. If only he would speak slower then he could possibly understand him.

"Wur awe starvin' here Frenchy, geh ah fuckin' move oan wae it."

'Frenchy' Oswald surmised was the Scotsman referring to his French citizenship, the rest was complete drivel. It made no sense. He knew the English language as well as his native tongue but he had never heard it spoken in this fashion. He turned to face him.

"How is your finger?"

Peering through the foot square gap in the cell door, the Scotsman gripped at the bars. "Gittin' beh-urr misttur monsieur fuckin' froggie. Noo urr wae gittin' grub ur wit?"

"If at any time in the future I have a fucking clue as to what you are saying we can speak then. Until that time, shut up."

Not one to lie down to a spat, he nodded to the cell opposite. "Ah bet the wee lassie's gittin ur fill eh? You goan in therr tae see tae ur?"

Oswald gave up trying to decipher his words. He laid the canvas and cord on the ground and searched for his keys. It took only one quick turn before the door became unlocked and he pushed it open.

He heard more rants at his back.

"An geez back ma fuckin' bed, am gittin pilez in ma erse lying oan this stane flair."

He ignored them and walked into the cell.

She was sitting, cowering in the corner on her wooden pallet. He looked across at her bowl. It was empty. At least she was eating. Her neck wound must be on the mend. He smiled at her and nodded backwards.

"Never mind his shouting. He's only mad because I used his pallet to fix up your window." He nodded in its direction. "Hope it did the business."

Her eyes followed his and returned in an instant. She smiled at him and gave a curt nod.

"Good, good." He stood for a moment fidgeting and as before, the awkward silence got to him. "Well, better get on."

But as he turned to leave, she rose to her feet. Her outstretched hand touched his arm and in an instant he felt a bond between them. The gentle touch of her hand on his coat sleeve was the only contact he had had with a woman in years. And as he looked into her pitiful eyes he saw her torment. 'What in God's name was she doing here'.

He could see through all the dirt and grime and what lay beneath was a woman of grace and beauty. His heart dropped when she smiled at him again and slowly nodded her head. He knew it was her way of thanking him and he felt touched by her gratitude. Whatever she was here for, he was determined to make her stay as comfortable as was in his power to do so.

"I will bring you some more food in a short while, but I have a duty to attend to beforehand."

He felt saddened when their connection was broken due to her letting go of his arm and walking towards her bowl. She returned with it in her hand and offered him to take it.

He nodded, but was surprised with her visual communication.

As she handed him the bowl she held her hand aloft with two fingers pointing up wards.

"You want two meals?" She was indeed on the mend to ask for double portions, he thought.

Her head nodded quickly in affirmation. But one more surprise was in store for Oswald. She pointed first to herself and then to him and with the same two fingers showing, she nodded once again.

"You mean you want one for me?"

Her head once again signaled 'Yes'.

He was shocked at the suggestion, but needed clarification. "You want me to eat here with you?"
Her smile meant that she did.
His heart beat at twice the speed, his mind racing. All he could do was nod. But finally the words found a route from his lips. "I will bring you breakfast in a short while, but when I bring you tonight's food…I will bring two."
His eyes scanned the cell to see what else he could do in the meantime. It stopped at her corner toilet bucket. And for some reason he felt embarrassed about it. Emptying it now would bring it to her attention and it did not seem appropriate after their brief but concise silent communication. He would leave it for now.
"Okay. Be back later."
She remained still until he turned and left the cell.
Locking the door home he felt elated. He was making progress with her and knew that she was adjusting to life here. But how long was her detainment he wondered. He remembered her first night and the rules regarding her sentence. They were very strange indeed. He would look into that in more detail and perhaps sneak a look into the Head's personal ledgers.
"So, ur we gittin fed ur wit?"
This man did not give up, whatever he was saying. After collecting the canvas and cord from the floor he looked over at the Scotsman.
"Eggs."
"Eggz wit? Wit aboot eggz, izzat awe wur gittin', jist eggz?"
Oswald was in a good mood now. It felt strange to him that in such a vile place as this that some humane elements can burrow their way in. He had just been invited to dinner by a woman.
"No, that is what Madame is having."
"In wit aboot me?"
Oswald stood still and stared at him.
"Funny talking Scotsman, you can have a bed."

*

Madeline 5

Chapter 1

A National Divide

Paris, France
Some time earlier

France was in turmoil.
No more so than in Paris, where a high percentage of its six hundred thousand residents lived in extreme poverty and privation. The squalid surrounds of their compacted existence consisted of muck ridden streets which were foot deep in excretia, both animal and human, and decomposing bodies of the pox ridden dead. What drinking water that was available from

its only source, the Seine, was contaminated with the entrails of the butchered animals from the local tanneries and the human waste which was emptied into it on a daily basis. With disease rampant, it was hardly any wonder that the death toll mounted at such an alarming rate. Under these conditions, the average male was lucky to reach the age of twenty five. Misery, filth and death were all encompassing and the cries of hunger were now commonplace with even the most basic of food; bread, being a scarcity. Unbeknown to most but the scholars of the city or the learned, what had happened hundreds of miles to the north had added to their already miserable existence.

The eruption of the Icelandic volcano 'Laki' had spread its ash cloud across most of Europe and had reached France the previous year. Most had just seen the dark cloud looming above and were ignorant as to what had caused it. But the harvests had failed and grain was now in such high demand that it had reached record prices. Bakers' premises were being raided on a daily basis as word had gotten out that the stockpiling for the best prices were now routine. This resulted in even more fatalities as many starving citizens frantically fought to death over a small sack of flour.

In complete contrast; just outside the city perimeter, sat the lush surroundings of *Versailles* where the Monarchy's decadence was known to all who hungered. The ill feeling towards the King had been for years uttered under breath by the populace for fear of reprisal. Lately though, they were not only speaking out, but the chants of *liberté*, *égalité* and *fraternité* appeared to be regular among many. And although the three words were often uttered in isolation of each other, they would soon come together to lead a nation in a revolt against the *Ancien Régime*. If France was about to explode…

…then Paris was the power keg laying in wait to start it.

*

King Louis XVI sat proudly on his solid silver throne within the *salon d'Apollon* of *Versailles* and rubbed his bare feet over the pile of the plush Persian carpet beneath. "Liberty? Freedom! They are free. All my subjects are free to go as they please."

Jacques sighed under his breath. "With respect your Majesty, they have no money to even pass through the city's numerous tolls which have been erected. They are not free, as they see it."

"They say they are destitute and starving. Are they not aware of the financial burden this country is in? Am I expected to feed them all?"

As Finance Minister to France, Jacques Necker was well aware of the state of the nation but sat quietly as he listened to his monarch rant further of the request put upon him. Much as he had tried in earnest to explain the severity of the matter to his king, he had not penetrated through the thick skull of a spoiled and weak man. He had for years stood loyal to him and had advised

Louis on many things. The cost incurred by the American Revolutionary Wars alone had so financially crippled the country that it had put it into debt of more than Eight Thousand Million *livres* alone. How do you explain that kind of loss to the masses with nothing to show as gain? Adjust the books accordingly, that was how. He had done so in the publication of his book *Compte rendu au roi* a few years earlier in which he had attempted to explain France's governmental income and expenditure. But the many falsities that lay within its pages showed that France had not fought the war against the British with tax-payers money, in fact they were solvent by millions at the time. The truth being that France had taken out many loans to fight the war and the interest payments alone had exhausted the coffers. The country was on its knees and funds had to be sought on an urgent basis. But from where would this come? This was the question that they now deliberated over.
Louis had formulated a plan two months earlier of re-convening *Les États-Généraux,* a general assembly representing the French estates of the realm. Not since 1614 had these three factions met - the Clergy, the Nobles and last of all, the common people. They had all sat head to head in a temporary setting within a courtyard in *Versailles* for several weeks but could not come to an agreement as to which estate held which power. The King's main objective was to discuss taxes to alleviate the debt, but this had been sided as the internal bickering mounted. Jacques had advised the King not to interfere and that a speech to the assembly would not be appropriate. Louis had refused and thus he himself had declined the invitation to attend on the day of his speech. He was not now as popular with the King of France as he once was. He knew his days were numbered as country's main finance advisor.
"Does your silence mean that you are deep in thought as to how we may proceed now? Or are you still upset about the voting."
Jacques looked up from the floor to face his King. "When you doubled the amount of commoners for the third estate, all had assumed that it would be a head vote, not one per estate. It is this reason we have found ourselves in the predicament we are in."
Louis sat unmoved by his words. "Your sentiments towards the people are touching Jacques, but they are not the ones that we can rely on to pay our debts, it is the wealthy." He stood and on bared feet walked around Jacques, seated on a lower chair. "Why should I; as King, be the one with the debt when all around me are nobles of wealthier standing? Let them aid the country that has for many years now protected them under *Ancien Régime.* Let them feed the poor, let them feed the hungry with bread."
Jacques eyes caught sight of the solid silver chamber pot sitting to the left of the throne. Selling that item alone would feed a family of four for months, he thought.
"Qu'ils mangent de la brioche"
This female voice had come from behind and as he heard it, Jacques closed his eyes tightly together. If his task of trying to convince his King on a way

forward wasn't hard enough already, then it was now an impossible task with her presence.
Maria Antonia of Austria had married the then Dauphin Louis-Auguste in 1770 and even as a young man, Jacques had mistrusted this woman from the beginning. Their marriage had been an alliance to prevent further conflict after the 'seven year war' between the two countries. When she had become Queen of France four years later, this Marie Antoinette had appeared to him to be as cunning a woman as he had ever met. Her loyalties to her home country of Austria over the country she now jointly ruled were apparent to him, but Louis seemed oblivious to this so he had said nothing. During their years of marriage, she had been, as was still now, naive to life outside her home at the palace. To say now, that in lieu of bread, the people should eat cake, was her total ignorance as to what constituted basic food and the costly ingredients as alternative. He sat in silence as he heard the King greet his wife as she entered the room – from the hidden door in the corner he assumed. The one he was not meant to know about.
"Ah Marie, you are a welcome face to these dull proceedings. Yes indeed, let them eat and indulge their fancy with brioche."
Jacques turned to face her before bowing and was met with the usual white powdered face, and equally white high raised wig. To accompany the colour, there sat a choker of pearls around her neck, the twin of which appeared to be sewn into the chest line of her deep black dress. As was the norm, he almost gagged with the smell of her heavily scented body. Unlike her foul smelling husband, she was known for bathing at least twice a day and Jacques was convinced that she must immerse herself in scent rather than clean water.
Their feelings for each other apparent - as neither trusted the other, she spoke to him in her usual condescending manner. "Come to twist the mind of your King for your own devices have we Jacques?"
It was quite the reverse for Jacques as he could not speak as such to the Queen of France. He cow tailed as usual. "I only seek to serve my King in the best way I can. I serve only for the good of France."
She flicked open her yellow patterned fan a mere two inches from his face and waved it in front of her own. "We shall see." She turned to face Louis. "Shall we not, my dear?"
The King resumed his seat on the throne and by way of an open arm, invited her to sit on his lap. Jacques stood like a child in front of the rulers of his beloved France as they toyed with his presence. With his hand on her left breast, Louis massaged the half exposed globe in full view of him before speaking. "It appears that we are at differences Jacques. Your loyalty to me is in doubt and as you know from me in the past, with doubts, I act upon them immediately."
Jacques knew what was coming. It had obviously been discussed between them both before he had been summoned. Her manipulative scheming had once again twisted his King against him. If France was on the verge of

collapse, she would undoubtedly be a contributory factor in it falling flat on its face. Did she not know that this would be her own undoing as well? He awaited further, his King's decision.
"To this end, I wish our country to relinquish its association with you as its financial controller. You are dismissed as of this moment."
Expected, it was still a shock to him. But even with the exalted position stripped from him, he still felt compelled to advise his King one last time. "The permitting of the double representation of the third estate of commoners was greeted by many with hope. But with the voting system changed, and the commoners having introduced the *Assemblée Nationale* legislation 'The Declaration of the Rights of Man and Citizen', many will fight for guaranteed equality of all."
Marie removed her tongue from her husband's ear. "Leave us. We grow weary of your *bourgeois* talk."
Jacques ignored her acerbic remark and concentrated on his King. "Your Majesty, revolution is close at hand. It is unwise to relieve me of my position at such a critical time. I wish only to remain by your side in these times."
It was not enough. King Louis XVI of France had spoken, albeit with words from others. "You have heard my decision Jacques."
Lowering his head to his King one last time, he turned and left the room.

"Damn fool."
He cursed further under his breath as he casually strolled through the *galerie des glaces*. Jacques looked to each side as he walked. His favourite room in the palace by far, this two hundred and fifty foot long room stood as a testament to the wealth of the monarchy. It had been the very place where; in the past, he would come to ponder over the problems and affairs of the state. And here he was now, devoid of all status, superfluous to use. He wanted one last look before he left for home and settle down to private life. His eyes ran over the spendour of his surrounds.
Seventeen mirror clad arches held within each, an arcaded window overlooking the gardens. And with twenty-one clad mirrors in total per arch, this room shone out like a beacon when in direct sunlight. Between each arch, marble pilasters stood proud, each bearing gilded bronze capitals including the *fleur-de-lys* and *le coq gaulois*. He seated himself beside one of the furthermost windows and looked out to the gardens. He sighed. Many a function he had attended here, be it official or private, with marriages and births being the happiest. But this had now ended. No more would he play a pivotal role in the future of France, nor indeed have a friendship with its King. He could see the doomed future of both even now and was in no position to help prevent any of it.
"Monsieur Necker."
The voice unfamiliar to him, Jacques turned from the scenic view to find the familiar face of a young servant boy in the palace's service. He did not need to ask what this boy wanted as the proffered letter in his hand spoke all.

Jacques simply took it from him and offhandedly dismissed him. Pulling his reading spectacles from his waistcoat pocket, he placed the middle grip on his nose. He peered down at the front. It was simply marked with his name and Paris. No title, no address, just the city name. It was apparent that this missive had been written from somewhere other than the city walls as whoever had delivered it here was clearly not the sender. He turned it over and broke the wax seal.

He reread it a third time. Pulling the lenses from his face, he rested both spectacles and letter on his lap. He tapped the frame on his leg and thought further. The peoples' revolt against the monarchy was closer at hand than he had thought. To resort to kidnapping a government official and ransom him for funds to arm the rebels was a sign of things to come…

…but who was this Gaston they were holding?

*

Madeline 5

Chapter 2

Sustenance

Gaston swallowed dry once again.
His throat parched with lack of water for what seemed like days now, he was almost at breaking point. Not since the first day had anyone come to the room, and with this, no food or water. He had been dehydrated even then with the brandy sweated from his body. Added to this, the heat within his confines from the scorching sun outside had him thirst to the point of him sipping at his own urine. His bladder now empty with the lack of fluids, he

lay half desiccated on the bed, his mind in confusion. The excruciating pain from his raw skinned ankle added to his misery. Unable to focus on a subject for any given time, his thoughts were intermingled with delirium and his hallucinations had him on several occasions holler out at the distorted images randomly gravitating around him. At least now with the evening's respite from the sun's rays he could breathe in some cooler air. Not one sound had he heard since being incarcerated and he had convinced himself that he was in such isolation that if he were to die now then no-one would ever know. It was for this reason that his eyes opened with a start at the sound of the door lock turning. He lifted his weary head from the pillow several inches, just enough to see across the room. The door was pushed ajar slightly and remained still for several seconds before being kicked open.

It was Sylvia.

She smiled at him as she entered the room. He noticed the transformation. Gone were the graceful looks of femininity he had first seen in the taverne. Her hair was now pulled back and held in place by a pale washed out scarf and her decorative dress now supplanted with a more rugged pheasant look, that of an insipid brown baggy top and loose fitting britches. But most importantly, she held within her grasp a tray, and what looked to him like a water ewer. His throat reacted at the thought. But on her approach, he also noticed the musket rifle slung over her shoulder.

"Bonjour Gaston."

Spoken as if this was an everyday occurrence; him held captive and dying of thirst, he thought only of damning her to hell for her part in it. But the words, 'Fucking Bitch' although thought of, could not escape his arid throat.

She laid the tray at the bottom of the bed. "Firstly I have to apologize for the way you have been treated. As organized as we are, both thought the other was attending to you."

Who this other person she was referring held little importance to him at the moment, neither was her apology. His main objective now was get to what he hopefully had assumed was water within the pitcher from there and into his system. He noticed her reaction to him staring at it.

She looked down at his naked form and studied him for a moment. "If I am to attend to you, then you will understand my need for this." Reaching to her side, she pulled free a length of leather cord which to Gaston appeared to have a noose tied at one end.

Sylvia explained further. "I am without doubt that you are upset with the way things have worked out and in particular my involvement. So this is necessary, for the time being anyway." Throwing the looped end towards him, she instructed him to place his clasped hands through the end. She would then pull the slipknot to tighten its grip on them.

Gaston understood her reluctance to approach him while unfettered. He would indeed; had he the strength, lash out at her. So doing as instructed, he found his bound wrists hauled up to the top end of the iron bed frame and secured there. Now lying naked on his back totally defenseless, he was at her mercy. She could do whatever she wanted to him. His eyes pleadingly looked towards the pitcher once again and to his surprise, his throat found the voice of a single coarse word. "Water."

Sylvia sat on the edge of the bed and let the water from the squeezed cloth drip slowly into his mouth. She dabbed it around his lips. "You cannot drink too much, too fast Gaston, your stomach would not take to kindly to it."
It mattered little to him how much he was being given, at least it took the thirst away and lubricated his aching throat. He heard her speak further.
"A fine state you are in given your short stay here. You have obviously led a privileged life where you have never thirsted for fresh water or lay with empty stomach."
If he could speak, then he would not have responded to such a derogatory remark as that. He knew only too well what the hardship of growing up in Paris was like. Life had not always been as pleasant as it had been up to a few days ago. As a boy, everyday life was as cruel to him as it was to the common people of the city nowadays. Although marrying into more money than he had ever expected, it had been his main incentive beforehand to get himself an education and eventually work in government. He wanted to make a difference to the lives of the people of France. The radical transformation of the country was imminent, he knew, and he had been involved in this before his needless trip to Salon. It had vexed him at the time as it still did now. He suddenly found himself able to speak. "I am on your side."
Sylvia lowered the cloth and let her arm rest on his chest. "Which side is that Gaston? The side you can make the most from."
He shook his head. "I seek equality for all, not for the few."
Sylvia threw the cloth to the side and rose from the bed. "You *are* the few Gaston." Lifting an edge of stale looking bread from the tray, she immersed it in the pitcher. Flicking the residue from her hand, she reseated as before and placed the moist bread to his lips. "You can barely manage to eat this due to your present condition. Many have to survive on something similar on a daily basis. The few do not."
Gaston pulled his mouth away in protest. "What makes you think I am one of the privileged few?"
Sylvia followed his mouth to the left and pushed it further to his lips. "You have to eat."
"Fuck the food. And fuck you too." He spat at the bread in retaliation. He nodded towards the musket leaning against the wall. "And what are you expecting to do with that. Shoot me. Well you'll have to, because I'm not the important person you take me to be. I'm low down the ladder of things, so who the fuck is going to pay a ransom for me, especially to a bunch of revolutionaries."
Sylvia tossed the bread to the side and lowered her hand in one swift movement. Clasping his testicles tight within her grip, she twisted them

slightly and watched him writhe in pain. "Do not underestimate yourself Gaston or us for that matter. Don't you think we had you investigated at the moment of your arrival here in Salon and both your political and private standing looked in to? You may not have achieved the laddered success in politics which you speak, but your family, and in particular your wife's family, have wealth in abundance. Now surely a loving wife would pay handsomely for the safe return of her husband?" She released the tension in her hand but still retained her grip. "It is sad in a way, as I have grown quite fond of you Gaston. Our brief time together I found very enjoyable." Transferring her palm to the girth of his penis, she clasped it tightly within her hand. "Very enjoyable indeed."

Gaston jostled his hips from side to side to free himself from her grip. "That was part of the set up was it? Bitch!" He clenched his teeth tight as the pain from his ankle shot up the entire length of his body. "Fuck, fuck, fuck."

Sylvia let her hand begin the slow rhythmic movements on him. "Relax Gaston. I wish this time we have together to be pleasurable for you…as well as educational."

His body exhausted, he lay still with the mixture of pain and elation. He tilted his head down to see Sylvia run her tongue up the full length of his semi erect penis. She stopped at the tip and stared deep into his eyes. "We shall have such fun together Gaston. Savour the taste of the water and bread now because all you shall receive in the future here from me is what the people of France have lived on for years. I shall eat and drink for us both Gaston…

…and you shall exist on my waste."

*

Many miles to the north, two empty stomachs sat around the campfire, deep within their own thoughts. Rubin turned the spit through ninety degrees. With each drip of fat that fell from the scrawny chicken to hit the embers below, there came forth a smell that would make the most replete of men salivate further. It had been a long time since he had eaten fowl and he looked on it with relish…unlike little missy seated at the opposite side of the flames. She had remained silent since her ordeal. Which was understandable, he thought. Although she had not seen him open the throat of the first, she had witnessed the brutal deaths of the remaining three. One of which had been vicious and at very close quarters. Thrown from a distance, he had driven the heavy knife deep into the man's forehead only a few inches from her face. It had startled her yes, but he had been given no choice in the matter. He had had to act as he had seen fit. But to him, these deaths had meant nothing, it had been routine as far as he was concerned. Whether they had died a quick painless death or writhing in agony at his torment, it was endemic with his lifestyle. You could show no mercy to people like these as you would have received the same in return. It was hard times they lived in and only the few who could endure through it and willing to do anything to survive, would prevail. He had done exactly that all through his turbulent life.

Having no family of his own that he knew of, he had lived by himself, for himself. Drifting from town to town in his homeland of Germany, he had used theft as his only means to survive. And when ousted from one place; be it the townsfolk or the authorities, he would move on to the next. He had not only wandered from town to city, but from country to country. His life had had no meaning until one spring afternoon on the outskirts of Paris, he joined the French army. It was to change his life forever.

Having volunteered as opposed to being French conscripted, he had put his age down as eight plus six; not knowing his proper date of birth, and had been accepted. It had been an eye opener from the beginning. A new word had been introduced into his limited vocabulary, and this word 'discipline' had been a shock to his system. Rising early in the morning and under so strict a regime as to work for two hours prior to receiving any breakfast had sent his mind in a spin. It had taken a few weeks to get used to its way of life, and especially the camaraderie he found that existed between fellow soldiers. And he was soon to be educated into their way of thinking, the hard way. He had been a loner throughout his early life and had found making friends a task which did not come easy. A brutal lesson had been learned after he was caught stealing from another soldier. He had been beaten to within an inch of his life by all others, and for four weeks had he been laid up in a bed within the makeshift infirmary. It had taken a lot of patience on his part to have his trust gained by the men after that. But during one battle he had saved the lives of two. He had been hailed the hero and was from then on, accepted once more into the fold. Never again did he turn on one of his own as it soon became clear to him that their lives depended on each other, both on and off the battlefield. It had been a valuable lesson and one he had never forgot, as you neither expected nor received any good will from the officers who considered all enlisted men to be nothing more than low life scum, and an expendable commodity. He did however gain the respect of both officers and enlisted men as a battle-hard combatant over a period of time. Having been trained in musket shot and pike, it was at close hand combat that he surpassed even his own reckoning. It had come natural to him. Adept with both long knife and dagger, he would cut and thrust his way through many a melee and although not owning or permitted to have one, he would use an enemy's sword to kill more of the same. It was during one such encounter that he received the mutilated face he bore now.

Raising his hand to his lips, he ran the fingers over the toothless gap and up the side of his face, the full length of his scar. He hadn't always been so marred, he remembered. If it wasn't too vain to think now, he had thought himself rather dashing as a youth. In fact, all the way up to receiving the injury, he had been popular with many a town wench he came across during his fighting days. But after his almost lethal injury, he had left the army and

travelled to Belgium, Spain and Prussia to fight as mercenary in which ever army paid him the most. His loyalties were, by then, to his pocket. And with it full of coin he would get drunk for days on end. In fact, had he not been in such an inebriated state one autumn morning, he would have found himself aboard ship sailing to the Americas to fight in the revolutionary wars there. To this end, he had found himself getting too far on in his years to be able to withstand the lengthy rigors of battle which could last for hours. Preferring an easier life, he had returned to Paris and to this day had survived by whichever means possible. And not until this time had he felt more concern about someone other than himself.
He looked across the fire at Madeline.
As he thought of her age and the life she was now enduring, he inwardly smiled at the thought of him knowing how old she was. Until recently he would have stated it as eight plus eight, but this young woman had introduced him to numbers in excess of this solitary digit. She was sixteen.
Being an acquaintance to many women of various ages, he knew the lives that they led and what they had to do to exist, his Annie being a prime example. But this young missy, having chosen the same profession in life, was still a child in his eyes and one that needed protection from the unsympathetic world that surrounded her. Not being raised in the city of Paris, she was immune neither to its harsh existence on the streets, nor the ruthless people who inhabited them. He on the other hand was expert in this field, but not just in the city, but out here in the wilds. He knew only too well that what had happened earlier was but a taster of what they could expect on a lengthy journey such as this. It was for this reason he had had her travel incognito, under the guise of a boy. But her lapse from reason to go swimming in the stream had led her into an unavoidable situation. He had seen her unclothed, and what this vision could do to unscrupulous individuals was not hard to imagine. Had it been any other woman with such a body, then he too would have succumbed to his body needs, as many others would do. This was not the case with the young missy. He had held her in his arms, but not as a lover or a would-be assaulter, but as a father consoling a daughter. And this was what he now considered her to be, as if this child had been given to him to guard over and protect as such.
He pressed the point of his small knife into the chicken and saw the juices run free of blood. "Almost done young missy, leg or breast?"
Madeline remained silent, seated on top of a fallen tree trunk and facing down into her tightly clasped hands.
In an attempt to make light of the situation, his voiced changed in tempo. "Come on now young Lander, got to keep your strength up. Long ways ahead yet and can't have you fadin' away to nothin'."
She shook her head. "I'm not hungry Rubin."
What could he do, he thought, he couldn't force her to eat. Taking the edge of the skewer, he lifted it from the frame and rested the bird on top of one of

the plates. "We'll leave it till it cools then. Hah, don't want you burning your pretty little fingers now, do we?"

His jests were in vain. She sat motionless and showed no reaction.

Under similar circumstances with anyone else, Rubin would have considered this tedious and one sided conversation unworthy of further effort, but he felt himself compelled to get her out of her mood. "How was the swim, I mean the water, for washing I mean?"

Madeline raised her head. "I put us both in danger Rubin, I'm sorry."

Rubin waved his hand out at her. "Ah, forget that. We all fuck up in life once in a bit, makes us better for it. The man ain't here yet that hasn't made a mistake. As long as you learn by them, and don't do the same thing again then that's fine. And don't go fretting yourself over them four, the bastards got what was coming to them."

Rubin followed her eyes to where he had hidden the bodies in the bush. "Don't worry little missy, they're dead. They won't be harming you no more."

Madeline turned to face him again and with a slight nod of acknowledgement, resumed her bowed head to face her hands.

Rubin stretched across the ground and dug into his coat pocket. "Ah well, would have preferred to have done this after we ate, but might as well do it now, along with a little swallow of something."

Curious as to what he was referring, Madeline raised her head.

Pulling a six inch long clay pipe from his pocket, Madeline watched as he packed the hole with what to her looked like dried weed. And with wide open eyes as he leaned forward and lifted a burning stick from the fire. He placed it to the hole and as he puffed, bellows of smoke came forth from its portal along with plumes from his mouth. She smiled. "My father smoked one similar to that. Well, when I was young that was, not now. Not since he became ill."

It had been one of the many things that Rubin had pilfered from the four dead whilst rummaging through their pockets and kit bags. He hadn't smoked a pipe since his army days. "Just need something to go with it." He uncorked the bottle which he had filled with the remains of the second that had been opened in his absence. Between them both, this amounted to about three quarters full, enough for him to enjoy the smoke with. He took his first swig then puffed at the pipe. After his second inhalation his lungs tried to compensate for the lack of oxygen and erupted accordingly. He coughed and spluttered over the fire.

Madeline laughed at his attempts to draw breath through the smoke. He continued to cough until Madeline heard the loud hiss as he spat a mouthful of brown phlegm into the fire embers. She cringed. "Yuck!"

She cringed further when he had pinched both sides of his nostrils and dragged the mucous along and out between his fingertips. The fire hissed again as he flicked the residue from forefinger and thumb.

"Oh for goodness sakes Rubin, that's disgusting."

Still coughing, Rubin tried to speak through laboured breath. "Oh so you'd…rather… I choke to death then?"

"No, but surely a handkerchief would be in order."

Not owning one, the remainder of his expectoration was barked into his shirt sleeve instead. He looked over at her. "That do you?"

"Oh, charming." It was apparent that she had roused from the doldrums, he noticed, as she chastised him further. "It appears to me Rubin that everything that enters your body in the normal way, exits in a more nauseating manner."

He lifted the bottle to his mouth, but paused before drinking. "Ah, but I draw the line at blowing off." He shook his head. "Now that ain't nice." He only did it to annoy Annie as he knew she hated it.

Madeline laughed again at the absurdity of his remark. "How can you be such a hypocrite Rubin? I've never heard such noises come from another as I do from you. To say that you don't…well, you know what I mean, that doesn't say much."

Rubin had swallowed more than enough. "Says a lot to me. You heard me do it yet?"

She sat forward. "That's hardly the point Rubin, there is a multitude of things that you don't do, but that doesn't mean you should be complimented on not doing every one of them. That would go for anyone. It's just a matter on common courtesy."

Rubin tried again with the pipe. This time his lungs grew accustomed to the smoke. "Then you don't do it then?"

She rose from the tree and sat cross-legged by the fire. "I fail to see what that has to do with anything. Whether I do or not is irrelevant, what would be is that I would do it in the privacy of my own surrounds." She held her hands out to get some heat from the flames.

Rubin swigged again, and with another puff, enquired further of her. "So if you needed to here, and now, you'd go into the bush yonder so I wouldn't hear you or would you try and make it a silent one?"

Madeline Tutt-tutted. "I would do neither."

It was Rubin's turn to laugh. His back arched. "Hah, so you'd squeeze and keep it in and hurt your belly would you?"

She shook her head. "I don't believe we are having this conversation. Only a few hours ago you killed four men and you are sitting laughing with idle talk of body emissions."

It had got her out of her thoughts, and that had been his intention. He nodded again to the bush. "Well they won't be blowing off anytime soon. Hah, just off." He refocused on her. "Got you talking anyway."

Madeline smiled. "I suppose so." She sighed. "I have a lot to learn Rubin, about who to trust…and when to do the trusting."

"Like I said little missy, you learn by the foolish things you do. You'll be much more aware the next time."

Madeline looked at the bottle in Rubin's hand. "May I try some of that please?"

Taken aback at the suggestion, Rubin remained silent for a moment, contemplating her request. He tilted the bottle in his hand. "You think you're up to this?"

Madeline lifted a small stick of wood and placed it on the flames. "I've tried a few drinks now."

"Not like this you ain't, you wouldn't even drink the wine in the taverne with me."

Madeline remembered the time he was referring to, after the scene with Jacques. She picked up another stick and laid it across the previous one. "The glass was dirty Rubin that was all. It had something sticking to the side."

"S'the reason I drink from the bottle."

"Well?"

"You'll not like this little missy, but I might have something you will." Laying the bottle to the side, he lifted himself to his feet, and walking towards Felix, pulled the food bag free from the side. He heard the faint clink from within. "Got these in town."

Madeline looked over at him. "I thought you said you only got the chicken?"

He walked back to the fire. "To eat, but leaving the taverne I found two bottles on the floor that weren't broken, couldn't resist it."

Positioning himself similar to Madeline, he crossed his legs and sat opposite. "Red wine. Well I least I think it is, the broken ones were. No idea what it's like though, but you'll soon tell me, eh?"

Madeline grinned. "I'll try my best." She looked at the bird. "Shall we eat as we drink?"

Rubin followed her eyes and then to the pipe in his hand. "Nah, we'll smoke and drink first, well me anyway." Placing the pipe in his mouth, he opened the bag and pulled out the bottles. "A warm fire, food to eat, drink to drink and a pipe to smoke, what more can a man ask for?..." He winked at her. "...and a pretty young girl by his side." He uncorked the first bottle. "Hand me your cup."

Madeline shook her head. "No, I want to drink from the bottle, just like you."

He nodded yonder. "Them cups are clean, no sticky bits on them."

"I know Rubin, I didn't mean that. I just want to do it the way you do. Please?"

He handed her the bottle. "Righty-ho then, if that's the way you want it, here, you have this one."

She shook her head once again.

"Fuck sake little missy, what's wrong now?"

Her head upwardly nodded at the bottle. "You go first."

He understood. "You're right, it may be bad. I'd know, wouldn't I?"

"It's not that Rubin, I just want to share the bottle with you, like friends would do, not have one of my own."

Rubin looked into her eyes and felt his heart smile. He pondered her words. It wasn't often he got something as good as that said about him, he thought. "Okay then. Here goes."

Madeline watched him raise the tip to his mouth and swallow. Then swallow more, and then swallow more. She could see his throat move each time he did it. He continued in the same manner. Was he going to drink the entire contents, she thought? "Eh Rubin, aren't we meant to be sharing that?"
He pulled the bottle from his mouth and burped. "Yip, that'll do just fine."
Madeline's shoulders lowered. "Huh, is there any left I wonder?"
Rubin spat into the fire and handed the bottle over. "Almost full."
"Almost full?" Her outstretched hand took it from him. "How can that be when," She realized by the weight that he had been feigning his swallow. "Oh! Ha-ha Rubin, very funny."
"To young Lander, and his first drink with his old Papa."

*

Madeline hiccupped.
She raised her fingers to cover her lips. "Oops, sorry."
She did it again, but made no further apology. She just looked across at Rubin and erupted with laughter.
He laughed back. "You're on your way to your first hangover young Lander."
She rested the bottle between her still crossed legs. "Why, what's a hangover like?" Her blurry eyes tried to focus in on him.
"Not good."
"Oh. Hic! That was short and sweet." She giggled as she gazed through one eye. "Just like you Rubin. Sweet," and with a grin, finished. "But not short." She laughed again and fell to the side.
"Think it's about time you were asleep young missy." They had been drinking for thirty minutes now.
Pulling herself up, Madeline raised her index finger and swung it pendulum wise. "Ah, ah, ah, not until we've finished." She lifted the bottle again and raised it to her lips. But only a drip came out. She upended it.
"Oh…all gone!"
Rubin had finished his original bottle and had shared the first red with Madeline. He uncorked the second and took the first swig as before. Satisfied, he handed it across to her. Why not, he thought. She needed some relief and a bit of escape would do her no harm.
Madeline took the bottle from him, but didn't drink. She just held it in her hands, resting on her leg. "I wet myself today Rubin."
She was staring into the fire as she said it. Rubin knew what she was going through. He also knew the signs of drink and the mood swings people go through while under the influence. You could be merry one minute and sad the next. "Don't you worry about that young missy, I've seen soldiers fill their britches with a lot more than that. Then have to go into battle stinking with filled drawers. Ain't no shame in what you done, fear does that to you. You've no control over it."
She sat silent.

"Good job you didn't have your britches on when you did it, eh?" He laughed hoping to evoke the same from her. And thankfully it did.
She looked up and smiled. "Given that I hardly know how to unfasten them, in my haste I would have."
"Ha-ha, then we'd have to call you Piddlin' Maddlin…"
Both laughed.
He added further, after another swig. "Or Leaky Lander."
Their laughter continued.
Madeline giggled and fell to the side again. "Hic! Or Pissy-missy."
All went silent.
Startled with her own outburst, she covered her entire mouth with her hand.
"I can't believe I just said that."
Rubin didn't hear her apology over his own outburst.
Embarrassed, Madeline tried to straighten herself up, but it didn't last long. In her half inebriated state her arm gave way and she fell over again.
"I reckon your gonna have one hell of a nippy head tomorrow young missy."
Madeline lay where she was, unmoving.
"Missy…you awake?"
She was drunk. He knew it. Within seconds of rising to his feet, he was over by her side. Taking the bottle from her grasp, Rubin lifted her limp body and laid her on top of the blanket. Pulling the remainder over her, he tucked the edges in at the side. He removed the boots from her feet and rose to stand over her. As he looked down, he muttered, knowing that she wouldn't hear a thing. "Don't think you'll need two blankets over you tonight."
He walked back to fire. "But you'll be suffering come morning."
He smiled.
That should be interesting to see, he thought.

*

Madeline 5

Chapter 3

Bread...or Lack of It

Madeline kicked at his side.
He mumbled something indistinguishable, so she kicked again. "Come on lazy bones, time to get up."
Rubin opened his eyes and was met by the dawn's early light. "Eh! What?" Confused and heavy headed, he ran his giant hand over his face to wipe the sleep from it. He adjusted his vision to see Madeline standing over him. His words this time were discernible to her. "You're awake."
"And why shouldn't I be?" She turned on her feet and made for the fire. "I have breakfast all prepared."
Rubin sat up straight and flicked the blanket from his legs. He leaned to the left to see passed her and saw two fish cooking on the skewer over the flames. "Where'd you get them?" It was a stupid question he knew, as they could only have come from the nearby stream. His point had been how did she get them?

She answered without the need to ask. "My father taught me how to catch fish without a line. We used to do it when we went camping overnight. I thought we would keep the chicken for later. Eat it cold as we go." She clapped her hands. "Now hurry, before they burn."

Rubin was dumbstruck. He'd expected her to be, well, like he felt now, he thought. He'd finished the remainder of the wine himself after she had fallen asleep. And the effects were apparent. He shook his head to waken himself fully then rose to his feet. Coughing and spitting as he went, he joined Madeline at the fire. He looked down. Two plates, two sets of eating utensils, two cups filled with clear water sat awaiting him. "How'd you light the fire?"

Madeline pulled her lips tight. "Um, sorry, I had to use your tinderbox. I got it from your coat pocket. I hope you don't mind?"

His shoulders shrugged. "Why should I mind? We're in this together, what's yours is mine and mine is yours." He sat down crossed legged as the previous night. He looked at the fish. "You carry on like this little missy and I'll enjoy this journey all the better."

Madeline leaned to the side and picked up his small knife. She passed it over to him. "I also borrowed this to clean them with."

Rubin's hand immediately felt to his boot. "How'd you get that?"

Madeline lifted her thumb to her mouth and sucked. "It's sharp. I cut myself earlier with it."

Rubin took the blade from her and sat tapping it in his palm. "Never mind how sharp it is, how did you get it?" He felt humiliated that this young woman was able to remove the knife from his boot as he slept and all the while oblivious to it. Was he getting that old? Were his natural survival instincts dwindling? Shit! Surely he hadn't been that drunk.

"You must have left it here by the fire last night, after you had tended to the chicken."

He felt his shoulders lower and muttered under his breath.

Surprised by his reaction, she commented upon it. "Why, did you think you had lost it?"

Rubin shied away from the question. He returned the knife to its rightful place within his boot. "I forgot about it, that's all." He changed the subject. "Right, the fish, I'm starving."

*

In contrast to the fresh country air, Parisians woke once again to the overwhelming stench of the city as it began to bake in the mugginess of the summer heat. And while the commoners of the city struggled for mere bread amidst it all, the wealthy broke their fasting with ham and eggs *al fresco* outwith the city perimeter.

Both let their empty plates be taken from them.

Janis looked across the breakfast table as her mother frantically waved her black coloured fan in front of her face.
"If you did not wear as much clothing as you do mother, then perhaps you would not feel the heat as much."
There was no faltering in her pace as she spoke out. "Pah! I have worn the likes of this since your Father died so I see no reason to change just because of the weather."
Janis adjusted the table's parasol to block out more of the direct sunlight. "Then at least sit within the shade."
The old woman shuffled back into the light. "Then I would become too cool."
Janis raised her eyes to the ceiling, there was no winning. With age came stubbornness, she thought. Lifting the teacup to her lips, she gently blew on its contents. "Will you be dining with us tonight? I have invited Alexis to dinner."
The mother eyed her daughter up suspiciously over her now static fan. "Oh yes, and since when have you taken to inviting Gaston's friends here in his absence. Alone."
Janis replaced her cup on the saucer and began folding her embroidered table napkin. "For goodness sakes mother, he is a friend to us both."
The mother leaned forward. "Yes, but when you are together."
Janis shrugged. "What is wrong with that? I just thought that with Gaston gone we might have some company at the house. Alexis is fun and we would not be alone if you were there, would we?"
Her fan now at double the speed, the mother spoke further. "He is well known as one for the women, I would not put it past him to…"
Janis threw her napkin on the table. She pushed her stomach out. "Look at me mother, I'm with child and Gaston is my husband. Do you really think that…?"
She was cut off as abruptly as she herself had done. "Janis, I know his sort. I have never liked him from the first time Gaston introduced him to me. It is he who has led your husband astray, you know that don't you."
Janis leaned back in her chair and closed her eyes. This was all she needed, an early morning argument and one which had come from nowhere. She had felt bad enough with the morning sickness first thing, and now this. Gaston was forever on her mind, but she just needed to smile or perhaps laugh out loud. The tedium of the last few days had had her maudlin. Some serious relief from the boredom was vastly overdue in her opinion. Yes, granted, Alexis was a ladies man and he had on numerous times in the past flirted with her. But this had been innocent and in Gaston's presence. Never had he said or hinted at anything out of earshot of her husband. Of course this had been in the days when she had been at her best, and not of late, when her dowdiness had apparently made Gaston's eyes wander from her. Her mind drifted. She dearly missed those days, when her husband sought no other in his sights but her. She wondered what he was doing now. This same thought

had entered her mind the previous night whilst lying in their bed alone without him. His thick pillow had been substituted in lieu of his body to warm against, but it had compensated little. It was the real thing that she had hankered to be holding in her arms, not fabric and down. Someone real, someone to embrace her the way she had willingly held it, a face to smile at, eyes to look deep into while their thoughts mingled and soft warm skin to hold against. With her eyes still tightly shut, her right hand unconsciously rubbed at her stomach to feel the child growing within her…Gaston's child.
"Are you in some distress Janis?"
Her eyes were pulled apart again. With a final tap on her stomach, she stretched out for her cup again. "No, but the sickness is becoming more frequent in the mornings. I shall rest for a while after breakfast."
"Perhaps you should postpone the dinner engagement until another time then."
Aware that this excuse could possibly serve her mother's own means, Janis stood up. "I will be perfectly fine come tonight. You are free to join us at the table, if not then you can tend to the children in my absence."
"Oh, so the children will not be joining you for this cozy late night repast."
Offended that her mothering responsibilities were being called into question, Janis spat out. "How can you say a thing like that? I have them all day, everyday, well apart from when they are at school. I just need some time with adult company that is all."
"Pah!"
"Oh, Pah yourself. He is coming and that is that."
She detested being rude to her mother, but whether it being her body changing with the pregnancy or her just plain missing her husband, Janis walked the few feet to the windowed entrance determined that her outburst had been warranted. If she did not understand what her daughter was going through then so be it. Passing though the outer parlour, she had just reached the door to the hallway when she was met by her elderly housemaid. The silver tray in her hand held two letters, neither of which had been written by Gaston she noticed. She could recognize his scrawled writing from afar and none bore any resemblance to his. One had caught her eye though. It was addressed to her alone. She picked it up from the tray and looked down at the last line. Paris. It had come from somewhere else in France she suspected, but on turning it over there was no other writing present. Now was not the time for reading or writing letters, she just wanted to lie down and rest. It was thrown back onto the tray. "Just put it with the others. I'll read it later."

*

"No fucking bread again?"
Rosie picked the last of the weevils out from her teeth. "Eh no, we haven't had any for days now." She lied.

In her second home from home, Charlotte rummaged her way through the larder. "Hate starting the day without bread."
Rosie flicked the offending crumbs from her lap just as Charlotte emerged holding a small leg of cooked meat in one hand and a lump of cheese in the other. Her muffled tones could only just be understood as her stuffed mouth spat out half of what she was eating. "This'll have to do then."
Rosie's eyes widened. "Have to do? That would feed us all. At least carve some meat from the bone, that way there won't be teeth marks left on it for the rest of us."
Charlotte sat across from her at the table and rested both elbows on top. "Won't be any left to mark."
"You mean you'll eat the bone as well."
Charlotte laughed. "Well I'm not against having a bone in my mouth, 'specially if there's plenty of meat on it." She nodded over. "Like your Frederick eh? Big bone Freddie, Frederick big bone."
"Here, that's my man you're talking about."
Charlotte pulled at the ham with her half filled mouth. "Only talking about part of him, well, most of him now come to think of it, ha-ha."
Referring to the size of his penis in addition to the removal of his leg, it did make up a higher percentage of his body mass now she agreed. She thought she could see through Charlotte's logic. "Yeah, I suppose so. When you work it out like that."
Charlotte spat a piece of gristle out onto the floor. "Work what out?"
Rosie had found her mind had wandered. "Him with no leg now."
It was the cheese's turn to be massacred. In one huge bite and with total disregard to its mouldy exterior, Charlotte had taken a fist sized chunk in her mouth and now attempted to speak through the remaining void. "I wov alking ah-out is coch."
Rosie could make nothing out of what she had just said. She remained silent until Charlotte had swallowed and was content for the moment to hand sweep together in a pile, all the pieces that fell from her mouth onto the table as she chewed.
Forcing the hard fermented curd down akin to a snake swallowing a mouse, Charlotte eventually made enough room to utter some semi-audible words. "I was talking about his cock, not his leg. Mind you, it's like talking about the same thing here." She laughed again.
"And I was talking about his leg. Or lack of it." Her cupped hand allowed the other to scoop the crumbs up into it and when satisfied she had the lot, casually flicked them onto the floor. She slapped her hands together. "We talked about it last night."
Charlotte laid both pieces of food on the table and wiped her mouth with the back of her right hand. "You talked about his leg?"
"No not the leg. What his future was without it. He wants to be a Doctor. Can you imagine, my Frederick a Doctor." She placed her chunky arched

fingers under each side of her bloated chin and tilted her head slightly as if in pose. "Me, a Doctor's wife."
The temptation of food in front of her too great, Charlotte began toying with the cheese again. "He proposed marriage to you?"
Rosie pulled her fingers from her face and thumped the now clasped hands on the table. "No."
"That was a quick enough answer. Do you think he will? After all if he's talking to you about it then he must have you in his plans to do so. Makes sense to me" A corner of cheese found its way to her lips.
Rosie joined her and picked at the edge. "No, but with his full attention on me again with that bitch Madeline out of the way, I'm sure I can coax him into it. Just have to show him my charm."
Charlotte added further on her friend's behalf. "As well as giving him a good seeing to every night, eh?" She winked.
Rosie leaned back in the chair and let her fingers tap on the table. "There's more to us than just a quick fuck Charlotte. We seemed fine until a few weeks ago, until you-know-who showed up and then it all went bad. I never knew how much I cared for him until I thought I was losing him."
Aware that the conversation had turned serious, Charlotte switched to sober mode. She reached over and took Rosie's hand in hers. "It can't be easy on either of you, with what's happened to him, but you don't become a Doctor overnight, a lot of things can happen in that time. It takes a long time to become one you know" She paused for a moment to let it sink in. "Maybe even as long as a month."
Rosie thought she had misheard her and tried to comprehend what Charlotte had just said. She lifted her eyes from the table to see her face grinning back at her. Both burst out laughing at the same time. "You're a fucking bitch Charlotte."
She nodded. "I know. Fun isn't it. Here…" Charlotte pushed the food across at her. "Have some cheese, you little mouse you."
Rosie laughed further. "Mouse maybe, little I'm not." She ran her hands down the side of her rolling dress. "Maybe I should lose some of this. Get myself nice and trim for him." She pushed her bosom up with both hands. "These are still alright though. He likes big tits so can't lose anything up here."
"Rosie. Don't do this to yourself. Frederick liked you the way you were when you two first met. You haven't changed since then so what makes you think he'd want something different to what you are now?"
Rosie sat forward again. "Then why was he after fucking Madeline then. Tell me that? If he still loved me then why look at her?" She pushed herself back again, almost sending the chair toppling over. "Just coz she made him come without having to put his cock in her mouth doesn't make her anything special."
"You have to admit Rosie she is one good looking young woman. Any man in Paris would want to fuck her. Look at us, what the hell are we compared

to something like her. We're fat, and I don't mind admitting it, we're getting on, if you haven't noticed." She pressed her own massive bosoms together. "We've got big tits for the guys to stick their cock between and come on our faces and fat arses for them to stick *their* faces in between so we can shit in their mouths. That's our lives with the bodies we have Rosie. You think yourself lucky you've got someone like Frederick. I've got no-one but the sick bastards I earn a living from. Don't try to become someone else. Just show him what you feel about him, show him you care. Show him you love him. He'll soon find his way back to you."
Rosie thought about what she had just said. "Maybe you're right Charlotte. I'm sorry I snapped at you. I'll just carry on the way things were before, only this time I'll keep a closer eye on him." She forced a smile, if only to reassure her friend. "And yes, I'll give a right good seeing to every night…just in case he forgets."
Charlotte smiled back. "That's better."
As she watched her best friend rise from the table to fetch boiling water from the pot, Charlotte thought of what she had seen the previous night. When she had finished work for the day, it had been one of her client's who had suggested her joining him for a drink in the local taverne. It had been much needed as she had been on her back all day. But as they searched for a free table she had noticed Frederick sitting alone in the corner, and he was not as sober has the usual upstanding young man she knew him to be. In fact he had been that drunk he had trouble keeping himself on the chair. This was definitely out of character and she could only assume that it was with him losing his leg. The taverne owner confirmed her suspicions. He had confided in him earlier that evening during a period of inebriated self pity. She now thought it wise to keep this from Rosie as it would only add to her self doubt and make her worry the more. Hopefully things would work out for the best, for her friend's sake.

*

Monique took note she had deduct the price of a full ham and cheese from Charlotte's wages.
Pulling herself free from the wall, she inched her way along the enclosed space and back to the spaciousness of the room. She sat on the armchair as she always did and contemplated what she had just eavesdropped upon. So that was why she had not seen Frederick around for so many days. He had lost a leg. How it had happened was the least of her concerns, it was of little consequence to her. What was important was his whereabouts. She needed to know where to find him as someone of prominence had asked after him, and she had been promised payment for this information. And she would provide it. Furthermore, and on a more personal note, she had lost a part time employee…to become a Doctor of all things. His size in the privates

department had made him valuable to her in the past, the tuition of inexperienced employees in the ways of pleasure his forte. Not that he was the stud he made himself out to be, no, it was only that if the girl could master his size, then anyone else would be less of a challenge to them. Her client's gratification came before all other. Apart from the prices she charged them, that was. And in that department she could not complain. Even in the absence of Madeline, her income had never been better. All the girls were working hard on their backs for her. Both Rosie and Charlotte were making her money on a daily basis with her more demanding clientele, but this new girl Monica was surpassing even their expertise in that particular field. She was becoming a much sought after favourite among many, with her tricks of the trade commanding a higher price than normal. What she called her 'three-hole specialty' was now commonplace among visiting parties and Monique had spied upon her performing this service on a few occasions now. This woman was determined to earn as much coin as she could. Her two children must indeed be eating heartily now, she thought. With the thought of food making her empty stomach rumble, she rose from the chair and climbed the stairs to dine on breakfast…one which would include fresh bread.

*

Monica pressed the damp towel between her legs and sat down to allow her body to absorb fully, its coolness. She winced with the initial shock of it. With her limited lubrication to ease the penetration of her various sized clients, and the subsequent friction thereafter, her back passage was aching, as was her front. She squirmed as she pressed it closer to her. How long she would have to keep up this pretence was anyone's guess, she thought, but her body would not withstand the pain of such for any length of time. It was a necessity though, as she had needed to make herself stand out from the others. Monique had fallen for it, and to such an extent that she had been given one of the best rooms in the house in which to perform her unique services. It had been perfect. She had been given free reign of the house, and thus, could fully exploit her liberty to find out what she needed to know. She had been guaranteed to be paid pro rata in accordance with her findings and when complete, she would hopefully return home to her two children a very rich young woman.

She looked around the single room which had been her lodgings for the last week. With furnishings limited to her aged and hard wooded bed, the chair she now sat on, a chipped basin on the floor at her side and the cracked chamber pot in the corner, it would not be hard to rise above her standard of living. To leave the comfort of the room at Monique's house each night and return to this had made her kick herself several times now. But the story about her evil father, the farm, her sister and her two children had been vital at the time. It was this she surmised had clinched the deal so she could not be too hard on herself. The money Monique had paid to her in advance of her wages had been enough to keep her with a roof over her head and food in her belly, but little enough for anything else. And although not having yet received her wages, the pouch of coins she had received as part payment from her additional source had made a great difference. Not that she needed much to live on that was. Her days were now spent fast asleep while her evenings and most of the night was spent lying on her back. Or on all fours as the case was now. It had surprised her how easy she had taken to do what she was doing for Monique. Not having much experience with men in the past; barring the father to her two children, she had to learn as she went along and had just asked what the men wanted on each occasion. This had given them the impression that they were tutor to a young lost girl. It was a game they all liked to play and one she soon came to master. She smiled in remembrance at her own audacity the first night she had suggested she take three in unison. She had even shocked herself.

Enamoured by her height, she had stood naked before this small rotund redhead; who had been kneeling before her, and had allowed him to push his face deep between her thighs. With his hands on her rear he had pulled her closer to let his tongue penetrate fully inside. She even remembered at the time deciding what she would have for supper that evening, such was the tedium. Thank heavens he wasn't her lover. If she were to ever get aroused by what he thought he had been doing, then it would be time give up. She had just stood there waiting his submersion, but had given up after ten minutes.

Pulling his head free of her, she looked into his eyes. "You going to be down there all night or are you wanting some real fun with me?"

His already reddened face flushed even further with the sweat, the man caught his breath and swallowed before answering. He had trouble using his tongue to speak. "What you got in mind."

Monica pulled away and sat on the bed's edge. "Well something a lot more interesting in what you were doing there, that's for sure."

Raising himself from the floor, he laid his hands on his hips in indignation and stood with his narrow, two inch long erection pointing straight at her. He struggled further with his words. "It's our money. We pay for what we want to do."

She looked down at his pathetic manhood, then up to his face. "That's all you want to do is it? You spent the first half of your time watching me undress. If I had done it any slower for you I'd be putting them on."

"Now see here." He swallowed again. "You're not the one who dictates what happens here. We do. We pay Monique the money and we all get what we pay for."

Monica crossed her long slender legs and sat with arms resting on them. "All I can see that you've spent your money on so far is your lack of breathe and developing lock-jaw." She shrugged. "But, like you said, it's your money." She thought further. "You keep saying 'we', who are 'we'?"

He sat by her side. "My two fellow friends in the next room, they await your pleasure when I have finished with you." He looked to the floor. "Or should I say when you have finished with me."

Monica considered what he had just said. They awaited her one at a time next door and not downstairs in the front parlour with Monique? This seemed strange, the usual protocol was to have drinks with her and afterwards ascend to the floors in turn. Why wait next door? And who was with them while they waited. "They are alone next door in the room awaiting your completion?"

He nodded. "We hire the room for our own pleasure as well."

Monica had no idea what he was meaning. She sat silent thinking it over. 'Their own pleasure, but surely she was their pleasure.' It was soon to be explained.

He smiled at her. "You are a digression my dear, something different, a deviation from the norm, so to speak."

From the norm, their norm! Then it hit her. She turned and looked into his face. "You like women as well?"

He took her hand and patted its back. "Off course we do, that is why we are here. We are here to be with you in turn." He scanned her body. "What man wouldn't? But we like to indulge in our own games in addition to yours."

That would interesting to see, she thought, and furthermore, fun to participate in. "Why don't you all come in at the same time then?"

His short podgy neck pulled back. "You mean us three, here, now, with you?"

"You may prefer the male form, but there is one thing a woman has to her advantage and that is the addition of a third opening. We seem to have a perfect match in numbers here do we not?"

It had been a perfect match as she had said. Unlike his slender penis which was not. When within her at the start, she could barely feel his presence giving his size and her expansion due to childbirth. This being so, he had been relegated to her rear, in a position she thought would be far more familiar to him given his natural proclivity and a lot easier for her to take in. The largest of the three she had in the normal way, but the youngest and by far the cleanest, she had cordially taken in her mouth. The various positioning of all within this quartet thereafter had had her giggle with joy. And it had been contagious. All three had laughed with her as the positioning became more extreme. She had found it strange at first to see one man with another's manhood in his mouth, but after a while it became a common sight. By the end of their play, Monique had earned three times the money in only half the time. She was well in her favour. And now the threesomes had become her specialty with groups appearing in that specific number. But it had its drawbacks she now knew. She pulled the cloth from her crouch and laid it on the floor. She looked down. It was still red and tender to the touch. Her stomach made noises indicating it was in need of replenishment. She was hungry for breakfast, so, rising from the chair, she walked, wide legged and sat on the bed. Pulling open the cloth which was lying on top, her hand tore at the bread. It was amazing how easy it was to get fresh bread in your mouth these days, she thought…especially if you had put a part of the baker in your own mouth beforehand.

*

"I'm sorry Father, but we've no bread."
Looking up to the waiter from his bible, the gaunt looking priest smiled at him. "I understand. But God has at least blessed me with meat and cheese, and for that I am truly grateful. You know, there are some who say that man cannot live on bread alone, I for one agree with that and on looking at this, it is a worthy substitute."
Happy with his acceptance of the situation; albeit it a bit long winded, the waiter placed the wooden salver on the table. "Glad you see it that way Father. Now, is there anything else I can get you before I leave?"
The priest shook his head and closed his leather bound book. "No, thank you, this is enough for any man. But perhaps some water if you could avail me of a glass, preferably untainted."
"Water here's real bad Father, milk's the best I can do for you there." He winked. "Daughter's got a goat out back." He leaned forward. "But don't be telling no-one, will you? Of course there's wine if you've a hankering for it, but…"
The priest raised his hand. "Your secret is safe with me. Milk will be fine thank you."
"Milk it is then." Pulling himself straight, he looked down at the Priest's feet and saw the travel bag he had noticed earlier. "Come far Father?"
'Indeed I have' he thought. 'But you are to know nothing of my travels to this vile city and the Lord's work that brings me here. If you were, then you would have to forfeit your life like all others who had bore witness to my presence in times past. A neat cut to the throat would hold your silence forever, like the others I am here to deal with in a similar fashion. A wife and mother would see my blade's edge some time soon and perhaps the children who were not in my plans, but would be a bonus for my own indulgence.' He smiled at the waiter. "Not far."
"And what brings you to Paris, God's work? Huh, you've got a lot of work ahead of you if you are."
"No, just delivering the sentiments of a loved one."

*

358

Madeline 5

Chapter 4

Uncertainty

The fish had been cooked to perfection and both were sated. With the bags filled with fresh water and four extra muskets wrapped up in the blankets and strapped to Felix's side, they made their way out of the woods to continue on the same path from the previous day. As the sun beat down upon them, both rode the first hour in silence.
It was Rubin who eventually spoke out. "You surprise me young 'en."
Madeline peeked over her shoulder. "Oh. Why?"
"Thought you'd have a banger of a head today. You supped the wine good an' proper last night. Till you fell over that is." He smirked.
With contrived indignation, Madeline faced forward again. "It was stronger than I thought. And anyway, it had been along day and I was tired." As pitiful as this excuse was, she still felt justified in saying it. It had been a long day for sure, and an eventful one. She had pondered over the previous day's scene in her head during the first hour of their journey. Was it any wonder she had felt like drowning her sorrows with the wine. If it had not

been for Rubin, heaven knows what kind of state she would be in now. If indeed she was still alive to feel it. She thought she was dead for sure. And once again it was Rubin she had to thank. It still played on her mind though, that she had not been fully open with him with regards to Ramone's letter. She had given him certain information from it and withheld the rest. Not that she mistrusted him of course, far from it, but preferred not to have to answer the questions Rubin would inevitably ask. She had showed him the two keys and revealed the location in which they were now travelling, but the rest she would tell when they reached their destination, if it was required.

Ramone had explained his feelings towards her in the letter. How he had changed as a person since meeting her, but of late, had wished for a hasty death. His life held no meaning with all the subterfuge and pretence. This part she had to think about as he had not expanded on it. What subterfuge had he meant? It was plain though that she had made such an impact in his life that he had bestowed all his worldly goods to her, and which were held deep within the vaults of an old abandoned castle. Why he would keep it hundreds of miles away and not where he had resided in Paris was a mystery to her. But then again, Ramone had been quite a mystery to her from the start. During there many excursions around the city, he had told her about his past. But several contradictions had crept in over a period and she had often wondered which parts were true and which were the fanciful thinking of an old man. She had at the time put these down to the forgetfulness of age, but now, and with their destination one of the numerous places he had mentioned, this could be the subterfuge he had written about. She was uncertain, but her life would be greatly transformed though, when and if they reach their goal. That was for sure.

She wondered what Rubin would do with his share. She smiled at the thought. Copious amounts of wine to begin with no doubt. But where did he live? Did he have a lady friend to spend it with? It suddenly occurred to her that of all the people she was familiar with in Paris, she hardly knew anything about any of them. Her question blurted out of her mouth before she had time to think about it. "Do you have someone special in Paris Rubin?"

The question coming from nowhere caught Rubin off guard. "Eh?"

Madeline expanded. "A lady friend. Someone close to you."

Rubin pushed his stomach into her back. "Well you're quite close."

She pushed back. "You know what I mean, someone you are fond of. A wife perhaps?" She knew for certain that he was not married but thought it amusing to ask anyway.

"Hah! A wife! Not a chance. I'm a free agent, and always will be." He needlessly hauled on the reins in demonstration of his thoughts. "A wife. Hah! The thought of it."

"Eh, yes Rubin, I get the point. Not a wife then. But someone you spend your time with."

Deliberately avoiding a proper response, Rubin toyed with her once again. "I seem to spend a lot of time with you don't I. If I'm not chasing after you round the city, I'm either on a horse with you or you curled up behind me round a fire."

Madeline snuggled her back against his stomach in affection. "Ah... that's a nice thing to say. Thank you."

Rubin smiled at her pretence, but considered her question once again in a more solemn manner. He thought of Annie. He spat to the right before answering. "Got someone I suppose."

"Oh!"

"She's like you."

Madeline inched her head round. "Like me?"

"Not like you in the way you look, more like in the way you are."

With this, her head and body turned to the extreme. She was almost facing him. "The way I am. You mean what I am with Monique?"

"Yeah, something like that. And sit straight or you'll fall off."

Doing as instructed, Madeline straightened herself and asked of him further. "It can't be just something Rubin, it is or it isn't."

"Okay, it is."

"It is what?"

"Like you with Monique, with the men."

Madeline remained silent for a moment to think over what he had just said. She had never seen Rubin with any of the women at Monique's house so assumed he didn't take advantage of her wares. But it did sound to her that he had someone with whom he did spend his time, and paid the price for doing so. "Have you known her long?"

"Who, Annie, oh yeah, long time now."

"I take it she, sorry, Annie, works in a place such as Monique's."

"Wouldn't exactly say like Monique's no, bit lower down the pecking order is where she works doing her thing." He thought further on it, then finished. "The pits more like."

Madeline was intrigued. Here was a woman who was doing exactly what she herself was doing to survive and yet Rubin appeared to have feelings for her. Hadn't she deliberated over something similar with regards to herself and Jacob? Or was she assuming too much here. She needed to press further. "So, Annie, is this who you will be spending your part of the money with? Have you plans for her?"

"Little missy, I don't even know what my share of this is, you've not told me much about what we're looking for. A vault with two keys isn't much to get excited about and make plans with."

He was right, she knew. Rubin had undertaken this journey on trust. It was about time she explained to him all that she knew. She decided there and then that she would disclose everything to him that very evening when they had settled down by the camp fire. He would then be as much in the dark as

she apparently was, she thought. But just as she had made her decision to do so, her thoughts were interrupted by Rubin's voice.
"Sit tight little missy, got company up ahead."
So deep in thought was she that she hadn't noticed the wooden bridge that lay further on up the trail. It was obviously used to traverse the stream which they had been following for so long now. But it was the two men seated either side of its vertical posts that had apparently bothered Rubin. Once again she heard his instruction for her to move round to his back, so in one rapid movement she was behind him with arms clasped tight around his waist. She peered round his massive frame. Even from a distance she could see the rifle muskets in their hands and she was clearly not the only one to have noticed it. Rubin had retrieved his own from Felix's hold. He pulled back a lever which she assumed was to make it ready to fire and now rode with the reins in his left hand and the musket in his right. With it facing upwards, he had the butt resting on his right leg. She squeezed him tighter at the thought of what may occur. She heard his reassuring words.
"Don't worry little missy. Things will be fine. Just keep you mouth shut, like before."
It was all the comfort she needed. She was safe in his hands, she was sure, whatever happened.
In such close proximity to each other as to be standing only three apart, the two men had advanced upon their approach. With Rubin bringing Felix to a halt, both now stood with barrels pointing directly at his chest. She felt Rubin lower his in reaction. He spat to the right before speaking out. "We seem to have a problem here."
It was one to their left who hollered out in retort. "No problem my friend, unless you make one for us."
This had been uttered through toothless gums Madeline surmised, as she could here the slurping of his loose jaw. She remained still, awaiting the outcome of this armed stalemate.
The second of the two broke his silence and pointed at Felix's side with the tip of his musket. "What's in the bag?"
She saw Rubin's head shake to the side. "Don't matter what's in the bag. You'll not get to see it." He paused. "You or your gumsy friend there."
Madeline shut her eyes tight together. Did Rubin know the quick way to start a fight, or what? She heard the stranger's voice speak further.
"We got two barrels here pointing at you. We could blow you're smart arse right off that fuckin' horse of yours if we wanted."
Apparently unconcerned with the threat, Rubin remained silent for a moment before she heard him reply. "And one of you 'ill die with me."
Unaware that Rubin had centred his aim between them and could at a moment's thought pick either to take his shot, Madeline opened her eyes again and peered round. She saw the two men standing with eyes fixed on Rubin. One had gulped deep at the thought of taking a shot in the chest, the other his musket shaking in his hands. Rubin spoke out once again.

"Well, do you want to know what's in the bag or not? You're wasting my time here."
Madeline could not believe her ears. Did Rubin have a death wish? Two muskets were pointing at him and he had only one to shoot back with. There was no way he could win a fight like this. But to her utter astonishment, she saw the toothless one lower his aim.
Still facing Rubin, he spoke out. "Put it down Jules. The big fella's got us."
Madeline noticed the other's displeasure and heard his rant.
"What do you mean he's got us? They're two of us here."
The elder turned to face him now. "I don't want to lose a son if he picks you to shoot at." His outstretched hand lowered the barrel for him. "Leave him be."
Reluctantly, the son let his musket be taken from him. The old man now stood with the two weapons pointing to the ground. "On your way stranger."
Madeline shuffled at Rubin's back urging him on. She wanted across the bridge and out of harms way as quickly as possible. But he remained still. She heard him speak again.
"Not much up to this bandit stuff, are you?"
The elder shook his head and once again spat out slurred words. "Ain't bandits stranger, just trying to get somethin' to feed the family with. Young ens are starving. Meant no harm to you..." He looked up in Madeline's direction and kept his eyes on her for several seconds. "...or your son."
Rubin lifted his eyes to look across the water and the barren fields beyond. He refaced them. "Farmers?"
Both nodded, but it was the son who answered. "Farmers with no crops for food, no money or anythin' left to sell to buy some." He nodded to the guns in his father's hand. "'cepting them that we need for huntin' and the likes."
Madeline noticed the old man's age and assumed he had been talking about his grandchildren when he had mentioned the young ones. She thought of the four muskets Rubin had wrapped up and were strapped to Felix's side. She leaned to the side and frantically hauled at the tight knots. Pulling the bundle free, she sat up straight with one them on her lap as the other three haphazardly clattered to the ground. Amidst the furore, she spoke out, with lowered tone. "Would selling four muskets get you enough money to buy food for the young ones?"
Madeline felt Rubin push his back into her stomach. She knew this was in reaction to her not remaining silent and more importantly that she was giving away items that he had intended to sell when they had reached the next town. But to her surprise, he remained silent. Not responding to her words directly, the two appeared to be staring up at him wide-eyed seeking his approval to her unexpected benevolence. She could feel Rubin sigh through his body movement. "Righty-oh..." He surreptitiously elbowed her stomach. "...son. If that's what you want to do."
On hearing Rubin's approval, the son made straight for the three muskets lying on the ground. The father; now holding both their own in his left,

outstretched his right to take the one from Madeline's hands. He nodded his thanks but remained silent, all the while staring straight into her eyes.
Madeline smiled back. "I hope your grand-children get better soon."
He nodded back as he took it from her.
Rubin pulled on the reins and steered Felix towards the bridge.
The old man stepped away to allow easy access. He hollered after them as they took their first step onto the wood. "Much obliged to your sir... and your kind son their, thinking of the young 'ens." As they clattered across the aging slats, they heard him finish. "...he'll make a good mother some day."
Madeline looked over her shoulder as they rode off. He was smiling at her.

"You know how much we could have got for those four muskets?"
Reseated at the front where she was happier, Madeline shrugged. "I don't care Rubin, as long as the children get fed. I do so hope they get a lot for them, means more food doesn't it?"
"If you say so, least old Felix'll be happier."
Madeline knew what he meant, the extra load had added to his already heavy burden with both riding on his back. She looked out to the flat open fields ahead of them. "Let's loosen his load further Rubin, I feel like walking for a while."
Rubin pulled on the reins and brought Felix to a halt. He let her dismount first before pulling his heavy carcass free as well. Standing upright to stretch his legs, he let Madeline take the reins and lead Felix on. Both took a leisurely pace.
"That was a very brave thing you did earlier Rubin. It took a lot of nerve to do what you did. How did you know the old man would give up?"
Rubin spat to his left. "I didn't, I took a gamble."
Madeline looked round Felix's front. "You took a gamble. You mean you weren't certain?"
Dawdling to keep pace with Madeline's shorter strides, Rubin kicked at some loose dirt with each step. "Nothin's certain in this world young missy, sometimes you just gotta take a chance, go with your gut feeling."
Madeline blew out through puckered lips. "Well it took some nerve."
Rubin remained silent but smiled inwardly to himself. Much more nerve than she would ever know, he thought, seeing as he had been given no choice in the matter. He did not have the heart to tell her that the barrel of his musket had been empty...
...he had forgotten to reload it that morning.

*

Madeline 5

Chapter 5

Perfect Afternoon

Denig held his wife's hand as she raised her foot onto the lowest rung of the carriage. Allowing her to take the narrow steps one at a time, he could not resist the temptation of patting her rump as she leaned forward to enter. Satisfied with her seated, he nodded to the carriage driver, and using only the bottom step for leverage, he pulled himself up and directly in. The door was closed at his back.
Caroline adjusted the thin blanket on her lap. "Pull the blinds down darling. I do not wish to be greeted by anyone on our journey."
Courteous to her requests as ever, he lowered both sides before sitting opposite. "Hardly a journey, is it? We have no destination in mind, remember."
Caroline raised her hands to her head and pulled the retaining pin free from her bonnet. "It is simply to be out of the house that is all. I feel the walls closing in on me these days."

As he watched her replace the pin in the hat and lay it on her lap, his outstretched legs rested on her seat. "I know exactly how you feel. Each time I hear word of a caller at the door I am dreading the worst." He dug into his waistcoat pocket and pulled out his silver drinking flask. "I'm amazed it's taking them so long to get to us."
Pulling the side of her cream dress away from his dust caked boots, she considered his statement. She knew he was referring to the authorities, but as he had remarked upon, surely the missing child's parents must have at least alerted them to that fact that they were her employers. It would only be natural for them to question anyone who may have knowledge of her whereabouts, so what was taking them so long to get here. Not that either of them knew of her whereabouts anyway, that matter had been dealt with by the two strange men in Jeanette's employ. She watched Denig sip from the flask. "We certainly have got ourselves in a jam, haven't we? I have never seen you drink so much as I have these last few days."
"Is it any wonder?" He looked about him. "I don't even know how long we will have this carriage. May have to sell it soon."
Caroline hated seeing her husband like this. Forever the optimistic since the day they had met, he had never once let it be known to her his worries. But now he had something to worry about. Their entire livelihood was in jeopardy, and all through greed and stupidity on her part. She was the one who had invited the Comtesse to live at their house during her stay in Paris. Knowing well that her plans had included gaining a fortune and with a percentage of it coming their way. But things had not transpired they way she had hoped. Jeanette was bleeding her husband dry with her demands and his wealth was dwindling rapidly each day. But to his credit, he had never once chastised her for her decision. Indeed he had taken it upon himself to accept the blame in her stead for being so naïve as to be taken in. If only she could find a way out of their predicament. She watched him drink further from the flask and with him noticing her stare, he extended his arm. She shook her head. "No thanks darling."
He took another quick swig and after replacing the cap, returned it to his pocket. "Where is the bitch today anyway, haven't seen her about? Hope she's still in the house, fucking cheaper for me there."
She wasn't. And Caroline reluctantly had to tell him she wasn't. "She left the house early this morning…in a hired carriage."
As his shoulders lowered, so did his head. "Fuck."

*

Jacqueline had seen them off on their well needed break from the house. Declining their invitation to join them on an excursion round the city, she had already made her plans for the day. And they included Jeanette.
Rising early as she normally did, it was around eight when she had looked out from the overhead window and seen the Comtesse leave in the carriage.

She considered the time. If anyone was to leave that early in the morning, then it was safe to assume that they were meaning to be away from the house the entire day. If not, then an appropriate hour sometime later would have sufficed. It was at that very moment when she had decided to do what she was doing now. Her intention was to sneak into Jeanette's room, have a rummage around and hopefully see what dark secrets she could unearth. Anything at all that could help Denig and Caroline out of the pickle she knew them to be in. She certainly did not want any of the house staff to know what she was doing, so waiting for the time she knew they would all be on the lower floor, she made her way along the hallway towards her goal.

After a quick look to both left and right, she turned the handle and pushed open the door. She was knocked back with the instant smell of body odour within the room. The combination of stale sex and sweat filled the air. Fuck! When was the last time that the window was opened in here, she thought? Clearly Jeanette held little value in respect of tidiness either. Her bedchamber was a mess. Gowns and undergarments lay strewn about the floor and her unmade bed a tangle of soiled sheets. She knew that Jeanette allowed none of the staff into her room to tidy up after her. If this being the case then wasn't it to be surmised that she must have something to hide? This was what she hoped.

By the time she had reached the middle of the room, she had decided where to begin her search. Like a fish drawn to a fly, the five layered set of drawers in the corner caught her eye in an instant.

It was evident that the Comtesse preferred to have most of her clothes near at hand; this by way of them scattered about the room, as the top three drawers were empty. By the time she had opened the bottom one, she had almost given up due to the fact that the fourth had contained nothing but bobbles, three pairs of lace gloves and an assortment of handkerchiefs, but her eyes lit up at its contents.

She had seen most of these sex devices before and was very familiar with their various uses. The eight inch ivory phallus drew her attention first. With this being the very article that Jeanette had beaten the young maid, it appeared to Jacqueline sick in the mind that anyone would want to retain it after it being used in this fashion. Her lips retracted when she spotted the tell tale specks of congealed blood on its surface. She bit her lip in thought. Could she take this and use it as evidence against Jeanette in Denig and Caroline's defense? She considered it, but taking it now would most likely cause trouble if it were seen to be missing. Later perhaps!

Her hand reached out for the string of inch wide beads in the corner. She smiled at past memories. On many an occasion had she inserted the likes of these into her back passage, and more pleasurable times using them on her lovers during fellatio. To pull them out rapidly at the point of ejaculation had had her men squirming in her arms she recalled. In fact, she had used this technique in her attempt to bring Ramone's old soldier back to attention. But alas, like all who had tried before and after, he had failed to rise to the occasion. They were thrown back into the corner and in their place she picked up a screwed wooden clamp.

Adjustable to suit the wearer's size, this type of penis clamp had always held her interest. Like many men of various age groups, it was used primarily to keep the erection hard as possible. The tightness of the grip restricting the blood flow held what was there, tightly in place. Others she knew savoured the delights the screwed clamp could offer in the way of pain, especially when a long thin pin was driven into the testicle bag at the same time. She had used something similar to this one's design before, only it had an additional feature, that of a rough edged side. This jutted out at such an angle as to rub hard against the clitoris during penetration, and especially good when astride your lover. It too was tossed back into the drawer in lieu of another phallus.

Smaller in both length and diameter, this did not have the smooth finish of the ivory, instead, the outer casing was that of course brushed leather. She noticed the small metal studs running down the sides. Jeanette liked it rough, she thought.

She had seen enough, this was not what she was looking for. Throwing it back to its approximate location she pushed the drawer in and rose to her feet. Her eyes scanned the room. Without thinking, she was drawn to the window and looked down. Yuck!

Two full to brimming chamber pots sat side by side, their smell nauseating. But it was the pile of blood stained rags that lay next to them that had her bite down on her teeth. It was obviously Jeanette's time of the month. Thrown in a heap with no consideration to the rancid smell which emanated from them Jacqueline winced at the thought of such unhygienic behaviour.

"Dirty bitch!"

She drew her fingers to her lips. 'Shit, she had said it out loud. What a fool. Hush, Jacqueline, hush.'

The four pillared bed was her next port of call, but seeing nothing on top save the twisted sheets, she went down on bended knees to look beneath. More soiled underwear lay on the floor, along with…along with. Her eyes squinted through the semi darkness. She could not make it out. What was that, she wondered?

Lying on her side, she stretched her arm in and now blinded to its whereabouts, searched at random with open hand. She felt its touch on the tip of her middle finger, so, pushing her arm to full extent, she clasped the item in her hand and pulled her body free. She pushed herself up and with her back rested against the bed, opened her clenched fist. Her eyes lit up.

…A small lady's pistol.

'What in God's name did she have this for?'

And whose life would be in danger had she a mind to use it.

Turning it around in her fingers she considered her options here with this. Unlike the items in the drawer that had a place, and had been put there intentionally, this was lost to the eye beneath the bed. If she were to take it

then Jeanette would merely think it still lost. Without further hesitation, the pistol found its way stuffed down the front of her dress. She tucked it home and rose to her feet again.
Although a good find it its self, she had not found what she needed. If indeed there was something to find. She walked towards the wall cupboard. Surely some dresses or gowns lay within. She had seen the Comtesse wearing far more clothes that what lay about the floor. The wooden slatted door to the right was pulled open and as expected, Jeanette's finer attire hung gracefully of wooden hangers. 'Bitch.'
Her envy apparent, Jacqueline ran her opened hand across the full range of evening wear on display. The various colours and cuttings had her jealous to the extreme. It would have given her great pleasure to take scissors to the whole damned lot, she thought.
'Who was being a bitch now?'
She shook her head and pulled opened the left. Further gowns hung there, alongside an array of ruff collared overcoats and tight fitting jackets. On the shelf above sat a display of hats and bonnets and as her eyes looked down, a selection of shoes and boots made her envy even greener.
"Fucking bitch."
This had been spoken aloud again and not thought. And as she said it she heard voices outside the bedroom door.
'Shit.'
This was thought of in her mind but she could have screamed it out loud. In panic, she looked around the room to find a place to hide. But before she knew it, she had backed into the cupboard and through the line of gowns. With both arms stretched, she pulled the two doors closed behind her. And even with the voices outside muffled in tone, she recognized the speaker as Jeanette.
'Fuck."

*

Denig swallowed the remainder of his brandy and tilted the empty flask towards the floor. "Need to get a bigger one of these."
Caroline smiled at him. "Yes, it took you all but fifteen minutes to empty it."
"Well you helped me."
"I took a sip Denig. But I cannot stomach it. I should have eaten a bigger breakfast. It may have helped if we had some bread. Where has it all gone these days?"
Denig shrugged. It was the least of his worries. "Maybe all the bakers are dead. Gone to baker heaven, with their small baker wings playing their dainty little baker harps."
Caroline laughed at his absurdness. This was more like the Denig she knew. She enjoyed his witty company immensely and was one of the main things that led her to marrying him. But the novelty of the carriage ride was wearing

thin and its confines restricting. "Shall we stop somewhere and have luncheon?"
Her suggestion brought a smile to Denig's face. "Sure." Any inn or taverne they stopped at would have brandy. He leaned to the side and pulled up the blind. "Need to know where we are first."
Both their eyes squinted at the suddenness of the afternoon sun.
Knowing the city well, Denig knew in an instant. "Fuck, we're near *Versailles*."
"How did we get here?"
"I don't know, we asked the driver to take us where his heart pleased him remember. I guess the fresh air was a want for him as well as us. Makes no difference, glad we're here, I know a place where the food is good and the…"
She finished his sentence for him. "The Brandy is served in clean glasses?" Leaning forward, he kissed the top of her head. "Exactly."
He banged on the roof with his fist.

*

With her view limited, Jacqueline peered through the slat at eye level and seen Jeanette enter the room. She had male company at her back but Jacqueline could only see his face. The young man was unknown to her but he was obviously drunk as he was walking in an awkward fashion. He was totally lost to view within seconds as he took a seat on the proffered armchair. Jeanette however was not. In plain sight, she had in an instant removed both bonnet and coat. And as was expected, they were thrown to the floor. Jacqueline knew what was coming, and she did not relish the thought of standing cooped up in the cupboard while they went about their business. In fact, with the restriction of the space and the clothes pressing against her, she could feel her body begin to sweat already. Jeanette meanwhile had removed her corset and dress.

*

With the gardens being in full bloom, they decided to sit outside in the sun and as both Denig and Caroline took their respective seats at the parasol table, the waiter tendered the day's special…wild boar.
"Just like me." Quipped Denig.
The waiter gave a conciliatory smile, unbeknown to its meaning.
Caroline however, did. "Perhaps my darling, but certainly never boring."
Lost to their banter, the waiter pushed Caroline's chair in and enquired as to their beverage requirements.
"Brandy. Large." He looked to Caroline.
"Wine, please, white."

Their order given, Denig nodded to the waiter as an instruction to leave. He pulled his chair in closer. "Not bad, eh?"
Caroline looked around at the well cultivated gardens. "We have dined here before Denig, I am sure of it, although I think it may have been winter as we ate indoors. I do not remember these gardens looking as they do now."
Denig shook his head.
Caroline extended some clarification. "We came here with Maxwell and Lauren, to celebrate their engagement, just the four of us."
Denig was none the wiser. He shrugged.
"It is hardly surprising you fail to remember since both you and Maxwell got exceedingly drunk."
This time he smiled. "Yeah, sounds like Maxwell."
Caroline tutted. "Sounds more like you, you mean."
"Good friends they were, we don't see as much of them as we once did, whatever happened to them?"
"They have a house in Marseilles. They moved there permanently. Probably to get away from you and for the good of Maxwell's liver."
Denig laughed. "Am I that bad an influence?"
"No, it's just that I miss the times we had together."
Denig clasped his hands over hers. "Happy days..." He smiled reassuringly at her. "And will be again soon, I promise."
Caroline forced one of her own. "I hope so Denig. I really hope so."

*

"Would you care for a drink before we begin?"
The young man looked up at the semi clad Comtesse and nodded. "Please, but begin what?"
"There is wine and goblets on the dresser yonder, fill two."
Her instruction a demand more than an invitation, the young man tried to pull his self free of the chair, but struggled with his affliction.
Jeanette noticed his predicament. "Remain seated, I will tend to it."
Through slurred words he asked further of his being there.
As she filled the goblets, Jeanette explained his presence in her bedchamber twofold. "First and more important, there are several questions I needed to ask you and which I am sure you will ably provided answers, but the taverne was not the place to talk of such. It is a delicate matter not to be shared with prying ears you understand."
Confused as to what she was alluding with regards to the questions, it was evident with her state of half undress what the second was. He asked further, regardless of it. "And the other?"
She handed him his drink. "Ah, the other. Well we will get to that forthwith." She pulled a nearby chair across to sit opposite. "There is a young woman residing here in Paris that you are familiar with."

He sat upright to drink from the goblet, but before he did, he replied. "I know a lot of women in Paris." He raised it in salutation.
Ignoring his remark, she continued. "Her name is Madeline."

Jacqueline's eyebrows rose at the sound of this. She had heard that name mentioned before by Caroline. The night she had returned from Monique's house. The new flesh they had called her. She adjusted her frame to both see and hear more clearly. The young man was obviously struggling to speak, his coughing persistent. But what made him do so at the sound of her name, she wondered.

The wine had been spat into the goblet faster than he had drunk it. He coughed to clear his throat.
"I am correct then."
Unable to speak, he nodded vigorously while hitting his chest.
"Very good." She allowed him a moment to catch his breath. "She is at present out with the city. I would like to know her whereabouts."
He shook his head. "I've no idea where she is." One last cough cleared his airways completely. And for a voice that was protective of Madeline. "Why, what do you want of her?"
"That is no concern of yours. I have heard that your relationship with her has been more than just a casual one. That a bond has developed between the two of you. It follows then that she would have taken someone like you; with a more personal connection to her, into her confidence, would it not?"
He pondered the notion. "I don't know where you're getting your information from, but it's severely inaccurate. I assure you, there is no bond, other than a mere friendship."
"Yes, but do not friends consider each other as confidante to the other? Disclose their personal feelings and perhaps their secrets."
"I have only seen her at Monique's house a few times. She does not consider me that close a friend. She hardly knows me."
Jeanette leaned forward. "Ah, but she sucked your cock…
…didn't she, Frederick."

*

Four large brandies and a roast boar meal had Denig full to bursting. He had actually finished off Caroline's as well. Now, the rocking of the return carriage ride had him queasy as the amalgamation of it sloshed about in his bulging stomach. He burped.
With the blinds drawn down once again and the carriage returned to semi darkness, Caroline removed her bonnet and unfastened her stay. "It is a wonder where you put it all Denig."

He silently expelled more of his trapped wind and patted his front. "Great though, wasn't it? And free as well." He moved his patting to the money pouch strapped to his belt. "…with extra coin to boot."
"You should have charged him interest on the loan. He has only been due you it for two years."
Lifting his feet onto Caroline's seat as before, he locked his fingers together and twirled his thumbs. "Old Gerard always keeps to his word. Lucky he spotted us sitting there, I'd forgotten all about it."
"Unlike others you have been equally generous to in the past."
Denig nodded. "You're right there darling, it's probably about time I called in these loans of mine. Trouble with that though is that I was always too drunk at the time to remember who I gave them to." He laughed at his own stupidity.
Caroline did not laugh with him this time. "Well make sure you do. We need all the money we can get now."
Denig nodded, but remained silent. It was always a safe bet to keep quiet and just agree when reproached by her. She always seemed to be right about things, unlike him who had been a fool in the past with his money. But at least he had been in control of his spending, whereas with Jeanette it just seemed to be an open account on his savings. His eyes dropped to the plunging neckline of Caroline's now loose fitting dress and the curves of her breasts. "They look nice."
Caroline followed his eyes down to her chest. She looked up. Her hand rubbed at her food filled stomach.
"Don't even think about it Denig."

*

"She didn't suck my cock."
"It was not necessary for her to do so I've heard. She must be some woman this Madeline."
He had heard enough. He placed the goblet on the floor and reached for his walking crutch. "I want to leave, now."
In a swift move, Jeanette had risen from her own chair and pushed him back. "I have not finished with you yet."
"Look, I don't know who you think you are and what you want from me, but you got me here under false pretence."
She stood over him. "And what pray tell did you think you were coming here for?"
Frederick remained silent, staring at the floor.
Jeanette reseated herself as before. "Monique has told me of your encounter with Madeline. You were of a size too great for her. She is a young girl who does not yet know the finer pleasures in life, where as I as veteran of such things, do. I can easily accommodate you."
Frederick looked up from the floor. "What?"

Jeanette rose from the chair and as she approached him, lifted her panniers to expose her naked front. "I can take all your cock in my mouth, but first you can oblige me by leaning forward and sticking your tongue deep into my cunt."
Angered at the suggestion, Frederick double handedly pushed her away. She lost her balance and fell to the floor. This time he reached his leg crutch and hauled himself to his feet.
"Fuck you old bitch."

Her mouth agape and eyes wide, Jacqueline was almost jumping within the cupboard. She had to stop herself from yelling out loud. Ha fucking ha, she thought. One person she was not going to win over with her so called Comtesse status. It was great to see her put in her place for once. 'Well done Frederick, whoever you are, tell the old bat where to go.' But as she moved to the left she felt something hard jab at her side. She shifted to the right just in time to hear him rant further.

"Madeline is the woman I hope to marry one day. Do you really think I'd mess that up by fucking an old trout like you? Look at you, you're pathetic."
Jeanette watched him turn in the direction of the door. "Then why did you come here?"
Without looking back, he hollered his reply. "I don't know. I was drunk, I don't know why."
"Because you were looking for a shoulder to cry on, that was why. Little lost boy was crying in his wine."
Frederick stopped at the door. With his fist clasped tight to the handle, he thought over her remark. He turned. "Perhaps."
"About what, you losing your leg, or that this Madeline plays heavy on your heart." She walked towards him. "Or is it a combination of the two?"
He looked into her eyes. "Why is all this important to you. Who are you?"
"Is it not obvious with me asking after Madeline's welfare?
…I am her mother."

'Her mother? Oh, fuck off. Don't fall for that old trick Frederick. Stand your ground, tell her to go jump in the Seine'. As much as she had to keep herself concealed, she felt like jumping out and slapping her for taunting the boy so. And once again she felt the hard jab at her waist when she altered her aching stance. She elbowed it back and listened further.

"Do you think I'm that stupid? Why on earth would Madeline's mother offer to stick my cock in her mouth?" He titled his head down towards her body. "And you looking like you fell out of a cattle slaughterhouse."
He felt her hand slap hard on his face.
"Don't you speak to me like that, young man, do you know who I am?"

"Yeah I do. You're some old woman who picks up strangers in a taverne, well not me. Goodbye."
He pulled the door opened and within seconds had it closed behind him.

Jacqueline was ecstatic. But she had to remain silent as the room had become likewise. She followed Jeanette as she walked to the corner and on bending down picked up a creased piece of cloth. Even with her back to her, Jacqueline knew what she was doing. Yuck! She was wrapping the blood rag round her thighs. 'And she had offered it to Frederick to put his face into. What a true bitch she was.'
Once fixed to her body, she pulled on her bedroom gown and headed for the door. 'Keep going, keep going.'
She did. And with it, Jacqueline made a sigh of relief. She was suffocating and she felt her body sweat run down her skin. She had to get out quick. But as she pushed the doors open, the very same hard article hit at her side again. 'What the hell was that?'
Once out into the relatively fresh air, she turned and checked the clothing. She had been standing beside one of Jeanette's coats. But it was the large side pockets which drew her eye. Pulling the side of it closer she dug deep into the right one. It was a book of a sort, and on pulling it out she noticed it leather bound and tied shut with identical cord. Hmm! She hastily undid the bind and on opening it at a random page stood with eyes wide open.
It was Jeanette's journal, a diary of a sort. She flicked through the pages and with opened mouth stared at it contents.
'This was more like it. This was what she had been after. Wait till Denig and Caroline see this.'
She fist jabbed the air "Yes!"

*

Denig fastened up his britches.
"Now that wasn't too strenuous on the stomach, was it?"
Caroline wiped the side of her lips with her fingers and pulled her head up. She rose from her kneeling position and sat back in her seat. "Just on the mouth darling, what took you so long? Am I losing my touch or is Caroline out of favour with Denig now?"
He loved her baby talk and laughed at her suggestion. "No, just the brandy." With his body stretched out again, he slouched down with hands up behind his head. "What a perfect end to a great afternoon."
"I'm glad you enjoyed it." Going by the time, and their imminent arrival back home, Caroline redid her stay and pinned her bonnet back in place. "We should be nearly home by now."
As Denig pulled up the blind, both squinted once again.
"You're right, almost there."

They sat in silence for the remaining few minutes, content to watch the scenery go by, until the carriage pulled into their street.
"What's happening there?"
He had noticed a commotion outside their house and as they drew closer he recognized two uniformed officers of the civil *Maréchaussée*.
"Shit!"
Caroline leaned forward. "What is it Denig?"
"The authorities have eventually paid us a visit
...a perfect end to an afternoon. Damn!'"

*

Madeline 5

Chapter 6

Supper

Janis looked approvingly at her own reflection in the full length mirror, pleased with the results of her efforts. It being one of her favourite dresses she had worn during the early stages of carrying Sylvian, she had altered it slightly to suit her more developed stage now. She turned to the side and drew her hand down over her bulging front. Her shoulders lowered at the sight. "Hmm…"
Should she wear something less noticeable instead, she thought?
She resumed her full on stance. Her eyes rose to her swollen breasts and with their prominent form, she smiled. Knowing that they were growing in line with her pregnancy, she was still pleased with their shape within the confines of her tight fitting corset. She appeared almost womanlike again. If only she

could cover the front somewhat without concealing her best asset. She considered her options.
"What am I doing?"
Taken by surprise at the sound of her own voiced conscience, she pulled herself back to reality. What was she thinking of, trying to conceal that she was with child just because Alexis was coming to dinner. This was preposterous, she was married. Whatever made her think of doing such a thing? She made for the comfort of her bedroom armchair and slovenly fell into it. Sprawled out with legs extended, she draped her left arm across her stomach and embraced its curvature. Because she was missing her husband, that was why. And not just in body, but to give her the attention she so dearly sought after. Make her feel special…the way Alexis would make her feel at dinner and afterwards by the fire with his witty tales and risqué asides. She sat up. What was wrong with that anyway? She was beginning to think like her own mother now. Why shouldn't a woman want to look her best? Why shouldn't she be given compliments and be flirted with. It was innocent but much needed fun. So why try to conceal the fact that she was pregnant?
Her mind in a spin with her own arguments and counterarguments, she sat straight and clasped her hands on her lap. What was happening to her?
A knock on the door left her question unanswered. She knew by the distinct short rapping who it would be. "Entrer."
As expected, the maid entered. "Madame, Monsieur Badeau has arrived."
"Very well Serina, please show him to the library and tell him I will join him directly. See to his needs in the meantime."
She curtsied. "Oui Madam."
Janis noticed her leave with a wicked smile on her face.

*

Having allowed Madeline to kindle the fire, Rubin had taken her step by step through the procedure of building it in a way that it would be less conspicuous by night. Now, content with her efforts, they had settled themselves by its side and picked at the remainder of the cold chicken carcass left over from their late lunch. Rubin watched Madeline suck at the scrawny leg she had been working at for over ten minutes now. "I think you've drained the life right out of that bird for sure young missy."
Madeline laughed at his quip. She threw the bone into the flames and rubbed the grease from her hands on the bottom of her britches. "Fresh country air certainly brings back your appetite Rubin. I am never as hungry as this while living in Paris."
Rubin lit his pipe and leaned back against a water bag. "The smell's enough to put a lot of country folk off their grub. Not me though."
Madeline pulled her knees up tight against her chin and wrapped her arms around her legs. She smiled at him. "Nothing bothers you does it Rubin? You just seem to glide through life, one day at a time."

Rubin blew a smoke ring and watched it drift up into the air. "One day at a time's good enough for me. If you wake up the next morning still alive, then you're ahead a day. If you don't, well…"
Madeline followed the circle of smoke until it had expanded so far as to dissipate. "You're dead."
Rubin puffed again. After a moment's contemplation, he nodded in semi-agreement. "Well, something like that."
"You are doing it again Rubin. 'Something like that', either it is or it isn't. You are dead or you are not."
Rubin blew another and watched it soar out in Madeline's direction. "You said dead, I didn't."
"Well, I just meant. I mean I thought that you…" She popped the smoke ring with her index finger before it had a chance to expand any further. She finished. "Well, meaning dead, that was all."
Rubin explained his thoughts the best way he could. "Waking up not alive don't have to mean your dead. Just means you're a different person to what you were before you fell asleep."
Madeline re-gripped her legs and thought about it. "Oh you mean change, as opposed to dying."
"Something like…" He re-thought his reply. "Yeah, exactly like that. People change. And it don't take a lot or long to do it neither. Can work the other way too, you fall asleep not alive and wake up alive."
Rubin knew it was himself he was talking about here. His life had changed dramatically after tending to and burying his Rosalind. There hadn't been a day since then that he hadn't thought about her wrapped up tight within his old tattered coat beneath the soil. And with Madeline reminding him so much of her, he had thought to protect her any way he could. He did not want to see what happened to Rosalind happen to her. People could change, and after all, he was a prime example of it.
Madeline had watched his look alter from that of carefree spirit to one of human solemnity. "You are talking about yourself Rubin, aren't you? I can see it in your face."
Rubin coughed and spat into the fire. Embarrassed with the possibly of being caught off guard with his emotions, he sat up straight and leaned to the left. "Yeah I change. Change positions here, got half a tree up my arse." He pulled a small three twigged branch from beneath him. "Must have missed that when we cleared the camp."
Madeline watched him throw it into the fire. "I didn't mean the twig. I meant you. You have changed since we first met." She tilted her head slightly. "Not in a big way mind you, just that I've seen lots of sides to you in the last few days that I did not think would have existed when we first met. You are not the big rough giant all the time. There is a much milder side to you it seems…gentlemanlike almost."

"Huh, I wouldn't go that far young missy. Ain't no part of me has manners in front of a lady, you said so yesterday didn't you. All the noises I make. And I curse like the old soldier I am."

Madeline sat forward to make her next statement more worthy of his attention. "Yes, granted, you do make the odd, well, frequent body emission and on occasions your language is choice, but you have never once disrespected me. As a woman I mean. When we slept beneath the same blankets you faced away from me all through the night. Even when you saw me unclothed in the stream, not once did your eyes wander from my face. Nor when you held me naked in your arms to comfort me, did your hand stray from clasping my back. That Rubin is what I class as your respect for me. Like a gentleman...a real gentle man."

Rubin sat up straight. "I'm no dandy if that's what you think."

Madeline laughed out at his insinuation. "I never thought that for a moment Rubin." She shook her head. "You are anything but a dandy, I assure you of that."

"Good." Resuming his leaning position, he puffed repeatedly at his pipe before sitting up straight again and adding further to reinforce his remark. "I like women just like any man does." He nodded.

"Rubin I am not doubting your word, you have Annie do you not, so how can you be a dandy?"

"Okay then, as long as we've got that straight." He sat back again.

"Goodness me Rubin, what has got into you tonight? You are definitely not your usual self. Do you want to spit into the fire again?" She had said this in jest in the hope that she would change his mood the way he usually did for her. Her eyes were drawn to the pipe he held in his right hand and she noticed it shake slightly as he pressed it to his lips. She scanned down to his left which was draped over his knee, it was shaking also. She had an inkling of what may be wrong with him. He had nothing to drink. She had seen this before in Paris, where people who relied on wine for their daily intake of liquid in lieu of water were prone to this type of symptom, it being the body's reaction to withdrawal from it. It was usually accompanied with sweating and as she looked at his forehead she saw the small beads of perspiration rapidly forming, several of which had started to trickle down his brow. He was also aware of it, she noticed, as the back of his free hand was raised to wipe it free.

"Would you like some water Rubin."

Pulling his eyes free from the fire, he looked across at her. "Huh!"

"I said, would you like some water, you look like you are burning up. Do you feel all right, you don't look well at all?"

He made efforts to drag on his pipe but changed his mind in mid puff. Leaning forward, he tapped it upended on the edge of a burning log to empty its contents. "No, I'm fine." Preparing to spit once again into the fire, he paused as if trying to muster some moisture to do so. He tried again. His eyes

moved to Madeline. "I've got no spit in me." He leaned back and coughed dry.
Concerned about his well being and his sudden malady, Madeline moved round beside him. In a feeble attempt to pull his heavy frame free from the water bag, she jostled with his elbow. "You need to drink some water Rubin, sit forward so I can get to the bag."
"I'm alright, stop fussin' over me young 'en."
"You are not alright Rubin, I can see it as plain as day." She stopped and looked directly into his eyes. "Has this happened to you before?" Deliberately avoiding mentioning his involuntary abstinence from the wine, she had hoped he would know what she meant without it sounding the way it could have. Being the proud and resilient man that he was, Madeline knew that it would be difficult for him to show, let alone admit to having a weakness.
No words came forth from his mouth in reply, but his stomach responded in a different way. In one violent outburst, he retched up a powerful vomit to his right. He retched again, and again, bringing the entire contents of his stomach up onto the ground. So violent was the sickness that his eyes began to stream and his entire body shook uncontrollably. Then, as if struck by a lightening bolt, his whole being became still and he slumped to the left onto the dirt.
Madeline had pulled back in fright and also in reaction to avoid the spray which had spilled onto her britches. But as he fell to the ground she shuffled round to his side. Fearful of him choking on his own vomit, she lifted his head to the side and laid his cheek to the dirt. She shook his body. "Rubin!"
His remained unmoving. She shook again. "Rubin, talk me. Rubin." Her pleas were not answered, his body motionless. Placing her hand to his cheek, she felt the searing heat from his skin and pulled back in shock. 'Oh my goodness, this was worse than she thought. These were no mere withdrawal symptoms as she had assumed, he was really sick. And sick bad.'

*

Alexis was standing by the drinks cabinet when Janis entered.
She was just quick enough to see his hand rise from Serina's bottom to her waist. Both turned around, startled by her presence.
"Janis."
"Alexis." She extended her right hand on her approach.
He took it from her and kissed its back. And where his lips remained a second more than protocol would dictate. He sniffed. "Ah, the scent of a woman, there is no other like it on God's green earth."
"Flatterer." She moved to sit by the unlit fire. "I see Serina has been tending to your needs." Referring to the brandy glass in his hand, she made her insinuation more specific. "The brandy I mean."

He raised his glass aloft and tilted it in her direction as acknowledgement of her implication. "Ah-ahh!"
Janis turned to Serina. "That will be all for the moment. Go and assist cook in the kitchen. I will see to Monsieur Badeau."
Placing the bottle on top of the cabinet, Serina curtsied once again and headed for the door. Janis could see her eyes look over mischievously at Alexis as she passed. When she had closed the door behind her, only then did Janis let her true thoughts be known.
"Still one with the women I see Alexis."
Alexis remained standing. "I am, Janis, one of the luckiest men living in Paris today. I have not yet had the misfortune of being married. Therefore I see it as my duty to attend to the needs of all women who crave pleasure from someone who knows how to fulfill their needs. Now then Janis, what may I get you to drink?"
"Wine please, a small one."
"Never given a woman a small one in my life, try again."
Janis shook her head at his quip. "Alexis you are incorrigible."
He left her with the last word. And as he turned to fetch her drink, Janis looked him over from top to bottom, taking in his physique, his demeanour and his well turned out garments. His suit of golden yellow pattern and cuffed sleeved shirt were set off by shoes which she was convinced she would be able to see her reflection in. He was indeed a fine looking man and one that any woman would have as her husband. If only he could tow the line to become one, that was. She knew that it would not be impossible for him to do so, just highly improbable. He approached holding a large glass of wine.
"Oh Alexis, I will not manage that, it will ruin my appetite."
"You needn't finish it." He sat opposite. "Is your mother joining us for dinner, or are we to have the evening alone with roguish talk?"
"I think not."
"And the children, where are the little terrors?"
She sipped at her wine. "In their own rooms, I crave adult company with mature talk tonight Alexis, not the petty squabbles of children. They miss their father so, and constantly bicker with each other. I just need a little break from it. Does that sound selfish of me?"
He leaned over and patted her right knee. "Not in the least." He sat back and rested his glass on his leg. "How is Gaston anyway? The old rascal hasn't been in touch with me since he left. I assume he is in regular correspondence with you?"
Janis thought of the missive she had received a few days earlier. By way of a brief and concise note to say that he was still detained in Salon on Government business, it was all she had heard from him. Nothing in it to say how he felt about her, whether he missed her or indeed asking after their children. "His letter said that he will be in Salon a few days yet, perhaps weeks."

Alexis balanced his drink on his knee and pulled free from his waistcoat pocket, a small case of snuff. "He may be more fortunate to be away from Parliamentary affairs than he thinks."
Janis watched him pinch a little of the powder between finger and thumb and press it to his nose. "Oh, why would that be?"
With a quick sniff up each nostril, Alexis continued. "Internal rivalry between the factions, that is why. They cannot decide on which way to proceed to appease the masses. Our time is close at hand I fear."
"Our time?"
Alexis pointed at several parts of the room with his head. "All this, all the money, the good living, all will be gone in the twinkling of an eye. This country is on the verge of change Janis, big change."
Janis adjusted her seating to accommodate the tightness of her dress around her mid rift. "You seem more solemn tonight than your normal self Alexis. Has something happened?"
The snuff case back in his pocket, he took the glass in his hand and leant forward. "Well…"
He was cut off before he had started. The door opened and Serina entered to announce that dinner was ready.
"Ah. Listen to me. Invited to dinner by a pretty woman and all I talk about is what state the country is in." He stood up. "Come, let us eat, drink and be merry, as they say."
Janis smiled. She proffered her arm to be led out. "That is more like the Alexis I know. I hope you like the venison."
He took her arm in his. "Venison! Now where on earth did you get that from?"
"You would be surprised how well connected my mother is in this city Alexis."
"Good, I'm starved. I could eat a deer."

*

Having pulled his limp body away from the fire and content that he had nothing left to bring up from his stomach, Madeline had laid Rubin on his back. She needed to get his temperature down she thought, so she had loosened and pulled free from him, his top garments. Here he now lay with his powerfully hirsute chest bare. She looked around her for something to use as a cloth to dab the cool water onto him. The blanket she had laid Rubin on caught her eye. She could use that she thought, but she would need something to cut a strip off. Rubin's knife! Pushing her hand into his tight fitting boot, she worked it around for a time before finally locating its presence. Adjusting herself, she held the blanket tight and drew the knife across its surface. The sharp edge of the blade tore through the cloth as if it was lard, and within seconds she had two strips in her hand. On bent knees, she upended the bag and poured the water onto each cloth, soaking them to full. Shuffling round on the dirt to reface him, the first strip was folded and placed on his forehead whilst the second was held above his chest. Squeezing the contents free, she proceeded to dab it on and around his skin, all the while with trembling hands.

What could have caused this? Surely it could not have been the bird they had just eaten that day, if it had been then would she too not be stricken with the same condition as he was. And as surmised, it was not the lack of wine that had him in such a state. She thought further. Her eyes pushed tight together as she considered the town he had visited the previous day and the pyres with the awful smell of the bodies burning at its outskirts. She remembered the man's words telling them of the sickness that had taken the town so quickly. Oh no, please no. And if that were the case, then would she too be at risk, here, now, with Rubin sick? Would she catch it from him? She looked at the splashed vomit on her britches. They would have to be cleaned, boiled in hot water. Her eyes moved to the small pot by the fire. No use, it as too small. She had to think, she had to think clearly. Rubin's life was in danger and she could not afford to be sick as well. Turning to face him again, she rested her hand on his chest and patted it. "You'll be alright Rubin. I'll take care of you. I won't let anything happen to you."

She bit the side of her lip. 'If only she knew what to do."

*

Janis laid her cutlery at angles on her dinner plate. She was struggling. Alexis meanwhile, she noticed, was still chomping his way through his third helping. "If there is anything left after you have finished, I'll have it sent home with you in a bag."

Alexis laughed out and lowered his own. He grabbed at his wine. "Is my gluttonous appetite that obvious? Forgive me."

"Gaston used to have the very same appetite as you do now. His taste for the brandy has killed it so. He eats very little these days. I worry for him."

Alexis pulled the tucked napkin from his collar and threw it on the table. He stretched his hand across the table to take hold of hers. "Nonsense Janis, he's as fit now as he's ever been. He likes the brandy just as much as we all do. I think you may be confusing this with his work. He's a dedicated man in government you know."

Janis let his hand remain on hers. "Do you think so Alexis, am I worrying needlessly?"

Aware of his touch being there longer than needed, he withdrew it and leant back in his chair. "Course you are. Nothing wrong's with Gaston. In fact, the break in Salon will be good for him. I assure you, he'll return a new man."

*

Gaston gagged.

He tried to move his head away from the flow but it was strapped tight to the bed frame. He could only face upright. And with his jaws held apart by two wooden splints, the more he tried to spit out the liquid, the quicker his mouth refilled.

Sylvia laughed at him as she continued to urinate into his mouth.

Squatting over him with bent legs either side of his face, she had begun her golden shower just as he had woken from his slumber. She now looked down at his frantic expression as he struggled for breath, fearful of swallowing her waste. She pushed hard with her pelvic muscle to empty every last drop from her bladder until the flow eventually subsided. He had swallowed half she was sure, but as he spat out the last of it from his mouth, he retched and his stomach brought up a surge which flowed down either side of his face. When he had coughed the remainder free, she heard him struggle with his favourite term of endearment for her.

"Ucking itch." With both arms and legs strapped hard to the corner of the bed, he could not move one inch from his outstretched self.

She lifted her left leg free and rolled to the side. Her hand pulled the splints from his mouth.

"Fucking, fucking, bastard, bitch." He tried to angle his spit at her from the corner of his lips.

"Now, now, Gaston, is that any way to treat a person who is nourishing you. After all, you are only drinking what the people of Paris have had to endure from the Seine for years now."

He tried to face her, but only his eyes found their way to his left. "What the fuck has that to do with me?"

She leaned over to but an inch of his face. Her tongue licked at the dripping residue on his cheek. "I want you to feel what it is like to live like a minion. A nothing in the eyes of French aristocracy, down trodden and stamped upon, starved of food and over-taxed, left with nothing and to die in the gutter. Like my husband."

"Is this what it's all about, your husband's death? Me being kept here is your revenge for what you think was the state killing your husband? You're fucking mad. I'm the one who's trying to change the fucking system and you've got me locked up here like some wild animal, with your sick fucking games. Now let me out of this fucking place."

Sylvia had let him rant without reaction. She was oblivious to anyone's opinion other than her own. It had been her idea from the beginning to kidnap and ransom him for the good of the revolution. The others had formulated a plan to abduct him and were deciding when the best time to do it when as luck would have it he had walked into the taverne. They had acted immediately. She was to lure him back to the designated house and there they would carry out their plans. But in doing this for them, she could also indulge herself with her own pleasure. It was highly unlikely that after the ransom had been paid he would be freed. They had sent two letters, one official and the other to his wife. Either of which money would be accepted but his death was inevitable. They wanted to make a statement, and returning a hostage back alive would appear weak. They wanted to be taken serious. His head would be sent to Paris minus his body. Meanwhile, she had him to herself. She had dreamed of such a thing since the death of her husband. With him taking his own life after all had been taken from him, she had been left alone with nothing. She now wanted revenge on the system that had instigated his death. And Gaston was a major part of that system. This isolated spot would be his eventual grave. But first, she had plans for him. His further rants pulled her from her reverie.

"Are you fucking deaf as well as thick, get me out of this."

She smiled at him. "Oh Gaston, Gaston." Lifting her naked body to a kneeling position on the bed, she pulled off the binding from his head. "You have had your aperitif Gaston so you may now proceed to your meal. I would not like to see you hunger." Stepping free of the bed, she leaned over at arms length and untied the strap at his left hand. She stepped back out of harms way as he automatically tried to grab at her. Her pendulum finger teased him. "Tut-tut now. Do not bite the hand that feeds you."

"Bitch!"

With his hand loose, he wiped his face free of the urine and spat to the side. "What, more mouldy cheese and stale bread?"

"Oh, much more of a delicacy than that Gaston."

She went out of full view for a moment as she bent down to the floor, but when she had risen again he could see a deep rounded dish in her left hand. Her right, she kept hidden behind her back.

"Piss soup is it?"

"Tut-tut Gaston, do you take me to be repetitive. Do you think my imagination is limited to just one dish? No, this is my specialty. I made it just for you."

"Fuck!"

His head pulled back in disgust as she laid the dish down on the bed at his side. She had defecated in it.

"Bon appetite."

His hand pushed out to knock it from the bed, but she was too quick for him. "Do not be too hasty to rid yourself of it Gaston or in its place you will rid yourself of something more vital." She laid the bowl to the side.

"You fucking sick bastard, if you think I'm going to…" His stomach tensed as she gripped the tip of his penis and pulled.

Stretching it to full length, her concealed hand became visible, and in it she held a six inch long knife. "I shall return in the morning Gaston and if this bowl is not empty…" She held the blade to his testicles.

"…these come off. Understood?"

*

Madeline 5

Chapter 7

The Bull by the Horns

Rubin was getting worse. His limp body had begun to shudder involuntary, but not continuous she noticed, but in spasms, and with each one, they became more violent. She knew he was losing a lot of moisture through his perspiration and had tried to get some water into his mouth by squeezing the cloth to his lips. But it was of little use, he needed to be seen by a physician, someone that could tend to him better than she could. But where could she find one? Where were they? She scrambled towards the bag and after rummaging through the contents, finally found the map Rubin had carried with him. She sat by the fire to see more clearly. Retracing their line of travel with her finger, she tried to pinpoint their exact whereabouts from the last time Rubin had shown her. She now kicked herself for not paying more attention and having just let him steer them on. Finally locating what she thought was the town with the pyres and the nearby woods where he had killed the four men, she moved her finger north along the side of the waterway where they had crossed earlier. She smiled. To the east, and not too far away by her reckoning was another town. Her eyes rose from the map. Hmmm, but which way was east she thought. She also noticed her legs which now lay bare after removing the soiled britches. There was no way that she could enter a town just wearing these drawers. She slammed a clenched fist into her knee as she thought further. Oh Pooh! She didn't even have one of her dresses to wear instead. Wait though. She looked up and peered round the fire at Rubin. He had britches on. Could something be done with them? It was worth a try, so, raising herself to her feet she made her way across camp. Looking down at his size, she wondered how on earth she would fit into them, but having no choice, she knelt and began to unbuckle his belt. Pulling them from him as gently as possible, she undid the money pouch which was tied to the top and placed it by the fire. She would have to take it with her to persuade the physician to come out back with her into the woods, she made herself remember. Holding the britches up at arms length, she considered the difference in dimensions to her own frame. They would be an overly loose fit she knew, and much too long in the length for her, but she would have to utilize them the best she could. So, once again, she found herself with the knife in her hand and hastily cut round the perimeter of each leg to shorten their size. She rose to her feet to pull them on and when she had tightened the belt tight around her waist, she looked down at the unevenly cut lengths. She sighed. It was ridiculous looking, but, with Rubin's need far out-crying her own vanity she simply accepted it and adjusted her top garments to cover them as much as possible. Grabbing the pouch from the ground, she rammed it into the right pocket and hurriedly looked around the camp. Okay, that was that sorted, was there anything else she would need? Her eyes stopped at Rubin and she found herself biting the inside of her right cheek. So much so that she felt the skin break and immediately tasted the saltiness of the blood. 'Oh, please help me find someone.' she prayed. 'Please.' Kneeling down in front of him, she pulled the blanket across his semi-naked body and tucked it in tight at both sides. "I will be back as soon as I can Rubin…with help." She leaned forward and kissed his forehead. "I promise."

Turning to face the fire, she stared at the dying flames. There was one thing for certain she needed to do though before she left.

The awkwardness of her clothes made her mounting Felix a difficult task, but she struggled on until settled. She patted his neck and leaned forward to whisper in his ear. "We have to find help Felix, so between us we have a hard task ahead of us. But we can do it."

Pulling the reins to the left, she led him out of the camp and up towards the high pastures she had seen earlier. If she had worked it out correctly then she would be facing east if she headed away from the path they had been following. Going by the approximate time and the position of the moon, by process of elimination she would hopefully be heading in the right direction. Fortune was in her favour, she thought, as the full moon gave just ample light for her to negotiate the way ahead. She hoped that further on, the lights from the town would give her a clearer indication and a more positive direction in which to head in. It would be in the lap of the gods whether she could find her way back again, but she put the thought straight from her mind and concentrated in the task in hand. She had to get there first.

*

With the wine on top of his pre-meal brandies, Alexis was tipsy, she noticed. He was slurring his words. But this was to be expected and he was always at his most frivolous when under the influence. He was making her laugh as she hoped he would do. His latest anecdote about an encounter with an obese lady at an out of the way tailor's shop had her chortle out loud.
"Enough Alexis, my sides will split right out of this dress."
He continued. "And she had the audacity to say that I was outrageous with my colour schemes. She was wearing bright orange for goodness sakes."
Janis had just sipped at her wine and had to place the glass on the table immediately, almost spilling it. She pressed her fingers to her lips to prevent the wine from ungracefully re-emerging, whilst her other hand waved at him in defeat. Her words struggled to escape through her laughter. "No more Alexis. Please."
He let the laughter subside before adding further. His outstretched hand picked up the decanter. "Oh!" He tilted it at an angle as if to prove to himself that it was in need of replenishment. "We appear to have finished off all your good wine Janis."
We, she thought. The look of childish disappointment in his face had her smile inwardly. "Shall we return to the library Alexis? I am sure we can find something there to satisfy your needs."
He laughed. "Oh, is Serina there?"
She lifted the glass from the table, and as she did, rose herself. "Your mind is never far from women Alexis. It is high time you were married and settled. Get your mind focused on things other than the fairer sex."
Alexis followed suit. "Fair, dark, blonde, it matters not to me. I'll have any of them." He walked round the table to escort her out.
"Talking to you is like talking to the wind." She let him take her arm. "It just blows back in my face."
As they approached the door, Alexis reached out for the handle, but after a curt knock, it was opened for them,
It was Serina. She promptly curtsied. "There is a caller at the door Madame."
Janis turned to Alexis. "A caller, at so late an hour?"
Alexis shrugged. "People do visit you know Janis. You may have been out of the social circle of late, but this does happen."

She smiled at his fake mocking of her. Turning to reface Serina, she enquired as to who the caller was, by way of their announcement.
"Madame, it is a Priest."
Janis stood with mouth agape. "A Priest?"
Serina nodded. "Oui Madame. I think he may have journeyed here as he has a travel case with him."
Although curious to learn more, she did not want to appear overly inquisitive to her maid's own postulation. There was protocol between employee and staff. "Very well, show him to the…" She thought of the library, but with them drinking there earlier she was fearful of it being too obvious. She was in no hurry to be castigated by a man of the cloth for imbibing, especially with the drinks cabinet being as prominent as it was and laden with the assortment of drinks Gaston had stocked it with. "…the Study. I will be there shortly."
As Serina left the doorway, Janis turned to Alexis. "It may be wise if you were to remain in the library. I would rather avoid your introduction as a dinner guest, especially when my husband is away on Government business."
"I understand. I'm sure I'll find something to occupy myself with in your absence. Meantime…" He leaned forward and whispered in her ear. "I need to pee."
She punched his shoulder as he passed.

*

Madeline could feel Felix struggle with the rough terrain underfoot, but to his credit, he carried on regardless. On two occasions now he had lost his footing and she had slipped to the right, so she patted his neck at every given chance along with soothing words of encouragement as they moved through the night. After thirty torturous minutes they had reached what seemed like level ground and peering down into the semi darkness, it appeared to her like a solid path. She paused for a moment. If, as she hoped it was, the road leading into town, then wouldn't it be wise to mark the spot where she had joined it, for the return trip. She looked about her person for something to leave but there was nothing, nothing that she didn't need anyway, well, apart from her boots that was. So, reluctantly, she undid her right one and threw it to the ground. If she hadn't looked a sight beforehand riding into town, then she certainly would be now. Continuing on, she kept to the road without fault and to her astonishment she eventually saw a glimmer of light ahead. Although the excitement in her grew, she could not afford to quicken the pace. She would have to be patient and proceed in the same manner as before. She wanted to get there in one piece.

After fifteen minutes of light gait, she reached the outskirts of the town and at such close proximity to it now that she was certain she could hear voices in the distance. If fact, if her ears were not deceiving her, she could actually hear the faint sounds of music as well. A far cry from the last town she had seen, she thought. Its distant light made the road beneath more visible, so heeling her heavy boots into Felix's sides just sufficiently enough to gee him on, she quickened his pace. As she reached what she considered to be the town boundary wall, she could hear singing up ahead, so passing through the wooden gates unchallenged, she headed in the direction of the revelry. It appeared to be a festival of a sort. A large circle of wooden benches had been formed in the main thoroughfare and in front of each had been placed a table, all of which she noticed were laden with meats and fruit. Not all of France was starving apparently, she thought. Heartily clapping, they cheered on the more boisterous of them who had taken to their feet to dance to the tune of a six piece band that appeared to have all its members playing with total disregard to each other. It sounded awful.

No-one seemed curious to a stranger's arrival and for several minutes Madeline sat patiently, waiting for the tune to end. But the cacophony continued unabated and eventually she dismounted. Walking lopsided due to the height difference in each leg, she led Felix by the reins to a nearby group of men. She had to cough loud to draw their attention. She did it again and tapped on the nearest shoulder. She was met by a smile through a thick grey beard.

"Yes ma boy, what can I do for you?"

Madeline hauled at the reins to placate Felix who was not overly enamoured with the music or the accompanying merriment. "Please monsieur, I am in need of a physician, and on a most urgent basis."

His tight, crow foot eyes looked bewilderingly at her soot caked face and then down to her loose, baggy britches held tight in the middle and showing several inches of bare skin above her ill fitting single boot. He looked up again. "I think you do ma boy, you seemed to have lost a lot of weight there, have you not?"

Ignoring his error in judgment as to the would-be patient, she explained further. "You misunderstand me monsieur, it is for…my, my father that I seek treatment for, not I."

His eyes looked to the sides and then up to the Felix's saddle. "Where is your father?"

"He is in the nearby woods. He is very sick and too weak to travel into town. I must get someone to him immediately."

The old man nodded towards the band. "He's the man you want. Him what's playing the fiddle…badly."

Madeline followed his eyes and focused in on the violin player. He was young to be a man of medicine, she thought. "The gentleman with the black moustache?"

"That's him alright, Simone, he's the one you want. Old Sol died two weeks ago. He's the new one here now, just got in two days ahead of you. Ain't much in the way of fiddling mind."

She could hear that for herself. He hadn't hit a right note yet. She nodded and turned to thank him. "Merci, you have been most helpful. I will speak to Monsieur…"
"Trabbia, Simone Trabbia."
"Oui, Trabbia." She thanked him again and turned to lead Felix around, but heard the old man speak further.
"Get some food down your neck while you're here, try and fill your britches again. Your arse looks like its fainted."
Madeline heard the others in the company laugh at his quip and at any other time she would have joined in the joke, but now was not the time. Hobbling, she led Felix over in the direction of the band which fortunately for her had started a gradual decline of the tune. With no definite finish to the piece, all appeared to just end their part at various stages of play, almost as if they had got bored with it and just given up. Madeline had never heard such disharmony in music before. Simone she noticed was still playing and was the second one to finish before the flute player. Both ended seconds apart. Hardly concerto material, she thought. She inched forward as he stepped down from the makeshift podium to a nearby table.
"Monsieur Trabbia."
Looking about him to see where the voice had come from, he could not see her as Felix had sidled in front of her and out of view of him. She nudged him to the side and called out Simone's name again.
This time, he did see her. Raising his goblet in acknowledgement, he hollered back. "I am Simone Trabbia." He walked in her direction. "If it is a request you want then you will have to wait for at least ten minutes." He grinned and lifted the goblet to his mouth in mid-step.
Wary of leading Felix through the crowd, Madeline had allowed him to come directly to her. She noticed the moisture of the wine on his moustache, and his disinclination to wipe the now dripping residue from it. She tried to ignore it. "You are a physician I believe?"
He made a silent and inward burp and side fisted his chest. "Pardon me. Yes, and hopefully a better one than I am musician."
It would not be hard, she thought. "My father is sick, I need you to come quickly and tend to him."
Simone pulled his head back. "Assertive little fellow aren't you."
"We have no time to lose, he has a fever."
"And where pray tell is this father of yours, nearby?" He raised his free hand to pat at Felix's head. "You needed a horse to travel but a few streets?"
She ignored his semi-mordant remarks and continued her plea. "He was at a nearby town yesterday, one that had a plague of a sort, they were burning the bodies. I think he may have caught it."
He shook his head. "I think the word plague young fellow is too harsh a description these days, pox or syphilis perhaps, but not plague. So where is he?"
She reached for the pouch. "I have money to pay for your services."

"I didn't ask you for money, I asked you where he was."
In her haste to acquire his services as quickly as possible, she had foolishly blurted out payment for such. "I'm sorry. He is...we are at..." She had to think in which direction she had come. "...west of here, in a wooded area not far from a deep flowing stream...a river almost. Please, please now, can we hurry?"
Simone shrugged his shoulders. "Means nothing to me young fellow, I don't know this area too well yet, I've recently arrived and just getting to know my way around the town."
Oh pooh! Of all the people she needed, she had to pick the one that did not know the surrounding area. She had hoped that whoever she had gotten to come back would have perhaps known the way.
Simone noticed the disappointment in her face. "Even if I did, are you certain we could find our way back in the dark? It would at least have to wait until sun up tomorrow. Until then, I will ask around and get a general idea of the area. Perhaps a map is available."
"I have a map." No she didn't. She had left it back at the camp, she now remembered. She stamped her heavy right boot on the ground in frustration. "Oh Pooh!"
In saying this, her voice had resorted back to that of a woman in lieu of the ersatz deeper tone she had spoken in line with her disguise. He had noticed the transformation, she was sure.
Simone scanned her from head to toe and when his eyes returned upward, they remained fixed, staring at her chest. "One thing about being a physician, you become very familiar with the human form and recognize in an instant the various shapes it takes." He raised his hand to her face, and with his thumb pressed to her lower cheek pushed up. He looked down at the black soot stain on his skin and then up to the white smudge of her cheek. "I dare say that the shape before me is not the one that presents itself."
Madeline had not been quick enough to pull her head away, or if she had, then her mind had been elsewhere. She raised her hand to her face to prevent her masquerade from being noticed. She spoke now in hushed tone. "It is not important who I am. What is important is that I get back to my father as quickly as possible. Now will you help me or not?"
Simone stared deep into her eyes and saw the heart felt pleading of a woman in distress. Never had he seen such dark eyes. As black as night and with a lustre of diamonds, he was momentarily struck dumb by their radiance. "I will do what I can, but as I have said, without knowing where you have come from, it is highly unlikely that we will reach there in the dark."
Growing impatient with both his negative; but rational thinking, and the constant hauling of the reins, Madeline countered. "I can't just sit around and wait until morning comes, he could be dead by then."
"I understand your frustration, but can you honestly tell me that you could remember the way back?" For a start, how long did it take you to reach town, did you falter in your original direction, stray from the road perhaps?"

Madeline bit her lip again. "Hmm, just over an hour I think."
"Okay, how much of that hour do you think you spent on the main road into town? Now think carefully here, how long?"
Madeline went through a detailed description of her journey to town, and a scattered account of her trek through the countryside. "Could we perhaps take a lantern with us?"
Simone sighed. "We could yes, but we still need someone with a far more knowledge of the area then me." He looked around him and hollered over to someone called Claude. They were instantly joined thereafter by a plump middle-aged man complete with lyre.
"Like a tune?"
Simone shook his head. "Later Claude. You know this area well, don't you? You've lived here a number of years."
Claude nodded. "All my life, was born just outside of town." He laughed. "On the side of the road to be exact, came as bit of a surprise to my mother I expect." He looked across at Madeline with eyes that automatically dropped to the crumpled fitting of her britches. They lit up with surprise at the absurdity of it. He refaced Simone. "Why, what do you want to know?"
"How far is the river to the west of here?"
It took but a second for him to answer. He nodded at Felix. "If you've got a horse then I'd say maybe only thirty minutes or so, at a pace. Go there fishing myself sometimes, good biting."
"And the surrounding area? Is there a wood nearby, perhaps a good place to set camp?"
Claude shrugged. "I suppose so, if you wanted to sleep at an angle, most of the wood is on a hillside, bit at the bottom though before it stretches out to the fields beyond. The river is a few miles further on. Why, thinking of going camping?"
Simone patted his shoulder with his free hand. "Thanks Claude." Courteously dismissing him, Simone led Madeline and Felix to a quieter part of the street. "Okay, so it seems a straight road out towards your stream and the flat part at the bottom of the hill. Does that sound familiar to you?"
Madeline nodded excitedly. "Yes, Felix had trouble trying to get up the hill, until we finally found the road leading us here. We are camped at the bottom I think. With a lantern we could find the way down the hill. I'm sure of it. It must be easier going down than up."
Assuming that Felix was her horse, he finally wiped the drips from his moustache and drew the cupped hand down over his chin. He blew out. "Well, never been one to shy away from a challenge. Give me a few minutes to collect my things."
Madeline smiled.

*

Madeline 5

Chapter 8

In the Dark

Janis' hand remained fixed on the door handle for a moment before pushing it open. She pulled it back in trepidation. A Priest! It seemed very strange, and at this time of the evening as well. She raised her free hand to her mouth and after breathing into her cupped palm, sniffed in quickly in order to spot the presence of the wine. Satisfied that she did not smell like a hussy; and with her only having two small glassfuls anyway, she finger brushed the front of her already spotless dress. Randomly dabbing her hands at both sides of her pristine hair, she felt herself presentable. She pushed the door open.
He had not taken a seat as would be expected of a guest in waiting, bur rather he had remained standing awaiting her presence. He turned to greet her from the middle of the room.
"Forgive the lateness of the hour Madame. My name is Father Parseur."
His dialect was noticeable to her in an instant. He was definitely not Parisian, she thought, and judging by the bag at his feet, Serina had been correct in her assumption. She let him approach and although she allowed the twinned kiss

to her respective cheeks, she thought the over familiarity of a Priest odd. She let it slip from her mind the moment she heard him mention Gaston.

"I bear tidings from your husband."

Her eyes lit up. "You are from Salon?"

He nodded, but remained silent.

"Please, please, sit." Her salutary hand offered him the nearest chair and once taken, sat opposite. "My husband is well?"

His smile offered an array of gleaning white teeth, which were in complete contrast to his rugged, gaunt face. And even though her words had been more a confident statement rather than a question, his returned smile did not convince her of Gaston's well being. It appeared to her more disconcerting than reassuring.

"At present, he is well. But…"

Janis sat forward. "But what, is my husband ill or is he in some sort of danger? Please, tell me."

He spoke further with his lilted accent. "My journey here is only to relieve him of the burden that weighs heavy on him. To alleviate him of certain obstacles that stand in the way of his future."

Janis considered his reply. She had feared the worst, his safety. She now realized he was talking about Gaston's visit to Salon. "My apologies Father, I assumed you were talking about his health. I take it you mean his role as visiting Government official to your town? Have you arrived in Paris with word of his endeavours?"

His smile had metamorphosed into that of a malevolent grin. "No, but I hope to return to Salon with good words about my own."

Janis fidgeted on the chair, uncomfortable with his cryptic remarks. "You are being very vague Father, if you don't mind me saying so. May I ask then the reason for your visit here tonight?"

He leaned to the left and took hold of his bag. "You may, but I cannot guarantee the answer will be to your liking."

She followed his eyes as he raised it onto his lap and undid the latch. "Then please, tell me."

"Very well…." He pulled a pistol from the bag and pointed it at her face. "…to end your life."

*

With Simone not owning a horse of his own, he sat behind Madeline who steered Felix through the town and out of the gates. Having borrowed a lantern from Claude, he held it down by his side with his right hand while his left gripped tight at his medical bag. This had left him nothing to hold on with except the grip of his legs tight against Felix. His body wavered with each movement.

"I'm going to fall off here, I'm sure of it."

Having resorted back to her normal voice since he now knew of her disguise, Madeline gave a suggestion. "Wrap you arm around my waist then, unless you want to walk ahead and lead the way."
Taking the former as the easier option, Simone joggled the bag round her front and let it hang from his hand over the right side. The weight of it pulled his body up tight to her back. "Sorry."
Madeline accepted his unintentional familiarity as negligible. She had more important things to worry about than a man pressing himself against her. Her mind was on Rubin. Fearing the worst, she tightened her grip on the reins and unconsciously heeled at Felix.
The lantern jolted in Simone's hand. "Hold on, hold on. You can't go any faster that we are. We want to get there in one piece."
Madeline was having none of it. "It is still bright enough to see the ground below, when it is not then I shall slow down and we can light the lantern, until then I want to make up as much time as possible. The hillside will be tricky and slow us down."
Simone raised his brows. "If we get there alive that is."
In comparison to Rubin as a travelling companion, Simone appeared to be a little sheepish for her liking. She had always depended on Rubin to make the necessary decisions and trusted his instincts and judgment at all times. She now felt as if she was the one in control and not Simone. But it was of little consequence, she needed him for one thing and one thing alone, to tend to Rubin. She would then be free of him. The road ahead darkened suddenly and as she looked up she could see why. A mass of cloud had obscured the moon. She was not the only one to have noticed.
"It's getting less light now, how can you see where you're going? We need to light the lantern."
"I am putting my trust in Felix until we reach the hillside. He got me safely to the town in the dark and he will do the same on our return." She patted his head as encouragement. "Won't you Felix?"
As if replying to her, Felix whinnied.
"We will need all its fuel to get down to the bottom. We will light the lantern only when I find my boot."
His initial reaction to such an absurd statement was one of disbelief, but as he thought further on it, he realized what she had meant by it. "Clever girl. Leaving a marker."
"It was all I had to leave."
"Good thinking, only one drawback though."
Madeline chanced a peek over her shoulder. "Oh, what is that?"
"How are you going to find your boot in the dark?"
Put in her place, she refaced forward. He was right of course. They could walk straight over it and never know. Reluctantly, but knowing it to be the right thing to do, she gave in to his request. "Okay, we will light it now then."

Happy that he had gotten one up on her, Simone leaned over her shoulder. "Pass me the tinderbox."
Madeline pulled Felix to an abrupt halt. "What?"
"Pass me your tinder box, so I can light it."
Her head shot round at him. "I don't have one on me, you borrowed the lantern." Oh no, please don't let it be so. "Simone, please tell me you have something to light it with, this is no time for levity."
Having got the upper hand in one swift move, he now felt the fool. He shook his head and twisted his lip to the side. "I forgot."
Madeline's head dipped into her hand. She could say nothing. He was an idiot. She was stuck with an idiot. It was all she could do but to pull his arm free of her and as she did so, the lantern slipped from his hand onto the ground. Madeline followed it. Slipping her leg free, she dismounted. "Get off."
"What?"
"Get off, now. We will have to walk, both of us. We need to find my boot otherwise the way down will be lost to us."
Doing as instructed, Simone pulled his leg free, but came off on the opposite side. He was not in her favour. It was best if he kept a wide berth. He let her lead Felix on and as she headed off in front, he bent down to retrieve the lantern.
Without looking back, Madeline gave another instruction "Leave it."
"But it's Claude's."
"We will get it on the way back. It is no good to us now."
It would have been hard enough to work their way down the hillside with the lantern, she thought, but to negotiate the steep decline in the dark would be perilous. She would meet that obstacle when they got there, she thought, but in the meanwhile she would have to continue on foot with arched back.
Simone had said nothing for the next ten minutes and it was not until the moon had appeared from behind the cloud did he utter a word. "Hey, a bit of luck, we've got some light."
Glad to have some respite from the aching back, Madeline straightened herself. Content that with her body fully erect she could still see the ground, she continued walking without acknowledging his outburst, her eyes scanning full ahead.
And then she saw it.
It had been closer than she had thought. "There it is."
Simone quickened his pace to catch her up. He had dallied behind knowing that she was still displeased with his folly and when he had reached her, saw her sitting on the ground pulling her boot on. "Well done."
Madeline looked up at him but ignored his congratulatory remark. She nodded to her left. "Down there."
Simone followed her lead and walked to the edge. He peered down into the thick dark wood. "How are you going to find your camp in that? I can hardly see a thing in there."

Madeline stood up and stamped her foot home. "We will keep going down until we see the fire."
Simone turned to face her. "The fire, what fire?"
"The fire I built up before I left. It was blazing earlier and hopefully it should still be now. It will be our beacon to follow once we see it."
Impressed with her forethought, he walked towards her. "I can understand your hesitance to trust in anything I say after the lantern fiasco, but wouldn't it be easier and a lot safer if we left Felix here. Trying to get down there would be a much simpler task."
He was right, she thought. There was no need to endanger Felix any further and after all, he had played his part well. She could simply tether him to a tree and fetch him later, come daylight. She nodded. "I agree, that would be the best thing all round."
Gripping the reins close to his mouth, she led Felix down to the nearest tree and once secured to it, bent forward to kiss his forehead. "Good boy, good boy."
As if knowing he was being left alone, Felix shook his main and snorted at her. She patted his head. "It is just for a short while."
Simone took hold of her elbow. "Okay, let's go."

*

Janis sat with mouth agape.
She could say nothing. Her entire body shook with fear. Her eyes had not moved from the tip of the pistol since he had withdrawn it from the bag. It was only his sudden move that brought her static body back to life. He pulled his chair closer towards her.
"You may be wondering why a Priest should be holding a gun to your face are you not."
Janis raised her eyes and swallowed hard. She nodded and uttered her words through trembling voice. "Please, I have children."
He pulled it closer. "I am well aware of that." With hushed tone, he changed the subject dramatically. "Tell me lady, are you nervous?"
His calm intimidation making her shake further, Janis pushed her body back into her own chair upon his approach. "Of course I am, wouldn't you?"
He stopped when their knees had touched. "Possibly, but I am the one holding the weapon, so I ask the questions. It would be wise for you to remember that, unless of course you want your children upstairs to meet an end similar to yours."
Repulsed with their body contact, Janis sharply angled her legs away. It was one thing to intimidate her, but as a mother, her natural protectiveness shone through. "Don't you dare threaten my children?"
He leaned forward and placed his free hand on her knee. "Such Bravado coming from one under such circumstances as this, but alas it will serve no purpose."

Janis felt her spirit rise. If this indeed was the case, then she had nothing to lose. "Then tell me why you want me dead? I see no reason a stranger; especially a Priest, if indeed that is what you are, would want to kill me."
His hand tightened its grip on her knee. "It is not I who wishes you dead. I am merely the instrument he would use to see it done."
He, she wondered. "Who is this 'he' of whom you speak?"
His hand began its slow its ascent up her leg and as it did, he raised the pistol to her mouth. "In time woman, at the point of death I will reveal this to you. Now lean forward and put the tip of the gun in your mouth."

*

With the overhead trees blocking out what little moonlight there was, both had groped about blindly in the dark during their descent. On several occasions Madeline had slipped on the loose undergrowth and had landed hard on the seat of her britches. It had happened again now and as she slid down the slope she caught hold of a low hanging branch which stopped her fall.
Simone had fared no better. He had tried to keep hold of her hand, but had; twice now himself, fallen on his back, the second of which he had lost grip of his bag. Fortunately after groping about for a few seconds, he had found it. His eyes squinted downwards. "Are you alright down there?"
After adjusting herself, Madeline hollered up "Yes, I just slipped again. Where are you?"
"Up here to your left, I think. Keep talking until I reach you."
After continuously calling his name, Simone eventually reached her. He could just make out her face. "How did you ever manage to get up there with Felix? This hill is torturous."
"I know, I don't remember it being as bad as this. I may have joined the road long before I knew it and left my boot further on."
"Well that's not going to make it any easier for us."
And it would be a lot better if she had decent footwear other than the boots she was wearing. Had she her flat leather sandals then she would at least feel the ground beneath her and negotiate a better foothold. As it was now, she just slipped with every second step.
Simone heard her fumble in the dark. "What are you doing?"
"Taking my boots off, I can't climb down properly with them on."
Simone considered his own, but after careful thought was reluctant to part with his shoes if he were to lose them. Being new to the profession, he did not have the luxury of owning a second pair. It would be of no advantage to him anyway as they were a good fit, unlike Madeline's which appeared to be of size well in excess of her feet. "You will struggle even worse trying to hold onto them."
"I will get them later. Are you ready?"

Pointlessly nodding at her, he took a tight grip of his bag and rose to his feet. "Here, take hold of my hand again."

Taking his grip in hers as instructed, both took there first cautious step forward and simultaneously slipped on the same loose earth. As they slid further down the hill, once again their connection was broken and as Madeline tumbled in the dark, she felt herself hit hard against the trunk of a tree. Her right arm took most of the impact.

Simone meanwhile had rolled down only a few feet before colliding with a similar wooded structure. His head had met it full on.

As both rubbed hard at their respective aches, it was Simone who called out first. "Are you alright?" It suddenly occurred to him that he didn't even know her name.

It took a moment before Madeline could muster the breath to shout back a reply. "I've hurt my arm during the fall. I don't think it is broken but it is very painful."

Simone rubbed at his head once again and hollered back. "Okay just do as we did before, keep shouting my name until I find you. Don't try to move your arm, keep it still, it may have dislocated."

Madeline leaned her back against the tree and clasped her hand to her shoulder. It was painful to the touch, but doing as Simone had instructed, she held her arm tight against her side. She heard his approach, as if scurrying down the hillside.

"Where are you, I said to call out my name." He landed on her lap with a crash. "Oh, here you are."

Madeline pulled her head back as the pain from her shoulder shot up through her neck. Her crown hit against the tree. "Ouch!"

Feeling as if he was constantly apologizing to her, Simone refrained from doing so this time and adjusted his seating accordingly. His outstretched arms attempted to find her frame. When his hands landed on her chest, he moved his palms over her front to get a bearing of where she was, and although feeling no softness of breast beneath his skin due to Madeline's tight fitting corset, he suddenly realized where they were. This time he did apologize. "Sorry."

"It's my arm Simone."

He inched forward. "Which, left or right?"

"The one I am holding."

His hands moved about until he felt the right arm down by her side. "Okay, just relax. Let me take hold of it."

After a brief examination; given his restrictions, he placed her arm back to her side. "Well I don't think you have broken your humerus, but your arm joint has been pulled free of the shoulder. I will have to reset it." He paused. "It's going to hurt…a lot. Are you up to it?"

He did not need to see her to know that she had nodded. He heard her sweet young voice give him her approval.

"Just do what you have to do Simone."

Brave girl, he thought. He had performed this procedure only once, in medical school, so he hoped he could make it as painless for her as possible. One swift turn and pull should do it. If only he had a splint of sorts to help support her arm. "Okay. What's your name?"
At first it had seemed a strange request at a time like this, but as Madeline thought further, she knew it would be his way of comforting her for what was about to happen. She did not relish the thought of it. "Madeline."
"Pretty name, now Madeline, this is what I want you to do.

*

Janis whimpered.
His free hand had risen from her leg to her left breast and as he massaged it within his palm, he pushed the tip of the pistol to her lips. "Put it in your mouth and suck it as if it were your husband."
Reluctantly, Janis did as instructed, and with shaking hand gripped the middle of the pistol. Tilting her head slightly forward, she put the tip an inch inside her mouth. She gagged at the taste.
"I said suck it."
His voice had become more threatening now in his demands and she could see and feel why. Like her own body, his hand had begun to shake as it held the gun and his grasp on her breast had tightened. His excitement with the proceedings was apparent. She was going to die, she could feel it. All that was needed was for him to squeeze the trigger and her head would be taken from her shoulders. She thought for a moment. Could she take advantage of this? Perhaps catch him off guard with a chance of escaping her doom. There was nothing left to do but try. As much as the taste was foreign and repulsive to her, she pushed her face forward to take in more of the pistol's length. And as she did so, she took hold of the middle with her fingertips and delicately ran them along the muzzle. With each stroke, she took more and more in until her lips were pushing in at least four to five inches. She could see from his face the pleasure he was getting from it, especially now that his hand had been pulled from her chest and clasped hard between his legs.
With both lost in their respective thoughts within the silence of the room, it was the sound of the door suddenly opening that pulled them back to reality. Their two heads turned round in unison.
It was her mother.

*

It had hurt.
Hurt so bad that she cried. Simone had removed his shoe and with his stocking sole pressed hard against the inside of her chest, had pulled hard on her outstretched arm and twisted it home. The popping sound had made Madeline momentarily gag, but was nothing in comparison to the excruciating pain she had felt as it did so. And having passed out with the

shock of it, she had, for several minutes lay unmoving until regaining consciousness.
Simone held her in his arms as she stirred. "Sit still for a moment Madeline. Give your arm time to adjust itself back into position."
She whimpered as the tears ran down her cheek. "It hurts Simone."
"I know, I know. But it will pass. You will feel some discomfort for a few days now, perhaps weeks, but you are young and have healthy bones. It will reset perfectly, although you will have to wear a sling for a time. I will tend to you properly on our return to town."
She continued to sob, but realizing their predicament, she sat up. "Rubin."
Reluctantly, Simone released his hold on her. "Who is Rubin, your father?"
Madeline knew what he must be thinking, but she had neither the time nor inclination to explain. "We must get down to him Simone."
With his hand still at her waist, he pulled her closer. "You are in no position to move tonight Madeline, not here in the dark. I cannot afford to let you damage your arm further. I will go down alone. You said something about a fire. Then I will find it. Find your father. I'll come back for you." And her boots and the horse and the lantern, he foolishly thought. This night was becoming farcical.
"But you do not know where to look."
"Do you?"
She did not. She was as much in the proverbial dark as he was. But it mattered little. "No, I am coming with you. I will not sit here all night waiting. I have to be with you when you find him."
If he could see her face clearly then he would have leaned forward and kissed her, so enchanted was he by her courageous stance. "Very well, but I'll have to make something to support your arm."
He slipped the shoes from his feet and pulled free his stockings. Tying the two ends together, he tugged hard to tighten the knot. "This will have to do. Don't worry, they're clean."
Having no idea what he was talking about, Madeline felt him take hold of her arm and with it at a right angle, bind it tight to her front.
"How does that feel?"
Madeline moved her arm slightly and felt its hold on her. "Fine."
Simone searched for his shoes and slipped them on. He felt the dampness from his sweat against the leather. "Just fine?"
It was Madeline's turn to apologize. She had sounded ungrateful and after all he had done and was continuing to do for her. "I'm sorry Simone. Yes, it feels secure, enough for me to move. Thank you for that. And everything."
Simone searched for his bag. "So I'm forgiven for the lantern?"
She smiled as best she could. "Yes. Now can we go?"
"I'm telling you Madeline, it's going to be hard moving down this hill with your arm the way it is."
She did not have a chance to counter his argument. Both jumped at the suddenness of the sound below…

A single musket shot.

*

Having suppered alone in her room with a small cut of venison and some bread, the mother; thereafter, had finished reading the small book she had started earlier that afternoon. Discontent to remain there with nothing further to amuse her, she had pulled on her thick bedroom gown and made for the library. It had not been to her liking to see Alexis pass her by on his way to their toilet room. He had been courteous enough yes, and had asked after her health, but it had been evident to her that he had more pressing things on his mind, namely emptying his bladder. He had made his leave as quickly as he had when greeting her so she had resumed her walk to the library.
She had in mind, the very book which she would spend the rest of the evening with, so upon entering, she had headed straight for the section she knew it to be in. Both Janis' and Alexis' glasses had been noticeable to her as she passed by the table.
Pah! What was her daughter thinking of?
But it was not until she had reached the side of the furthermost armchair that she had noticed something odd on the floor. It had looked like a pair of legs jutting out from behind. And as she inched forward, the rest of a human torso came into her view. Her recognition of who it was had been instant…the uniformed body of their maid Serina. Her hand had pulled to her mouth in surprise, and as she moved closer round the chair she had seen red.
A pool of deep crimson ran free from Serina's neck and it had weakened her already frail legs at the sight of it. Sliced open to the bone, her throat had been splayed from ear to ear.
'An intruder, there was an intruder in the house, Janis, the children!' She had thought of nothing else but to run as quickly to the aid of her daughter as was possible. The dining room had been her first port of call, but upon seeing it empty, had ran to the study.
And when she had pushed the door opened, a further horror awaited her.
The blast from the pistol was deafening, and she felt the impact of the ball in her left shoulder.

*

Deciding it would be better to glide down the hill gradually on their rears rather than on foot, both pushed on further. Not a word had been mentioned since the shot. With both on them having their own thoughts of what may have happened, neither wished to say it out loud for fear of it being true.
Could Rubin have awoken from his state to find himself in such a delirium as to have taken his own life? This had occurred to Madeline. The thought of him pushing the tip of the musket into his mouth and pulling the trigger had

her move even quicker down the hill. And before she knew it, they had hit level ground.

Somewhat relieved that this part of the ordeal was over, Madeline pushed herself to her feet and with her free hand, brushed her clothes free of the twigs and bracken. Her arm was aching, but the thought of Rubin had pushed the pain to the back of her mind. Out from beneath the trees now, they had reached a clear spot where the light from the moon lit up their surroundings. She turned to find Simone.

He was by her side, and looked totally disheveled. "Well we made it. How's your arm?" He placed his bag on the ground.

"It's very painful." She nodded to the left. "It came from that direction."

Knowing what she meant, he remained silent. He moved closer to inspect her sling, and as he did so, he felt Madeline pick free the twigs and grass from his hair with her free hand. Satisfied that it had not loosened any he pulled back. "Looks okay."

Madeline's eyes looked down to the sling. It was the first time she seen it. "Your stockings?"

Embarrassed with the recognition of it and the gratification in her tone, Simone stamped his feet. "Was getting too hot anyway."

Her smile brief, she was pulled back to reality. From the corner of her eye, and over Simone's shoulder, she thought she had seen a glimmer of light in the distance. As a reaction, she made a move with her bound arm to point in its direction and winced.

Simone had seen the look in her face and turned round just in time to see it as well. Then it was gone. "I saw it too Madeline. It must be the fire."

In the expectation of him being right, Simone hastily picked up his bag. "Let's go." And leading Madeline with him, they headed in its direction.

A relief to be walking on solid ground, they made headway through the semi-thick bush desperately hoping that would not err from their course. The way things had gone tonight, he thought, it would just be their luck if they did. He offered words of encouragement as they went. "I don't think it should be too far now."

With her bare feet scratched to bleeding and her arm aching, Madeline hoped so. She felt totally drained of life and if it were not for her concern over Rubin she could have gladly sat down and slept right there where she was. But she pushed on regardless. Rubin had been there for her when she needed him and she had promised him that she would come back with help. She was not about to let him down now...

Whatever they found when they reached the camp.

*

Madeline 5

Chapter 9

Life or Death

With the pistol having been torn hard from her mouth, Janis had felt two of her teeth crack as the rough edged barrel ground against the upper tips. Her immediate reaction was to raise her hands to clasp her face, but as she saw her mother take the impact of the shot she tried to pull herself free of the chair.
She felt the back of the Priest's fist on her face instead. And also the snap of one of his finger bones as he did it.

Stunned by the suddenness of the old woman's entrance, he had yanked the pistol free, turned and shot her. Without thought, he had fired the weapon which had been in complete contradiction to his professionalism as an assassin. It had never been his intention to use the gun on any of them. Instead, his choice of weapon was to have been his knife, as it had been with the maid. Quick and silent as always, save the gargling of the throat as it opened up. But he had panicked. Had been totally absorbed in his own bodily pleasure and with the person he was here to kill. His misplaced anger had taken itself out on her and he now stood clutching his aching fist after drawing it hard across her cheek. He had broken the bone in his little finger he was sure. Angered at his own stupidity, he threw the spent pistol to the floor and grabbed at his bag.

Fearful that further weaponry may lie within its hold, as was the pistol, Janis; although in abject pain, leapt from the chair and grabbed at his arms. She felt his elbow dig deep into her chest as she jostled with his wrists. Her body doubled over and she felt herself thrown; like the pistol, arbitrarily to the floor where she lay, momentarily stunned by the force. But she could not give up now. Not only did her own life depend on disarming him, the lives of her children did too. She had to find the strength from somewhere. So, pushing her body up through sheer determination, both hands clutched at his left ankle and with one tremendous pull, heaved him off balance. And as he fell to the floor with her, she caught sight of the glimmering blade in his hand.

*

Alexis had been in the midst of shaking himself dry when he heard the shot being fired.
"Fuck!"
Having no idea where it had come from, he was still in the process of fastening up his britches when he ran free of the toilet room. Looking from left to right in double quick time, he had hoped for a clue as to where he should start. 'The dining room, no they had just left there, the library possibly, no it couldn't be there…the Priest! …the Study.'
As he ran at full speed across the hall, he was met by other members of the staff, who; in reaction to the shot, had emerged from their respective workplaces. The cook complete with spatula in hand and her young assistance were held in place by the live-in gardener, all of which stood only a few feet from the study door.
It was the elderly carriage driver that pointed the way for him. "It came from in there Monsieur."
It was the study for sure. Alexis nodded and headed for the door.
The first thing he was met by was the body of Janis' mother slumped on the floor. His face drew back in horror. Her shoulder was exposed to the bone through her thick robe. But before he could react any further to her state, his eyes were drawn to the melee in the middle of the room. Janis was on the floor also, but with her was who he assumed was the Priest. It was hard to tell. Part obscured by the armchair he did notice a knife raised high above and was evidently held there in preparation of a downward thrust. And Janis was the intended victim. He leapt forward as quickly as his brandy wary legs could carry him, but as he approached, he saw the knife holder turn in his direction.

With his upper half moving faster than his legs could carry him, his momentum continued on well after he had tried to stop. And in defense of the swinging blade coming towards him, he lifted his arm to shield the blow.

It was too late. Released from his hold on her, Janis pulled herself free just in time to see the tip of the blade cut across Alexis' face. The skin parted in an instant and the flow of blood was immediate. She heard him scream. Her rage at the situation now at boiling point, her left leg swung round with such a force as to kick their assailant off balance. And as he fell to his left, Janis lunged forward to grab at the knife yielding hand. She also felt the edge of its blade. Catching it an inch high of the hilt, her thumb ran up its length cutting deep into her skin. The Priest's free hand meanwhile; once again, made impact with her cheek with such a force as to send her reeling on her back, where she lay unmoving, stunned and bleeding.

The keen edged blade had run effortlessly up from Alexis' top lip, through the skin of his cheek and sliced its way into his right eye, the punctured orb of which now made him blind on one side. Howling with the amalgamation of his eye deflating, the enormity of the pain and the copious amounts of blood that ran into his cupped hand, Alexis, stood momentarily shocked. But on seeing Janis thrown to the floor once again by the force of the Priest's fist, his temper rose. He charged forward and with all his weight behind him, pushed the Priest to the ground. He heard the sound of the knife clatter to the floor. Tilting his head to the left so as to take in as much vision from his good eye as possible, he caught sight of the knife by the Priest's head. His bloodied hand grabbed at it and without thinking, twisted his body round so as to drive the point into the side of the Priest's neck. As the body convulsed below him, he pushed the blade in deeper, and pulling the hilt towards him, he opened the throat up further until the body twitched no more.

*

Madeline 5

Chapter 10

With Bated Breath

It had taken them only fifteen minutes or so to reach the edge of the camp and as was expected; with no further glimmers since the initial one, the fire had gone out. In her haste to run to Rubin's side, Simone grabbed her loose arm and held her at bay. She struggled with him but he stood his ground.
"Wait, Madeline. Something's wrong here."
Even in the faint light of the moon she could see across to the other side of the camp were Rubin was lying. The blanket was still wrapped around him.
"He is there. Rubin is there. I can see him from here. It is where I left him."
He reluctantly gave in to her wishes but with due hesitance, took hold of her hand so as to stop her from getting too close to the body. If indeed he had the symptoms that she had described to him earlier then he did not want her anywhere near him and exposed to it. He would have to check him out first. They moved in closer, all the time his eyes alert to danger. When they had reached the fire, both noticed that it was out completely, with no embers glowing.
"Strange! How could the fire go out so quickly? I had it full blaze before I left."

Simone thought it odd as well. "Stay here. I'll go and see to your fa…Rubin."

"But…"

"No buts' just stay here."

As she watched him cross towards Rubin, Madeline moved round the fire to her own blanket which was still spread where she had left it. She sat down as ably as should could befitting her encumbrance and proceeded to wipe her feet free of the bloodied dirt. If anyone in Paris could see her now, with her hair pinned back, soot smeared face, oversized men's britches cut at irregular lengths and tied tight with a belt, blooded bare feet and her arm in a sling, then who would recognize as the pristinely attired woman they had known beforehand? Not many she knew. But Simone had seemingly seen through her many faults and downcast exterior and now, in retrospect, she had noticed the way he had looked at her on several occasions earlier. Her initial thinking of him being a bit lily-livered had been proved wrong as he had taken control and seen them safely; albeit with slight injury, to the camp. She was certain that if anyone could treat Rubin, it would be him. Giving up the hopeless task of wiping her feet, she looked across to see Simone bent over, his head to Rubin's face. She closed her eyes tightly shut. 'Please make it not be the town ailment, please? If need be, just make it something bad but curable, please?"

She sensed Simone in front of her. As she opened her eyes he was crouched down on his knees, a mere foot from her face.

"Will he alright? Can you make him better? Please Simone, tell me that you can."

"Madeline."

She looked round his shoulder in Rubin's direction. "Tell me he is alright, Simone, please."

As she tried to stand, Simone took hold of her arm. "Madeline, wait." He hesitated before continuing. "He's been shot in the chest."

"But…but, who could have done that to him? I must see him, tell him he will be alright, that you will save him. Make him better."

He rose with her and steadied her in his arms. "Madeline, I can't. It's too late."

"But…"

He shook his head. "We're too late Madeline…

…he's dead."

*

Madeline 5

Chapter 11

A Thought for the Dying

The smaller of the two led the horses towards the other who stood watching the flames rise. He took the reins in his hand.
"Good heat on a summer's night."
The other stood by his side. "Sure is. You waiting to smell the flesh?"
He shook his head. "Nah. Seen and tasted enough tonight. You?"
"Me neither. We got what information we needed. Got to be making tracks, but at least we're headed in the right direction."
"The lady put up a fight to end fights. Woman had spirit."
Something within ignited and sent the flames even higher. Neither of them flinched at the booming sound, but pulled at the reins to settle their horses.
"She said nothing, even when I took the skin from her thigh. Woman had guts."
"You taste them?"
His eyes stared unerringly into the fire. "Nothing so deep, only flesh. Cut off thin, took a second of heat each side to get it perfected. Way I like it. You fuck the man?"
"Yeah, straight up the arse. The way I like that."

"He did not put up the good fight his woman did. He was weak."
"The moment I pulled the eye from the socket he screamed like a baby. Madeline this, Madeline that. Fucking dandy."
As the flames got more severe, they felt the heat on their faces but neither pulled away. And although their skin was searing, it was nowhere near the intensity of the heat on the skin of the two strapped to their chairs within the inferno. They heard the screams of the dying man as the singed and burning skin fell from his body, the dead woman meanwhile immune to the suffering.
"Time to go."
The other agreed.
Mounting their horses, they turned towards the open plains beyond, but before setting off, something caught the taller Raul's eye. A glimmer of light was reflecting off something on the fencing. They rode over. He looked down.
A few coins had been placed on top of the fence post.
"Strange place to put money."
The other looked towards the flaming cabin and thought of the two within.
"Call it payment for the ferryman."
They pulled at the reins and rode off in search of their prey.

*

Madeline's story is continued in book 6

Printed in Great Britain
by Amazon